The ROCKETEER®
JET-PACK ADVENTURES

Created by DAVE STEVENS

THE ROCKETEER
JET-PACK ADVENTURES

Editors: JEFF CONNER and TOM WALTZ

Editorial Consultant: SCOTT DUNBIER

Associate Editor/Design Consultant: JUSTIN EISINGER

Designer: RICHARD SHEINAUS

Associate Designer: ROBBIE ROBBINS

Cover Design: JAY BONE and RICHARD SHEINAUS

Cover Illustration: JAY BONE

Ted Adams, CEO & Publisher
Greg Goldstein, President & COO
Robbie Robbins, EVP/Sr. Graphic Artist
Chris Ryall, Chief Creative Officer/Editor-in-Chief
Matthew Ruzicka, CPA, Chief Financial Officer
Alan Payne, VP of Sales
Dirk Wood, VP of Marketing
Lorelei Bunjes, VP of Digital Services
Jeff Webber, VP of Digital Publishing & Business Development

ISBN: 978-1-61377-907-1   17 16 15 14   1 2 3 4

www.IDWPUBLISHING.com
IDW founded by Ted Adams, Alex Garner, Kris Oprisko, and Robbie Robbins

Facebook: **facebook.com/idwpublishing**
Twitter: **@idwpublishing**
YouTube: **youtube.com/idwpublishing**
Instagram: **instagram.com/idwpublishing**
deviantART: **idwpublishing.deviantart.com**
Pinterest: **pinterest.com/idwpublishing/idw-staff-faves**

THE ROCKETEER JET-PACK ADVENTURES

YVONNE NAVARRO ◈ DON WEBB
GREGORY FROST ◈ SIMON KURT UNSWORTH
CODY GOODFELLOW ◈ NANCY HOLDER
NANCY A. COLLINS ◈ ROBERT HOOD
NICHOLAS KAUFMANN ◈ LISA MORTON

Illustrations by
JAY BONE

Edited by
JEFF CONNER and **TOM WALTZ**
Editorial Consultant
SCOTT DUNBIER

Created by
DAVE STEVENS

San Diego 2014

SPECIAL THANKS TO

Jennifer Bawcum
Michael Lovitz
David Mandel
Kelvin Mao
Emelie Burnette
and
Lauren Gennawey

CONTENTS

THE RED, WHITE & GREY

by

YVONNE NAVARRO

Saturday, October 21, 1939

The waters of the Pacific spread below the plane, a sun-sparkled azure blanket that covered nearly everything in the view from the cockpit of the Aeronca C-2. Cliff Secord had managed to rent the aircraft from a guy named Jack, one of the mechanics at the airfield back on the mainland. "Rent" might be stretching the truth a bit, since that translated to the exchange of a hard-won five-spot for the keys for the next three days. Jack's warning to Cliff to bring it back on Tuesday morning in nobby shape wasn't something to shrug off; the guy was twice Cliff's size and looked like he routinely snapped stunt pilots in half just to exercise his muscles. Cliff had never been what anyone could call an artsy guy, but the sight of the water below made him wish he was so that he could somehow combine what he saw with what he felt—nothing made him happier than flying.

"Where did you say we were going?"

Well, *almost* nothing.

He could barely hear Betty's sweet voice above the exhilarating sounds of the engine and the wind streaming over the plane's wings.

"Avalon," he yelled back. "On Catalina Island."

He glanced at her and was rewarded by her dazzling, red-lipped smile. "It sounds like something out of a legend!" Her eyes were shining, and it was hard to say if it was a reflection of the ocean below or happiness.

"Almost," he told her. "King Arthur was supposed to have gone there to die, accompanied by Morgan le Fay."

"Oh my, how romantic." She sat up straighter, trying to see over the dash. "Is that it already?"

Cliff laughed. Leave it to Betty to find romance in anything and everything. "Yep, already. It's only twenty-three miles from L.A." He'd fueled up completely before leaving, so on impulse he banked to the right and headed northwest, following the island's jagged coastline. Today the ocean was relatively calm, but they could still see small waves pushing against the rocky outcroppings that showed beyond the tree-crowded shore; here and there were small beaches, mostly deserted except for the occasional fishing boat. Betty stared down, entranced by the glistening waters surrounding Catalina; they were clear, a deep indigo blue that lightened to a beautiful turquoise every time the waves pulled back into the Pacific, especially on the southernmost part where the current was strongest.

His girlfriend gestured downward. "Is that where we're going? It looks awfully small."

"It isn't, and it is," he replied. At her confused look, he continued. "That's Two Harbors. Not much there but old Army barracks right now. I hear sometimes Hollywood people stay there when they're working on movies." He pointed ahead of the plane's nose and a little to his left. "We're headed to Avalon, back where we were before I turned to give you the island tour."

Below them the trees had thinned and been mostly replaced with a barren landscape littered with gray rocks. "It looks pretty inhospitable down there," Betty noted.

"This part, definitely." Cliff banked to the left, heading for Buffalo Springs Airport. The water swung out of sight on Betty's side of the aircraft, but not before he glimpsed a cozy little bay that sported a wide, sandy beach. There was a small building not far from the beach; he'd done a little advance research that told him that was the Eagle's

Nest Lodge, the old stagecoach stop. If he could get his hands on some transportation other than a cab, that had definite possibilities. As Betty would say, *romantic*. "Look ahead. The airport's coming up."

Betty was silent, looking down as the runaway drew nearer and Cliff finally touched down and coasted to a stop. It took awhile to get the plane squared away and their things unloaded—even though it was only a three-day stay, Betty had a full suitcase. By the time a taxi finally pulled up to take them into Avalon, it had started to rain; the precipitation wasn't much more than a fine mist, but it still had Betty shivering beneath her lightweight, Paris-style black coat.

Cliff opened the door for her and let the driver put their bags in the trunk. The car's interior was cool but dry, a definite improvement. To take his girlfriend's mind off being chilled, Cliff decided a little juicy movie news was in order. "Avalon's become quite the relaxation spot for the movie stars these days," he said. "I heard a rumor that Clark Gable and Olivia de Havilland were going to be around this week. Errol Flynn, too."

Betty had been hunkered down into her collar, but now she perked up. "Really?"

The first part was true, but the second...okay, there might be some movie stars around, but the *who* of it was stretched as far as a rubber band could go. "We should do some shopping, explore the stores along the beachfront," he said. "If the Hollywood types are around, you know that's where they'll go first."

Her smile was back, but then it dissolved as her teeth chattered. "S-sorry."

"Let's stop somewhere and get a hot bowl of soup and some coffee before we check into our hotel room," he suggested. When she nodded gratefully, Cliff leaned toward the front seat. "Say, any suggestions about a place to grab a hot lunch?"

The driver was an older guy sporting a crew cut gone gray above bushy eyebrows about ten shades darker. He rolled the unsmoked half of a coarse-looking cigar from one side of his mouth to the other before answering. "Yeah. Where are you staying?"

Cliff saw the man's gaze drift to Betty in the rearview and didn't like how long it lingered. "Beachfront," he said sharply. The driver's gaze shifted back to Cliff, and he gave a curt nod before refocusing on the road. "There's a little place at the start of the pier called Larry's. Nothing fancy but they got decent sandwiches and clam chowder." He paused, then offered, "Nice view of Avalon Bay, too."

"Larry's it is," said Cliff. His voice was pleasant enough, but when the man glanced in the rearview again, Cliff made sure he had a *Don't monkey with my girl* scowl on his face.

It must have worked, because in another quarter hour—without more conversation or looking back at Betty—the taxi pulled to the curb in front of a whitewashed cafe that had curtains decorated with tiny blue sailboats framing its three windows. After paying the driver and collecting their luggage, Cliff and Betty climbed out and, despite the chill, stood for a moment gazing at their surroundings. The drizzle had stopped, and the sun was trying rather unsuccessfully to push a few golden rays through slits in the clouds. The times that sun did break through gave everything outside—buildings, sidewalks, streets, even the people—a thin layer of shine, as though the world had been sprinkled with glitter.

Betty shivered as the sun disappeared again. "Let's go in," she said. The café was fronted by a wooden platform fenced off and finished to look like the decking of a boat, and he followed her across it. "I think we could both use a hot cup of coffee right now."

"Sure thing." Cliff held the door for her, then pushed their suitcases through and pulled it shut behind him. The café was warm and welcoming, and the door did a fine job of cutting off the elements; he could picture huddling at one of the tables on a blustery January evening, watching the whitecaps on the ocean whip the sea into froth at the hands of a winter storm. Kind of like what they wanted to do now, except that every table in the place was occupied.

"Damn," Cliff muttered under his breath. He scanned the tables, but everyone looked solidly into their meals or coffee or whatever. A few people glanced at them but went right back to their meals and conversations. Betty might be cold, but he was already overheating; he pulled down on the zipper of his leather flight jacket and ran one hand across his forehead to wipe away the layer of moisture while he tried to decide their next move.

Betty nudged him with her elbow. "That man over there is waving at you. Do you know him?"

Cliff followed her gaze and saw a guy sitting at a table in the far corner. He was older, with a strong jaw below plentiful white hair swept back from a well-weathered face. When their eyes met, the man offered Cliff a welcoming smile and gestured enthusiastically to the empty seats at his table. Cliff hesitated, then glimpsed a leather jacket much like his own draped over one of the empty chairs—there, he realized, was the connection. "Let's go join him," he said. He shoved their luggage off to the side where no one would trip on it, then ushered Betty forward. They made their way through the tables to the back corner.

The older gentleman pushed back his chair and stood. "Zane Grey," he said, offering his hand to Cliff. The two shook before Grey said, "Please, join me. You won't get a table for hours otherwise, and it's not the best weather to wander around Avalon. This time of day, most of the restaurants will be full." He moved to the side and pulled out a chair for Betty. "Miss?"

"We'd be delighted," she said sweetly and settled onto the offered seat. She shrugged out of her coat at the same time Cliff took off his flight jacket and hung it over the back of his chair. He scooted up to the table, trying to figure out where he'd seen this guy before. It only took another few seconds for Betty to jump in and make everything click. "I'm Betty," she said. "This is Cliff, my boyfriend. You're the Western writer, aren't you?" Grey nodded, and his expression made it clear he was pleased that she recognized him. "Cliff, this man is *famous*. He's written dozens of books!"

"Well, more than that, actually—"

"*Riders of the Purple Sage*," Betty cut in. "That was you, wasn't it?" Her hand flew to her mouth. "Oh, I do apologize—I didn't mean to interrupt. How rude."

Grey laughed easily. "Not at all, Miss. Writers have two favorite subjects: their work and themselves."

Betty smiled. "I'm glad you're not offended. And please, call me Betty."

"Betty it is." Grey turned to Cliff. "Speaking of favorite subjects, I couldn't help noticing your jacket. That looks well used."

Cliff nodded. "Well, it's definitely my favorite. Wear it every time I fly a plane."

Grey's expression brightened. "So I was right—you're a pilot."

Cliff nodded. "Small planes, stunt stuff."

"He's an *excellent* pilot," Betty put in. She actually looked like she was preening.

Grey chuckled. "I see someone who's biased." He sat back as the young waitress came over with a couple of menus, giving Cliff and Betty time to order hot coffee and the café's specialty of homemade chicken and dumplings soup. The girl came back a second time with two cups and a full coffee pot so she could refill Grey's cup, too; when she poured, the comforting smell of the brew seemed to chase away the last of the drizzly chill, and Cliff could almost see the tenseness fall away from Betty's shoulders. The three of them chatted a bit about local stuff—tourist spots, restaurants, hotels—until the soup came. Like the coffee, the scent of the chicken soup was comforting and helped both Cliff and Betty relax. The people at the next table were talking about the Nazis and the war in Europe and some big Navy warship that was supposed to dock in Los Angeles next month, but that wasn't something Cliff wanted to get into while on this island mini-vacation. Now that they were warm and dry, he thought he could even give a pass to that lecherous taxi driver—after all, who wouldn't want to look at a woman as beautiful as Betty?

"So you two are here for the weekend?" Grey asked. When Cliff nodded, the older man leaned forward again. "I've got a big place here on the island, more rooms than I know what to do with. There are already a few people staying over for a couple of weeks. Why don't you join us? Great company, excellent food, and save your-selves a few bucks. I even have a car you can use while you're here."

"We're planning to head back to the mainland on Tuesday morning." Cliff raised an eyebrow. "That's quite a generous offer, Mister Grey. Especially to a couple of people you just met a half hour ago. What's the catch?"

"Cliff!" Betty said in a dismayed voice. "Don't be rude!"

But Grey only chuckled and folded his hands on the tabletop. "Please—call me Zane. And don't worry. I'm not offended. Cliff, if you could find time during your stay, how about a flying lesson or two? It's something I always had a little interest in but never did anything about."

Cliff considered this. "Well..."

Betty touched his arm. "Oh, let's do it, don't you think? It sounds marvelous." Her eyes were shining again, a sure sign that she was convinced and there was no way they were going to do anything else. She probably thought they were going to meet some movie stars at his house or something, and in reality, maybe she was right. The guy *was* pretty famous—even Cliff knew that plenty of Grey's books had been made into movies. He seemed like a nice-enough sort, and if he wanted to be the butter-and-egg man for their trip, why not?

Cliff pushed his empty soup bowl to the center of the table. "We can give it a shot, I guess. But I'll tell you, it's gonna take more than an hour to get you in the air on your own."

Grey nodded. "I'm smart enough to know that. But it'll be a good time just to be flying in a small plane with someone who could tell me the basics."

"I could do that," Cliff said. "Plus I'm flying an Aeronca C-2, pretty easy to learn as long as you don't try anything whacky."

Grey beamed. "Excellent." He glanced out the window. "Look— my driver just pulled up. Let's get your stuff and head to the estate." When he stood, Cliff and Betty followed suit, but when Cliff pulled out his wallet, Grey waved him off. "I've got this." He lifted a finger toward the woman behind the register on the other side of the room, and when Cliff glanced in that direction, he saw her nod. "It'll go on my tab."

"That's very generous of you, but—"

"Really, it's no bother. If I can't spend a little green on some newfound friends, what's the good of working all these years, right?" He made a show of offering his arm to Betty, and she took it daintily, flashing Cliff a look that said, *Hush now, and just enjoy it!* He gave her a crooked smile and followed them, grabbing the biggest of the bags by the door for the driver to load in the back of Zane Grey's car, a cream-colored Lincoln convertible that was so beautiful it could've just come off a new car lot. Grey climbed into the front seat while the driver held the door for Betty, and Cliff then went back for the rest of their stuff; while the man put their bags into the trunk, Cliff tried to relax against the light leather upholstery and hoped his old, worn jacket wouldn't leave a dirty smudge. Betty, on the other hand, looked right at home, a dark-haired beauty with ruby lips reclining in her princess carriage.

The drive took them right along the coastline, with no pauses or side trips for a scenic route. They hadn't gone far among the quaint shops and small homes before the car headed west on Marilla Avenue and shortly after that took a right turn onto Vieudelou, a street name Cliff wasn't even going to try to pronounce. The two-lane road curved a couple of times, and then the pavement dropped away at a wooden sign that proclaimed they were rolling down the rain-sodden dirt of STAGE ROAD. The driver steered the Lincoln around a final bend, and suddenly, just that quick, they were there.

There was no mistaking that Grey had not used the word "estate" lightly in his invitation. The building was a sprawling pueblo with too many windows and patios to count; the house itself and its main entrance were above them, up a hefty flight of narrow stairs that looked rather treacherous, covered as they were in moisture from the recent drizzle.

"Oh my," Betty said. "It's so big."

Grey glanced at her from the front seat and smiled. "I suppose it is, although it doesn't seem that way to me. There are always guests in one part or another, and of course there's the housekeeping and kitchen staff, so the place is never really empty." Whatever else he was going to say was forgotten as his driver came around and opened the door. Grey climbed out and waited while the man did the same for Cliff and Betty. "Andrew, take Cliff's luggage to the Canyon room and Miss Betty's to the Tonto Rim room." Grey beamed at them. "The two best rooms in the place for very special guests. Why don't we all relax for a bit, then meet for cocktails in front of the fire in the main room in an hour?"

Cliff opened his mouth to protest and got Betty's sharp elbow in his ribs as she nonchalantly hooked her arm around his. "That sounds wonderful, Mister Grey."

"Zane."

"Of course." Cliff caught Betty's pointed glance. "Doesn't it, darling?"

"Ye-es." He hoped his answer didn't come out sounding as glum as he really felt. So much for a few nights of romance with his girl. If he'd known Grey's invitation was going to gum the works like this, he never would've accepted it. Well, no sense dwelling on it. This was the way it had played out, and they were stuck pretty good. But why did that kind of stuff always seem to happen to him?

The air smelled green and fragrant, heavy with the scent of leaves, moist earth and a few late-season flowers blooming here and there on the hillside. The steps were steep and plentiful, but he wasn't complaining too much, because Betty held onto him the entire way. A good part of him was afraid this was as close as they were going to get during their stay, so he was glad to make the climb last, stopping now and then to point out something nice in the view. They parted inside when the driver motioned for Cliff to follow him and a maid appeared to show Betty to her own room. He saw them head down a hallway on the opposite side of the great room. He wondered why Grey would use the length of the place to separate them; Betty was always reading those movie-gossip magazines, and Grey had been on the cover of one not so long ago. It was pretty well known the old man had several mistresses, so he couldn't be all that stiff about Cliff and Betty acting like a couple.

"Don't worry," Grey said from behind him. When Cliff turned to face him, he saw a corner of the older man's mouth lift. "You'll have plenty of alone time with your lovely lady. Let me show you to your room—which, by the way, has its own private entrance." Grey's lips widened into a full smile. "As does Betty's room, in case you were wondering."

Cliff chuckled. "Is it that obvious?"

Grey shrugged. "I wouldn't put it that way, exactly. But let's just say that I still understand." He motioned for Cliff to walk beside him. "You know, I always wanted to learn to fly. I'm afraid I'm too old now."

"You're never too old," Cliff said. "As long as your mind's clear. It's more a matter of being willing to put in the time for the flight lessons and the hours."

"Well, I've certainly always been interested in airplanes. I will admit that my real passion for free time is fishing, though. Still..." The writer's voice trailed off, and Cliff could hear the yearning in it.

"I could take you up today," he offered. "Show you the basics. It wouldn't be like real lessons, of course, but you'd probably get the gist of it. The plane is set up for a copilot. If you're a quick study, maybe even give you the yoke for a minute or two."

Grey's forehead furrowed. "I realize you agreed to that back in the café, and it's quite a generous offer. But I don't want you to think that my hospitality is contingent upon anything like that. I'd be happy with a few stories around the fireplace and maybe a ride over the island."

"But it's the least I can do," Cliff told him, "and easy besides. Like I said, the Aeronca is easy to fly. I've heard some guys claim a newbie can have it up in the air alone with only five or six flight hours."

Grey looked thoughtful. "Not sure I'd bet my life on that one, no matter how tempting. Still, I know you came to Catalina to spend time with your girl. I'd love a lesson or two, but I don't want to cut into that."

Cliff chuckled. "Sir, that was the agreement, remember? And if anything, you're doing me a favor. Betty will want to go shopping, and at least this will delay the agony of having to go with her."

Grey had led Cliff down a wide, cool hallway lined with richly toned Saltillo tile, and now the white-haired man stopped at a heavy wooden door. He pushed it open and stood to the side. "Your room," he said. "If you need anything, there's a buzzer on the desk. Ring it and one of the staff will be along immediately. We'll meet in the main room in an hour and discuss my miniature flying lesson and make sure we can fit it into your schedule."

After Grey left, Cliff inspected the room. It was nicer than anyplace he'd ever stayed, and certainly more than he would have been able to afford on his pay as a stunt pilot. He hadn't seen much of the estate so far, but this room was the same as the rest: rugged and western in style but subtly opulent. Displayed in an upright frame on the desk was a pristine copy of the book Betty had talked about earlier, *Riders of the Purple Sage*, and Cliff realized that the colors around the room—the curtains and matching bedspread, the paintings, even the rugs—had been painstakingly coordinated to go with the book's cover. Also on the desk were some touristy things—a couple of maps of the island and Avalon, some outdoorsy guides for hiking and bird-watching and the like. The decor was pleasing, decidedly masculine, and he wondered what Betty's room looked like, if Grey's decorator had somehow managed to soften things up to suit a woman's tastes. On the wall opposite the door were two large windows and another door that led outside to a small private patio with a gate that was locked from the inside. Beyond the gate was an expanse of lawn that was still bright green and ultimately gave way to the wilder, untended hillside, which meant he was on the back side of the hotel. If Grey was as savvy as he made out, Betty's room would be on the same side, albeit on the opposite end of the building.

One way or another, Cliff had every intention of checking out Betty's decor later this evening.

When Cliff had freshened up, he headed back the way he and Grey had come. There was no way to lock the door behind him, so before he left, he hid the jet pack as best he could, pushing it into a tangle of ivy out on the patio rather than choosing someplace obvious like the oversized burl-wood wardrobe. He heard voices, quite a few more than Zane Grey's and Betty's, long before he crossed the threshold into the great room; when he did, he remembered that he and Betty weren't the only guests in their host's home tonight. In retrospect, Cliff thought he should have known better— the man was a rich and famous author who'd had movies made from his books. The estate was enormous, more than large enough to accommodate at least a dozen more visitors, and there was a full staff besides. A guy like that was used to entertaining a loaded house and probably did it all the time.

Tonight a good-sized group of people was gathered around the massive stone fireplace, chatting in low, amiable tones. As he strolled across the room to join them, Cliff could hear glasses clinking and an occasional soft laugh. The lamps around the room cast enough light to cut through the shadows, and the fire, not too big and not too small, was stoked to just the right size to hold off the chilliness of the damp fall afternoon. It was such a welcoming scene that by the time Cliff spotted Betty, he was eager to join the conversation.

His girlfriend had changed into a strapless black dress that showed her generous curves to perfection. She smiled when she saw him and reached for his hand. "This is my boyfriend, Cliff Secord," she announced to the others. "Cliff, you must meet Zane's other houseguests." She gestured at each of the people in front of her as she introduced them, demonstrating a knack for remembering names and facts that Cliff had to admire. "This is Helmut and Ingrid Roehm," Betty said. A tall, middle-aged man with a lean face and dark blond hair nodded at Cliff; his wife, a pretty thing with lighter blond hair and blue eyes set in a plump face, smiled pleasantly. "They're originally from Germany, but when Hitler began gaining power, they relocated to Brazil with their friends, Ilse and Janni." She indicated the two women on Helmut's other side. Both had light brown hair and stern gazes, similar builds and blue eyes like their companions, and they looked like twin librarians. "They're sisters," Betty told him. Close enough.

Cliff shook hands all around, a little surprised at the sense of suppressed strength he felt in each of the women's grips. "Pleased to meet you."

Grey came forward and offered him a glass, then poured a measure of scotch into it from a crystal decanter and topped it off with a splash of cool, fresh water. "The McCallan," he said with pride. "I've had this cask for nearly ten years, so it's about forty years old. Great stuff." He saluted Cliff with his glass. "I save it for very special guests."

"Absolutely," Cliff agreed. He raised the glass to his lips but inhaled deeply before sipping. The smell of the expensive liquor was intoxicating by itself; adding the smooth taste made it downright exquisite. It warmed everything on the way down to his stomach. He looked toward Helmut. "South America, huh? That must be quite the change from Germany. What line of work are you in? I bet it's hard to find jobs down there."

He had something else to add, but Betty's elbow gouged discreetly into his ribs and drove it from his mind. "Don't mind Cliff," she told them. "He's like a child sometimes. Always too curious."

Helmut chuckled. "No worries, Miss. It's a natural question. But we are very fortunate." He inclined his head toward the three women in his group. "You see, I am an investor, so my business can be done from anywhere there is a telegraph available. As a matter of fact, that is how I met Mister Grey. I specialize in new companies, the smaller ones run by common people. Ilse and Janni work for me, teaching German and English to those whose companies I back when the need arises." His blue eyes were steady, and he held Cliff's gaze without faltering. "I am what one would call the salesman, while Ingrid keeps the books and manages the employees."

"Sounds exciting," Cliff said, although he thought it was anything but. He didn't say anything else, just listened to Betty and the three women talk about the island and sightseeing. He hadn't liked Helmut's use of the phrase "common people," wording that made it clear the investor looked down on those who had less money to invest, although he certainly took advantage of that. But there was something else about Helmut that was rubbing him wrong, something more that he couldn't quite identify. Was it the too-direct gaze? Even if they didn't consider themselves shy, most people couldn't help averting their eyes now and then when they talked to new people, almost like they were afraid something secret would be revealed if they stared too long. Helmut had said he was the salesman of the outfit, but still...That unwavering look had a fake feel to it, like the guy was trying to say, *Look at me. I've got nothing to hide. Absolutely nothing.*

Really? Because hotshots like Helmut were *always* hiding something. And the women didn't strike him as any better; their eyes were too hard, too...calculating. Even Ingrid, who could probably pass as someone's nanny, had a coldness to her blue eyes that was unsettling. It took him another moment to figure out, but then he realized that when she smiled, the expression never reached her eyes.

Betty turned to him. "Would you mind terribly if I went shopping for a few hours with the ladies?" she asked.

"Of course not," Cliff answered. He shot Grey an *I told you so* look.

"I'm told that Greta Garbo is on the island for a couple of days. Jimmy Stewart, too. The Hollywood people are always coming over. You might run into someone in Avalon, perhaps catch an autograph or two." Grey nodded at Helmut's wife. "Ingrid, especially, is a huge movie fan. I'm not sure how she does it, but she definitely has a knack for keeping track of where the stars will be."

Betty's expression was radiant as she looked at Ingrid. "Really?"

The German woman nodded. "Yes. I have certain friends in the industry who let me know. It's not always on the mark, but the information is correct enough to make it useful most of the time."

At her side, Helmut looked at his watch and then at Grey. "I don't want to be rude, but I have some business to which I must attend, and it will require me to also go into Avalon. Is there a way...?"

"Absolutely," Grey immediately picked up on the unfinished request. "You can take one of my cars. The Cadillac or the Lincoln—your choice."

Helmut nodded. "Very kind of you to accommodate."

"I'll have a driver waiting for the three of you in..." Grey glanced at a handsome grandfather clock between two of the windows. "Will a half hour be too soon?"

"That's fine," Ilse said without waiting for input from the other women. "We'll be ready."

All smiles, the ladies headed to their rooms. Betty stopped to give Cliff a quick kiss on one cheek before she followed. "Are you sure this is all right? What will you do while I'm gone?"

Cliff inclined his head toward their host. "I believe I'll give Mister Grey his first flying lesson."

"This is it," Cliff said as he and Grey walked around the orange and white Aeronca C-2.

Grey plucked experimentally at one of the wires running from the wing to the plane's body, then peered into the cockpit. "Not much to it," he said doubtfully. "I've only been on a plane once in my life, so I'm certainly no airplane expert, but I was expecting something...I don't know. Sleeker, perhaps? Sturdier?"

Cliff chuckled. "Sorry, but today, this is what you get. In the industry, they nicknamed this baby a Flying Bathtub. Like I said before, the upside is that it's easy to learn to fly." He grinned and leveraged himself into the pilot's position. "Climb in."

After a moment's hesitation, Grey did just that, settling next to Cliff and following suit as the younger man belted himself in, then donning the leather cap and goggles Cliff handed him. That done,

Cliff motioned to the man waiting in front of the plane's nose; the engine caught with the first spin of the propeller, and in a few more minutes, Cliff had them pulling upward through the currents of air dancing over Catalina Island. He waited until the airport had faded behind them before leveling off at respectable altitude, and then he cruised there for a while until he could see Grey starting to relax. Once he thought the old man felt sure the Aeronca wasn't going to fall apart beneath them, he started explaining the dials in the cockpit and showing how the aircraft responded to manipulation of the yoke. The island spread out below them as they headed roughly southwest, shades of gray and green along small hills spotted with trees and occasionally cut through with roads. Cliff kept their course steady and easy, circling around Mount Orizaba then heading to the eastern side of the island and following the coast on its northwest edge. At the isthmus he turned the airplane west again, then south to follow the coast on the opposite side.

Grey was a smart man, and he was catching on in no time at all. When he joked about the padding in front of them, a feature put there to keep the potential jolt of a landing from becoming too painful for the pilot and passenger, Cliff decided the older man was comfortable enough to get a little hands-on time at the yoke.

"Take it," he instructed Grey, raising his voice to be heard over the wind rush and the buzzing of the propeller. "No sudden moves—keep her steady. I'm right here." Grey did as he was told, although Cliff could see the man's nervousness return. He grinned; most people didn't get to pilot a plane their first hour in the cockpit. "Don't look so surprised. You're doing fine."

"I certainly hope so," Grey said. "Let's hope this is the last surprise for the day."

Cliff laughed. The coastline was starting to turn; rather than take the yoke, he put his hand over Grey's and turned the plane to the left, following the angle of the island westward to its tip before guiding it more tightly around; from up here, it resembled an arrowhead. When the coastline below straightened out for a bit, he pulled his hand away and let Grey go on his own again. Rather than make the man try to follow where the ocean and island came together, he let Grey stay on course straight across the water, not trying to make conversation or disrupt his concentration. Below them, the color of the ocean changed as they put more distance between the land and the plane, shifting its shades of blue from vast indigo in the west to a clear, exquisite turquoise where the waves broke against the rocky shore and the water filled with oxygen. They flew past the isthmus again, farther out on the left side of the plane this time, and from this viewpoint it looked like a jagged aquamarine slash in the land that nearly cut the island in two.

"We're going to aim toward Little Harbor Bay and turn east," Cliff told Grey. "That'll put us on a straight line south of the runway so we can circle around for landing. Do you know where Little Harbor is?"

"I could find it blindfolded," Grey answered. "But not from up here. Other than for fishing, I'm afraid I've never really studied the coast topography of the island."

"Got it. I'll take the controls back when we get close, give you a chance to pay more attention to the rock you've been living on for... how long now?"

Grey lifted one shoulder. "Twelve, thirteen years." His expression was a little sheepish. "To me, it's just home, you know? Where I live, where I write, entertain. You understand."

"Sure," Cliff said agreeably. But he didn't understand, not at all, and it took everything he had not to visibly shake his head. This old guy lived on an *island*, for crying out loud, in a house that was the size of a hotel. He had the kind of bulge that nobody in Cliff's circles had ever experienced, and they likely never would, either. Yeah, he'd worked for it—Cliff understood that—but did he even really appreciate it? Maybe at one time he'd been a regular Joe like Cliff, but if so, it seemed like those days were so far behind him he'd forgotten.

Ahead Cliff saw the coastline where the far side of Little Harbor Bay jutted back out. "I'll take it from here," he told Grey. He banked the Aeronca hard to the east so Grey could see and motioned for his passenger to look down. "That's Little Harbor Bay. It has two parts— a mini-bay with a beach slightly to the north and then the main one that bears its name. There's an old stagecoach stop there. I already knew about it, but it's also mentioned on a guide map on the desk in my room."

Grey peered over the side. "Ah, I know where we are!" he exclaimed. "I've actually been here recently with Helmut and Ingrid. I don't know if you can see it, but over there—" Grey pointed, but Cliff couldn't tell at what—"is a bit of construction, a small site where there will ultimately be a small marine research base."

"Really?" On a whim, Cliff turned the airplane back to the north, coming around in a circle so that he could take a look at the spot Grey was talking about. Yeah, there it was, tucked between two outcrops of rock that were steep enough to qualify as cliffs. There wasn't much to the site beyond a tiny wood building and a pile of what was probably construction materials covered by a dark-colored tarp. The location was ironic—that little mini-bay had caught his eye on the flight in, and here this marine research base was right across from it. Probably not such a romantic spot after all.

He frowned suddenly. "Did you say you'd been there with Helmut and Ingrid?"

"That's right."

"Why were they at the site?" He gave Grey a sidelong glance. "I guess that sounds nosy, doesn't it? It just seems strange, but it's probably none of my business."

Grey laughed. "I don't see the harm in telling you. You recall Helmut saying he invests in small companies?"

"Right," Cliff said, although the way Helmut had put it wasn't nearly that nice.

"This is one of his investments," Grey told him. "He said it's a small company from Canada that wants to study whale population and migration. Their start-up money came from a research grant by the Canadian government, and they have a number of universities donating to it. Once construction is completed, the universities will compete against each other to send their best marine biology students to intern there for a semester at a time, oversee the equipment, man the boat, whatever's needed."

Cliff looked at him doubtfully. "That's going to shape into some kind of a building? Looks more like a shack to me."

Grey nodded. "Right now, true. But it's still in the planning stages. It won't be a huge facility, just a couple of rooms and a dock that can service a small research vessel. Right now I think they're doing a lot of surveying, and maybe the underwater pouring of the concrete footings for the dock." There was a satisfied tone to Grey's words. "In my opinion, the world could use a lot more projects like this one—which, by the way, has the full blessing of William Wrigley, Jr., who owns the island."

"No kidding."

"Yep. No one can build on Catalina without his consent."

By now Cliff could see the airport runway on his left; one more circle and he could bring the Aeronca down. "Interesting." Cliff gave the head pad a companionable thump. "Now let's get back to your flying lesson. You're about to see why the Flying Bathtub is a favorite for both new and experienced pilots. It's as easy to land as peach pie is to eat."

Although he kept going, giving pointers to Grey about reading the indicator gauges, keeping the aircraft level, reducing their altitude and more, it was all autopilot droning, standard stuff that he could basically relay in his sleep.

And none of it could derail the deeply unsettling thought that the too-smooth Helmut and his ice-behind-her-eyes wife were financing construction in a conveniently hidden spot only a little over twenty miles from Los Angeles.

Dinner had been both a blessing and a curse.

On the one hand, Cliff had been seated next to Betty, who as always looked positively delicious. Tonight she was wearing a dress she'd obviously picked up during the day's shopping expedition, a black-and-white striped number with a full skirt that rubbed against his legs and a spaghetti-strap top with just enough of a gap between the fabric and her chest to be juicy. The food was pretty posh, double main dishes of swordfish steak and prime rib, with vegetables and salads that had been fancied up so much that Cliff could no longer tell what they'd started out as. And who could resist a spread of cobblers and little chocolate-and-cream mini-cakes—Betty called them *petit fours*.

On the bad side...*two hours*. No offense, but Cliff was used to grabbing a burger, fries and coffee from Millie at the Bulldog Café; most of the time he was in and out of there in a half hour at the most. But he'd been stuck here. They'd started with drinks, then had been served some kind of tiny thing with a French name—*amuse-bouche*, he thought it'd been called—that was supposed to do something to your taste buds but had been barely big enough to chew on. After that had come the real appetizers, shrimps damned near as big as a fist and saucer-sized oysters baked with cheese and spinach. Then lobster bisque soup, a salad course and finally the main event, all followed, of course, by the dessert spread and more drinks. At the end of it, Cliff not only felt like he was going to burst, but also he was stiff as a block of cement from sitting for so long. Did the old man eat this way every night? If so, how come he didn't weigh four hundred pounds?

Finally the conversation had dwindled and people began excusing themselves to head to their own rooms. Grey stayed, but he looked tired; Cliff thought that if Helmut and Ingrid had any manners—they were over in one corner, talking quietly—they'd retire so Grey wouldn't feel obligated to wait up.

"Ready to call it a night, Cliff?" asked a sweet-as-honey voice from behind him. As always, Betty was right on the mark. You could always count on her to know when it was time to make a graceful—usually—exit.

He turned, grinning at her unspoken invitation. "You bet."

One of her eyebrows lifted momentarily, and her mouth stretched into a smile. "I'm going to head to my room. Want to walk me there?"

Cliff almost agreed, but his gaze touched on the last three people in the great room, and at the last second he remembered the construction project over by Little Harbor Bay. "I'll come by in a little while," he told her instead. "I want to clean up a bit, brush my teeth."

Although she didn't say a word, this time the lift of Betty's eyebrow was a lot higher.

"Seafood," he added, trying to sound sincere. He made a show of poking at the inside of one cheek with his tongue, like he was trying to dig out something that was stuck. Not exactly attractive, but maybe it would do the trick.

Betty tilted her head. "I see," she said. There was a hint, just a bit, of frost in her words. She lowered her voice until only he could hear her. "Fifth door on the left. Don't keep me waiting too long." With that, she turned on her heel and headed out, pausing only for a brief good-night to Grey before disappearing down the hallway. Cliff frowned as he watched her go, wondering why she didn't stop to say something to Helmut and Ingrid. It was curious enough that he'd be sure to bring it up later.

Speaking of which, if he didn't want seeing her to be too *much* later, he needed to get a move on.

Back in his room, he slid open the patio door and dug the piece of luggage containing the jet pack out of the greenery at the side of his private patio. In two more minutes he'd donned his leather jacket and the Rocketeer helmet and had the jet pack strapped in place. He opened the gate and stepped through, pausing to listen to the night sounds—mostly crickets but other insects, too, the small rustlings of nocturnal creatures and the occasional far-off sounds of traffic from Avalon, the foghorn of a boat. No one else was around, and the woodsy hillside was camouflaged in a damp darkness that leaked onto the back of the house, fighting to overtake the glow from the occasional softly lit window. With his hands securely in the familiar metal fittings, Cliff made his way into the trees as quietly as possible, searching for a clearing big enough to use for takeoff but far enough from the estate so that the jet pack's ignition wouldn't be noticed.

As many times as he'd used the jet pack, takeoff was still a bit of a shock, that deep, swirling feeling in the pit of his stomach that he couldn't compare to anything except, maybe, the trickiest of his daredevil stunt jobs. In a plane, he felt secure, surrounded by metal-work and braces, belted in and able to steer; with the jet pack propelling him, everything he felt was precisely the opposite: there was nothing but the helmet and leather jacket to protect him if he fell, and let's face it—his old flight jacket would be sad and sorry padding if he dropped out of the sky at a thousand feet, and the helmet wouldn't save him if he landed and snapped his neck.

But it was all worth it.

The jet pack fired, and Cliff headed straight up, toward a million stars he knew were there even though they hid behind a high, thin cloud cover. The night air was sweet and blissful as it bathed his face and left behind the smell of spent fuel. He didn't have to go very high before he could see enough lights here and there to guide him in the right direction, west toward Little Harbor Bay. He'd double-checked the map and flight distance before he'd left—a little over eight air miles—and he had more than enough fuel to get there, poke around a little, and return.

To make his adventure even easier, Cliff saw that his destination was lit up like a soft-focus Main Street on Saturday night. Lights, not too bright but still visible, were strung along the rocky coastline, illuminating the whole construction site. Oddly, although the area they'd flown over earlier in the day had looked to be dusty and empty of all but a small shack and a tarp-covered mound, it now had an abundance of bodies in it, swarming like busy bees around a hive. Working this late at night was strange to begin with, but since when did construction workers dress in all-black uniforms and boots? The WPA workers he'd seen in California were wearing their clothes until they were little more than dirt-stained rags. Sometimes they had hard hats, but only if the job site provided them. Most times they kept the sun off their scalps with well-worn poor boys or used Ben Hogan hats.

Cliff circled around and came back from the other side, trying to get a better look but still keep enough altitude so he wouldn't be noticed. The "shack" had grown considerably and now had a frame connected to it that was at least three times bigger than the original structure. There was a ship not far from the rocks at the shore, but it didn't look large enough to be the research vessel that Grey had talked about, and like everything else, something was off about it. At first glance it looked like any other small ship, except it was painted a dark enough gray so that if not for a pitiful few lights along the deck, it would've blended into the sea. And what were those protuberances on each side of the forward cabin—

Something black streaked into his vision from the right and knocked him out of the sky.

What the hell was that?

Cliff's thoughts were tumbling as fast as his body was headed face over feet for the water.

Some kind of bird? An eagle, or—

Sky.

Giant mutant seagull?

Ground.

Sky.

A man?

Cliff managed to right himself and shoot upward, aiming for the stars and as much distance as he could put between himself and his attacker. He hadn't just been knocked aside; he'd been really hit, and hard—he could feel his ribs aching beneath the sturdy leather of his flight jacket. Who—or what—could do that and fly at the same time? Well, besides himself?

He leveled off and looked down, then used the accelerator button in one hand to jerk sideways, just before something whizzed by him again. The air displacement pushed him back, but at least this time he didn't drop like a sack of wet flour, and Cliff managed to track it and climb a bit higher. When the flying thing swung back around and aimed for him a third time, it was below him; the lights from the construction site made it into a sleek black silhouette, but he could finally get a decent look.

It *was* a man!

At least...mostly. It had to be, right? There was a head, helmeted like Cliff's own, arms bent at the elbows and likely holding onto acceleration buttons or levers, just like he was. Human legs trailed out behind the thing, dragged out flat by the speed of acceleration, but that was the end of any resemblance to the shape of a man. Were those wings? No, of course not...some kind of gliding or parachute device?

This time Cliff saw the shape head-on when it came hurtling toward him again. A man, thank God, with some kind of device strapped to his back, a jet pack of a different kind. Bigger, heavier, painted black like his outfit and helmet to help him blend into the night, and yes—there was some kind of gliding mechanism incorporated onto the fuel tanks to help him maintain lift. He flashed by

Cliff on the right, turning expertly at the last second so as not to kill them both in an aerial version of the old chicken game. But his passing was more than just a whoosh of air; this time, the guy swung at him. And he *connected*, giving Cliff a solid punch that whacked him in the right shoulder where his arm joint met the muscle of his upper chest.

Cliff grunted in surprise and instinctively backed off the accelerator buttons; that, in turn, dropped him a good seventy-five feet before he managed to regain control. His attacker came at him again, this time from above, using Cliff's loss of altitude as a weapon in itself. The black-suited man drove both booted feet heels-first into the top of Cliff's Rocketeer helmet.

Beyond the fact that he was almost knocked silly, Cliff lost another sixty feet or so, fighting to climb at the same time he struggled to orient himself. His ears were ringing, his vision was blurry and spotted with white and yellow dots and he felt lucky to still be headed up toward the skies when he desperately slammed his thumbs against his acceleration buttons.

The ground spun across his gaze, and he realized there wasn't a whole lot of grace space left. The construction workers—and he didn't for a second believe that's what they were anymore—had seen him and were pointing upward and running back and forth below him like a hungry pack of hyenas waiting for an injured ape to fall out of a tree. But if he ended up landing among them it might be a better end, because the edge of the cliffs weren't far off; going over them would likely mean crashing against the sharp, half-submerged boulders and having the Pacific's waves grind him to hamburger. Neither choice had been included in his plans for the end of the evening.

Wait—were those *rifles* in the hands of the men charging across the beach below? You betcha, and they were bringing them up, no doubt hoping to make him the bull's-eye in a nighttime game of target practice. Great.

Something tiny moved in the corner of his eye, and Cliff twisted instinctively away from it, veering hard to the left and away from the construction site to head toward the open ocean. The other man streaked after him, steadily gaining, and even though he knew it was useless, Cliff couldn't stop himself from pressing harder on his accelerator buttons. Five seconds, ten, twenty—

The fog bank!

Cliff felt his breath expel from his lungs in relief as he suddenly cut into the thick, nightly band of fog that rolled toward the island. He swerved to the right, climbed, then went back to the left, holding himself level and slowing until the noise of the jet pack became almost imperceptible in the moisture-laden air. He could see the coastline of the island below him, the tiny dots of light coming from the piers and houses set far apart, but he was careful not to drop too close to the ocean, below the camouflaging layer of white mist. It was only a minute or two until the noise of the other guy's jet pack faded; no doubt the attacker didn't want to stray too far from home base and chance being seen.

Although the fog had helped Cliff escape, it was also obvious it was a major asset in hiding whatever they were up to at that phony construction site. Was Grey involved? Cliff didn't think so; the old man seemed pretty oblivious to the island's goings-on beyond the greatest spots for fishing. He probably had accountants and lawyers who handled his money and investments, or maybe that was taken care of by Mrs. Grey, who didn't seem to be around this weekend. But someone trying to disguise a project like that wouldn't have been so unconcerned when Cliff had flown over it.

In another quarter hour, Cliff was back in his room with the jet pack secreted in a slightly different location—variety never hurt—on the securely locked patio. He cleaned up as quickly as he could, changed his clothes and shoes, then slipped into the hallway and pulled the door shut behind him. There were still lights on in the hall and the great room, but they'd been changed to nighttime illumination, just enough to make sure a wandering insomniac guest didn't trip over a wayward ottoman and break something. A slow-burning log still glowed in the enormous fireplace, the smoldering orange wood occasionally cracking and sending a shower of sparks against the hearth screen. Normally Cliff would have thought the sound comforting, but something wasn't right in the place, and the popping sound that came from the wood was just short of spooky. There were too many shadows in the oversized room, too many dark places where things unknown could blend into the dark.

"Mister Secord?"

Cliff spun, barely holding back a yelp. Helmut Roehm stood in just such a shadowed area to the right of the fireplace, where the throbbing red-orange light couldn't reach. "Uh...yeah. Hi. What are you doing here?"

The other man stepped closer and pulled a silver cigarette case from his pocket. He flipped it open and held it out to Cliff, who shook his head. Helmut slid out a snipe and lit it. "I suppose I'm not ready to sleep. More of a night person, I guess. You?"

Since it would reflect badly on Betty to tell the truth, Cliff said, "The same."

"Ah."

A corner of Helmut's mouth turned up knowingly, and for an instant, just that, Cliff had to resist the urge to backhand him. Since that would make him a very poor houseguest, he asked instead, "How do you like the California climate? It must be very different from Germany."

Helmut shrugged and dragged on his cigarette. "Yes. But remember that we have been in Brazil for some time. From there to here is not such a shock." He glanced at Cliff. "We left Germany to get away from the Nazis. We came here for the same reason, the Nazi party trying to establish control in Brazil."

"Right," Cliff said. He kept his voice agreeable, although he felt anything but. Roehm sounded as though he was trying too hard to be convincing. His dislike of the German was rising with every ten-second span he had to be in the man's company, more than could be justified by their limited interaction.

"Well," Helmut said, "I think I shall retire to my room. Perhaps a little reading will relax me. Good night, then." He tossed the remains of his cigarette into the fireplace and touched one finger to his forehead, as if in salute.

Cliff nodded and stayed where he was in the front of the hearth, watching Helmut out of the corner of his eye. What was it about him? He was somehow involved in the goings-on at Little Harbor Bay, but how so? As an investor? Or as a full participant in the surreptitious nighttime construction of...what exactly?

He sighed. Interesting questions that required more research, but he wasn't going to get any answers tonight. Was it too late to join Betty? No way to know unless he tried. That decision made, he turned toward the hallway, stepping into the space Helmut Roehm had been standing in when Cliff had first been startled ten minutes earlier. He'd just tap very lightly on her door, see if she was still awake—

Crunch.

Cliff stopped and looked down, then rubbed the sole of one shoe lightly across the polished wood floor. It moving with a slightly grainy feeling, like...

Sand.

Beach sand, to be precise.

Well, that answered one of his questions.

Sunday, October 22, 1939

By mid-Sunday morning the fog had burned away to reveal a cloudless, cornflower-blue sky. Cliff was up early and drinking coffee in the dining room with Zane Grey well before Betty, the Roehm couple and the sisters joined them. His sleep had been broken, his mind muddled with thoughts of his night visit to Little Harbor Bay, the sandy debris left at the side of the fireplace by Helmut's boots, and a twinge of nervousness that Betty would be annoyed at him standing her up since she'd already been asleep when he'd peeked into her room. But she greeted him with a smile and a kiss, then sat next to him, chatting with the others and squeezing his hand every now and then.

After the meal, everyone split up and drifted off to do their own things. The three German women grouped together and asked Betty if she wanted to go with them to Avalon for another shopping expedition, but Cliff had been with Betty long enough to recognize a certain less-than-enthusiastic set to her jawline, even when her smile looked genuine.

"I'm sorry," he said, stepping forward before Betty could reply and taking her arm, "but today is ours." He gave the other women his most engaging smile, but it did nothing to warm up the ice in their eyes. "You understand, I'm sure."

"Of course," Ilse said stiffly.

"Have a wonderful day together," Ingrid said with at least a little more warmth.

"Thanks for rescuing me," Betty said when the trio of German women had moved away and there was a little distance between her and them.

"I could tell you weren't comfortable," Cliff said. "I thought you had a good time yesterday. What gives?"

Betty shrugged. "I don't know." She hesitated. "Something is odd about them. It's like everything they say is carefully considered before it comes out of their mouths. There's no spontaneity to it, no true feeling." She laughed, but it sounded brittle. "I know that must sound strange, but it's more than just putting on airs. With everything they say, all their comments about America and the war in Europe, it's like they're trying overly hard to convince me of who they are, who they support."

"Funny," Cliff said thoughtfully. "I got the same impression from Helmut."

"Yeah," Betty agreed. "I didn't want to be rude and say anything, but I have to wonder if Mister Grey is picking up on this, too."

"Maybe. If he is, he probably wouldn't say anything. It might be stepping over the line, since he's in the position of host, having opened up his house to them."

"True." Betty seemed to give herself a mental shake, then brightened. "But let's not talk about them anymore. What are you and I going to do today?"

"Well, if you've brought along some clothes that are a little sturdier, how about we do a little hiking? It's a nice time of year for that, not too hot but not too cold. It might get a little drizzly, although it looks pretty clear right now."

"That sounds like fun," Betty said. "But I'll tell you right now that I don't want to do any camping, stay overnight or anything like that. I like my creature comforts."

Cliff laughed. "Me, too!"

After Betty had changed her outfit, she and Cliff went to find Zane Grey. Their hunt was unsuccessful, but they managed to run across one of the staff, a young man at one end of the hotel who was working a heavy coat of wax onto the newly washed Lincoln they'd ridden in yesterday.

"Do you know where we can find Mister Grey?" Cliff asked him. "We wanted to see if we could borrow a car, something that would be okay to drive on some of the rougher roads so we can get a look at the less-populated parts of the island. We thought we might drive up to Little Harbor Bay and check out the research project he told us about."

The young fellow was probably no more than nineteen, likely earning some extra money to help pay his way through college. He wore a standard worker's blue shirt with the name BILL stitched over the left pocket. "You won't be able to talk to Mister Grey at this time of the morning," Bill said, glancing at his watch. "This is his writing time. He won't come out of his office unless there's an emergency. But he'll be down for lunch." Bill motioned at the closed garage doors. "He left instructions that you could take one of the other cars. There's a Ford pickup truck that should do just fine for you. It's a little bouncy, but it'll take you where you want to go whether you're on paved roads or you get more adventurous and drive on some of the dirt ones. And Maggie can pack you a lunch if you're not planning on being back by noon." He grinned, showing a generous gap between his front teeth. "She makes the best chicken salad sandwiches you've ever tasted."

Cliff checked his own watch. "I think we'll be back in plenty of time. We definitely want to have lunch with Mister Grey and the other guests. I also owe him one more flying lesson."

Bill nodded. "I'll go get the keys for you. Tank is full, so you don't have to worry about that. And don't bother going into Avalon to fill it up before you bring it back."

As they waited, Betty glanced at Cliff. "You're really giving Zane Grey flying lessons?"

"Just one so far," Cliff told her. "The Aeronca is easy to learn, and it's the least I can do after he's putting us up for the weekend with food and cars and all."

Betty nodded. "True. So he was serious about what he said in the café."

"Yeah," Cliff said. "I think he wants to learn how to fly more than he's letting on. I can't help him that much, but as long as I'm with him, I can let him take over in the Aeronca for a few minutes at a time, keep an eye on it."

"Well, you be careful up there," she said. "Don't let him get over-confident."

"Not in my lifetime," he said.

Across the driveway, Bill slid one of the garage doors up, then backed out the Ford, turned it around pulled it in front of them. The good-sized vehicle was a nice, respectable gray color. "Here you go, sir," the young man said as he got out. "Have a great time."

"Thanks," Cliff said. "I think we will." Bill walked around and opened the passenger door for Betty, then closed it after she climbed inside. A few moments to get situated to where things were and they were headed to Little Harbor Bay for, unbeknownst to Betty, a little ground reconnaissance.

The interior of the island was a lot different from Avalon and the more populated areas just outside the town. Cliff expected that, of course, but he was surprised at how dense the forest was, at the sense of untamed nature that increased steadily the farther they traveled from Zane Grey's mansion. The trees grew tightly together, providing heavy shade across the roadway where the branches on both sides of the road arched over it and met. The brush at their bases was dense, thoroughly packed at the roadside. Even so, now and then they would catch a flash of movement— a mule deer, fox or some other creature fleeing from the intruding sound of their motor vehicle. There were almost no structures, and the few they did see appeared to be little more than weathered, abandoned shacks, with no indication of what they once might have been used for.

Cliff had picked up the map from the room and tucked it in his pocket to make sure that his mental image of the island as seen from overhead matched with the reality on the ground. It was a quiet, beautiful drive, and it didn't take that long for them pull up by the old stagecoach stop at Little Harbor. He parked the car, and he and Betty got out and went into the lobby of the inn just to take a look. It was nice enough, although nothing like the Zane Grey estate. He bought a couple of Coca-Colas for them to take along on what he already knew was going to be a very short hike. Betty didn't know it, of course, but all he wanted to do was get a closer view of the construction site for the so-called marine research facility. It was an odd construction site, indeed, that had armed men guarding it at night. Perhaps it was some kind of a government thing, a secret setup that Grey might or might not know about. If that was the case, Cliff could easily enough turn back when he got more of an idea about the truth. On the other hand, a secret government facility wasn't something he thought a German on the run out of Brazil should be investing in. And definitely not something Helmut Roehm should be exploring late at night.

When the tiny bottles of Coke were gone, Cliff clasped Betty's hand. "Come on," he said, "let's go this way." He pointed to a small pathway off to the side of the inn. There was a well-worn, canted wooden sign stuck in the ground with faded painted letters announcing BEACH THIS WAY with an arrow pointing away from the building. It seemed like a good place to start; he'd flown way too high to note any foot paths and certainly hadn't been thinking about it anyway, since he'd been trying to evade the black-suited flying man chasing him, a figure he'd come to think of as the Black Phantom because of the way he could seemingly disappear and reappear. They could follow the path down to the beach, and then he could rely on his memory to take him around to the southwest and the area where the construction was going on. He really needed to get a closer look at the covered mounds that had dotted the area on his flyover, see what they were. Hopefully they would turn out to be nothing more than two-by-fours and normal construction materials; then he could be done with all this mystery and truly enjoy himself with Betty.

They followed the path where it led around the back of the inn and through a less densely greened area down toward the ocean. Although they were well into fall, the climate was good for growing, and wildflowers still dotted the area. The clear sky seemed to magnify the occasional sweet calls of birds back and forth. After a while the soil got sandier, and they could hear waves lapping against the shore before they came off the path and stepped onto an expanse of golden sand. It was a beautiful area, with the sun turning the surface of the ocean into a shimmering mirror broken only by the occasional tip of a wave. With very little wind right now, the sun was warm and welcoming; it was a scene that made Cliff wish he and Betty had brought a blanket and the picnic lunch Bill had suggested. How nice it would have been to spread the blanket so that he and his girl could lie back, smooch a little, and speculate about what the future might hold.

But although that was a sweet and romantic thought, the notion dissipated when, far to the left where the sand started to give way to a rockier surface, Cliff saw the tarp-covered piles. As if she knew what he was thinking, Betty pointed and said, "Look—I wonder what those are."

"Let's go find out." He took her hand again, and they walked along the shore, just at the water's edge, with Betty laughing and trying to dance away from the occasional wave that reached for her shoes. Cliff grinned at her, but inside he couldn't help being a little worried. He didn't want to get her too close to something that might turn bad, and the guns last night had certainly been that. What had he been thinking?

Finally they reached the first mound. *Interesting,* Cliff thought as they examined it. There were two tarps covering each mound. The top one was tan-colored to match the sand, and the one underneath was dark, as if someone would come out and flip the covers to camouflage the piles from day to night. Be that as it may, as he and Betty wandered from mound to mound, there was really nothing that odd about the materials. There was some wood, two-by-fours, two-by-sixes and stacks of plywood, although the majority seemed to be steel beams and sheets. Grouped as they were, it was all pretty innocuous, with nothing to indicate any sort of sinister purpose. The building that was taking shape was large but as bland and featureless as everything else, not much more than a roofed rectangular structure that looked like more of a warehouse than what Cliff thought a research facility or offices should be. Then again, what did he know of such things? A research facility would have labs; it would need space for aquariums and large tanks of water, steel tables, things like that. Perhaps the men on the ground had simply been guarding the site against potential theft, although even as he thought it, Cliff knew that was a stretch. Security would likely consist of only a single guard, two at the most; the notion of such an endeavor being controlled in the air by someone with a jet pack similar to the Rocketeer's was flat-out absurd. But if it were something secret set up by the government, wouldn't they guard it during the day, too?

Unless it wasn't the government at all.

Unless it was someone else.

Speaking of guarding it during the daytime, he and Betty had come to the opposite side of several other buildings that were still being erected and a few tarp-covered piles beyond it. Past those was a stretch of shoreline where the water deepened sharply from the light blue of the beachfront to who knew what depth. Here was where a dock would be constructed for the research ship. So far, Cliff didn't see anything that indicated such an endeavor was being started, even though he knew he'd seen a ship there last night. What he did note was a pair of dark-clothed men about fifty yards up the shore past the last covered mound. When he and Betty stepped past the last pile, the two men started toward them.

"I wonder who they are," Betty said.

"No telling," he responded. "But let's turn around and go back. This is some kind of construction site, and they're probably out here to make sure no one swipes anything from the site." He decided it would be better not to go into the whole marine research facility thing.

"Really? Why would someone do such a thing?"

Cliff shrugged. "Times are hard. I suppose if you know the right people, you could sell this stuff and make a few bucks. Best not to tangle with them—there's no reason for it."

"It's getting toward lunchtime anyway," Betty noted. "By the time we hike back and then drive, there'll be just enough time to clean up and change."

"Sure," he agreed. "Let's go."

They turned as one and headed back the way they came. As they moved down the beach and away from the nonexistent pier, Cliff glanced over his shoulder. The guard duo had stopped and was watching them leave, hands on hips, faces shadowed by dark workers' caps.

"Okay, Zane." Cliff's voice rose over the noise of the Aeronca's engine. "Your turn to take the yoke."

"Already?" Grey sounded like he was joking, but Cliff could hear the note of anxiety beneath the question.

"Don't worry. I'm right here. I'm watching everything."

"All right."

Grey's hand closed hesitantly around the yoke, and the plane wobbled a bit. Cliff steadied him by putting his own hand over the old man's for a few seconds then releasing it. "You're doing fine."

Grey took a deep breath, then asked, "Where are we headed?"

"Little Harbor Bay," Cliff answered. "It's a pretty area, so let's take another look at it."

"That it is."

"Do you know where you're going?"

Grey nodded. "Yeah, I do now. I never had reason to do it for the island before, but I can make a pretty good map in my head when I need to. It comes from all these years researching my books, keeping track of where my characters are and where they're going."

"I'll bet," Cliff said.

"It's not far," Grey told him.

"Let's decrease our altitude," Cliff said.

"What?"

"Decrease our altitude," Cliff repeated. "Go a little lower and see if we can get a closer look at the construction of the marine research facility you invested in."

"Uh...how do I do that?"

Cliff showed him, keeping a careful eye on the altimeter as the plane went lower. "No sudden moves," he instructed. "Just slow and steady."

"Isn't that it?" Grey asked. "Right down there?"

"Yeah," Cliff answered.

"Looks like the construction's moving along."

"I suppose," Cliff said. "Although I don't really know what it all encompasses."

"Me, neither," Grey admitted. "I've got a little money sunk into it, but not that much."

They buzzed overhead, not much more than a couple thousand feet of air separating them from the beachfront. "Aren't we a little too low?" Grey asked nervously.

"We're okay," Cliff said, "but let's go ahead and climb back up. I'd like to come around—"

Something long and black darted into his field of vision from the left side of the plane, and Cliff resisted the urge to jerk the yoke out of Grey's control. A bird? Or something else? "Head to the left," he instructed. "We'll turn over the ocean, then pass over the site again to head in the direction of the airport."

"Will do," Grey said.

"I want you to climb, too. Bring it up higher than we are now."

"Okay."

There it was again, and there was no mistaking it for a bird this time. It was definitely the Black Phantom of the previous night, dive-bombing the wingtips on the pilot's side of the plane. Did he really think he could somehow force the Aeronca out of the air? Not likely—he had to know that if he got too close, the propeller would suck him in and chew him into a million pieces at the same time it took down the plane.

"I'll take the yoke now," Cliff said. So far, the Black Phantom had stayed on the pilot's side of the plane and Zane Grey hadn't seen him. For the old man's sake, he needed to make sure it stayed that way. Maybe, Cliff thought, this was the Phantom's way of warning them away from the construction site. If so, it would work right now, but it wouldn't keep Cliff away permanently. One way or another, he was going to find out what was going on down there.

Cliff looked down again, this timing focusing on where a boat pier should be, but there was nothing above the surface of the water. Still, the water was clear and mostly calm right now, and even in his quick overhead pass, he could see something beneath the water, a shadow of something being constructed. Underwater construction would only block the docking of a boat, so what exactly was it?

What kind of vessel could move into place against a below-the-surface structure?

An interesting question, but right now he needed to keep Grey from noticing the Black Phantom. The fewer people who knew about this, the better. He suspected it would be best for his host all the way around not to be involved in this. It wasn't easy, but under the guise of showing off a little, Cliff managed to keep the Black Phantom out of Grey's line of sight. When they finally left the flying man behind, Cliff exhaled in relief. He hadn't realized he'd been holding his breath— that's how badly he wanted to keep that character's existence away from Zane Grey. Lost in his own thoughts, Cliff didn't say much on the return flight to the airport, but neither did Grey. Maybe the older man was tired. He was getting up there in years, and a sort of fast track to learning to fly was probably pretty taxing. Although he was sure they had different reasons, Cliff thought they both seemed a little relieved when the Aeronca was finally down on the runway and coasting to a stop in front of the hanger.

If Cliff had thought last night's dinner an elaborate affair, tonight's was nothing short of a feast. It was almost as though Zane Grey was celebrating something, some unknown holiday or event his very lucky guests knew nothing about. Everyone dressed up, including Cliff as best he could. Betty looked even more stunning than normal in a pencil dress patterned with marbleized roses that tied around her neck and set off every generous curve in her body while highlighting her pale skin, dark eyes and cherry-colored lips. Spread before everyone were lobster tails drizzled with hot, sweet-smelling butter; more huge prawns; escolar dusted with finely grated Parmesan cheese; and, for the seafood-challenged, filet mignons wrapped in bacon and stuffed with garlic and mushrooms. An array of grilled and sautéed vegetables accompanied the entrées, as well as an enormous, freshly made Caesar salad. Dessert consisted of huge wedges of luminous key lime pie, the perfect, citrusy end to a spectacular meal. Grey plied his guests with fine wine, warm liqueurs and coffee after the meal, seeming to bask in everyone's enjoyment.

But all was not quite right. Cliff could feel an undercurrent of unease around the German guests. Not just the women, but Helmut, too. They put on a good show for Grey, and, they thought, for Cliff and Betty. But there was a tautness to the muscles in Helmut's jaw and shoulders, a steeliness in his gaze when it met Cliff's. The German women seemed more determined than ever to get Betty to be friendly with them, but the more they pushed, the more Cliff could see his girl backing away. There was a weird sort of desperation to their charm, as if there were some sort of secret prerequisites they needed to meet or test they had to pass with regard to her, something that was critical to whatever was going on beneath the surface of their visit. And Cliff had no doubt that there was, indeed, something going on, something nefarious that did not just bode ill for Zane Grey, but that also would affect them all on a much larger scale. It had taken awhile to turn it over in his mind, but he was now convinced that the construction at Little Harbor Bay was much bigger than some purported marine research station. There was only one thing that he could think of which would require an underground docking station...

A submarine.

At first the idea seemed ridiculous—no way could anyone get a full-size submarine here without detection. But what if the Germans somehow managed to bring in a smaller vessel in pieces, then assemble it in place? He didn't have to try hard to recall people at the café talking about the warship that was going to dock in Los Angeles soon. What if they were gearing up to attack that warship when and where it was least expected? Such a hit would destroy the ship, yes, but to be attacked on native soil would also be a major blow to the morale of the entire U.S. services. And why stop there? If the Germans were able to bring in even just a single mini-submarine loaded with ordinance, it could also potentially do major damage to the ports of Los Angeles, striking right at the heart of one of America's major coastal cities. It might set America up for a surprise invasion on the West Coast, making it difficult to defend Los Angeles from a direct land, air and sea assault. It was clear they'd successfully created their own version of a jet pack. A single small squadron of jet-pack-suited German soldiers armed with something as simple as grenades could do irreparable damage. And what if they were armed with something more deadly, like small bombs? They could be dropped on bridges, highways, sure—but only *after* the German fliers made sure to decimate everything they could at March Field in Riverside.

If there was even a chance that something like this was in the works, Cliff had to take steps to ensure that it never came to fruition. So first thing in the morning, before breakfast, he would have a talk with Zane Grey, tell the older man what he knew, and have him use his considerable connections in Avalon and Los Angeles to investigate this and, if necessary, end it.

The evening got a lot better when Cliff and Betty finally managed to cut the invisible cord that the Germans seemed determined to wrap around Betty. They said good night to Zane Grey, and then Cliff took his girl for a lovely evening walk. The weather was still clear, with just a hint of a breeze ruffling the leaves and sending little whiffs of sweet-smelling scent here and there from the fuchsia, crocus and other flowers planted around the Grey estate. Now and then a few night birds would twitter and whistle softly, calling out to each other above the sounds of the late-season crickets. He and Betty held hands at first, and then Cliff slipped his arm across her shoulders when the temperature dropped. She snuggled against him as they turned and made their way back. By then most of the house was dark, with only night-lights and the ever-present small fire burning on the hearth in the great room. Cliff walked Betty to her room, then was pleased when she pressed her lips against his and gave him a small, inviting smile. In another moment, she had tugged him through the door and closed it behind him. For the next couple of hours, there was only him, and Betty, and their quiet sounds of lovemaking.

"Back after another night of flying?"

Cliff had left Betty in a contented sleep and was moving quietly past the fireplace in the great room when Grey's voice came out of the shadows next to it. He jerked to a stop—why did everyone seem to hide in the same spot next to that damned thing?

"Flying?" he repeated dumbly. All he could think of was somehow hiding the fact that he and Betty had been pitching woo in her room, and no matter that the old man probably took it for granted. After all, a gentleman would never advertise such a thing. "No, of course not—"

"I know about your strap-on flying machine, Cliff."

About-face on what he was thinking, and now Betty was the furthest thing from his thoughts. How could Grey know? And did he really, or was he just digging, bumping his gums in the hopes that Cliff would spill everything?

He opened his mouth to tell Grey that he didn't know what the old man was talking about, but Grey held up his hand, making a long-fingered silhouette in front of the low fire. "I saw you take off in it the first night you were here, saw the helmet, the whole deal. I know you're the Rocketeer." Grey paused, and Cliff thought he heard a strange mix of amusement and wonder in the man's next words. "Imagine that—a real-life superhero, right here in my house."

"I'm no superhero," Cliff said. "Just a regular Joe." The denial had come out unbidden, but now it was too late to take it back. He might as well have signed a confession.

Grey chuckled. "You may say that, but a lot of people think otherwise. And don't worry; I'll keep your secret. I do want to know for certain where you've been going on the island, though. I have an idea, but I want to hear it from you." He hesitated, then added, "See if it matches up with what I've been thinking lately."

Cliff rubbed the knuckles of one hand with the other, thinking it over. He was cornered here; if he denied it, his host could get angry and do something unpredictable, like order him and Betty out of the house. He'd been planning to tell Grey everything in the morning anyway, so what difference would it make if he told him tonight? Same result—get Grey to talk to the right people and put an end to the shenanigans going on at Little Harbor Bay. If Grey was a man of his word, they could work out the details to skirt around how Cliff had managed to get all the juicy details, say all his knowl-edge came from flyovers in the Aeronca and his hike with Betty. Besides, this was Zane Grey, the author of dozens of solid American Westerns. For God's sake, the man wrote about cowboys and Indians and the Old Wild West. You didn't get any more American than that.

So Cliff told him everything...almost. He wasn't sure why, but he thought that maybe Grey was safer not knowing that Helmet Roehm had his own type of jet pack and was not only capable of flying like Cliff, but was, perhaps, even a little better at it. On a subsurface level, the German certainly seemed more bloodthirsty, more experienced at combat if not the actual jet-pack-flying itself. Cliff wasn't sure if his pride or his desire to keep Grey out of that part fueled the omission, but there it was. Or rather, there it *wasn't*.

"So that's it," Cliff finished. "I was going to come talk to you early in the morning about getting in touch with the appropriate authorities."

Grey's face was dark and troubled in the slowly dying firelight. "Absolutely," he said. "Breakfast is at eight. I'd suggest you be in my office no later than seven."

"You can set your watch on it," Cliff said. He tipped an imaginary cap to his host and headed to his room to grab some sleep.

Monday, October 23, 1939

As he knew he would, Cliff woke early with the day's task right up front in his thoughts. He dressed quickly and, just for giggles, stuck his Mauser C96 into the back of his belt. He was determined to meet up with Zane Grey well before breakfast so the author could make whatever calls were necessary, but first he wanted to stop by Betty's room and make sure she knew how wonderful their time together the night before had been. There was an emptiness to the place that Cliff didn't recall feeling before, and he wondered as he strode to Betty's door if the Germans had risen even earlier and vacated the premises. Perhaps they had realized Cliff was on to them and their goals were destined to fail. It would be unfortunate if they were to escape, but the major thing was to put an end to whatever they were building at Little Harbor Bay.

But when Cliff raised his hand to knock on Betty's door and it pushed open a few inches, his whole plan got turned on its head.

"Betty?" He swung the door wide without waiting for her to answer. The room was a disaster. The bedcovers were scrambled on the floor, and the ceramic lamp that had been on the nightstand was now in pieces strewn across the tile. The desk chair was overturned, and various knickknacks looked as though they, like the lamp, had been thrown. Even books had been pulled from the built-in shelves and tossed everywhere; the reading chair and footstool that had been in front of those shelves were both tipped on their sides, the cushions tumbled out. And Betty was nowhere in sight.

Cliff spun, heading toward the door in search of someone, anyone, who could help him. He was almost there when a folded piece of paper taped to the inside of the doorjamb caught his attention. He yanked at it so frantically he almost tore it in half, and when he finally got it open and his hand steady enough to read it, he felt the air stick in his throat when he tried to inhale.

Little Harbor Bay.
Drive alone or you
know what will happen.

Furious, he wadded up the paper and threw it across the room, then ran to see if he could find Bill and wheedle a set of car keys out of him. He made it as far as the garage where he'd seen the young man the day before, and then he heard Zane Grey's voice behind him.

"Looking for me?"

Cliff stopped short and turned to face the older man. "Uh...no, not yet. Later, after..." His words faltered as he tried to concoct something that would satisfy his host. "If I could get a car, I thought I'd run into Avalon and...pick up some flowers for Betty. A surprise. You know." Even he knew it was a lame-sounding story, but Grey only raised an eyebrow then seemed to accept it.

"Sure," Grey said. He glanced at the expensive timepiece on his wrist, making Cliff remember his own words of last night. "No problem. Take the Packard; the keys are in it. I don't think Bill had a chance to gas it up, but you should have plenty of fuel. It's a small island. You can go a lot of places on only a half a tank."

"Yeah," Cliff said. Although his heart was hammering, he remembered to add, "Hey, thanks. I really appreciate it."

"No problem," Grey said again. "I'll talk to you later. When we get together, we'll have a late breakfast and take care of that situation we talked about last night." His eyes narrowed. "It seems my other guests have decided to leave without saying good-bye, so there's no sense in serving a full breakfast anyway." He raised his hand in farewell, then turned and headed back to the house.

Cliff wasn't surprised to hear the Germans had left, but he didn't wait around to talk about it. He was in the Packard and backing out of the garage inside of a minute. He had to force himself not to floor the accelerator and spit gravel everywhere—he didn't want to call attention to himself. He felt his Mauser C96 dig into the small of his back beneath the leather jacket but didn't try to adjust it—the pain would keep him sharp. If those jerks had hurt Betty, had even touched a hair on her head, he was going to put an end to a lot more than their damned construction project.

The drive to Little Harbor Bay looked a lot different when he was doing it to save Betty's life. Although the morning sun was just as bright and the sky was just as clear as yesterday, the trees that whipped past the car seemed a hundred times darker, the underbrush more dense and unfriendly. If they had killed her, would they dump her body in the woods somewhere? Or would they chuck her into the ocean like so much useless driftwood? He couldn't think about that; he couldn't bear to imagine life without her, to know that her spectacular smile and those beautiful blue eyes were gone for all time. She had to be alive. He had to get there and do whatever it took to save her.

Cliff slid sideways and kicked up dirt everywhere when he ran over the wooden sign and forced the car onto the pathway leading to the beach, a trail that was never meant to accommodate a vehicle. Whatever route Helmut and his cohorts were using to get to the construction site was unknown to Cliff, so this was his only option. The car bumped on the path, lurching over half-buried rocks until it finally slogged to a stop in the sand on the beachfront. Cliff lunged out of the car without bothering to shut the door, running for all he was worth toward the biggest building. The others were still in a state of framing, so the big one seemed the logical place to go. He was almost to the door when a shout made him skid to a stop. Before he could say anything, he realized that four men had come around the corner of the building and now he was surrounded. Each had a rifle barrel trained toward Cliff's chest. Helmut Roehm stood to the side, a lit cigarette hanging from one corner of his mouth.

"I think you should stop right there, Mister Secord," Helmut said in a congenial tone. "I believe we must have a conversation before you proceed any farther."

"You can say that again," Cliff snapped. "Where's Betty?"

"She is unharmed...so far," he said. "The question is did you follow the instructions I gave you?" He looked at Cliff with half-closed eyes. "Did you come alone?"

"Of course," Cliff retorted. "I would never do anything to endanger Betty."

"Ah. That is most excellent."

"Take me to her," Cliff demanded.

"In due time, Mister Secord, in due time. First I must ask to whom have you imparted information or, shall I say, speculation, regarding my marine research facility?"

"I don't know what you're talking about," Cliff said.

Helmut Roehm laughed. "Do not take me for a fool. I have seen you on your many *visits* to my site."

Cliff's eyebrows rose. "Really? And how could you have done that?"

Helmut's mouth turned up in a smirk. "Do I really need to go into the details? We both know what I'm talking about."

Cliff didn't answer. So Helmut Roehm was the Black Phantom. He had a jet pack similar to Cliff's, but still different in important ways. What did it use for fuel? And who had come up with the idea for the wing-like appendages that seemed to give it a better ability to turn and glide? Interesting questions, but not the focus right now.

"I don't believe I'll share that information with you until I see that Betty is all right."

"Fair enough," Helmut said. "Were I in your unfortunate shoes, I would probably take the same position." Helmut gave the slightest incline of his head, and Cliff was suddenly grabbed on both sides. A quick rough search and he was stripped of his gun and his only defense. No matter, he would fight with his fists and his teeth if he had to.

"Come along, Mister Secord," Helmut said. "Let me take you to your lady friend." The German turned and strode toward the area farther down the beach where Cliff knew they were constructing the docking station. Cliff was pushed along behind Helmut, his arms firmly gripped by two of Germany's Nazi finest. Another two men followed behind them. He could almost feel their weapons aimed at the center of his back. As the six of them came around the last and largest of the boulders, he saw Betty up ahead. Her hair was disheveled, and she was still in her nightgown, with not even a robe to keep her warm. Her hands were tied behind her back, and she was the most beautiful woman Cliff had ever seen.

"Cliff!" she cried. The German women were her guardians, and they looked like they'd taken more than a few good whacks in overpowering her. As they got closer, Cliff could see a bruise along one of Betty's cheeks, but the worst of it had gone to the others. Ilse had a solid knot above her left eyebrow, and Ingrid's bottom lip was split in two places. The third woman, Janni, cradled her left arm in her other hand and kept unconsciously rubbing at her noticeably swollen elbow. All three still looked a little shocked at how the morning had gone for them; no doubt they had expected to waltz into Betty's room and have her follow their orders without question. Cliff had learned a long time ago that Betty wasn't the kind to jump when someone said so.

"Are you all right?" he demanded. "Have they hurt you?"

"I'm fine," she retorted.

He could tell by her tone that she was seriously ticked off. If they thought she'd given them a hard time earlier, they should let her loose now and see what happened.

Before Cliff could say anything else, Helmut cut him off. "So now that you see she is unharmed, I repeat my question: to whom have you talked about this...*situation?*"

"If by *situation* you mean your little hidden Nazi camp, quite a few people have been told about it," Cliff shot back without hesitation. "The authorities will be here any minute."

Helmut Roehm laughed. "I seriously doubt that. If what you say is true, I would expect you to have brought them with you." He smirked. "And believe me, this will be much more than a tiny military camp."

Cliff scowled. "A docking station then, for a—"

"—submarine," Helmut finished for him. "Yes, we have been making plans for some time." He gave Cliff a sly look. "You are a smart man. I'm sure you have already deduced what else is in the works."

Cliff's stomach lurched, but he'd be damned if he'd let this German see his reaction. "Flying soldiers."

Helmut beamed. "Like you, but better. More experienced with both flying and fighting, and their apparatus will allow them to carry such weapons as will devastate any defenses Los Angeles might be able to gather on short notice. By then we will have either destroyed or commandeered the warship and any other worthy vessels in the ports. We will make German history and rewrite the future of America." The Nazi looked at his watch, then made a show of gazing at the sea, the sky, and finally back in the direction of the lodge. "No, Mister Secord. I do not believe you have told anyone. Nor do I anticipate any so-called authorities coming to rescue you."

"I told Zane Grey," Cliff said quickly. "He expects me and Betty back at his house within the hour. If we don't show up, he'll call the coppers."

Helmut waved his hand, dismissing Cliff's statement. "Grey is a foolish old man who does nothing but make up cowboy-and-Indian stories, idiot things about a world which no longer matters. Even if you were telling the truth, no one would think he was doing anything other than what he does best...make things up." He turned to address one of the men who had a rifle aimed at Cliff. The guy was tall and angular, and his light blue eyes displayed as much warmth as the Arctic Ocean. "Get two of the smaller steel beams," Helmut directed. "Chain one to each of their waists. The supply boat should arrive in fifteen minutes. When it gets here, take them three or four miles out, and push them into the ocean."

Cliff heard Betty gasp as the other Nazi strode toward a pile of beams not too far away. "Even if you kill us, you'll never get away with it," Cliff said. It wasn't much, but it was all he could think of to say. There was a sound in the background that was registering in his brain as vaguely familiar, but he didn't have time to think about it. He had to stall for time until he could figure a way out of this mess. "Someone else will discover what you're doing and put a stop to it. When we don't come back—"

Before he could finish, the source of the noise swelled loud enough to drown out his words. Helmut and the other Germans all looked up as a plane, flying almost dangerously low, buzzed over their heads, close enough to kick up a cloud of dust and even make a few of them duck.

The Aeronca!

"Who is that?" Helmut screamed. "Shoot it! Shoot it out of the sky!"

The two men holding him let go without thinking and raised their rifles. Cliff didn't hesitate; he lunged forward and knocked the last guy to the ground, hoping the man would let go of his rifle when he fell. When that didn't happen, Cliff spun toward Betty, but that was no good either. The three German women had already forced her to the ground and were dragging her in the opposite direction. For a few precious moments, everything was in chaos, and there was enough time for Cliff to do only one thing that might lead to something better all the way around.

Escape.

He was at the edge of the closest bluff before the man on the ground could scramble to his feet and come after him. A split second for him to change his mind—he didn't—and he leaped into space, hoping to God he had enough momentum to clear the rocks at the base so very, very far below.

Cliff had heard people talk about how time slowed when you were in a life-and-death situation—car accidents, drowning or falling, like now—but he had no such luck. He dropped fast, and when he hit, it felt like the water was a hammer and he was nothing more than a fragile finishing nail; the air went out of him from both the impact and the water temperature, and he went down and down and down.

But he came back up, and he swam for the open ocean because his life depended on it.

45

◆

Panting and trying not to choke when the small whitecaps hit him in the face, Cliff pulled himself forward. Something zinged into the water next to him, and he glanced back at the face of the cliff; several men were standing there and shooting at him. He could only hope their aim was lousy and also that the boat Helmut had talked about was late...not that he had any answers beyond that. What was he going to do, swim all the way around the island to Avalon?

Another bullet splashed close—too close—by his head, and then Cliff registered the sound of the plane again, coming back from a different direction and running another drastically low flight path. He looked up without breaking stroke, trying to put as much distance as he could between himself and the Nazis. What he saw surprised him so much he nearly sucked in a lungful of water sprayed into the air by the plane's passage: Zane Grey was solo-flying the Aeronca.

He thought disjointedly that Grey didn't have enough flight time or knowledge to land that thing by himself, plus if the man didn't pull up, he was going to fly into the side of the bluff; then something heavier than a bullet thunked into the water off to his left. Cliff turned his head and saw a white life ring bobbing on the surface of the water as the plane pulled up. He swam toward Grey's unexpected package without hesitating, hoping the thing wouldn't give the Germans a bigger target to aim at. Something was tied to it, a canvas bag, and as he hooked his arm into the ring and yanked open the bag, he wanted to yell for joy when he saw his jet pack and Rocketeer helmet. He had never suited up so quickly, and in barely fifteen seconds—and damned grateful that the apparatus could even fire up while immersed—Cliff surged from the water in a cloud of fine, salty mist and a proud spurt of orange and yellow flame.

Grey had managed to miss the face of the cliff, and the Aeronca was out of sight. Cliff circled around and headed back toward the construction site, his mind fixed on one thing: saving Betty. A noble scheme if there ever was one, but as short-lived as an ant under a German jackboot: the Black Phantom hit him like "King Kong" Charlie Keller had smacked the ball in the World Series earlier that month. Cliff flailed in the air and fell, then righted himself and came back around to meet the flying Nazi full-on. They pounded each other, falling and climbing, sometimes getting knocked backward and almost upending as the blows both connected and missed. More and more, Cliff found himself fighting to stay airborne instead of dodging, taking hits instead of swinging; as his ribs and the muscles in his thighs and arms were battered and bruised, and after the third or fourth savage punch to the side of his head left his head ringing despite his helmet, he knew he was on the losing side of this aerial fisticuffs match.

Cliff swung around to ward off the next blow, then realized the Black Phantom was gone. He saw a streak from the corner of one eye and jerked toward it, only to see the Nazi climb straight up, almost stop in place, then turn and rocket straight for him. He pulled back, but it was a useless effort. He'd taken the brunt of the fight, and the German had already knocked him nearly senseless—his sense of direction was off, his anticipation slow, even his reasoning was muddled. At the end, he couldn't make himself do anything but hover in midair and stare at the doom that was headed straight for him.

But his death was still a thousand feet away when Zane Grey hit the Black Phantom head-on with the Aeronca.

Cliff cried out as the aircraft and the Nazi disintegrated in a dazzling orb of fire and light. Pieces of metal and burning bits of unidentifiable matter fell through the air, and it only took the first small piece burning through the arm of his jacket to yank him out of his daze and speed him the hell out of there. He headed straight back to the construction site, where Helmut's black-suited lackeys were running back and forth like cats with a snarling dog in their midst. Betty was still there, and still with her hands tied behind her back; even so, she was holding her own against the taller and more formidable Ilse as the German woman did her best to get close enough to push Betty over the cliff's edge. They'd never gotten a chain around her, but the odds of his girl surviving a backward swan dive—or shove—were pretty slim.

Ilse darted in again, this time intentionally absorbing Betty's kick to her thigh to get close enough to shove Betty's right shoulder. It was just enough to make Betty stagger backward, and Ilse grabbed the chance to aim a kick of her own at Betty's stomach. Betty turned to the side, but it wasn't enough, and in another second she was falling sideways into space—

47

◆

—and Cliff snatched her out of the air and lifted her up and away from the wet, rocky death that waited below.

Zane Grey, it came out, had indeed taken it upon himself not to wait for Cliff's return to contact the people he knew and bring the might of the U.S. Navy down on the would-be secret base that Helmut Roehm had believed would change the future of Nazi Germany. A Navy vessel and a Coast Guard vessel were speeding toward Little Harbor Bay before Cliff managed to get Betty out of sight; luckily they were concentrating on the ocean, where pieces of the wreckage still floated like mini-islands of flame, as well as the construction site and the people trying to flee the premises. Those folks were easily rounded up by the police and loaded into official vehicles that had already been positioned to block their retreat, and Cliff later learned that it took the Navy less than an hour to demolish the would-be Nazi attack base and leave nothing but dust and rubble. They wouldn't spill the details, but they'd done something to cover the loss of the Aeronca with its owner and Jack back at the airfield on the mainland. Even the death of Zane Grey, which should have gone down in America's red, white and blue history as a famous man's heroic end for his country, was quietly morphed into a reportedly peaceful demise at his mainland home in Altadena by the Feds. Cliff figured one of the housekeepers had reported the condition of Betty's room to Grey; the old man had found the note Cliff had wadded up and tossed aside, and had known damned well that Cliff was handing him a line of booshwah about having to go into Avalon.

It was a damned shame, Cliff thought. A man like Zane Grey ought to be known for what he'd sacrificed. Sure, everyone would remember him as a fine writer of American Westerns, but his greatest accomplishment would never be known. Not his books, or his movies, or his stories.

His greatest gift: the red, white and grey.

NAZIS IN PARADISE

by

DON WEBB

January 1940

The Nazi spy plane was making its second sweep along the
Black Jade River. This was the one spot where his Tibetan
hosts had been silent about, so it was the one spot that was
interesting. Suddenly there was a cloud, a patch of fog off port.
Lighting crackled out of it, hitting the *Zornige Adler*'s wing and fuselage. They were all going to die, so far from the fatherland...

Her hair was the most wonderful thing in the universe, until you
saw her eyes. Betty was more exciting than flying the jet pack on the
night of a full moon over the Pacific. Cliff knew he could take credit for
many of the good things in his life, but he couldn't take credit for love.
A gentle rain fell outside; both were reading magazines and enjoying a
dying fire. The almost empty glasses of red wine threw beautiful red
shadows on the wall. All was good (well, except for a slightly thin
wallet). All was loving and great. Cliff was reading an article on Hornet-
powered Lockheeds in *Aviation*. A few months ago Hughes had flown a
Lockheed, a Super Electra, around the world, even over Russia.

Betty, resting on the cream-colored sofa, was once again proving that she must be his gal by reading *Astounding Science Fiction*. Her imagination, like her beauty, was above, far above, the norm and seasoned with just the right touch of strangeness. Cliff felt love, or something very like it, flush through his veins like rocket fuel.

"Hey, sweetie, what're you reading?"

"A story by Don A. Stuart about scientists in Antarctica and a telepathic monster. They discover a spacecraft trapped in the ice and burn it free with thermite, but then its pilot hides by being able to become anyone of them."

"They get the spacecraft?"

"No, it caught fire because of magnesium in the hull. Why?"

"Are you kidding? Think what could be learned from something like that."

"Well, Stuart does mention antigravity and atomic power."

"Atom power, huh? If we humans had that, we would live like gods."

"You already live like a god. You can fly, can't you?"

Cliff responded, "Yeah, but more importantly, I can call the most beautiful woman in the world 'sweetheart.'"

He crossed over to her, grabbed her off the sofa and kissed her warmly. Her mouth tasted of the wine, the fire, the night. Her mouth tasted like freedom. This tussle went on for a few minutes, and then both were sitting on the sofa.

Cliff picked up the copy of *Astounding*. He paged through it, reading the taglines of the stories.

"Hmmm. 'Hell Ship.' *Josh McNab, good Scots engineer, finds himself against a cracked rotor-shaft and a bull-headed skipper—aboard the Spaceship Arachne*—why do they always make those guys Scottish? In the real world, engineers aren't heroes."

Betty said, "You're partially an engineer, and you're my hero."

"I thought I was your hero because I was a pilot. Besides, Peevy is the engineer—do I need to start watching how you look at him?"

"You know I am only for you, honey. But speaking of engineers, heard anything more from your friend Howard?"

"Yeah. Forgot to tell you—supposed to see him on Thursday."

"Well, that's fine. Any clues?"

"He's still hinting about a 'big secret.' Could be a mission, maybe just a special test flight. Maybe something else—the man has secrets."

"Still, you're good luck for him, Cliffy."

"Good luck or just lucky. I just hope it's some hush-hush test job and with no Nazis involved."

Cliff Secord put down the magazine and returned to the more important business of the night.

The Sunset Strip wasn't Cliff's usual stomping ground, even when he had a paycheck in his pocket, but it seemed like every Angelino knew where 8225 was—if not by number, then by name: The Players.

The club was situated at "the top of Strip," just west of Crescent Heights, adjacent to the elegant Chateau Marmont, and catty-corner from the Garden of Allah residential complex, an exotic compound of villas and apartments catering to writers and actors. Housed in a three-story white stucco structure with high curving arches of the Moorish school, The Players was a fairly recently addition to the Playground to the Stars, being the pet project/unhealthy obsession of Preston Sturges, a playwright from "back East" who had "made good" in Hollywood, becoming a successful writer and director, and well-known for his Algonquin-tested caustic wit. Boasting a restaurant on every floor, The Players had quickly become a popular watering hole for the Hollywood crowd, thanks in no small measure to its owner's policy of serving some of the strongest drinks in town—and the steaks weren't bad either.

Though it was just early evening, the Strip was already hopping like it was Saturday night. This mile and a half section of Sunset Boulevard connected western Hollywood to Beverly Hills and, by a fortuitous fluke of zoning, was situated safely outside the Los Angeles city limits—and thus the grip of the profoundly corrupt LAPD. With the more congenial Los Angeles County Sheriff's Department overseeing this "strip" of pavement, it had, since the twenties, boasted a colorful concentration of casinos, nightclubs and shops, making it the destination of choice for pleasure-seeking Angelinos.

Cliff parked in The Players' lot and walked casually to the club's main entrance. Citing her superior knowledge of Hollywood culture, Betty had convinced him to put on a dinner jacket and clean slacks, and as he took the measure of the other patrons, Cliff had to admit that once again she had been right. After mentioning to the tuxedoed maître d'hôtel that Mister Hughes was expecting him, Cliff was escorted without delay past the bustling Blue Room—the club's main showroom—and up to the quieter, more exclusive, third floor.

Upon his arrival, the first thing Cliff noticed was a cluster of starlets and men Cliff recognized from the celebrity columns huddled around a small dining table. He moved closer and saw that Orson Welles was conducting a magic trick. The filmmaker and actor placed three items on the table's crisp white dinner cloth: a shot glass with a brown liquid in it, a tiny globe and a silver letter opener. These were situated in front of a man in a blue seersucker suit who, Cliff noted, looked a little lit up.

"Now Bill," intoned Welles in his best radio voice, his way of reminding his audience that he'd played Lamont Cranston, The Shadow, for nearly two years, "as you know, I have studied the powers of the mind for many years, even traveling to the Orient for instruction in the esoteric art of mental control from a revered Chinese *sifu* by the name of One Hung Low. I will now demonstrate how my telepathic powers can influence your waking mind. To that end I've written a prediction and sealed it in this envelope. It's just a short piece of writing, Bill, no 'Rose for Emily.'" Welles smiled and winked at his rapt audience. "In brief, it simply describes the results of our little experiment. Not a prediction, not a guess, but a clear statement of fact, which I now ask you to place in your breast pocket."

Mister Faulkner took the envelope from Welles and did as requested.

"Excellent. Now I will rearrange the objects to your specifications. Simply tell me when I have them as you like."

Welles shifted the objects around on the white tablecloth. When the shot glass stood on Faulkner's left, the globe in the middle, and silver letter opener on the right, Faulkner said, "Stop."

Welles seemed to stifle a grin. "You all saw it, ladies and gentlemen—though I moved the items, my friend Bill here chose their placement." There was general agreement, and Welles continued with his instructions. "Now, please pick up any two of the objects. Select what is dearest to you."

Faulkner's hand started toward the shot glass, but then the writer paused, smiled, and picked up the other two objects.

"Okay, Bill, again of your own free will, pass one of the items to me."

Faulkner handed the globe to Welles, keeping the silver letter opener.

"So, ladies and gentlemen, you all have witnessed that Mister William Faulkner *thinks* he has acted under the sole agency of his own free will—but I can assure you it was really the magic of One Hung Low. Now, Bill, would you be so kind as to employ that letter opener to unseal the envelope?"

Faulkner retrieved the letter. With suspicion flickering across his face, he carefully sliced open the envelope and removed the folded single sheet of paper inside. He unfolded it and looked at it with a bemused express, then read it aloud: "You chose the silver letter opener."

Sounds of awe, then everyone clapped with delight. Welles beamed as he began his next trick.

Cliff was tapped on the shoulder. He turned and was greeted by Howard Hughes.

"Hello, Secord, glad you made it," Hughes said. "My table's over here." Looking back at Welles, he added, "I love those magic gags he does. You believe in magic, Cliff? Besides the magic of movies, I mean."

"Not really, but I do believe in miracles," Cliff replied, thinking of Betty.

Two glasses were waiting like sentries at Hughes's table, perhaps guarding a bottle of a single malt Scotch whiskey that had been aged for eighteen years. "Have a seat, my friend. Still take your liquor neat?" Hughes poured them both two fingers of the amber liquid.

Without preamble, the aviation magnate said, "Cliff, I need a pilot."

"Really? Just so happens I am one," Cliff grinned. "But you knew that, so don't keep me in suspense."

"I'll try not to, but it's a bit complicated. You see, I need someone who's not only a damned good pilot but also who I can trust to the fullest—and who's crazy enough to do something very special for me. For our country, really."

Cliff took a sip of his drink, trying to appear nonchalant. "A test flight then, or some kind of secret mission?"

Hughes's natural intensity focused on his favorite pilot, outside of himself, of course. "It's a bit of both, actually. I need you to deliver a team of men, trained specialists, to the roof of the world."

"You mean Tibet? Wow. Your men or Uncle Sam's?"

"Does it make any difference?"

Cliff shrugged. "Trained specialists, huh? Trained in what?"

Hughes motioned to a man seated at a small corner table. One of his executive secretaries, Cliff guessed. The man quickly brought over a leather briefcase, then just as quickly retreated to his station, all without a word, just an exchange of nods.

Hughes opened the satchel and handed Cliff a file that was fat with papers and photos. "Here, let me show you," he said somewhat grandly. Cliff opened the file and looked, but all he saw was a marquee for the Texas Theatre glowing in the night. *Angels with Dirty Faces* was playing, last year's big Bogart and Cagney crime film.

"Sorry—wrong file," apologized Hughes. "That's one of my movie palaces in Dallas." He retrieved another folder and passed it Cliff.

Cliff opened it and saw a glossy black-and-white photo showing a roomful of Tibetan monks, apparently hosting a modest dinner for a group of Germans, six or seven men. Some the Germans were in officers' uniforms with SS insignias. *Oh jeez*, thought Cliff, noting the triangular banners of the swastika tacked to the wall above the group.

"What the hell is this, Howard?"

"Nazis in Nepal, my friend," Hughes joked grimly. He pointed to one of the civilians. "That one is Doctor Ernst Schäfer, director of this little expedition. Last year, Heinrich Himmler, the Reichsführer of the SS, personally sent this research party to Tibet. It was organized by the Ahnenerbe, a so-called 'scientific' institute cofounded by Himmler, and their mission is to find evidence of Aryan habitation among the indigenous peoples of the Himalayas."

"No kidding," mused Cliff, looking at more photos. "Never heard of these Ahner-whatsits—or their expedition."

"The American papers, at least those published in English, weren't much interested," noted Hughes. "The Ahnenerbe funds various made-up research foundations, all dedicated to proving that the ancient Nordic peoples who first settled Germany were descended from the pre-Christian gods who once ruled the world before recorded time. How they figure into Nepal still confuses me, and I've been briefed by experts."

"Sounds like something out of *Argosy*," said Cliff.

"If only that were so, but it's the Nazi brand of nationalism, uniting Germany in a crusade to reclaim its 'lost birthright.' Claiming that pure Germans are descended from gods and everything they do is divinely inspired creates the perfect excuse for taking over the world. Who are the rest of us to deny them their destiny? As they tell it, these ancient gods spawned the so-called Aryan race, and that's why Nazi scientists are poking around Tibet: they're looking for scientific evidence to support this Aryan origins thesis and thus further their propaganda program. It's very important to Himmler and his coterie."

"That's quite a justification for evil."

"Isn't it, though? And they're not the only ones who use it," said Hughes dryly. "The SS operates like an elite cult, run by Himmler and worshiping Hitler, and its initiates believe they are on a holy crusade. This fantasy about divine Germanic origins dates back to at least the 1880s. In the aftermath of World War I, the theory was revived by radicals, caught up in the worldwide spiritualism craze at that time."

"Sure, I remember my mother and her friends having séances when I was a kid, and later the traveling circus I was with had a fortune-teller who did that sort of thing with a crystal ball," said Cliff, looking up from the folder. "But I thought all that hoodoo was either a carny con or a parlor game to amuse people before there was radio."

"In most countries, yes," said Hughes, "but the peace treaty that ended the Great War was also an extension of it, punished Germany harshly, crippling their economy even further. It was humiliating, and this Aryan origin story held a special appeal. The Nazis cleverly adopted key elements into their own propaganda, and Hitler's impassioned oratory was effective in spreading their seductive message. Americans often forget that Adolph and his crowd didn't seize power until after he was elected chancellor."

Cliff had been leafing through the file during this impromptu history lesson. Now he returned his attention to Hughes. "So how does this expedition figure into this? They're still in Nepal?"

"Actually, this group arrived back in Berlin a few months ago. They filmed themselves searching for signs of 'Cosmic Ice' and measuring the craniums of monks. Germans have always been nuts about documenting their achievements. However, see him? The one with the impatient expression." Hughes indicated one of the SS officers. "That's Herman Blumenkraft, a weapons and security specialist attached to the Ahnenerbe. Soon after this photograph was taken, he left the expedition and returned to Berlin posthaste. A week later, Hitler underwrites a second expedition, a very hush-hush one, run by Blumenkraft."

"A secret Nazi raid on Tibet? You can't be serious."

"I *am* serious, and so are a few other people I trust, including some you know as well," said Hughes, meaningfully. "There are two schools of thought on what they're up to. If it's like the previous excursion, then their primary interest is to acquire mystical objects for the Reich, or at least Himmler's private collection. Special amulets, ancient scrolls, crystal skulls, ceremonial weapons—that sort of thing."

"But you don't attend that particular school," suggested Cliff.

"No, I don't," Hughes confirmed. "Given his abrupt return to Berlin and the immediate launching of a new expedition, I believe Blumenkraft is searching for something else entirely, something along the lines of the valley of Khembalung."

"And that's where I'm going, *a lost valley?* You don't need a pilot; you need a medium."

"I know it sounds like something H. Rider Haggard would write," said Hughes, "but nevertheless, legends from all over the region, not just in Tibet, tell of a hidden valley, or series of valleys, high in the mountains, blessed with a miraculously warm climate and inhabited by an ancient race of long-lived people. Himmler's circle of occultists believes this is where the high priests of Atlantis escaped to after their continent sank, which makes it a leading candidate for the birthplace of what would become the Aryan race. I'm not sure how this squares with the 'gods on earth' theory, but then none of it makes any sense in the first place."

Cliff looked dubious. "Atlantis? Really, Howard?"

"Wouldn't you head for the highest spot you could find if the sea just swallowed up your home?"

Cliff laughed. "Look, I appreciate the history lesson. Gave me a whole new perspective on Nazis and confirmed how contagious insanity can be, but you still haven't told me what your angle is in all this. You don't really believe in some 'lost paradise' fairy tale, do you? It's like a yarn by Burroughs or Howard."

"Doesn't matter what I believe," Hughes answered. "It's the lengths that Hitler and Himmler are willing to go for *theirs*. Hitler didn't just underwrite Blumenkraft's secret expedition; he supplied him with an experimental high-altitude aircraft. Only a skilled pilot can fly it—and I want it."

"Sure you do. And I'm to a ferry a team of your 'security experts' over to Tibet so they can hijack it then I bring it back—all unofficial like. Why didn't you tell me that in the first place?"

Cliff regarded Hughes carefully. Patriotic feelings and a deep dislike for Nazis aside, Hughes was "asking" him to commit an international crime, a covert act of war, without any official sanction other than his word. Cliff wasn't so sure that this mission was a good idea. In fact, he concluded that it was absolutely insane.

Hughes returned Cliff's gaze, then poured another drink. "You and I go back some, don't we? Know each other's secrets. That's why you're the only one I can trust with this. Don't you think our 'classified aeronautical technology' can beat Hitler's?"

So *that* was it. The Rocketeer was to be part of this show, not just Cliff's flying skills and discretion. Was he being ordered, in the nicest way possible, of course, to become some kind of sky pirate? He began to wonder if Hughes really *had* off-the-record military approval. Cliff knew the aviation giant didn't like being told what he could and couldn't do, which made it more than likely that any real authorization would only come *after* the German spy plane was parked safely in a military hangar somewhere or scattered over a Himalayan mountainside.

"Well, Howard," Cliff finally said, "while this Scotch whiskey sure is nice, snatching a German superplane from halfway around the world is a pretty tall order, specially when it's full of SS men. We're not exactly at war with Germany, you know. And Roosevelt says—"

"Don't be simple, Cliff," interrupted Hughes. "In order to win reelection, Roosevelt pledged to keep the country out a war—unless we were attacked. That's the key clause, because while most Americans don't want another war, the president knows that sooner or later, like it or not, we'll have to send troops if the Axis is going to be defeated."

Cliff was searching for something clever to say but decided it wouldn't be well received. Hughes was working up a head of steam on this subject.

"Nobody wants war," continued Hughes, "but we can't allow Hitler and Hirohito to simply divide up the civilized world. Roosevelt may be a damned union-loving, Wall Street-hating socialist, but the man is no idiot. He knows that a war would end the depression, rescue our industries, and put everyone back to work. Japan is an island nation whose only natural resource is the water that surrounds it. You watch. The New Dealer will order his pawns in Congress to impose an oil embargo on Japan, calling it retaliation for invading China. With the life's blood of their war effort cut off, the Japanese will be forced to take some kind of drastic military action, and they don't believe in half-measures. They know they'll have to fight us at some point; they must have plans in place even now. That's why this mission is important. German engineering and technology are way ahead of ours—we need to do whatever we can to learn what they're up to."

Cliff didn't quite know what to make of this impassioned analysis. Could President Roosevelt really force the country into a war it didn't want? That didn't seem possible, but aside from having a general suspicion about authority figures, Cliff wasn't very political, taking things as they came and preferring to leave that area to Peevy and Betty. Was Hughes merely stating a pet theory—or giving Cliff a peek behind the curtain at how the world worked?

Hughes finished his drink and appeared much calmer. "Cliff, it's an experimental aircraft full of specialized Nazi engineering. All right, perhaps I was getting too emotional. I know you're not an assassin, and stealing that plane under the noses of a bunch of SS elite without killing them all is probably impossible. So how about you just get me photographs, some film of it in flight. What do you say?"

Now Cliff had finished his drink as well. "That's more like it, and if I can tweak the Führer's nose at the same time, so much the better. Now, if this second German jaunt is so secret, how do you know where I'm supposed to go?"

"After collating reports smuggled out of Germany with other intelligence from Europe," Hughes explained, "and using elements in the core Khembalung myth itself, we have a pretty good idea where Herr Blumenkraft and his SS teammates are heading."

"Just 'pretty good'? Sounds about right."

For the "Eastern jaunt," as Hughes referred to it, the aviation entrepreneur had supplied Cliff with a specialized plane, as well. Codenamed Thunderbird, it was designed for long-distance, high-altitude flying and could carry a crew of eight. Unknown to everyone else, Thunderbird had a newly installed compartment in the aft section that would allow Cliff to don his rocket suit and exit the ship while in flight. Though he believed in the mission, Cliff couldn't help feeling as though he'd been manipulated by Hughes.

The high altitudes involved meant intense cold and the need for oxygen bottles. Cliff had only been able to put in a few rushed hours getting familiar with these new obstacles, which were further complicated by the cameras he was expected to use—one still, one for motion pictures. Hughes had wanted to rig something to the Rocketeer helmet, but Peevy said it would interfere with Cliff's ability to maneuver. Instead, a chest pack was devised. It housed the cameras, which Cliff could trigger in flight, and two small oxygen bottles. A third camera, a small Leica, could be attached to Cliff's left wrist as backup.

It was Cliff's hope that none of this would be necessary, for the primary plan was to locate the Nazis' plane on the ground. That provided many more options, including commandeering the aircraft as Hughes originally intended. Cliff had made it clear that he was not an assassin. "Of course you're not," agreed Hughes. "That's why I'm sending some with you."

At the very least, they could take better pictures on the ground, even from a distance, then lob a mortar on it and skedaddle back home. But if an aerial encounter was their only option, then it was the Rocketeer's mission to get those photographs, and Cliff knew he better be able to deliver.

On that point, Cliff thought it unlikely that he could exit the Thunderbird, photograph the German plane from all angles, and then fly back without anyone on either craft noticing. Revealing his Rocketeer identity to the rest of the team wasn't ideal, but not fatal, either—they'd all been selected with discretion in mind. What worried Cliff more was if the Germans had the ability to attack them in the air. The Thunderbird had been built for exploration and research, not military missions, so it had no weaponry. Stealth was their only real strategy, and there was nothing stealthy about a man wearing a jet pack.

While in Calcutta preparing for the last leg of the trip, Hughes sent them a telegram:

"Chinese General Ma Bufang has discovered Japanese agents in Manchuria led by Jinz Nomoto have likewise begun a secret expedition to Tibet, probably seeking the same goal as you. STOP."

"Well, boys," said Cliff, "looks like Tibet is getting right popular."

Besides Cliff, the team consisted of three aviation engineers, a geologist who had surveyed the Kunlun Mountains and the Taklamakan Desert, two specialists in long-range photography, and a linguist who spoke Amdo Tibetan, Mandarin Chinese, Balti, Puric, Tcho-Tcho, and Russian. The "pretty good idea" from Hughes's researchers centered on the Kunlun Mountains and the Taklamakan Desert. If there were any hidden valleys around, this would be the area, so it was likely that Blumenkraft's expedition would be looking here. Of course, maybe the Germans knew exactly where to look and were already in the hidden valley of Khembalung, well hidden from the Americans. Cliff kept these views to himself. The mission was supposed to take no more than two weeks, so the odds of finding the Germans were not great, unless Hughes was not telling all he knew.

The photographers were clearly spies—a matched pair, one American and one British. The aviation guys were Hughes's men; Cliff had seen them around the Culver City airfield. The geologist, Doctor Barnes, worked for Royal Dutch Shell and, like Hughes, had attended Rice Institute in Houston, though unlike Hughes, he'd actually graduated. The linguist, Doctor Emme, struck Cliff as a decidedly odd bird. The other men were all in their twenties or thirties, while the tall Doctor Emme—with his mane of silver hair and purple (yes, purple) eyes, which had the slightest suggestion of epicanthic folds—was impossible to classify. The man didn't drink or smoke, and he took his tea salted, Tibetan style. And unlike everyone else, he didn't mock the Nazis' outré brand of "mystic science."

The night before they flew out of Calcutta, the group enjoyed a meal of rich curries and sweetened milk drinks. Doctor Emme gave his thoughts (unsolicited, Cliff noted) on the Nazis' Aryan home-land theory. "Our German friends like to believe that their beloved 'über-race' originated from this region. It sounds far-fetched, yes, but fifteen hundred years before the Chinese established the famous Silk Road, a group of tall, redheaded people who spoke Tocharian made the area a trading paradise."

"What did they trade?" asked Alan Smythe-Turing.

"Silk, yellow amber, sheep, art, horses, iron, salt and, above all, knowledge," replied Doctor Emme. "Without realizing it, Hitler and Himmler are probably right about Germanic precursors being in central Asia, but this doesn't make them 'Aryan.' The records show that these peoples liked trade and knowledge more than killing and destruction, while the so-called 'Aryan race' the Nazis are obsessed with is nothing more than a fiction they adopted, a useful tool to further their goal of world domination."

Now Doctor Barnes piped up. "It's a weird region. The volcanism of the zone might possibly create a warm valley—a sort of Tibetan version of Yellowstone."

"I don't like the credence you're giving this hogwash," said Cliff. "I just want to find the spy plane."

"The world is a much stranger place than we in the West give it credit for," Doctor Emme said, smiling. "I am sure that some of us here have knowledge that would amaze others." He glanced briefly at Cliff while the American and British spies glared at each other.

Cliff ignored the doctor's gaze as best he could. "Well, Doc, we're not here to amaze each other—just grab some pictures of a rare German bird and fly away home. Can we all agree on that?"

"Of course," said Doctor Emme. "That is our mission."

After an awkward silence, Doctor Emme began musing on the exotic customs of the region—cremation, polyandry and the couvade. The doctor expounded on the redheaded mummies, the strange stone "books" that are cut in the shape of a spiral, and the magical mountains. *Who was this guy working for?* thought Cliff. *Did Howard really send him?*

Cliff flew them out at dawn, heading toward western Tibet and clear skies. They should be able to make a good pass over the desert before nightfall, returning to a secret British airstrip in Nepal. The Thunderbird was smooth and fast, easily cruising along at 30,000 feet. *Another Hughes triumph*, thought Cliff admiringly.

Doctor Barnes sat in the cockpit with Cliff, talking about the region, pointing out the major mountains. "Your best bet is along the Black Jade River," he said, reading off map coordinates. "Six years ago I found evidence of oil there for Royal Dutch Shell. The natives told us about travelers in distress who sometimes saw a green valley, a paradise normally invisible. It's a regular feature of such stories."

Cliff frowned. "Stranded and lost, half-dead from starvation— who wouldn't hallucinate? Did you find any *real* evidence?"

"Of course not," Barnes snorted. "For my money, the Nazis are looking for oil fields, not some lost Aryan godhead. Their petroleum sources in the Middle East could easily become unstable. The German military knows that the country that runs out of gasoline first will lose the war."

Cliff was reminded of what Hughes had said about an oil embargo on Japan. Was Roosevelt going to put a gun to their head and dare them not to respond? But if there was no embargo, wouldn't that be aiding Japan's war on its neighbors? *This is why I hate politics*, thought Cliff.

Doctor Barnes hadn't stopped talking. "So, no," he continued, "I don't believe there are any mystical truths hidden in the deserts of western Tibet, but there might be gas and oil deposits. The Germans would certainly want to control them."

In the late afternoon the plane reached the Black Jade River, a dark line bordered by green in a brown desert, fed by scattered streams, tenuous lines of life in a harsh world. Then Cliff saw it.

Or, rather, saw nothing. Where a small tributary fed the river, there was a patch of land that seemed to elude the eyes, make them move away. Cliff would scan the desert in a long continuous movement, but when he hit a certain spot, his eyes twitched and lost focus. He looked three times, four times, his heart rate jumping each time he tried to focus on the little patch. This was crazy. How could his perception have a gap in it?

He banked the plane around for another pass. Then another. Everyone in the plane stopped talking. The photographers finally realized they should be taking some reference shots of the landscape below.

"I see it. No, wait, I don't see it," said the American spy.

"The rocks don't line up," noted Barnes.

"I don't see anything," commented one of the aviation guys.

"It's a trick of the light," said Alan Smythe-Turing.

"I am going to make a low pass," announced Cliff.

Doctor Emme spoke up. "Don't waste your time, Mister Secord. This region has no inhabitants. You're just seeing quartz outcroppings reflecting the sun. The mineral has optical properties, you know. Your eyes are just tired."

Cliff thought the doctor's voice sounded like a sideshow mesmerist. He closed his eyes, shook himself awake, and began spiraling down for a closer look.

"You are wasting time. There is nothing there. This maneuver is becoming dangerous."

"Shut it, Doc. There's something down there," yelled Cliff.

Down and turn and down and turn. Each circuit bought more comments.

"I'm sure there's something."

"I saw it. White buildings along a river. Green fields."

"Some kind of steam or mist. I see it, then I don't."

"Please, don't do this," said Doctor Emme.

A cloud, a little cloud with glowing lights, suddenly seemed to be on the right of the airplane. It was matching their speed! It was not a cloud, but it was hard to look at. Lightning flashed out, three times—cutting off a section of the right wing like a hot knife through butter. The cloud seemed to disappear.

The plane shuddered hard as Cliff wrestled the joystick. The craft went into a steep, spiraling dive. Seven screams in different pitches reverberated throughout the Thunderbird's cabin. Emme seemed to be praying, the only non-screamer. Cliff thought of running for his suit, but there was no time.

And then Cliff saw it. A beautiful green valley stretched out below, dotted with white domed buildings, smaller white houses and shining silver geysers that shot high into the air. Cliff didn't have time to enjoy the odd scenery—he was looking for a fairly level patch of land before it was too late. But it was too late, Cliff realized. His insides turned to ice. The damaged plane was falling too fast to land, or even to manage a good crash.

"Hold on!" Cliff yelled, angling the Thunderbird toward the softest-looking patch of foothill he could find. He started praying, and a light flashed on the port side of the aircraft. It could've been lightning, but the sky was clear. The plane began to violently jink left and right before scraping hard on the side of the mountain Cliff was trying so hard to avoid.

And then there was blackness.

He woke in pain, in darkness and in restraints. No, there was a little light. A little green night-light. It could be a hospital, but it smelled of incense. He moaned, then passed out again.

"Good morning, Mister Secord. I am glad you are with us. Not many manage to come here uninvited."

A very tall, smiling middle-aged man stood beside him. Cliff lay on some version of a hospital bed. The lights were on. A yellow-robed nurse was quietly adjusting a machine in the corner of the room. The man looked half Chinese, half white. He wore a yellow garment that resembled a martial arts blouse, and thin-legged silk jeans. He had purple eyes and could have been Doctor Emme's son.

"You may call me Mister Smith, for now. Although I am sorely tempted to have you call me One Hung Low," he said with a charming smile. "We will discuss much later. I am sure you have questions."

"Did anyone else make it?" asked Cliff.

"Yes. Doctor Emme survived. So did Doctor Barnes and a man that calls himself Smythe-Turing. I am told you performed heroically during your rapid descent."

"Only if you call being panic-stricken 'heroic.'"

The nurse turned and looked at Cliff with frank curiosity. Her features were more strongly Chinese; her eyes were black, but her hair was a light red. She seemed so worried for his well-being that Cliff thought he could almost feel her concern. His pain had lessened a good deal, but he was still bound. She crossed to him and laid a cool hand on his brow; for a weird moment he thought she was Betty. She drew her hand away as though she had just touched a hot stove and went to adjust some dials on the mechanism in the corner of the room. Cliff pulled against his restraints.

"The tethers," said Mister Smith, "were to keep you from hurting yourself as you awakened. You had broken both arms and cracked three ribs, I believe." He murmured something in another language to the nurse. She moved a lever to its highest position, smiled and came forward to remove the ties.

Cliff asked, "How long since the crack-up?"

Mister Smith paused for a moment. "You crashed into the sacred mountain a week ago. We forced sleep upon you to speed your healing."

Cliff took stock of himself. Neither arm seemed broken. He had cracked his ribs before and knew what that pain should feel like. Either this man was lying to him about his injuries, or he was in the best hospital in the world.

"My plane?" he asked.

"I should think the plane was not entirely yours, Mister Secord. Mister--" again the man paused, as if looking for a missing word, "—Mister *Hughes's* plane could not be saved. After we pulled the survivors out, it caught fire. A total loss, I'm afraid."

"Really? *Everything?*" Cliff said, trying to keep his voice even. He didn't want to specifically mention his Rocketeer gear.

"While the aircraft could not be salvaged," answered Mister Smith after another bothersome pause, "your personal flying device was much more fortunate. The trunk it was in proved quite protective...Mister Rocketeer."

Cliff opened his mouth.

Cliff closed his mouth.

"Where am I, exactly?" he asked. At this point he wouldn't have been surprised with Barsoom or Hyperboria.

"There are many names for our humble community. I suspect you might know it as Shamballa or Khembalung."

"Then it *is* real."

"That depends on what one means by 'real,' but putting that aside, yes—we are as real as Washington, D.C. or Berlin."

Cliff let this information settle. "What are you going to do with me?"

"Heal you, of course. Then add your knowledge to our own. That has always been the bargain."

"Am I prisoner?"

"Of course not, but few decide to leave."

Cliff nodded. Suddenly he was very tired.

The next day Cliff was out of bed. The valley was beautiful, peppered with geysers, making the air as warm as a hothouse. It did stink of sulfur, and every home or dwelling smelled of incense. In halting English, Tashi, the nurse who had been in Cliff's room, offered to take him on a pony ride. "They're Tibetan ponies, very hardy. Would you like to visit a farm?" She had clearly prepared this speech.

Out of the hospital or temple or lab or whatever they called the place, Cliff saw dozens of the native folk—all having a beautiful blend of European and Chinese ancestry—much as the architecture of the valley could boast. When they saw him, they frankly stared, as one might at a particularly ugly ape in the zoo. They would smile, say little and definitely not engage him.

"What's wrong with me?" he asked Tashi.

"We view the outer world as corrupt. You are too much like *asuras*—demons—short-lived and too full of passion. We have little passion."

"Do you like having little passion?" Cliff asked, flirting being a habit. *You can always look at the menu, just don't order*, Betty always teased.

Tashi stared at him. "No," she said.

It was weird; when she looked directly at him, he had the craziest thoughts. For a moment he seemed to remember sitting by the fire reading magazines with her talking about telepathic monsters. She urged her pony from a slow gait into a trot; his pony followed along. Soon they arrived at the farm. The land between the farm and the village was garden-like—full of flowers. Some of them Cliff knew well, like roses and daisies, others were tall, multicolored lilies that he had never seen. He wished he could pick some for his girlfriend.

Now, that was odd. Right now he couldn't think of her name, though her face was clear enough in his mind's eye.

The farms had amazingly high-yielding crops. Cliff wished his grandfather could've seen them. After the tour, she took him to a small pond surrounded with pink flowers and offered a simple lunch of some cooked grain dish, cold tea, and peaches.

"Do you grow everything you need in the valley?"

Tashi nodded. "It has ever been so. I am sure you will find our food rather plain."

"I doubt that," said Cliff. "How did you learn English?"

"We have...*ambassadors*, you might say, that live throughout the world. English is a very important language."

"How many languages do you know?"

"Only fourteen," Tashi replied, without missing a beat. "I am not good at languages."

Cliff looked at her as she smiled shyly. "Doctor Emme...is he one of your ambassadors?" he asked.

"Yes. He is my...relative."

"And Mister Smith, is he your relative as well?"

"He is my...teacher," she said. "But yes, also a relative. An ancestor—I think that's the English word. Ancestor."

When he had asked about Emme, he felt for a moment as one feels in the early morning awakening from a particularly vivid dream. He could tell she didn't like the questions, or perhaps he didn't like her answers to them. Suddenly he remembered Betty's name. How could he have forgotten his best gal? Something was fishy here in Eden. Tashi was staring at him very intensely. She leaned across the grass and touched his forehead again as though checking his temperature.

She was so lovely, and the pond and the flowers—he could easily believe that no one wanted to leave. The war-bent outer world seemed alien and unnecessary. He wanted to know about this valley, he wanted to know the hows and the whys and its history. But he would have been very happy just to eat his peaches and listen to the sounds of the birds in the trees.

A local bird in the tree above them made a hissing call, and Cliff's love spasm was interrupted.

Then Cliff saw a man approaching them. His clothes were different, military—a black SS uniform that had seen better days.

"It can't be," muttered Cliff as Herman Blumenkraft, Himmler's special operative, boldly joined them. The first thing Cliff noticed was that the German's face was now quite scarred, as if by fire.

"*Guten Tag*," said Blumenkraft with a slight bow. "I was told that the American pilot had made a full recovery. I am glad to see this is so." The German's cold eyes did not match the warm tone of voice.

Cliff stood and regarded the German. His hands ached for a pistol, especially when he saw the Nazi wearing a sidearm.

"As you can see," continued Blumenkraft, gesturing at his face, "my entry into this 'valley of plenty' also involved a violent crash. I was not as fortunate as you, however. The healers say that in time my face may return to its original handsomeness, though I like to believe that scars give a man more character. Perhaps your new friend here has already told you about the special properties of this beautiful valley?"

"No," said Cliff curtly. "We have not discussed it."

"Then allow me to enlighten you," continued Blumenkraft, oozing solicitude. "The legends did not exaggerate, for the valley's inhabitants appear to live for hundreds of years. They do not know the memory loss and dimming of mind that so often afflicts the aged in our world. This really is *Himmel*—and we didn't have to die to enter it."

"Yes, we are lucky men—Herr Blumenkraft."

"Ah, I see you know me," said the German. "In this you have the advantage."

"Clifford Secord. Cliff," said the Rocketeer.

"A member of the United States Air Force?"

"No. A civilian pilot."

"Civilians rarely come to Tibet. Alone."

"I was badly off-course."

"Off-course but not out of luck, my fortunate friend. The ruler tells me that not even one in a hundred can see through their 'perception veil.' I am most impressed. We shall talk of it again. You and I are very alike, Herr Secord."

"I don't know what you mean," said Cliff, knowing exactly what he meant. He wondered what Tashi was making of this cat-and-mouse conversation.

"Angels are made for heaven," said the SS officer. "I doubt that you are more of an angel than I. But then, you have been here but a few days; perfection in all its glory has not yet begun to bore you. Or perhaps you have already found other distractions," Blumenkraft mused, momentarily directing his gaze at Tashi.

"Mister Smith told me that I was not a prisoner here—I doubt you are either."

The Nazi smiled. "Oh, I will leave, Herr Secord. But there is so much to learn first. So many amazing things here."

The SS officer gave another slight bow and then strolled away. Cliff stared after him, glowering. *He must have been testing me,* he thought. *No one can be that naturally insufferable.*

What the hell's wrong with me? I haven't even checked in with the other survivors. I haven't gotten my jet pack back. I haven't looked for the Nazi plane. How many days have I been here?

Cliff looked at Tashi, who was looking intently at him. Suddenly he felt oddly self-conscious.

"Do you understand who that man is?" Cliff asked.

Tashi nodded. "His plane crashed here seven weeks ago. The crew died. He ran burning from the wreckage before collapsing. At first our doctors did not believe that he could be healed. He hovered between life and death for many days, but then came out of the mending sleep. They said he has amazing powers of will. This added to our doctors' knowledge."

"If 'powers of will' means 'massive ego,' then I totally agree," said Cliff. "Say, who is this 'ruler'? May I meet him?"

"But you have, Mister Cliff," laughed Tashi. "He is the man you call 'Smith.'"

"Of course, I should have known. Then, can I see *him* again?"

"Anyone can see the Great Teacher. I will arrange an audience for you tomorrow morning."

"Also, I need to see Doctor Emme and Doctor Barnes and Smith—er, Smythe. Smythe-Turing."

"Certainly. You can you see them as soon as we leave the farm, if you really want to," said Tashi. She reached out to touch his forehead again. Cliff drew back.

"Hey, touchy girl, you know I have a girlfriend, don't you?"

Cliff thought she looked a little sad when she said yes.

"You paused a lot with your words when we began talking... yesterday, wasn't it? How did your English get so good?"

Tashi smiled, "We have been studying how the mind works for over a thousand years."

Telepathic monsters? Hadn't he and Betty joked about telepathic monsters recently? And snow? Had he been talking about her?

A shadow crossed Tashi's face. "You looked angry when the burnt man spoke to you. Is he your...enemy, maybe?"

"He is the world's enemy, no maybe about it. Haven't your ambassadors told you about how men like him are spreading evil, threatening the entire world?"

Tashi did not reply, taking Cliff's hand instead. And giving him that look...

He was going to compare Blumenkraft to the snake in the

Garden of Eden, but maybe the serpent isn't the only source of deception here. It would be good to see—

To see.

Wasn't he supposed to go see somebody about a barn and a blacksmith about turning something?

Oh, just hang out with the pretty girl here in this valley; you have all the time you need.

True to Tashi's word, Cliff met "the ruler" the next morning. On the way there, he remembered wanting to see the other survivors— odd that he would have forgotten that. Mister Smith had no exalted throne room, no secret passages filled with chanting monks, strange incense and grotesque, jewel-encrusted idols. *Where's Edgar Rice Burroughs when you need him?* wondered Cliff. His fiction reading had always included a selection of adventure pulps—*Argosy, Weird Tales, Adventure*—so he couldn't help but feel a bit disappointed at the lack of exotic pageantry.

Instead, Cliff and "Smith" sat on a marble bench in a park before two white domed buildings about twice the height of the Taj Mahal. While the mending pilot expounded on Hitler and the growing Nazi menace, small deer grazed on the lush green grass, white peacocks sought insects, and birds chirped in the trees.

"So you see, Mister Smith, we can't just do nothing. This affects everyone, even you folks way up here," Cliff concluded.

The leader simply smiled.

"Calm yourself, Mister Secord. We *do* understand the Nazis. They are cruel and awful, just as you so eloquently stated. But what happens when they are gone? The United States and the Soviet Union will divide the world, then plunder its resources and pollute its air and waters. In time they too will fade, and China and India will make a much worse mess. And so it goes. But it is not our concern."

"How can you not be concerned? Last time I checked, we were still on Earth. It's your world too."

"The original inhabitants of the valley were Tocharian traders. They were tall, redheaded, and had violet blue eyes, which should please the Third Reich. The valley changed them—gave them long lives, made them more aware of the workings of their brains and nerves of their bodies than other humans can comprehend. When the Buddhists found us, we were already an advanced people. But we were warlike, like the Nazis, and convinced of our right to rule the world.

"We had made great breakthroughs in physics. We did what your scientists are just imagining possible—split the atom. We had learned techniques of lessening the effects of gravity. We had learned how the directed thoughts of one mind, or a group of minds, could influence others. We were vain; we were becoming evil. The Buddhists saved us. They taught us peace. Superior technology does not make you a superior man, for the dark side is not mastered; this same technology will eventually destroy its creator."

"I can appreciate that," said Cliff earnestly. "I understand the need to control power or it will control you, and that's very well and good, but the world is in real trouble, the kind that well-meaning platitudes won't fix."

"A single human can do better than a group of humans," replied Mister Smith. "We learned that we must decide, as a group, to turn our swords into ploughshares, as your Bible says."

"Okay, but what do you do if your enemy is making better swords?" asked Cliff.

"We choose to be unseen to our enemies. We do not desire the world. We observe it, allowing some of its artists, scientists and philosophers to find us. Occasionally we interfere in subtle ways, trying to keep mankind from destroying itself."

"So we're on our own, then? Because 'observing' Hitler and Tojo isn't going to stop them from taking over the world." Cliff was becoming increasingly exasperated with how this was going.

"In the West you think of God as simple goodness," Smith continued. "Pet a puppy, give soup to a hungry man. Have you read the *Bhagavad Gita*? God shows Himself to Arjuna as the Infinite during a time of war. Death the Many Armed and that Infinite can only represent the crisis, the destruction and the breaking of everything that has a finite, conditioned, mortal character—rather like a voltage that is too high and burns out the circuit through which it passes. The Nazis serve the will of God by giving you a role. The Gita adopts this view not to justify evil or perversity, but to metaphysically sanction warlike heroism against humanitarianism and sentimentality. If there was to be no war, there could be no means for such as you to find your destiny. It simply is not *our* destiny, so we live apart from it."

"Jesus! Are you saying that the Nazis are part of God's will? Which God is this, exactly? I'd rather skip finding my destiny if it means not having another war, thank you very much. Maybe it's my destiny to kill Blumenkraft, help stop the Nazis that way."

"If it is, then you shall, but not here. No violence happens here; no karma is accumulated."

"You are an idiot, sir. The Nazis would take everything you have—every science, every technology, every piece of art, every stored jar of preserved fruit—and leave all of you dead or enslaved."

"Of course they would. So would the Americans. Just more slowly, beginning with missionaries and Western medicine."

"Most American Indians would agree with you, but that's in the past. This is now, and you have to choose. Your days of peacefully hiding away from the world are coming to an end. We live in the age of the airplane, and soon the rocket. You will be discovered. You *have* been discovered."

"We have other ways of avoiding notice," said Smith with a smile. Then suddenly Cliff found himself staring at an empty bench. He did not like being made a fool of.

"Stop your magic tricks. The Nazis found you, and so did I. Isolationism just doesn't work anymore." Cliff thought of Roosevelt, that maybe the president had figured that out awhile ago.

Now Smith was sitting next to him.

"Science, Mister Secord. Not tricks. The science of awareness. Your nerves are sending signals to your brain. For example, you are getting a signal from your left pinky toe right now, but your brain ignores it, no reason to pay attention. But if I gave you—what is the phrase?—a 'hot foot,' then you would notice that toe swiftly enough. Your brain makes this kind of processing decision automatically, while our people are trained since birth not only to be conscious of these signals, but also to control them. Once that is mastered, it is relatively simple to influence the minds of others, as well. I could teach you to do so, in forty or fifty years."

"Yet both Blumenkraft and I saw through this 'perception veil' of yours."

"You are both remarkable men. The shadow of the war that is to come is already purifying and strengthening people such as you. We will have to increase our vigilance. There is a disadvantage to this. It gives dreams."

"Dreams?"

"A kind of dream. Why do you think so many writers and artists have visions of Secret Tibet? While we distract the world from looking at us, there are those who react differently to the techniques used in doing so. Religious fanatics, certain writers and artists, the outright insane, among others—they begin to *fascinate*, one might say. The cohort within Hitler's circle who seeks out mystical objects and arcane knowledge, his ultimate goal is to have an unstoppable weapon, a *Wunderwaffe*, that will win the war for them. We know that is why the German came to our valley."

"I am not going to stay here. I *can't* stay here."

"That is your right, of course."

"And I would not be quiet about my visit."

"True. You might talk about it. But you would soon forget, and our people in the world would discredit you. Maybe you could get a few crackpots—how I love your slang—or you might try to lead an expedition here, only to get lost in the desert."

"And would you visit my bones?" asked Cliff.

"I'm afraid I couldn't, Mister Secord. I have lived here so long that I cannot leave. The valley both contains and maintains me."

Cliff regarded Mister Smith with a frown. The man was smug and infuriating, not like the German, of course, but still annoying as hell.

Cliff stood up to leave. His anger and frustration suddenly fled, leaving his mind clear. And then he knew...

"Wait a minute, Smith. I didn't just crash here, did I? You made lightning hit my plane! Some kind of Tesla stunt. I bet you brought down the Germans, too—you and your plowshares. You're up to something, some kind of experiment. Maybe just entertainment."

"Mister Secord, although you and Herr Blumenkraft are most entertaining, we did not bring you here for our amusement. You came here on your own, yes? Yes, we wanted to study your minds, to know what an American and a Nazi were like, especially on the eve of the war that is to be."

"So you still think you are godlike men, fit to play with destinies of others? Not that different than when the Buddhists found you."

"Humans are weak. We may be stronger at some things, and much more patient than our short-lived cousins, but we are not perfect."

"I will meet with the other survivors today."

Smith just smiled up at him. Cliff turned and walked off, his anger and confusion fully returned. Sure, the place was extraordinary, Smith was right about that, but couldn't its properties be studied and replicated elsewhere? Howard Hughes might make an even bigger fortune here, but mankind would surely benefit in the end. But if Blumenkraft managed to steal even one of their secrets, it could determine the outcome of the war. Aside from his jet pack and some experimental planes over at Hughes Aircraft, Cliff hadn't really seen much in the way of advanced technology, but he knew it when he saw it, and here it was all around him.

Smith's people made electricity by splitting the atom, their hospitals seemed hundreds of years in advance of the West, and the agriculture they practiced could feed the world. Smith's disappearing trick bugged him, but he doubted it was some "science of mind" thing, just another magic routine, like Houdini or Blackstone.

Cliff decided he must find Tashi and see if his Rocketeer gear had really been "repaired." Then he had to talk to Barnes and Smythe-Turing. He wouldn't bother with Emme; Cliff realized that what had at first struck him as strange was that he looked like the valley dwellers. Clearly it was time to leave, get out of this damned valley and back to Los Angeles. He'd figure out how later. Oh yeah, and it would probably be a good idea to kill Blumenkraft.

Cliff had started making his way to the small hospital when he almost immediately ran into Tashi. Coincidence? Cliff was too grateful to question it.

"Tashi, I need you to help me, really help—not just dull my mind with dreams I don't want to dream."

She looked down at the ground. It was the first time Cliff had seen the valley dweller show embarrassment.

"Cliff, I am so sorry. I was supposed to simply monitor you, but then I began to have feelings that I hadn't felt in a very long time. You are a good man, and I hope you can forgive me. How may I help you?"

"I need to see Doctor Barnes and Smythe-Turing."

"No, you really don't, but I'll show you," she said.

It was early evening, and the smell of spicy vegetables filled the air. The villagers were not vegetarians, but ate meat sparingly—whether from Buddhism or the difficulty of keeping herd animals, Cliff knew not. The one-story homes had white or pastel outer walls plastered over wood and stone. They used electrical power to light spiral-shaped bulbs. Cliff never saw wiring entering the houses; either it was buried or the villagers used the sort of "broadcast power" that Tesla had dreamed of. Tashi led him to one of the few two-story homes.

As was the custom here, they entered without knocking. The bottom floor was filled with shelves of fossils and mineral samples. Tashi sang a phrase that was answered from above. A woman that could have been Tashi's sister descended the stair, followed by Doctor Barnes in his yellow silk suit.

Barnes smiled at Cliff and walked over, extending his hand.

Barnes said, "You're—let me think—you're Cliff Secord, the pilot who brought me here, aren't you? I owe you a big debt of thanks. Dechen, can they join us for dinner?"

"Yes, of course," the woman said, looking daggers at Tashi.

"No need," said Cliff. "I just had a question for Doctor Barnes."

Barnes smiled at him.

Cliff said, "I know this is the darnedest thing, but I can't remember why we came here. Why was that, Doctor Barnes?"

Barnes looked puzzled for a moment.

"Oh yeah," he said. "You were taking me here to help these nice people learn about geology. But as you can see, they already have a great mineralogy collection." He gestured at the shelves.

"Wasn't I supposed to take you back?" asked Cliff.

"Now, why would I want to go back? I love it here."

Cliff smiled. *I thought so.* "Well, that was all I needed to know. Sorry to have bothered you. Come on, Tashi."

"No bother at all," said Barnes. "Come by anytime."

When they left the home, the sun had begun to set. Tashi stared at the ground.

"I suppose Smythe-Turing is the same," Cliff said.

"Happier even. The life he came from was awful and depressing. Here he writes poetry and farms."

"Tashi, you must help me. I need to leave. I don't want to become a vegetable for Smith's hothouse."

The young woman blanched. Tears welled up in her violet eyes. "I am sorry that you have so chosen," she said. "The other man from your world studies hard here. Isn't there anything here that interests you?"

"Tashi, I want to take you with me. There's more to life than this valley, as wonderful as it is."

She crushed her body to him. "I will spend my last days with you. I can't be your lover, but I will at least be your friend."

Cliff reached a new resolve. He would go back home until the war was over, keep his trap shut, and then return here with Betty at the first opportunity. Smith was probably right—men like Howard Hughes *would* see the valley as one big treasure chest, ripe for the taking. The natural order of things for people like them.

"Tashi, you make it sound so glum. You can see the outside the world. I will come back."

"With your Betty?" she asked.

"Yes, with Betty."

"You'll forget this place long before then. You will even forget Tashi." She smiled sadly.

"How can I forget you? I am taking you with me, if I can."

"I will help you, Cliff Secord. Because I love you. And your friends need you."

"I—uh...My flying suit. The jet pack. Do you know—?"

"Our engineers have been caring for them," said Tashi quickly. "I will take you there."

The sun stood directly over the valley, yet as Cliff had observed, the air temperature never increased nor decreased by more than a few degrees, night or day. Tashi took him to a large, red brick building in the shape of a pentagonal frustum. It had large glass doors and was brightly lit inside. The main hall held disk- and bell-shaped crafts, none of which looked like they could fly, as least as far as Cliff could tell. The place seemed deserted, even though it was the middle of the day.

"These are special vehicles," explained Tashi, though Cliff didn't quite believe her. "The engineers don't work on them here."

In a much smaller room, a lab of some sort, Cliff found Blumenkraft, Emme, and two of the tall natives inspecting the Rocketeer suit, its duffel bag on the table nearby.

"Hey, just a damned minute here! That's mine!"

Blumenkraft smiled broadly at Cliff, putting down the distinctive helmet. "Ah, I'd hoped you were the Rocketeer. You are quite famous within certain circles of the Reich. You have encountered the Luftwaffe's own version of this technology, yes? I believe they use a different type of fuel. A hydrogen peroxide derivative."

"Just put it down, Blumenkraft. I'm not here to talk shop."

"But we *are* in a shop," laughed the German. Smirking, he set down the helmet with exaggerated care. The pair of engineers stepped back a few paces and watched the two men.

"If you'll permit me the observation, Herr Secord, your equipment is rather antiquated compared to the standards here. Have you seen the vimanas?"

Cliff said nothing as he began gathering his gear into its duffel bag, which was also on the table. The small trunk he had used on the plane was missing, probably damaged in the crash. Tashi stood in the doorway, a look of concern on her face.

"The monks were just explaining the vimana's propulsion," continued the German, ignoring Cliff's silence. "There's a mercury-filled motor in the center of those domed crafts. A solar broiler heats the mercury as it is spun very, very fast. This creates a field of..." He paused, searching for a word.

The taller of the two natives said, "*Laghima.*"

"*Ja! Laghima*, which not only lifts the vehicle, but also provides the life-sustaining force that permeates this valley. Think of it, Herr Secord. It draws power from the sun and grants long life. It is like the *Vril* in Bulwer-Lytton's novel. This is the Holy Grail of German science. What am I saying? Of *any* science."

"This technology will stay here, with these people," said Cliff. "You can't steal it from under their noses."

"Oh, my dear Mister Secord," clucked Blumenkraft, as if indulging a small child, "I see 'these people' have gotten to you. Their talk of destiny and God's will. Did you really fall for it? Think, my friend. You are a man of practical experience. With this technology under our control, you and I could rule the world. Truly rule it—for the better! Do you not think we could do a superior job of it than Hitler and Stalin or Roosevelt and Churchill put together? I told you we had much in common. We know how the world works. The strong rule the weak and the clever control the strong. Are we not both strong and clever?"

"I am not interested in ruling the world, you fascist bastard," said Cliff.

Blumenkraft laughed heartily.

"*Ja*, this is where you fail. No will to Power. What *do* you want, then?" The German looked at Tashi. "Love, perhaps? If women are all you want, think of how many you could have if you possessed the secrets of the ages. You could even keep that one," he said, nodding toward Tashi. "Her sisters, too, I'm sure."

Cliff lunged toward Blumenkraft, aiming to wipe that smug grin off his wretched, scarred face. He managed to plant a solid right hook on the Nazi's left cheek. The German staggered back with a groan. One of the natives stepped forward and simply tapped Cliff with two fingers on the back of his neck. He fell to the floor, stunned but conscious. Emme burst into laughter. He stepped forward to kick Cliff, but the other native stood in his way.

Still laughing, Blumenkraft dusted himself off. "Our hosts do not permit violence, remember?"

Tashi helped Cliff get back to his feet. He shook off the paralyzing effects of the native's attack, then stood glaring at the natives and the Nazi. "Their so-called ruler told me that if it is my destiny to kill you, I *will* kill you," Cliff told Blumenkraft. "And I'll do that very thing before you loot this place for Berlin. These people might not fully understand you and your kind, but I sure do. Plenty."

"They guard their valley quite well, I grant you," conceded Blumenkraft, "but mind tricks won't stop bullets. That is why they are more pathetic than even you. You say your destiny is to destroy me. You are welcome to try—I would never stand in the way of deny one's destiny, even yours. The Reich's destiny is divinely inspired; we Aryans are born rulers. These people, this valley, prove it. You would do well to reconsider my offer. Choose the winning side, and reap the rewards."

Blumenkraft strolled from the room, whistling a tune from a Wagner opera. Emme left with him, like a puppy trying to please its master. The tall redhead with the two-finger haymaker spoke to him softly. "We can not allow violence in our valley. You understand."

"Sure, I get you, Mac," Cliff replied sourly. "But you better hope that people like me can keep people like him out of here. Your studious guest is a damned Nazi. Those rats are grabbing up as much real estate in Europe as they can, and he's eager to tell his pals back in Berlin all about your kingdom in the sky here. You heard what he said about bullets. He was talking about using them on you—understand? You can't trick bullets into thinking you're invisible."

The two engineers simply smiled.

"We enjoyed studying your flying toy," said Two Fingers. "Primitive but quite clever."

"It should work even better now," added the other.

A toy! First they stand around while Blumenkraft practically declares war on them, and now they call the rocket suit a toy! *Unbelievable.*

With Tashi looking on, Cliff inspected the jet pack. It had been cleaned and polished, and a small gray metal tube ran alongside the combustion chamber. It wasn't clear if it was fuel, cooling, or something else. Cliff debated whether to thank the engineers or bawl them out. Now he noticed Tashi staring at him.

"You are a warrior, like Arjuna. It is your destiny to fight. Like Gesar of Ling. Like George Washington."

Cliff wasn't too sure about Arjuna and Gesar, but George Washington had been his hero since second grade. He and Lincoln.

"Come on, Tashi, I need some fresh air. Fresh as it gets around here, anyway."

Cliff stuffed his jet pack and flight suit into the duffel bag and walked out of the workroom. He and Tashi left the great hall and found a bench outside, underneath some trees that bore a small red fruit that Cliff didn't recognize.

"Tashi, is it true that the vehicles I saw can really fly? Leave the valley?"

"Of course they can, but those vimanas are seldom used. We have others for our ambassadors or if a youth has too much of the warrior spirit in him and we must send him forth."

"But they're still maintained, right? Blumenkraft could take one if he wanted to?"

"He couldn't fly it himself."

"What about me? I'm a trained pilot."

Tashi laughed. "The controls are not like ones you are used to. They can be...difficult."

Cliff took that in. "So, if Blumenkraft wanted to use one..."

"He would need a pilot, but no one wants to leave the valley," replied Tashi. "Perhaps if he persuaded a hot-headed youth."

"Could *I* find someone...?"

Tashi silently regarded Cliff before replying. "That someone is before you."

"You? Great! Can we go tomorrow morning?" asked Cliff, before it occurred to him to ask why she'd even want to help him...*escape* was first word that came to mind.

"Why not tonight?" Tashi said.

"Aren't they powered from the sun?"

"Yes, but we know how to store such power. You think we only fly in the daytime? Two of them use a poisonous ore for energy. Not as safe, but very quick—some say maybe better."

"Faster but not as safe, huh? Sounds just like my Gee Bee."

The moon rose full and silver over the valley of Khembalung. It turned the small river into ink and polished the domes so beautifully that it hurt Cliff's heart to think that he would be leaving this place so soon. Smith had to be wrong; there could be no force in the universe able to drive this image from his heart. Cliff vowed he would stop Blumenkraft, then return to the valley as quickly as he could. Smith was right—mankind was heir to wars—but surely mankind could grow up. Couldn't what had accomplished here be duplicated elsewhere? Cliff found this line of thinking made him confused and frustrated. Still, this was a dream to fight the nightmare of torch-lit rallies in the heart of Germany.

Cliff hefted the duffel bag with his jet pack as he and Tashi neared the front door of the hall that housed the vimanas. It suddenly dawned on Cliff that in his week here, he'd seen no guards, no soldiers—and no children. Did extended lifespans mean fewer births, or were they being trained somewhere else, honing their mental skills?

More importantly, no one was watching any of the buildings, or even the valley itself. The two natives he'd encountered with Blumenkraft seemed to be monks or scientists, not guards. Cliff had to admit that Smith's "mental tricks" were effective. But he also knew that tricks wouldn't be enough to shut out a world at war. Would anyone be inside to stop him?

As Cliff began to push on the great glass door, a sharp noise— the sound of stone scraping against stone—came from deep in the main hall. Tashi drew close to him. "I think someone is opening the roof," she whispered.

"Blumenkraft must be making his move," murmured Cliff grimly.

The hall was largely unlit, but as the massive roof began to slide apart, a bright shaft of moonlight lit up the dull gray metal of the vimanas. Cliff saw Doctor Emme pulling on a lever set in the floor.

Now Blumenkraft appeared from the shadows and moved to stand by Doctor Emme, watching him closely. Cliff and Tashi ducked behind one of the saucer-shaped crafts near the hall's entrance, the grind of the machinery covering the sound of their footsteps. An eerie blue light had begun to glow along the base of one of the two bell-shaped vimanas near Doctor Emme and Blumenkraft. As the glow grew brighter, symbols or strange letters about a foot in height were revealed along the craft's thick metal. The cryptic figures filled up with bright blue light, glowing with pulsating inner light that rotated counterclockwise. A strange vibration filled the room, a mix of almost-palpable air pounding and strong static electricity.

From their hiding place, Cliff and Tashi watched Doctor Emme and Blumenkraft approach the glowing machine. The German was wearing his sidearm and carried a chest or small trunk of some kind. As they neared the vimana, a trapezoidal panel swished open before them.

"How soon before they can take off?" Cliff asked Tashi in a whisper.

"Not long. We must hurry."

"Wait. Blumenkraft is armed. Let them go, and we'll follow in one of the faster ones."

"I must try something first. I have a duty," Tashi said quickly. She darted from hiding and ran toward Emme, yelling at him in a language Cliff had never heard before.

Startled, Emme turned and confronted Tashi. Blumenkraft pointed his pistol at her. They continued their intense conversation, which ended with Emme laughing dismissively. Cliff didn't need a translator to understand that.

The vimana's light rotated more swiftly, insistently. Emme pushed Blumenkraft's gun down, and Tashi moved closer to him. She started to speak, but Emme slapped her so hard she fell to her knees.

"Hey!" Cliff ran out toward them. Blumenkraft raised his gun and shot. Cliff felt the bullet whistle by his midsection. He dropped to the ground close to Tashi, feigning grievous injury. He could see the look of horror on her face, illuminated by the pulsating blue light. Cliff winked at her. She moaned and pretended to faint. Blumenkraft and Emme turned and boarded the vimana, the panel swishing closed behind them. Now the vibrations increased. The bell slowly levitated a few meters into the air, positioned itself under the opening in the ceiling, then shot away into the starry sky with a loud swoosh.

"We must be quick," urged Tashi, her fainting charade over. "My grandson is not adept in operating that vimana; he will fly slowly at first."

Cliff went to get his flying gear.

Had she said grandson?

Tashi sang a syllable, and the second bell-shaped craft began to glow. A large panel slid open. Cliff exchanged a look with Tashi, and then they both entered. Inside, a bank of jewel-like lights stood blinking before a central column of silver metal. Six large screens displayed all directions outside the craft. Cliff carried his suit in. She placed a diadem on her head. In its golden circle, it had small lights, which blinked in unison with some of the lights on the control panel.

"What kind of armament does this have?"

"None, of course," said Tashi. "This isn't a war vessel like the ones in the Mahabharata. It only emits a mild electrical discharge, mainly to frighten off outlanders. Please stand here; the vimana is almost at full power."

"You—you shot down the Thunderbird!"

Tashi was silent for a long moment, her eyes avoiding Cliff.

"The discharge can disable primitive flying machines. I tried to be careful, to avoid casualties. Our Lama wanted specimens from every side. He hoped for Japanese subjects, too, but their plane was not sturdy enough to reach us."

The vibrations increased, resonating up the scale like a musical instrument, soon becoming inaudible to Cliff. A moment later Tashi said, "We are ready." Cliff looked around for something to hold on to.

The machine rose, moved to the center of the hall, and then shot into the night. Cliff observed that the screens showing the craft's direction were a brighter hue. To the south, he could see the other vimana. Blumenkraft was apparently heading toward India.

"Tashi," he asked, "did you say *grandson?*"

"Yes," she said with a laugh. "We live longer than people on the outside, but not without a price. We need the energies of the valley. And we lose our passions."

"What will happen to you? Now, I mean."

"Nothing—as long as I remain with the craft."

"And if you leave? What then?"

"I will age. Rapidly. As Smith told you."

"And Emme, has he aged?"

"When he was but a young man," answered Tashi, "my Emme chose to leave the valley and live as one of our agents. The valley's influence dissipates over time. He spent too long among outlanders, I think, succumbing to the stories of Aryan rule by divine right. How fragile the mind is, to believe such things, though clearly it would be a simple matter for us to dominate the world with our technology. But we would be destroyed—first by becoming like Hitler, then by the revolution that would follow."

"So Emme is with Blumenkraft by choice?" asked Cliff. "He's not being forced?"

"Of course not. He can overpower the burned man easily. This was part of the Lama's test, and it shows that we still can't afford contact with the outer world—that's why no one would talk to you."

"No kidding," said Cliff. "But if you can fix that Nazi's face, why not his mind, as well? 'Influence' it, like Smith said. Only an idiot buys that fascist nonsense. And don't say 'destiny'—I'm tired of that excuse."

"We cannot force someone to think a certain way, only show them the consequences in their decisions."

Cliff watched Tashi as she piloted the craft, but there wasn't much to see. Her hands were out, palms down, hovering over a bank of lights arranged like six jewels; she never seemed to touch anything, yet the lights were responding to her somehow.

"Hey, how come no one is following us? Doesn't Smith mind people running off with his flying bells?"

"You're not 'running off.' I'm taking you."

They were flying almost due south—Cliff couldn't guess at their velocity, nor could he understand the apparent lack of *movement*. It was uncanny. There weren't even chairs or benches in this thing. So either their flights were short, or they just loved standing. Whatever the case, Cliff could see that Tashi's superior piloting was enabling them to gain on the other bell.

The moon was setting now, disappearing behind large peaks of the Himalayas. "He is very stupid," said Tashi. "To fly so low over these mountains is dangerous."

"Where is he headed?"

"Wherever the German is telling him, I suppose. But it won't be anywhere populated. Even Emme will not allow the craft to be seen if he can help it."

Cliff stared at Tashi's flawless face, lit by the glowing controls. He kept expecting her to deny the remarks about her age, say she was joking. Cliff began to notice that every time the bell changed its course, a different sequence of lights flashed. Six jewels, six directions. That made sense.

Now they were nearing the other vimana. Suddenly it veered, shooting straight up rather than southward.

"Good!" said Tashi. "He is showing sense."

"You still care for him, then?" said Cliff.

"You always love your children, even when they misbehave." Tashi looked at Cliff with tenderness. He was trying to frame a reply when a piercing alarm went off. The second craft plunged downward and rammed them. The impact was brutal and destabilizing, driving their bell into the mountainside and its jagged rock face.

Cliff and Tashi were thrown violently to the floor. The bell began to slide down the cliff face but then suddenly began to spin, stopping in midair and hovering in place next to a large, sharp outcropping. The bell began emitting a throbbing hum that wavered up and down the scale in a rapid repeating sequence. The view screens flickered, going in and out of focus, making it impossible for Cliff to spot the other bell. He hoped that it was at least as damaged as their craft but feared that was not the case. And where was Tashi?

Cliff saw the woman lying motionless at the foot of the navigation console. He scrambled over to her, fearing the worst. He let out a sigh of relief when he saw that Tashi was still breathing. She must have slammed her head pretty hard during the crash, and there wasn't much Cliff could do about it at the moment, other than try to make her comfortable. He noticed that four of the lights on her diadem had begun blinking in a fixed pattern, and guessed that the bell's rapid spinning and humming was some kind of emergency response triggered by the crash. Hopefully it was sending out a rescue signal, but Cliff didn't want to wait to find out.

The flickering view screens stabilized, allowing Cliff to see the other vimana swooping toward them. A second ramming could be fatal.

Cliff instinctively pulled the diadem off Tashi's head and put it on his own. "I don't know if this going to work, but we can't just be sitting ducks."

Imitating what he'd seen Tashi do, he *willed* the craft to move to port. Nothing. Then Cliff whistled, trying to match the notes he'd heard Tashi use. Nothing.

The other bell rushed at them. Cliff grabbed the navigation panel, bracing himself. Suddenly the control panel lights blinked in a simple sequence and the bell lurched to port, neatly evading Emme's assault.

As the other bell swished by, Cliff tried for elevation, willing the craft to rise. Eureka! Up the craft went, shockingly fast, quickly clearing the mountainside. Emme followed, climbing high into the skies over the Himalayas.

"Okay, Doctor Emme, you may be a great linguist, but when it comes to flying, I know what I'm talking about."

Cliff swung the bell down and starboard—almost clipping the other craft. Then he shot up again. As Emme's belle followed, he did a power dive toward it. Again, at the last second, the other bell spun away.

The more Cliff focused on directing the vimana, the easier it was to control it, as if the craft itself was becoming familiar with him rather than the other way around. Seeing the six lenses—above and below and at the cardinal points—gave him an idea. He swooped down toward the mountains, watching as the other bell also began to drop, positioning for another attack. As it came closer, Cliff visualized lightning bolts shooting from his vehicle at Emme's three closest lenses. With any luck, he had taken out Emme's cameras. Then he arced up toward the other vehicle, a dive bomb in reverse.

Emme didn't maneuver out of his way, resulting in another shattering impact. Though Cliff struck the other craft hard, it wasn't enough to bring the other craft down.

Cliff wasn't about to let this technology get back to Hitler. Better to die here now than allow millions to perish later.

The other bell wobbled in the air, then shot upward. Cliff tried to pursue, but something was wrong; his craft wasn't as maneuverable. The bell was only rising very slowly.

Tashi began to groan. Maybe if she regained consciousness, she could give Cliff some help, but for now, he couldn't track Emme's bell.

Then he saw it—in a power dive directly overhead. Cliff willed his craft forward, but it barely moved. He hurled lighting upward, but the other craft continued its dive.

There was a crushing impact between the bells, and then they struck the cliff face and tumbled down the sheer mountainside. The navigation screens went black, and then Cliff blacked out as well.

Cliff didn't know how long he was out. He slowly became aware of several things at once: freezing-cold air, the sharp tilt of the floor, the dim red light bathing the craft's interior. Thankfully, the alarm was silent now. Then he saw Tashi lying across from him, still breathing. Cliff felt something sticky on his left arm; his ribs were probably cracked again.

There was a large gash in the side of the craft, the source of the freezing draft. Cliff could see stars, snow and someone coming in, a figure in shadow.

Then he heard Blumenkraft's voice.

"Herr Secord? Are you still with us, Herr Secord?"

Cliff remained silent. The Nazi switched on a small flashlight and began inspecting the wrecked interior. Cliff closed his eyes, feigning unconsciousness. He could sense the beam playing over the small navigation area. The light stopped—Blumenkraft had found what he wanted. Cliff dared to open his eyes and saw Blumenkraft picking up his rocket suit. With flaring anger overcoming his pain, Cliff rolled to his feet and hurled himself at the German, screaming like a wild animal.

Blumenkraft reacted quickly, half turning at the first sound of movement and then swinging the suit's helmet at Cliff's head. He slid underneath the countermove and caught Blumenkraft around his belly, sending them both down the slanted floor. The German let go of the helmet and pummeled Cliff with both fists, hammering on his neck and shoulders. Cliff fought back like a creature possessed, charging again, flailing at the Nazi in the red-tinted gloom.

Blumenkraft struggled and twisted, elbowing Cliff in his face. But the American was not to be stopped. He bounced the German's head against the floor. Once, twice, thrice. Blumenkraft made a little strangled sound. Then he fell limp. Cliff pushed his body off. The flashlight, still lit, had rolled under the flying suit. He lifted the suit up a little and retrieved it, then went to Tashi.

She was lying face down, her breathing sounding wet and ragged. Cliff said her name gently, checking to see if there were any obvious injuries. He'd been present at enough crack-ups to have a pretty good idea when a pilot's spine was damaged, and he didn't think Tashi would be in danger of further injury if he rolled her over. He had to talk to her.

Cliff attempted to make Tashi more comfortable. The bell was really beginning to get cold. As he covered her with his jacket, he heard her whisper, "Cliff..."

He knelt beside her and took her in his arms. "Tashi, I'm so sorry. Hold on, I can fly you back with my jet pack. They can fix you."

Tashi slowly lifted up her face, and then Cliff saw it. Dark age spots and wrinkles were beginning to appear on face. Her hair faded to white, came loose in his hands. Her eyes began to twitch and water. To Cliff's horror, he saw her body shrinking as muscle groups denatured. Everything she'd said had been true, and he hadn't listened. With the bell disabled, she was no longer under the valley's protection.

"Cliff, hear me," she struggled. "I don't have much time. The Lama was watching you from the time you left Culver City. In the hospital, I was assigned to monitor you, like my sister was for Barnes. But I fell in love with you, even though your heart beats for another."

"Tashi...hold on. We can leave right now."

She smiled at that. "Remember me," she whispered. "At least sometimes. Betty is so lucky. If I was just three hundred years younger..."

Then her breathing stopped and her body fell in on itself, like a deflated balloon. Cliff could hear her bones crack, and air whistled out of her mouth and nose. Her skin went slack, and her eyes turned grayish brown. He carefully laid Tashi's body back onto the floor.

Damn, it was cold. He hated to do it, but he had to retrieve his coat from Tashi's body, or he'd freeze to death before he got his jet pack, and even if he did, he'd freeze to death flying to safety. To his dismay, he saw that the ship didn't seem to have any emergency gear. How was he going to survive the night up in this thin air?

Despite the crushing pain in his chest, Cliff knew that his only hope was to risk frostbite and take flight immediately, before he lost any more strength or body heat. He guiltily got his suit and jet pack on, feeling terrible about leaving Tashi's body. Surely Smith would send his people to retrieve it, if only to salvage the missing craft.

But damn, it was cold, the air so thin. Cliff realized that anoxia was setting in and that without oxygen bottles, he might not have much of a chance at this altitude.

Cliff left the vimana the same way Blumenkraft had entered it. Outside, he saw that the two bells were crunched together, their perilous slide to oblivion halted by a large rock outcropping, jagged cliff walls on either side. Occasionally a light flared over the bells— a cold fire that looked like mother of pearl. There were large gaping cracks in both bells, and snowy footprints explained how the Nazi had been able to get to Cliff's craft with relative ease.

Fighting the cold, Cliff looked through the wide crack in the side of Emme's craft. Using the German's flashlight, Cliff scanned the vehicle's interior. Emme lay facedown on the floor near the control station, his head at a very bad angle. *So much for super-science*, thought Cliff. He shook his head, gritted his teeth against the pain to his ribs, and activated the jet pack, soaring up into the thin cold air.

Cliff was less impressed by The Players this time. Howard Hughes was late, and Cliff had ordered a T-bone, mashed potatoes, and a draft beer. Hughes wanted to debrief him, but Cliff had little to say. It seemed his memories of the hidden valley were dimming; every day a little more was lost. This morning Cliff woke up thinking that the name of the guru king was One Hung Low.

At a nearby table, three reporters were quizzing Preston Sturges about his new picture from Paramount, *The Great McGinty*. Was the dictator a send-up of Hitler, Stalin or Mussolini? The talk went on until someone suggested that Hitler was some sort of hypnotist or magician.

Preston Sturges said, "Don't you buy any of that. Magic is the bunk. When I was a kid in Paris, I saw my mother spend way too much time with Aleister Crowley. I saw through his phony act then, and I was only thirteen. Poor Mom—for a few years, she bought anything that creep was selling."

Howard walked up carrying a book.

"I see you ordered, Secord. Good job. I love the steaks here. You know Sturges over there is right—magic *is* the bunk."

Cliff stiffened, stung by the implication.

"Howard, I never said anything about magic. Just that the people I met have science and technology that we have yet to discover."

"Cliff, I'm sorry, but I just can't buy it. When you were brought to the embassy in New Delhi, you were suffering from frostbite, oxygen depletion and near starvation. I mean, *something* happened to you, but..."

Howard Hughes slid a copy of James Hilton's novel *Lost Horizon* across the bar to Cliff. Its handsome brown and cream dust jacket featured a drawing of Himalayan peaks.

"Most of what you claim to remember is laid out in this book," Hughes continued. "A warm valley, longevity, ancient technology superior to our own, a beautiful woman aging to pieces because she left the valley. Quite a yarn, and Capra made a nifty movie of it, too, which I just bet you saw. Sam Jaffe was the High Lama—you made 'Sam' into 'Smith.'"

"So I've been told," Cliff began, "but they explained that their 'thought screens' can cause artists to dream of their world. Bulwer-Lytton's *The Coming Race* came out well before Hilton's book. None of that matters to what I experienced."

"Cliff, think about what you're claiming. And isn't your memory growing less sharp every day? That could be due to surviving your ordeal."

"That's why I wrote everything down as soon as I could. And you can't argue that the jet pack hasn't been modified. How could I have done that with no tools, much less even knowing what I was doing?"

"That part's true enough," said Hughes. "It's why I haven't had you committed to a sanitarium so you can rest your overheated brain."

"Look, Mister Hughes, I know how it sounds, but I found your valley and met the people there. The jet pack modification proves it, even if I can't remember all the specifics. They said their influence in the outer world was subtle, and this is one example of it. Of that I'm sure."

"Okay, Cliff. Calm down. You're right—the modification promotes cooling and helps fuel efficiency. Maybe now our jet planes will go a little further and faster, perhaps even shorten the war."

"Right, *shorten the war*. Then I'll go back and prove it to you."

Hughes gave Cliff the grin he only unpacked for his close friends. "Shangri-La, Cliff. Shangri-La. I'll be right there with you."

Far away in *Das Kehlsteinhaus* (the Eagle's Nest) in the mountains above Berchtesgaden, Germany...

"*Mein* Führer, I learned amazing things, things that will change the course of the war. I knew they'd try to alter my memory, but I kept a record, wrote down everything I learned, everything I saw."

Hitler looked up at the man. Blumenkraft's survival was shining proof of Aryan superiority. If even half of what Himmler had told him about the SS man was true...

"What sort of things, Colonel?" demanded Hitler.

Blumenkraft put his right hand on his scarred face.

"Watch the chessboard, *mein* Führer."

A gift from Eva, the lovely chessboard, beautiful piece of Oberammergau wood carving, sat in front of Hitler. He loved the set, even if he was a poor player—he hated losing.

Hitler saw that the SS colonel had an odd expression on his face; his eyes were strange now, and sweat was starting to bead at his temple. Was it sweat?

Then one of the black pawns wobbled...and moved forward one square.

A drop of blood slid down Blumenkraft's right temple. Hitler saw that the pain of this mental exertion gripping the man. Now a white pawn jumped forward.

"*Mein Gott!*" exclaimed Hitler. "It *is* true."

"*Ja, mein* Führer," uttered Blumenkraft. His face relaxed, and he dabbed away the drop of blood that had now reached his jawline. "They have the ancient Aryan sciences. Their flying machines, the bells, will win the war for us. Once we arm them, we will rule the world. I ask only one thing."

"The fatherland always rewards its heroes," said Hitler.

Blumenkraft managed a smile. His scar was greatly diminished, but a shock of his hair had gone white. "The Rocketeer left me for dead, and I would like to return the favor. I want the head of Clifford Secord."

(Dedicated to the memory of Louis Pauwels and Jacques Bergier.)

FAREWELL, MY ROCKETEER

by

GREGORY FROST

May 1940

Cliff Secord nose-dived his Gee Bee "Z" like an old-time barn-
stormer. Down out of the clear blue sky he plunged,
shooting lower than the ridgetops and lookout points of the
Grand Canyon. Then, as if effortlessly, he leveled her off high above
the shining snake of the Colorado River.

Mules and tourists would be going up and down the narrow
trails on both sides, but none of them had a view the equal of his.
This was living!

The beauty of the striped and jutting promontories—the pinks
and reds and the golds—helped him cast off the low spirits that had
dogged him since leaving Ottawa.

He should have been ecstatic. He was heading home from
Granville's Air Show, where he'd won all but a single race and
impressed the Granvilles so much they'd asked him to fly the lead
biplane in a mock dogfight on the last day of the show. That had
been such a hoot. He had $600 in his pocket for his week of partici-
pation, and the Granvilles wanted him to come back next spring to
do it again. According to them, by the last day, 10,000 people had
seen him zipping through the pylons.

Air races and shows were still big business in Canada. What had gnawed at him the whole week, though, was knowing he'd been invited in the first place because the show couldn't book enough homegrown flyboys. Canada had been at war with Germany for six months, and while he zoomed around a grassy field for the entertainment of children, Canada's best fliers were somewhere engaged in *real* dogfights. He felt like a fraud, and the six hundred bucks weighed a lead anchor in his pocket.

The beauty of the Grand Canyon lifted his spirits some. And there was still one bright spot left on the trip home: Pineveta Intermediate Airfield—more specifically, Sue Ann, who waitressed at the airfield diner.

Olle, who ran the place, had told him she had a crush on him, which he hadn't exactly failed to notice. She wasn't Betty, of course, but she was awfully nice, and he looked forward to spending the rest of the afternoon with her before he headed back to Los Angeles. His ego needed the company of someone who was sweet on him.

He threw off the last of his gloom then and told himself how nothing was gonna mess that up.

Well south of Phoenix, he zeroed in on the airfield's four-thousand-foot north-south runway and started his descent. Intermediate fields like Pineveta were all dirt runways and nothing like Glendale or Santa Monica. Even on a day like this, if you weren't watching closely, you could miss 'em.

He pulled a grandstanding little loop-the-loop on his approach on the off-chance Sue Ann might be watching the Gee Bee's descent.

It was while upside down that he spotted the Ford Trimotor parked off to the side of the shorter east-west runway. That sure hadn't been there last week. Good, he thought, the little airfield was getting some business beyond the local biplane crop dusters.

Knowing the crosswinds over the field, he was ready for the brief jolts of turbulence when they came. The blue and yellow Gee Bee twisted a little, but he wrestled her straight and bumped down comfortably, then taxied in toward the hangar.

He gave the Trimotor the once-over as he passed. "Wow," he muttered, "a real Tin Goose." Looked like a *Mexicana* logo on the fuselage. He wasn't aware that Mexicana planes landed at intermediate strips.

At the end of the runway, Cliff turned the Gee Bee around and then cut the engine and came to a halt near the hangar. He popped the door fasteners on the cowling as Olle Jacobsen pushed rolling stairs up against the side of the plane. Olle seemed to be in a hurry. Before Cliff even had his hands on it, Olle had slid the cowling forward, away from the stabilizer.

Cliff took the opportunity to stand up for the first time since Rapid City. His knees complained, and he groaned. Flying cross-country in something as tight as his Gee Bee was like being folded up in a matchbox.

"Clifford," Olle said, "I want you to get back in your plane and—" He stopped, and his eyes shifted as if he was trying to see behind himself. He manufactured a smile and said, more loudly, "What a— what an unexpected surprise."

"It is?" Cliff blinked. After four hours of flying, Olle's behavior left him a little dazed: he was *sure* Olle knew he'd be back through after Ottawa. Was Peevy's old pal losing his grip?

"Is everything all right?" A soft voice snaked up from below and behind Olle, who swallowed behind his stiff smile.

Cliff looked around him to find another man, short and swarthy, standing at the foot of the steps, dressed in airfield coveralls but with a tidy bow tie at his throat.

"Everything's hunky-dory up here," Cliff answered, as if he failed to see the concern, the fear, in Olle's eyes. He shook the dust out of his brain, and tried to make little of the situation. "So, ya got yourself a new assistant, hey, Olle?"

"Yah, my—my assistant. Mister Ganos. Cliff."

"A pleasure to meet you," said Mister Ganos. He had an accent that made the words sound the opposite of what he said. "What should I be doing now, Mister Jacobsen? Perhaps you could...show me."

Olle turned, but before he could speak, Cliff pointed at the side of the runway. "You could toss them chocks under my wheels, keep her from rolling if the wind picks up." As if to prove his point, a crosswind gusted over the airfield, kicking up dirt. "See what I mean?"

With obvious reluctance, Mister Ganos strode over to the chocks.

"What's the lowdown?" Cliff asked in a whisper.

"Oh, Clifford, I am sorry it's you. Sorry I told them about you."

Not sure what that meant, he replied, "S'okay, don't worry."

Cliff glanced at his duffel bag on the floor, debating whether to bring it inside with him but deciding it was better off hidden. He slid over the side and onto the ladder, then helped Olle drop the Fiberloid canopy back into place.

Mister Ganos had chocked both wheels by now and met him as he stepped onto the ground. "Did you have a good flight, Mister Cliff?"

"Swell," he said as he came down the steps.

Mister Ganos led the way off the field to the diner, and when they reached it, he held open the door with such formality that Cliff almost felt he should tip him.

The group of people inside the diner all stopped whatever they'd been doing and looked at Cliff. He pretended not to notice, instead fastening his brown eyes on Sue Ann with such intensity that, despite obviously being as scared as Olle, she blushed.

"Hey, babe," he called and headed straight for her. He swung around the end of the long counter, and in one quick movement, grabbed her around the waist and hoisted her in the air. He planted a kiss on her and held it for a long minute, which was at least two minutes longer than he'd ever expected to kiss her. By the end of it, he knew that she knew that he knew something was up. He set her feet back on the floor, looked into her shocked eyes and winked. "I am so glad to be back," he announced, then slipped around the counter again and sat down on one of the spinning stools, turning and twisting it like a lovesick kid. "Think Olle'll let you come out back with me for a minute?"

He'd given himself time to count the five strangers in the front of the diner, including Mister Ganos, and one more looking out through the porthole window of the kitchen door.

Of the five, one was dressed in a bespoke suit, with slick brown hair perfectly parted; one was blond and would have had a seven o'clock shadow if his beard had been darker; and one was a dark woman so gorgeous and self-possessed that Cliff could feel the icicles circling her. Like him, she wore jodhpurs and boots, though there was something severe in the look of those pants on her. Her white blouse was loose and silky. She also wore a holster on her hip. Behind her, lying on the bench of one of the booths, was a man in a leather bomber jacket who looked to be asleep—or dead.

Cliff swung around to Olle. "You don't mind if we, uh, have a moment?"

Olle shook his head.

"Great. Set down the coffee pot, sweetie, and c'mon." He took Sue Ann by the hand and headed for the pantry exit. Out back were two concrete steps. He turned around on the lower one, no longer giddy.

"Oh god, Cliff, we're in so much trouble." Sue Ann clung to him.

He whispered into her ear, "Who are they?"

"Don't know. They flew in about seven this morning, barely got on the ground in one piece. Their pilot—I don't know—he had a stroke or something."

"Where were they *supposed* to land?"

"I don't—" She was interrupted by the back kitchen door opening. The man who'd been in the kitchen with Idris, the cook, stepped out. He'd stuck a cigarette in his mouth and now lit it up, whilst staring straight at them. He was muscled, wearing a shirt and tie, his sleeves rolled up and sweat under the arms.

"Look at the lovebirds," he cooed.

"What's it to ya?" Cliff shot back. "I've been up north, and I missed her."

"No kiddin'. Funny she and the geezer didn't mention how you was her boyfriend an' all. Just how you was some kinda great flyboy they was expectin'."

"Yeah? Well, maybe they didn't tell ya 'cause it's none of your business. You a G-Man or somethin'?"

"What if I was?"

"Got a badge?"

"I don't gotta show you no stinkin' badge." He flicked his cigarette at them. "Now, why don't we all go back inside, Cliffy? Mister Bauchmann wants to meet you."

101

◆

"Who?"

"G'wan." He jumped toward them.

Cliff knew better than to get into a brawl with him, not when he didn't know what was going on yet. It couldn't be G-men: the ones he'd encountered weren't thugs, and they'd likely have recognized his name, since he still had possession of a certain piece of government property. He was sorry now that he hadn't packed Peevy's "bootlegging" Mauser.

He turned Sue Ann around, and they ducked back inside with the thug close behind. Cliff held the door till the thug came charging up the steps after him. Then he slammed it hard. Outside, there was a yelp followed by a soft thud.

Cliff turned around, and the ice queen had snatched Sue Ann aside and now stood two inches from him. Her scent was like night-blooming jasmine. If he'd breathed in enough of it, he'd have stopped touching the floor.

She looked from the door to him. "Have you hurt Dundy?" she asked.

"Oh, was he supposed to come in with us?"

She smiled as if the idea of Dundy being injured appealed to her, like she would pay money to watch people get hurt. Sue Ann moved off behind the counter again, looking on with fear. The well-dressed man had come up beside Olle. He didn't say or do anything, but his bearing implied a threat—to Olle or to Sue Ann or to both. He made it clear to Cliff that *someone* would pay for any further shenanigans.

"You Bauchmann?" Cliff asked.

Before the man could answer, the door at Cliff's back burst open, and Dundy stormed inside. Cliff just had time to turn and see that Dundy had torn his pants at the knee before Dundy's fist slammed into his jaw.

He awoke with Sue Ann pressing a towel wrapped around some ice against his face. Her brown hair enclosed him as she bent down and kissed him. For a second he considered it could be worth falling down regularly if she kissed him every time it happened.

Betty was off doing her Hollywood thing, so he didn't see how she could complain if he got kissed now and then. She was probably kissing guys every half hour in front of a camera.

Sue Ann suddenly drew sharply away, and he saw that he was lying on a booth bench, and on the bench across from him was the guy who hadn't looked so good when he'd arrived. The guy looked less good now. Dead, in fact, and Cliff wondered how they planned to put him on ice. It had to be over ninety degrees.

Remembrance of the situation roared back, and he sat up much too fast.

Sparklers spun in front of him. His jaw throbbed. He was facing the window, looking out at the bunkhouse across the road and the old cars parked there. He slid his boots down off the bench and then sat leaning on the table.

"Mister Secord," said a voice above and beside him.

He turned to face the dapper man in the suit. Bauchmann. He remembered. The guy reminded him of Jonas back in New York—the long, thin face and beak of a nose, the cultured voice and sense of control. He even had a half-amused look that could have graced Jonas's puss. How could someone wear a suit like that and not be sweating? Guy must be part Gila monster.

"Mister Secord, let's not have any more fisticuffs, hmm? Because Dundy would mop the floor with you, and I fear he dislikes provocation. It makes him quite useful in his job, but not particularly... pleasant company."

"What *is* the mook's job?"

"Oh, let us speak instead of *your* job, shall we, dear boy?" Bauchmann leaned on the table. "Mister Jacobsen told me all about you. He claims you can fly anything. I believe he said something along the lines of it being so in your blood that you almost don't require a plane."

For a second Cliff had to think if Olle had somehow twigged that he had the rocket pack. Nah, that was crazy. Olle had never seen inside the duffel. No, it had to be because of their conversation when he'd refueled on his way up. Olle had called the Gee Bee a flying death trap and had named Boardman and Allen, who'd both crashed in theirs. Cliff had countered by quoting Jimmy Doolittle: "the sweetest little ship I've ever flown." And Allen, he pointed out, had messed with the plane's design. And then he'd bumptiously added the brag that he could pretty much fly anything from Goose's gyro to any of Hughes's experimental test planes. Yeah, that probably hadn't been wise; but Sue Ann had been listening, and, well, he liked the admiring way she looked at him.

"Okay, yeah, I'm a swell pilot," he admitted. "So?"

"So, as you can see, dear boy, our pilot has now flown off with the angels, which leaves our group with something of a dilemma."

"You need somebody else to get you where you're goin."

"There, you understand perfectly." He straightened up.

"Tell ya the truth, not really."

Bauchmann said, "Then come and sit with me over in the corner, and I'll explain the details of our venture. I'm positive you'll see the light by the time I've finished."

Cliff dutifully got to his feet. This time the jaw ached but nothing sparkled. He kept the ice on it as he walked past the lineup of Ganos, sneering Dundy, and the ice queen in her riding costume. They followed him with their eyes. The blond mug went over and started to haul the body out of the booth. He was strong.

Bauchmann sat at one of the small round tables, his back to everyone. Cliff sat watching the booths. Dundy got up to help carry the pilot's body out. Skinny Idris in his dirty cook's apron was left standing behind the counter with nothing to do. He met Cliff's eyes. Cliff gestured a "chin up." His dark fingers trembling, Idris took out and lit a smoke.

Ganos, eyeing Bauchmann's table suspiciously, came over and drew a chair up between them. Without looking at either of them, he said, "I feel I should be a part of this conversation. There is so much to discuss, and *you* might leave something out." He made a small laugh as if he hadn't disparaged his partner.

A moment later, the woman dragged another chair over, forcing Ganos to move sideways to accommodate her.

Drily, Bauchmann said, "Well, now that the principals are all gathered, perhaps I can discuss matters with Mister Secord?"

"Unless you got a deck of cards," Cliff remarked cheerfully. When they stared back at him, he added, "Well, it's too late in the day now to be flying anywhere."

"You wouldn't fly in the dark?" asked the woman.

"Not if I can help it." The look she gave him made Cliff think that maybe she hadn't been asking about planes.

"Indeed," Bauchmann agreed, taking back the conversation. "Thus we have time for a tall tale, do we not?"

Cliff shrugged. "Sure." He stretched his legs out, acting as relaxed as possible.

"Very well. Our story starts in the sixteenth century, when the explorer Hernán Cortés took as his prisoner the king of the Aztecs, Montezuma. You've heard of Montezuma?"

"I've heard of his curse."

Ganos tittered.

Bauchmann impassively continued, "Cortés's actions were taken without the approval of Spain and its representatives, with the result that he was forced to battle the Spanish army. In the end he triumphed over them, but while he was thus engaged, Montezuma set to work. Cortés and his Spaniards had made it plain they wanted all the gold and precious stones, and by all accounts the Aztecs had more riches than the whole of ancient Egypt. They had mines, you know. Advanced metallurgical skills. Imagine it, Mister Secord."

"Sure, and I've heard there's gold up in the Sierra Madres if you don't mind killing yourself to get it."

"When the totality of the trappings of wealth of the Aztecs was collected and amassed in one place, there was so much gold and so many jewels that the Aztecs had to assemble seven separate caravans in order to carry it off. And that is what they did. They took their riches, and they headed away, most likely in seven different directions, but no one will ever be certain of that. All that wealth vanished, and it has never been found. To Cortés, the Aztecs pretended that it was tossed in a lake, from which nothing has ever been recovered either. Cortés certainly found nothing."

"You gonna tell me you think Montezuma's treasure's hidden under a diner in Arizona? I think I'd try the pie first."

Bauchmann finally laughed. "I do like a man with a sense of humor, but you shouldn't overplay it, Mister Secord. Are you not a man of vision, dear boy?"

"You know, when I was a kid, the papers were full of stories about a guy name of Freddie Crystal. He had a treasure map. Had people running all over Utah, crawling into caves and stuff. Even had me dreamin' of running away to join the circus. Hundreds of people lookin' for the same Aztec treasure you buzzards are talkin' about and nobody ever found nothin'. And I don't think he was the first, either."

Ganos drew himself up. "I take umbrage at being called a *buzzard*, young man."

Bauchmann ignored him. "As a matter of fact, your Mister Crystal *wasn't* the first, though he was misinformed, or else he'd have purchased a map off some charlatan. The person of more interest to us is one James White. I wager you haven't heard of him."

Cliff shook his head. He had to admit he couldn't help being a *little* intrigued by all this. He had a pretty good idea where it was all leading.

"You've not heard of him, because Mister White entered the history books in 1865. He was found, starving and completely delusional after spending three weeks on a raft on the Colorado River. He had no idea how he'd stumbled into the town where he was nursed to health and had no idea just what he had seen."

"And what *had* he seen?"

"Treasure, Mister Secord, what else? He described finding thousands of golden idols, trinkets and other objects. The array of things he described suggests he was not lying, for who would know to fabricate the details so well? Rather, suffering from malnutrition and heat stroke, he confused the time and place of the discovery. He convinced everyone, including himself, that he'd only recently made his discovery, and that it must have been in the lower granite gorge of your Grand Canyon. Prince Ferry was his reference point. As with Mister Crystal decades later, the treasure hunters found nothing at all."

"Okay, so you wouldn't be telling me this if you didn't have something those people missed."

"How perceptive of you. I do like a fellow who sees the point. Our Señorita Diablessa has a map on her person." He nodded to the dark ice queen. "Hard to believe in that outfit, I know, but she does, I assure you, and she is disinclined to part with it."

Her two partners stared at her. Her eyes smoldered.

"What, is it tattooed?" Cliff ventured.

Diablessa said nothing.

"Oh, if it were *just* a treasure map, we'd be no smarter than Freddie Crystal, would we?" Before Cliff could agree, Bauchmann asked, "Would you mind, my dear?"

With obvious reluctance, she undid the cuff of one shining white sleeve, her turquoise and silver bracelets jingling as she reached into it, tugged on some string, and drew out a parchment that had been wrapped around her forearm.

"Nothin' up *your* sleeve, huh?" Cliff said.

Ganos snorted. No love was lost between those two.

Her slender fingers unrolled the parchment, and Cliff realized it wasn't paper at all, but an old leather skin of some sort onto which a lot of symbols had been inked in red and black. He studied it. The landmarks maybe didn't mean anything, but at a glance they seemed vaguely familiar, like he'd flown over them. He asked, "What's all this stuff on the side that looks like dominoes?"

"The right side is a calendar in the Nahuatl system of writing," said the woman. "It details how long it took those who created this document to make the journey from Tenochtitlan to where they hid the treasure. From it, we—or rather, I—am able surmise how far north they must have come on their journey." And with that she rolled the skin loosely again around her wrist and pulled down her sleeve.

"But you said there were seven caravans."

Bauchmann smiled. "Good, you were paying attention. Yes, you're correct, and this is the map for only one of them. It is possible that it's the only one that has survived. Even now, associates of mine seek to learn of the existence of others. Whether this corresponds with Mister White's discovery in the last century, we can only speculate."

Ganos said quietly, "People have already died for these maps, Mister Secord. It would be terrible for anyone else to suffer, don't you think so?"

"Now, Ganos, we needn't be so melodramatic. I'm sure Mister Secord will happily assist us in return for Blaine's share in the proceeds." Bauchmann glanced idly around at Sue Ann behind the counter. "Won't you?"

Cliff spent half a minute trying to calculate the odds. They couldn't fly out till morning. That gave him the night to try to get Sue Ann and the others out of here. Anything could happen, especially as it was clear none of these crooks trusted one another.

"Heck yeah," he said finally. "You need a pilot, an' who doesn't need a pot of gold?"

Bauchmann nodded. "There. You see, Ganos? I've found gold is *always* persuasive. Welcome to our little group of players, Mister Secord."

"You're gonna to have to let me go over that Trimotor stem to stern, though, if you expect me to fly 'er to, uh," he gestured at Señorita Diablessa, "wherever on her forearm we're goin'. I got no idea what sort of landing your pilot made. And, gold or no gold, I don't figure to take off and watch my wheels stay behind on the runway."

"Naturally. Of course, you'll understand we cannot leave you alone while you're doing that."

"'Course. I'm gonna need Olle to come along, too. We got three engines to check, not one, and we're already losing the light. Unless you want to waste time tomorrow morning."

"Whatever you need, Mister Secord, by all means."

Cliff got up. Dundy, at the door, crossed his arms like he had no intention of letting him out. Cliff looked down at Bauchmann. "The first thing I need is, you keep your pet monkey off me."

"Dundy," Bauchmann called. "Sit down at the counter. Where's Hans?"

"Covering up Blaine's body."

To Cliff, Bauchmann said, "I'll have Hans join you at the plane when he's finished."

Cliff started out. He waved Olle to come along, gave Sue Ann a wink that everything was under control, which he didn't for a moment believe, but it was what she needed.

From outside, he watched the woman, Bauchmann, and Ganos argue around the table. "Olle," he said, "go get your rolling steps from the Bee, and while you're at it, I got a duffel bag stashed in the cockpit. Bring that with you, will ya? Like it's part of your tools."

"Sure, Cliff. But you know, by golly, they ain't gonna share wit' you."

"The deuce, you say." Then he grinned. "They also can't live without me till we get back here."

The interior of the Trimotor was shiny aluminum, the front divider walls corrugated. The eight seats were wide cane chairs clamped to the floor. It was like the plane had been outfitted in Cuba.

There was a small shelf-lined luggage section between the passengers' cabin and the cockpit. On one side lay a large rucksack with shoulder straps. He opened the flap and peered in: canteens, tin plates, flares. Well, they'd come prepared for a *short* trek, anyway.

On the other side, a stack of Mexicana brochures in Spanish lay on the upper shelf and was held in place by a coconut. He could only wonder about the coconut. The lower shelves contained parachutes in canvas packs about the same color as his duffel.

Olle leaned through the rear hatch with the duffel and an inquisitive look on his face.

Walking back to grab it, Cliff wondered if he'd peeked inside. But Olle said nothing as he handed it over and withdrew.

Cliff tucked the bag deep behind the 'chutes, out of sight. Unless someone went pawing through them, they would never notice it.

The cabin was efficient. Two seats, for the pilot and copilot, and behind them, a drop-down seat for a stewardess who would face the passengers. He sat behind the left-hand steering wheel, looked out at the Curtis-Wright engines, the exterior gauges, the control-panel gauges, then the skinny pole of the "Johnny" brake between the seats like some crazy shift lever growing out of the floor. In his head he went through the takeoff sequence, closed his eyes and felt the wheel in his hands. This was going to be different from anything he had flown, however much he'd bragged for Sue Ann's benefit.

When he got up, he found Señorita Diablessa sitting in the first of the cane seats, her left leg crossed, boot extended as if she expected him to polish it. She held a cigarette between her fingers, expectantly.

"Sorry," Cliff told her. "I don't smoke, so I don't carry a lighter."

"Mmm." She reached into the big thigh pocket on her jodhpurs and drew out her own brass Zippo. She watched him over the flame.

"You my personal guard? I thought that was Hans."

She exhaled. "I could be so much more if you let me."

Despite trying to maintain his cool, Cliff felt his face flush. Good thing it wasn't bright in here at the moment. "How you figure?"

She got up. He noticed now that she'd unbuttoned two more buttons on her blouse for his benefit. That kind of thing probably worked with Dundy. "What would you say to partners?" She shook her hair out, waiting to see what he would do. He couldn't get past her in the aisle without climbing over the chairs or her.

He scratched behind one ear. "I, uh, I thought we already was partners. Like Bauchmann said, right?"

"Bauchmann." She said it like a curse word. "He is *loco*, you know? He wants treasure for all the wrong reasons."

"Wrong reasons like what?"

"Oh, for the glorious fatherland, of course."

"So he *is* a Nazi."

"You had guessed?"

"He's not the first one I've met."

She concentrated on squashing the cigarette underfoot, and then suddenly she pressed up against Cliff. "Me, I want to sink naked into a great pile of gold coins and make love with someone." She pushed her fingers into his hair, pulled his head to her. Cliff's eyes went wide, and hers never closed, locked upon his gaze while her lips melted into his. She tasted like nicotine. Then she pushed away from him as if he had made the play for her. He swallowed. "*You* have the skills to take me anywhere I want to go. Bauchmann can't even drive a *car*. He has to have Hans take him everywhere. Like a little boy. You and I, we can have all the treasure and all the time in the world to spend it."

"*Fraulein?*"

They both turned as Hans stuck his head through the open hatch.

"Yes, what is it, Hans?"

"You are to come back to the *speisewagen* and let Herr Secord finish his preparations."

Cliff understood now why Hans didn't speak much. Bauch-mann could pass himself off as a well-educated Brit, but Hans was practically a cliché.

Diablessa gave Cliff a final sultry look and touched one finger to his lips. "You might want to wipe that off before your little girl sees you." Then she walked down the aisle and swung out of the hatch.

Cliff pressed his hands over his face. "Whew!" he hissed. "Cool down, Cliff, before she lights you up like one of them flares." He wiped his palm over his mouth and looked at the red on his fingers. "I gotta get back to someplace sane. Like Los Angeles."

He climbed out of the plane.

Hans stood outside the door, legs apart, hands behind him, in a stiff military stance. "You are satisfied, then?" he asked.

"Brother, and how."

Olle was on the rolling stepladder next to the portside engine. "So," Cliff asked. "How's she lookin'?"

"This plane's in very good shape. Someone's taken good care of 'er. Sure not this lot."

"Probably whoever they stole it from."

"You get everything stowed?"

"Yeah, so long as Hans doesn't go snoopin'." As if on cue, Hans came around the nose of the plane, and Olle got down off the steps. They rolled the ladder back into the hangar with Hans striding along like a shadow behind them.

As they started back to the diner, Hans said, "No. Herr Secord is to sleep over there for the night." He pointed to the bunkhouse.

"You have any other guests?" Cliff asked.

"Nope. It's only you and them, lad."

"Maybe we'll play some cards after all." Then, more quietly, "Look, Olle, if something does go wrong, like nobody comes back? You make sure Peevy tells Betty, right? I wasn't ever workin' with Nazis. Tell 'im 'Remember Catalina.'"

Olle glanced at him in round-eyed comprehension. "Bauch-mann...Oh, Clifford," he said.

The sky was blue and cloudless. Cliff shared the cockpit with Ganos, who passed the time nattering about his travels through Istanbul, Greece, India, and Egypt. Bauchmann and Diablessa, in back, scrutinized their map, and periodically one or the other of them would come forward and announce the identification of something conforming to a feature on it—a formation of rock, a river, a small body of water—and Cliff would alter or maintain his course accordingly. Bauchmann had traded his suit for a more reasonable outfit: a linen shirt, khakis, and ankle boots. And Diablessa had replaced her white blouse with a military-style desert shirt with epaulets, sleeve tabs and pockets.

Dundy had been left behind at the diner. He had orders to "clean everything up" if they didn't return by sunset tomorrow. Cliff had hugged Sue Ann. She was crying, but he promised her everything would work out fine and he'd be back long before the deadline arrived. "Save me a piece of pie, okay?" This time she wrapped her arms around him and gave him a kiss. Whatever else, he was logging a lot of quality canoodling time on this trip.

Olle stared at him with barely concealed terror, and Cliff wasn't sure whose life he feared for. With Olle, it was probably his. Cliff slapped him on the shoulder, then picked up his leather jacket and walked out like a condemned prisoner hemmed in by the other four.

"Sunset!" Dundy shouted at him as he crossed the dirt.

Cliff turned and yelled back, "That's sunset *tomorrow*, ya goon!"

Ganos, beside him, had laughed his strange fragmented chortle. "Really, I am liking you quite a bit, Mister Secord."

Liking him, as was obvious now, meant telling him every detail of every strange adventure Ganos had ever had—and there seemed to have been quite a few, including the pursuit of some sort of large bird figurine—until finally Bauchmann shouted "That's it!" so loud that Cliff heard him even over the engines. Bauchmann rushed forward as Ganos pressed his face to the windshield.

Off to the right, Cliff made out a hook-shaped string of mountain peaks rising out of the desert floor ahead. He was sure he'd passed over it before at some point, but it hadn't meant anything. Bauchmann leaned in and pushed the map in front of him. No question the formation on the map matched what he was looking at below.

"Okay, then," Cliff yelled and banked to swing around. "Now we find someplace close where we can land."

Fortunately, this proved relatively easy. Less than a mile below the base of the mountain, the ground leveled out fairly quickly into something like a fluvial plain between the mountain and the bend in a nearby river. Cliff wasn't sure what river it was or if it fed into the Colorado—thinking about James White, the guy Bauchmann had mentioned, wondering if this small river could have been part of his journey.

He made two low passes to confirm the plain didn't hold any surprises and offered enough length, and then carefully he set the Trimotor down. They bounced a few times along the way. If they gave him the opportunity, he would walk the makeshift runway before they left.

He cut the engines as he brought her around and pulled to a stop with the full runway's length ahead of him. At his back, Bauchmann said, "I see Jacobsen knew what he was talking about. Blaine couldn't have brought us down half so well as that."

Cliff said nothing. Ganos, who had looked fairly terrified during the descent and landing, mopped his face and made his strange little laugh as he got up. Cliff stayed seated. Maybe they would forget him now that they were on the ground; but abruptly Hans was there, silent as always. They exchanged a look, and Cliff nodded and got up. Hans stepped back against the shelves and let him pass, then followed him out of the plane.

The string of mountains wasn't by any means the highest in Arizona, assuming they still were in Arizona. The tallest peak, he guessed, was maybe three thousand feet. The triumvirate of Bauchmann, Diablessa and Ganos held the map between them as they discussed the proposed ascent. Cliff wondered where in the stretch of upland terrain their destination lay. There was no reason to assume the hypothetical Aztecs had climbed the highest peak to stash their treasure. He tried to recall what the map had shown.

Three dots, he remembered, more or less where the formation hooked. If no one had climbed it since—if paths hadn't been formed already—he wondered what difference it made which approach they took.

"Hans," Bauchmann called. Hans wasn't about to go without his charge, and Cliff found himself being hauled along by a surprisingly strong grip.

Hans let go of him and saluted, clicking his heels together, though in the pebbly rock he almost lost his footing as a result. Bauchmann addressed him in German and pointed at the map. Hans looked from it to the mountains ahead and back again. He poked a finger at the map, and his finger snaked up to the dots. Cliff looked up again. He wished he'd brought his aviators along. It was way too bright out here.

The conference seemed to be at an end. Bauchmann said, "*Der Rücken.*" He'd hauled two different rucksacks from the plane: the one with the canteens, which Hans distributed, and an empty one. Hans slung them both over his shoulder.

"Hans, lead the way," Bauchmann ordered, and they all started off toward the mountains.

The base comprised broken boulders and rock that had likely tumbled down over centuries from above. Sparse scrub grew in and around them. Ganos commented that he'd anticipated there would be clues, indications or carvings of some sort, but now he felt that anything carved in stones four centuries earlier would have been buried under rubble. Bauchmann commented how much he loved mountains, but no one except Hans seemed to share the sentiment.

Early going proved exhausting, though the boulders were fairly easy to climb, and Hans seemed to know exactly how to navigate them with practiced ease. None of the others seemed to have anticipated what climbing a mountain, even a low one like this, might entail.

Once they got above the broken rocks, the way became easier. There were numerous plateaus or ledges, and there was something like a natural path winding toward a broad chute up the side. On perhaps the third plateau up, Hans pointed to a place where a bowl shape had been chipped into the rock. It wasn't a natural depression and drew the interest of Diablessa. Not far away, under a protective outcropping, she found another, larger one. She knelt there, then ran her hand through the depression.

"What are they?" Cliff asked.

"Mortars," she explained. "It means people were here at some point, people who ground corn."

"Your Aztecs?"

She shrugged. "Someone. Also, they must have remained awhile. Why else go to the effort of carving such things?"

"They sure didn't grow corn around here." He had little time to think about it, as Bauchmann soon sighted some glyphs carved into the nearby rocks and nearly fell in his excitement to scramble on up the chute.

At the top of it lay another seemingly natural, narrow path, or else one so old that erosion had worn it to almost nothing in places—in particular one spot where they had to squeeze around an outcropping dotted in more petroglyphs. The images didn't mean anything to Cliff, but Diablessa suddenly clutched his arm and held him back as the others edged around the outcrop.

"This," she hissed, "is the symbol for Tenochtitlan. You see? Those represent cacti, growing out of a single stone. It is true. There *is* treasure." The way she said it, he half expected another kiss. Instead she pushed him aside and quickly edged around the outcrop ahead of him.

"Jeez, thanks a heap," he said to nobody. They'd left him alone. Right then he could have turned and dived back down the chute and maybe lost them on the mountain; but Diablessa's excitement was contagious. She'd been holding back, hadn't truly committed to believing in this "Tin Goose" chase until now. Now there was proof, carved in stone. The stories of the treasure were real. He wanted to know, too.

Cliff put one arm around the outcrop. Something grabbed his wrist and yanked him off his feet. For an instant he thought he was going to be dropped down the mountainside. Instead, still caught in Hans's iron grip, he stumbled upright on the other side. Hans eyed him suspiciously. Ganos, behind him, said, "When she came through ahead of you, we feared you might be planning to leave our little party."

"Nuts to your party," Cliff replied, and Diablessa shot him a glance. He saw that he was standing in front of the three dots on the map. They were maybe eighteen hundred feet up.

The slope of the mountainside before them was steep, almost sheer. It also featured three cave mouths. They were approximately ovoid and might have been natural formations save for the images carved between them.

Hans shrugged off the rucksack, dug into it and came up with two military flashlights. He gave one to Bauchmann and kept the other.

Bauchmann said, "Ganos, you come with me. You two go with Hans. We'll start with these tunnels; leave the final one to explore together. Be careful. It's more than conceivable that the way is protected."

"Protected?" asked Cliff.

"He means booby-trapped," Ganos clarified.

"Oh. Terrific."

They split up, with Bauchmann entering the left-hand tunnel and Hans the middle one. They had to crouch somewhat to walk, and the floor angled steadily downward. A cool breeze emanated from ahead.

Cliff, at the rear, could only see a little of what Hans's light revealed. The floor of the cave was rough, rock-strewn and curved, which suggested that maybe it *was* a natural formation. Soon enough it bore left, and they saw dancing light ahead of them. Within a few moments they were facing Bauchmann and Ganos. The two tunnels formed a single loop.

They stood, turning about, looking for anything, more symbols, a secret passage. There was only a small hole, penetrating deeper, maybe worn there by water, and nothing larger than Butch back in Los Angeles could have entered it.

Frustrated, they turned and walked back out, and for a brief time Cliff was in the lead.

Outside again, they considered the third tunnel. "Hans, take the lead. You follow him, Mister Secord. Then Ganos and Diablessa. I will make up the rear. That way there is a light at each end as we go." Cliff was thinking, *Booby traps. If there are any, Hans triggers 'em, and I'm the guinea pig.*

This tunnel began the same as the other two. Everyone had to crouch to go. But the floor didn't slope, and the space quickly widened, accommodating two people abreast. Someone had worked on the walls here with chisels. Shortly, they encountered a barricade of broken rock. Hans muttered, "A cave-in or just where they deposited what they carved?" He swung the light around, then up at the wet ceiling. It did seem that a section above them had long ago collapsed. Peripherally Cliff swore he saw something move, but Hans lowered the light straight at him, and he had to shield his eyes.

"Hey! Cut it out!"

Hans was shining it back at Bauchmann. "We have to climb over!" he called.

"Yes, all right, be careful!" Bauchmann called back.

Cliff blinked until he could see again. Ganos nudged him impatiently. "Keep yer shirt on, will ya?" He turned and clambered up onto the nearest boulder.

Where the debris tapered off, it looked like the tunnel narrowed to a kind of doorway barely large enough for one person to enter. Hans had stopped there and was shining the light in through the opening. Cliff couldn't be sure if he looked terrified or thrilled. Cliff leaned around the edge and peered in. "Wow," he said. Whatever he'd imagined, it sure wasn't this.

In the low-ceilinged room lay a mass of shining objects, ingots and little statues, spears and plates and assorted things he couldn't identify. The light glimmered off dusty gold and reddish, almost coppery surfaces everywhere, all of it piled up around a red-gold chair of some kind in the middle, on which sat a skeletal figure. That was enough to make Cliff take a step back. He bumped up against Diablessa and Ganos. They swarmed around him and kept going, in their zeal pushing Hans into the chamber.

Bauchmann called, "Be careful, you!" which might have been at any of them, but no one seemed to be paying much attention. The notion of booby traps was forsaken in the face of real treasure.

Cliff stood beside Bauchmann in the doorway. He said, "Seems to me it's awfully unguarded, just sittin' here like this."

Bauchmann replied, "Oh, the one who was killed and left in the chair was to guard everything, from the spirit realm."

Cliff stared at the empty sockets, the half-mummified face. "I don't think he's up to it."

"There *is* a curse associated with this treasure, you know," Diablessa said.

Bauchmann replied scornfully, "There is *always* a curse."

Hans was kneeling and scooping as much as he could from the pile into the empty rucksack. In his excitement, he overfilled the pack and found that he could not lift it.

"We don't need to take all of it at once, you fools," Bauchmann yelled at them. "We have all the rest of the day and tomorrow, as well. Just fill what you can. We will bring more with us next time."

Cliff thought of his stowed duffel. They would root around, find it and its contents. He needed to be the first one back to the plane.

Ganos was filling his pockets, and Diablessa even slipped small ingots and jewels into the swooped hip pockets of her jodhpurs. She'd taken out her cigarettes and lighter, and, after lighting a smoke, had dropped them in the pockets of her blouse.

Hans emptied half of his rucksack and then carried it to Cliff. The bag nearly pulled him off his feet. "Geez, it's gonna take *two* of me to get this off the mountain."

"I'm sure Ganos will help you with it. Hans has the other bag."

He was already emptying the second bag of its contents, flares, rope, and even pairs of sun goggles. Cliff said, "Hey," and snatched a pair. "Would have been nice to have these on the climb."

He was getting up when in the flashlights' glow the ceiling started moving. There was a deep niche around two sides just below the ceiling. Cliff hadn't thought anything of it. Now a lot of small shapes with long, angular black pipe-cleaner legs were skittering out from the recesses, clinging to the ceiling and swarming the chamber. "Um..." he said. "Folks."

Bauchmann looked at him, then at the ceiling. Hundreds of the spindly legged creatures were pushing silently overhead. It was probably inevitable that some of them would be knocked off. They dropped randomly. Diablessa screamed and flung away her cigarette. She batted at herself. Ganos shrieked and stumbled over Hans's half-filled second bag, sprawling across the skeleton in the chair. The skull tumbled off the spine, and the chair tipped back.

Something deep in the rocks rumbled.

Bauchmann and Cliff stared at each other; then Bauchmann cried, "*Schnell!* Get out of here now!"

An instant later the ceiling exploded. It couldn't have been suspended more than a foot off the ledge, but that was enough for it to crack apart when the weight of the unleashed boulders above struck it. The chair, weighted with gold, had acted as some kind of fulcrum. Bauchmann was right: the corpse *had* been guarding the chamber.

Ganos tried to get up but only made it to his knees before the middle section of ceiling smashed him flat. Diablessa sprang for the door. Hans refused to let go of the second rucksack, and Bauchmann, ignoring the arachnids raining over him, reached out and grabbed the sack, even as a chunk of ceiling dropped like a metal press onto Hans. It would have crushed Diablessa, as well, but Cliff had grabbed her around the waist and all but thrown her from the chamber, using the momentum to pull him out the doorway, too.

Skittering harvestmen crawled all over him. He expected to be bitten, poisoned, but none of them did anything except fall off harmlessly and flee. Bauchmann pressed against the doorway, coughing in the cloud of rock dust. He gripped the second rucksack at his feet. Hans's hand, extending out of the rubble, still clung to the strap. Coldly, Bauchmann bent down and pried the fingers open. The hand flopped, lifeless.

The roaring soon stopped. The dust floated in the tunnel. The room was nothing but a pile of debris, exactly like the section of tunnel they'd climbed over.

Only three of them had survived, covered in gray dust and with the two heavy bags to carry between them. Bauchmann stared wistfully back into the room. "I knew there would be a trap, but I thought— hoped—the place where the rock had fallen...that someone before us had sprung it already. Now I see, it was the test for their chamber. Of course they had to make sure. Next time I will bring more men. We'll dig out the rest now that we know its location." He lifted the larger rucksack. "This is a good start. Enough to fund many future expeditions."

Through his talking, Diablessa slapped at her clothing and whined in her throat. No harvestmen were crawling on her, but she seemed to feel them anyway.

It took them over three hours to get down again. They let the bags slide down the chute, and one came open and dumped its treasure, which had to be gathered up, redistributed so the bags were more or less equal in weight. They had to rest frequently, especially on the boulder debris near the bottom. By then Cliff's arms and shoulders were screaming from the effort, and his shirt stuck to his back.

The sun was low in the sky by the time they reached the Trimotor. Maybe a few more hours of light. They all looked as if they'd taken baths in gray dirt.

Cliff collapsed in one of the cane chairs until he had the trembling strength to lift his canteen and drink a little, splash water over his face. He sat and let it evaporate.

When he looked up, Bauchmann was leaning on the back of the chair in front of him. "We need to leave, Secord." Cliff stared at him like he was nuts. "Now." He drew a Luger, the first time Cliff had seen him with a gun. Trying to aim it, Bauchmann's hand trembled. Cliff pointed at him loosely.

"See how you're shaking? If I tried to hold onto the wheel or that brake right now, I'd crack us up for sure."

Bauchmann seemed to absorb this. "How long then?"

"Dunno. Gimme half an hour." *Yeah*, he thought, *give me time to figure* somethin' out.

"Half an hour then. No more." He walked down to the side exit hatch and climbed out.

After a while, the *señorita* came and sat down across from him. She'd washed her lovely face, but there was dirt in the creases. Her arm moved toward him, and he found that she was offering him a small metal flask.

He took it and knocked back a swig. His eyes bugged out, and he hissed out a breath he felt sure could melt paint.

"*Añejo*," she told him, "have another. It's fortifying."

"Well, it turned *your* hair gray." She laughed. He probably looked worse. After a second, more cautious sip, he handed it back. "So, got enough gold to bankroll yer Nazi pals?"

She flashed an angry look but quickly realized he was ribbing her. "I have enough to bankroll *me*," she said, "and you. That's all I care about."

"Seems like a lotta work when he's taking most of it. Partner."

Her eyes searched his face as if trying to read him, to decide whether she dared trust him. "What do we do?"

Cliff tried to work out how he could get alone for the few minutes he needed. "I don't know. Once we get back to the airfield, he'll have Dundy rub me out for sure." He sighed. "I gotta think."

He laid his head back against the seat then and pretended to sleep. Maybe she would go outside. If he could get both of them to go out for even five minutes, then he might get to the rocket pack. Yeah, that was all he needed...five minutes.

He awoke with a start. Bauchmann had kicked his foot. He waved the Luger, this time with a steady hand. "It's time we were on our way, dear boy."

Trying not to show how annoyed he was with himself for falling asleep and how tired he was of Bauchmann calling him "dear boy," Cliff stretched and looked around. Diablessa was in a chair nearer the cockpit. She, too, had drifted off in the heat, exhaustion, and tequila. He yawned. "Close up everything. Let's get going."

He strode stiffly up the aisle. On the way, he casually grabbed his leather jacket and put it on, buttoned up the bottom few rows. He still had no idea how he would pull this off, but he had to be prepared.

Both the rucksacks were on the shelves above his duffel. And the parachutes.

Diablessa followed him and sat in the copilot's seat. He flipped switches, glanced at the gauges. "Whatever I say," he told her softly, "follow my lead." He started the engines, then released the brake. He rubbed his eyes. They began to taxi along the rough dirt flat. He remembered he'd wanted to walk it. Too late now. He pulled on the wheel. The nose lifted, and they ascended.

As they reached the top of their climb, he threw the wheel a little bit so that the plane lurched. Bauchmann called nervously,

"What in hell was that?" He came up the aisle, frightened and angry. Cliff repeated the movement before he could see.

Bauchmann stumbled and jammed his way into the cockpit.

"Aileron, maybe," Cliff said. "Thing about the Trimotor is the wires are all strung externally. Out there, see? If we've snapped a wire, then I need to know about it before we make another turn and end up slammed into a hillside. We might have to set down again." He indicated that Diablessa should take hold of the wheel in front of her. Once she had, he stood up. To Bauchmann he said, "You, too. I need for you to sit here and hold her steady, while I go check the elevators and rudder, while we still have the light."

Bauchmann squinted and looked from one to the other of them as if trying to assess whether they had cooked something up between them.

Cliff said, "Look, we're at five thousand feet. Where am I gonna go? Although, come to think of it, might be a good idea if we all three had our 'chutes on. I'll get 'em while I'm checking. Okay?" Bauchmann still hesitated to sit. "Look, Bauchmann, all I want's to get back with Sue Ann, ya know? I don't trust Dundy."

"Very well," Bauchmann said, looking more worried. "What is it I do, Secord?"

"Sit here. Hold the wheel steady. She pulls all of a sudden like before, you guide, level her out." Bauchmann—who didn't even drive a car—had gone pasty. Diablessa observed him with silent contempt.

Cliff brought two parachutes back into the cabin. "Here, put these on, you two."

He waited until they were wrestling with the harnesses to step back, grab his duffel and toss it into a chair in the passenger compartment. One of the rucksacks lay right in front of him. He really couldn't help himself. He snaked one hand in and felt around, then one at a time brought out four of the ingots, followed by a statuette of some crouching figure, dropping everything out of their line of sight behind the corrugated aluminum divider.

In three minutes he'd put on the rocket pack, strung the controls down his sleeves and buttoned up the chest panel of his jacket. "Still checking!" he called out.

He dropped the ingots and statue into the duffel bag and closed it up. Head down, he carried the bag and helmet ahead of him to the side hatch. At the last moment he put on the helmet.

As he reached for the door, he saw Diablessa. She'd come out of the cockpit and stood staring at him in astonishment—for a second. Then she flipped open the holster at her waist.

"That's what I thought," he called. "So long, partner!" He shoved the hatch open, and the plane suddenly tilted. Behind him a gunshot went off, but the pitch flung him out the hatch. He barely hung onto the duffel as he palmed the thrusters and zoomed away from the Trimotor, looped around and passed it along the opposite side. Even as he did, the plane's nose dipped, and it began flying erratically. Bauchmann had already lost control of it, or they were fighting inside, with nobody steering.

Cliff veered left and shot away, toward the southwestern horizon. The plane wasn't even flying in the right direction now as it stalled.

They could stay with the gold, or they could save themselves. He'd given them the choice.

At the very last second, he glanced back and saw a small figure leap from the hatch. It dropped way too fast. He or she had jumped with the gold. That wouldn't work any too well.

A moment later, the chute opened, and an even tinier shape plummeted away below the figure. Whoever it was had wisely let go of the rucksack. The plane was going down now almost as fast.

But the sun was low, and he had no time to go back. Anyway, they'd shoot him. Which of them had killed the other? He didn't know, but he worried that they wouldn't be the last to die tonight if he didn't turn up the juice.

He blazed like a fireball across the evening sky.

Cliff came in from south of the field, landing behind the bunkhouse. The first thing he noticed was a cream-colored sedan parked in front of it. Bauchmann's associates?

He crept across to the brightly lit diner. Sue Ann, Olle and Idris had been tied to three chairs. Otherwise they looked to be okay. No sign of Dundy, though. He didn't dare go inside till he'd found the thug.

He noticed the glow of the hangar lights throwing the shadow of the Gee Bee. He crouched down and scuttled to the corner of the diner, peered around it.

Two new people stood beside the Gee Bee: a tall, black-haired man and a similarly tall, willowy blond woman. Dundy was holding them at gunpoint while he spoke to them. Cliff grimaced. If he shot at them there, he was going to hit the plane.

Dundy seemed to be enjoying himself, strutting back and forth. The man was bleeding from a cut lip. The woman, who looked to be no older than Cliff, stood apart as if hoping to circle Dundy. She looked like, if she got the chance, she would pounce.

Cliff tugged off his helmet. He set down the duffel bag and stuffed the helmet inside. His hand brushed the cold, hard ingots. He pulled one out. His fingers wrapped perfectly around it, leaving the thruster button operable beneath his thumb. It could have been made for his grip.

He slid along the side of the diner, into the deep shadows behind the steps where he'd stood below Sue Ann just yesterday. Seemed like weeks ago.

He inched his way forward until he stood at the edge of the shadow—the next step would be into the glare of the hangar lights. Twenty feet maybe between him and the trio.

He got into a position like a quarterback ready to spring, cocked his left arm back, then pressed the thrusters.

The rocket pack blasted him full force at Dundy.

At the roar, the thug twisted about, the gun swinging away from the two hostages, but not fast enough. Cliff's punch cracked against Dundy's nose, lifting him straight off the ground. The gun fired at nothing.

Cliff cut the thrusters, but he and Dundy skidded past the couple and under the Gee Bee. Dundy's head smacked the fuselage, and he folded in half with Cliff sandwiched against him. They plowed across the packed dirt on Dundy's legs and backside.

Cliff pushed him aside and rolled, getting up shakily.

Dundy's pants were shredded. Assuming he wasn't dead, he wouldn't be able to sit right for quite some time.

Cliff turned back. He found Dundy's Mauser laying just this side of the plane. Geez, did everyone pack a Mauser?

Rather than crawl under, he walked around the nose, boxing the two people between himself and the wing. He held the gun on them just in case.

The man had taken out two cigarettes, lit them, and passed one to the woman. He seemed not in the least bothered by Cliff holding the gun. He said, "That's quite the new way to travel you have there. Are they making those for everyone this year? What d'you think, Pat, would you like one?"

"Not if I have to roll in the dirt as much as you have," she said to Cliff.

He wiped at his face, which only smeared the dirt more. "Who are you two?"

The man replied, "Someone who doesn't tolerate the ungodly. And you would be?"

"Secord. I'm a pilot."

"You're the one they forced to join their treasure hunt. The girl inside told Pat about it while I was entertaining Dundy." He touched his cut lip. "This is *your* plane then. I hope he didn't ding it much with his skull." He took another drag on his cigarette. "My guess is if you're hurtling around here like a bullet, you've managed to elude your playmates."

Cliff nodded. "Bailed. Didn't much like the company."

"Bauchmann?" The name came sharp as steel.

"He or that woman—one of 'em made it. I was too far away to tell which."

"Ah, the aptly named *señorita*. What about Ganos and—?"

"Buried in the treasure room when the ceiling caved in."

This brought the man up short. "Treasure room? You mean to say they found real treasure?"

Cliff nodded. "All kinds o' things. Little statues, ingots, lotsa red-gold stuff."

"That'll be tumbaga," said the man. "Not worth quite so much—still, you're claiming that map led them to real Aztec treasure."

"Yeah, why?"

The blonde replied, "Because Simon here made that map. He copied pieces of some documents he came across in the Palacio de Bellas Artes and then ensured Bauchmann heard his forgery existed."

"He's a slippery eel. You likely didn't know, but he's a—"

"A Nazi?" Cliff said it with affected nonchalance. "So you're government, huh?"

"Let's call me a free agent, as the actress said to the bishop. I take it without their pilot, the plane went down."

"Yeah, way out in the desert. Even if Bauchmann's the jumper, he's not going very far draggin' two hundred pounds of gold around with him."

The man's blue eyes blazed. "Well, *there's* incentive, right, Pat? Time you and I went prospecting." He flicked away the cigarette. "Oh, Secord, you probably should let your friends in there know you're alive. They're well convinced of your demise."

"Yeah, I should," Cliff agreed. He realized suddenly that he was about ready to collapse. He turned away and walked unsteadily, heavily toward the front of the diner. As he went, he unbuttoned his jacket, shrugged out of it and slipped the controls from his hands. When he reached the duffel bag, he knelt and stuffed everything into it. The jacket covered the jet pack. He stood again, with effort, pausing a moment against the wall. His shirt was plastered to him.

He saw Sue Ann's eyes go wide when she spotted him through the window. Olle and Idris looked up.

Entering, he set the gun on the counter, then untied Sue Ann. His fingers fumbled at the knots. The second she was free, she sprang up, hugged and kissed him. "Oh, thank god, Cliff!" His dirt mapped her face. She mussed his hair, and dust exploded like an insect swarm. Olle cleared his throat. Cliff said, "Can you untie him, Sue?" His legs were going rubbery. They must have sensed him slipping, because they both leaped to catch him, then set him on the chair Olle had vacated. Sue Ann untied Idris.

"Man," said Idris, "you look like a walkin' dust storm."

Cliff lolled. "Yep, just blew in." He grinned.

"What happened, Cliff?" Olle asked.

He asked for some coffee, then related a condensed version of events that left Olle asking the same question as the man outside. "They found real treasure? Oh boy, that's going to excite people, huh?"

"Prob'ly, only I can't tell you where, 'cause the map's gone down with the plane." He almost dozed, then sat up straight. "Hey, wait, guy outside—I bet he has a copy."

He turned in the chair, facing the windows. The new car parked by the roadhouse had gone.

"Rats. Who was that bird, anyway?"

Sue Ann said, "The woman was called Patricia; that's all we found out. Dundy dragged 'em both outside when he caught her talking to me. *He* knew who they were."

"Yeah, we can ask him. Anyway, we gotta tie him up before he wakes up. C'mon." He lurched upright, and the four of them went out and around Cliff's plane.

Dundy's body had disappeared.

"Why, those two musta snatched him. Brother, doesn't that beat all?"

"Some strange stuff, all right," Idris agreed.

Looking out across the field, Cliff announced, "I need a bath," and then collapsed.

When he woke, it was noon, and sunlight was flickering in his eyes as his washed shirt and pants flapped on the clothesline in back of the bunkhouse. He reclaimed some fragmentary recollections of sitting in a big tin tub and having water poured over him, but mostly it was a blur. After wrapping the blanket off the cot around himself, he went out and retrieved his clothes. He found the duffel bag stashed in the corner. Someone had closed it up for him.

Olle met him on the way to the plane and nodded at the bag. "I found that 'round by the back steps. Figured you'd left it there last night."

"Thanks. Where's Sue Ann?"

"Not here, Cliff. I telegraphed Peevy early this morning to let him know you were all right." He unfolded a telegram and offered it.

Glad to hear Stop Betty real worried Stop Wants him home Stop -P-

Cliff stopped. "Sue read this?"

"Yah, I'm sorry. I left it on the counter and..."

"That's okay, Olle. I woulda just had to tell her good-bye anyway."

"I think she'd like if you stayed awhile."

"Look, she's really swell. I hope she knows that. But *you* know I gotta go home."

"Yeah, I know. Rocketman."

Cliff winced. "Ha, yeah. Listen, tell Sue Ann...I dunno. Tell her we'll always have Pineveta?"

Before climbing up into the Gee Bee, Cliff knelt and opened the duffel to drop the rocket pack in. Feeling around, he counted two ingots and the Mauser taken off Dundy. The small statue was gone. Instead there was a sheet of paper tucked inside the bag. On one side, a crude stick figure had been drawn.

He held it up and saw writing on the back: *Secord, you're on the side of the angels. ST* "Well, what d'ya make of that?"

Olle read it, scratched his head. "Golly, I don't know."

"Side of the angels. Ha!" Cliff folded it back in the duffel on top of the rocket pack.

Okay, so maybe he wasn't flying dogfights, but he *was* fighting. *On the side of the angels.* Yeah. That didn't sound so bad.

He lowered the canvas bag into the cockpit and climbed in after it, ready to help secure the cowling. But Olle was holding something out to him: the other gold ingot.

"Sue found this when she washed your pants last night."

He had no memory of what he'd done with it after clobbering Dundy. He shook his head.

"Look, you guys keep it," he said. "Whatever it's worth, split it three ways, okay? Just don't get crazy on account of a little gold."

"Certainly not. We trust each other completely."

"Yeah," Cliff replied. "I'm pretty sure that's how it always starts."

THE
END

◆

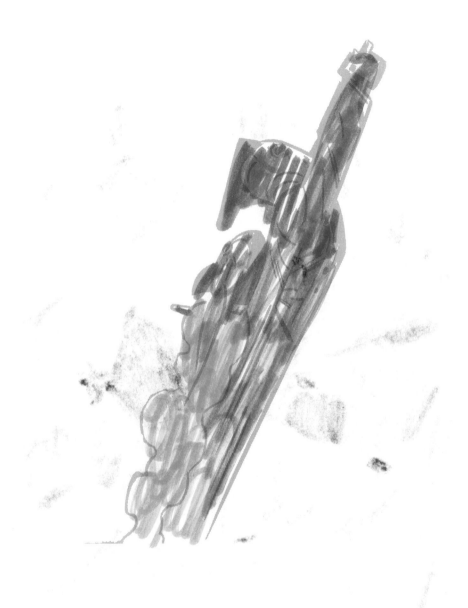

ATOLL OF TERROR

by

SIMON KURT UNSWORTH

July 1941

PART ONE: Wildlife

"**F**oreigners," muttered Cliff, watching ungainly birds circle
through the skies above one of the Widows, and sighed again.
He looked down at the copy of *Popular Mechanics* lying open
across his knees but could raise little enthusiasm for the article on a
new type of nut that he had been reading. It was too hot to read. It
was too hot to do much of anything really, the sun a merciless eye
glaring at him as he tried not to stare at Betty.

Boy, but that was hard.

The curvaceous brunette was in a swimsuit, lounging backward
on an upturned wooden dinghy the size of a small car, as Jones
took yet more photographs of her. Her skin gleamed, tanned a light
brown, and Cliff knew that if he was closer to her, he would be able
smell coconut from the sun lotion and the clean scent of shampoo
from her hair. But no, he wasn't allowed any closer than this,
because Jones had banned him, saying, "You're too distracting, my
boy. Go sit up there and stay quiet. There's a good chap!" Jones, with
his annoying British accent, Jones with his camera and his "Turn

this way, Betty!" and "Just one more, Betty!" Jones, always looking, always *leering*.

It had been like this throughout the entire trip, island-hopping across the Caribbean before finally ending up at this remote (*derelict, really*, thought Cliff) island group—the *Les Sept Veuves*. The Seven Widows, whatever that was supposed to mean. At every port they had put in, Swinney and Markham (neither of whom he had heard speak, apart from the technical mutterings they shot at each other or at Jones) would film endless hours of the local flora and fauna while Jones would scribble notes for his voice-over. When they finished, Betty would be brought out from the ship for the film-maker's "little side project." Travel between the islands was on a ship that was little more than a tramp steamer, and their cabin was small and hot and smelled of engine oil, Betty's lotions and Cliff and Betty themselves. And they argued. Well, not "argued" so much as *bickered*, Cliff decided. A parade of little irritations about each other: too *loud*, too *quiet*, not enough, too much. Yesterday, Betty had slapped his upper arm and called him a "big galoot." It sure wasn't the "tropical getaway" Cliff had imagined back in Los Angeles. Sighing again, he returned to the magazine.

There is a risk that a nut's grip may relax, potentially leading to mechanical problems or a decline in efficiency when repeating lateral pressures are applied to connections, joints or armatures. Recent research, however, has led to the development of a new type of nut that can remain tight even under the greatest strains. Doctor Alfred Seymour, of the Marbury Institute, explains: "We have created a nut that locks itself shut and can withstand a far greater amount of repeated transverse shifts!"

"You mean, it won't loosen no matter how hard you shake it?" muttered Cliff to himself, dropping the magazine again. "Then why not just say so? Can't anyone speak English these days?" He looked back along the beach, studiously avoiding peering at Betty, who was now sitting on her knees in the surf, leaning back with her chest thrust out. Water ran down her brown smooth skin in dreamy rivulets.

"More *American*, Betty!" called Jones. "More teeth! More smile! Let's show the boys what they're fighting for! My God, Betty, you're so *gorgeous*!"

Gorgeous? That little limey bastard, thought Cliff, his fists clenching. He wanted to say something, but it would only annoy Betty, and he couldn't face another row. It was too hot.

"Keep it coming, Betty, keep it coming!" Cliff couldn't stand it any longer. Dropping the magazine, he rose and turned his back on the photographer and his girl and walked off along the sand.

It was beautiful here, he had to admit. The water was deep, clear and blue, the broad beach white and soft—much nicer than the ones at Catalina Island. And it smelled good, too. The bright, fresh scent here that was a distinct relief from the pungent bouquet of the *SS Panama Shore*, the ramshackle vessel that Jones had optimistically described as "luxury accommodations" back before Betty had signed her modeling contract (with Cliff added on in a rider clause).

"Just a few weeks," Jones had said, "taking photographs of the ideal American beauty for the benefit of the Allied troops. Something to encourage them in the fight against the Nazis and to amuse me while making *Nature's Paradise: The Hidden Caribbean*, my latest travelogue. You'll have a holiday, I'll get my footage, the soldiers won't be stuck with Betty Grable, and we'll all make a spot of money. What more could one want, eh?"

Something to do, thought Cliff, *other than read old magazines and watch you eye up my girl*. The problem was that wherever they dropped anchor, it was unspoiled—"unspoiled" meaning *quiet* and *empty* and *damn near uncivilized*. There were no nightclubs, no cinemas, no radio stations, no shops, and the only bars tended to be seafront shacks full of locals drinking beer with unpronounceable names that tasted like fermenting fruit. (No beer should taste like that, should it? It wasn't right.)

To Cliff it felt like they were skulking around, darting from island to island. Technically speaking, they were in a warzone, though the action was an ocean away, and Jones had shown them some paperwork that he claimed was Defense Department permissions and approvals. "If a stuck-up phony like Flaherty or that fool Fitzpatrick can shoot down here, so can I!" Jones had declared, referring to Robert J. Flaherty, the pioneering filmmaker known for recording remote native cultures, and James Fitzpatrick, who turned out a line of the Technicolor travelogues for MGM. Cliff had learned that the mere mention of Fitzpatrick's name was good for a twenty-minute tirade from Jones, and if the filmmaker had had a drink or three...

What had seemed like a needless worry back in Los Angeles now stuck Cliff as a very real concern. Did Jones really have official permission to roam around down here, or was he pulling a fast one "for art's sake"? With that pretentious little jerk, who knew?

The beach curved, and soon Betty and Jones were lost from sight. Birds still circled in the distance, their black shapes stark against the endless sky. Animals moved in the palms lining the beach, the grasses rustling and the undergrowth crackling lightly. Cliff felt himself relax. It was good to be away from everything, that much was true. He hated to leave the flight school at Grand Central, but with more military instructors finally becoming available, he could afford to take a vacation with Betty, something they hadn't done in a long time, since Catalina, really—and that hadn't turned out quite as planned either. He took a deep breath, savoring the clean air in his lungs, then let it out and breathed in again, this time through his nose.

"Jesus H. Christ!" he spluttered as the stench of something rotten hit the back of his throat like a wet, dirty rag. He gagged and spit, hoping to rid himself of the smell. No such luck. The stench was foul, thick, cloying and strangely familiar. Cautiously, he sniffed again, feeling for the breeze. It was blowing from ahead, bringing the smell with it. Cliff sped up slightly, following the curve of the shore, until he came upon the cause of the disgusting odor.

A dead whale.

Cliff thought it must be a whale because he didn't know of any other sea creature, besides a giant squid maybe, that came that big. And this beast was big—at least twenty feet long, fat around the belly, and with big fins that flapped across the sand like rubber. The whale's carcass was covered with ragged holes, some a couple of feet across, bloody torn crescents that exposed pink and gray flesh beneath the dark, thick skin. Blood trails stained the ground around the creature, hard-edged in the pale sand. The whale was on its back, and one large eye, eerily close to a human's, seemed to peer at Cliff reproachfully. Flies, sluggish and noisy, crawled over it—one landing on the eye as Cliff watched, taking a tentative taste before flying off again.

There was a group of Caribbean men standing around the whale. They weren't arguing, but they were upset, speaking to each other in what Cliff had come to recognize as French, the sound of it like listening to words coated in molasses rolling over each other. One of the men was gesticulating at the sea, holding a large and torn fishing net. Another, older, saw Cliff and hushed the pointing man to silence.

"Hey, fellas," said Cliff, nodding at them in what he hoped was a friendly way. None of them replied. "Something took a fair few chunks out of this big boy, didn't they?"

"It's a female," said the older man in thickly accented English.

"Gee," said Cliff, not entirely sure what to say. "What happened? Sharks get her?"

"No," said the older man as one of the others said, "Yes!" in an even thicker accent.

"*No*," repeated the first man. "This was not one shark but many. There are many different bite sizes on this poor creature's skin. It is odd..." He trailed off, the words sounding as though they were pouring into a crack in the earth.

"Odd how?" asked Cliff, not sure if he was really interested or just hoping for something that might break the boredom.

"They haven't eaten," said the man. "Just bitten. It's not the first, either."

"There've been others?"

"*Oui*. Five or six over the past weeks. Things have been spotted in the water around the Widows as well, moving fast, never clear enough to see. Some new kind of shark, maybe. Maybe they are what ate Claude."

"Claude?" said Cliff, now thoroughly confused. Sharks? Claude? Between the sun and the smell of the whale's blood, the buzzing of the flies, and the man's accent, he was getting a headache.

"My brother. He went out to fish two nights ago," said the man holding the torn net, his accent making the words near impossible to separate from each other. "We found his dinghy earlier today. It was wrecked, barely afloat, and stained all over with blood." He held up the torn net again as though this offered proof. The other men remained silent, looking sullenly at Cliff.

"We have to take care of this," said the older man, gesturing toward the whale. The men around him pulled machetes and, in one case, a cleaver from their belt loops and started chopping at the corpse. The sound of each blow was like nothing Cliff had heard before, rich and moist and somehow *deep*. Each piece the men sliced free, they hurled out into the sea. Old, thickening blood spotted the men's arms and face, spattered across their sleeveless shirts, dropped like rain to the ground around them. The older man, seeing the look of disgust on Cliff's face, took him by the arm and walked him back along the beach.

"Better this than we leave it here to rot," he said quietly. "We won't eat this meat, so the fish can have it. I am Leonard, by the way, and it is a pleasure to meet you."

"Cliff," said Cliff, surprised, as the man took his hand and shook it solemnly.

"I don't suppose this has given you a very good impression of our home? It is a good place, *Les Sept Veuves*. You should enjoy it and not worry about what you have just seen."

"Yeah," replied cliff, thinking of Jones and *more teeth, Betty; more chest, Betty; turn this way, that way, turn every way, and more teeth, more teeth.* "Your island's great; it's just the company I keep that's not so hot."

"Come to Charlie's Bar later," said Leonard. "I will buy you a beer and hopefully improve your experience of the island and the company."

"How do I find Charlie's bar?" asked Cliff.

"Simple," said Leonard, with a throaty warm laugh. "Walk up from the dock and you will see it. It's the only bar on *Les Sept Veuves!*"

"He's a damn shifty piece of work, and he's always staring at you!" said Cliff in an almost-shout.

"Of course he's always staring at me, you big idiot," replied Betty in the same almost-shout. "He's a damned photographer!"

"Betty!" said Cliff, shocked at her language.

"What? Cliff, you're impossible. You knew that this trip was work, that he'd be filming and taking my photograph. And he's paying us well for the privilege, don't forget."

"Yeah," said Cliff. They were at that point where he could either say something and they'd argue all night, or he could stay quiet, bite his tongue and force back his anger, and they might be able to have a nice night. *That damn Jones*, he thought, but kept his lip buttoned.

They were in Betty's "cabin," a fisherman's hut that Jones had arranged to be made at least habitable for her, set back from the beach. It was as basic as Cliff's, with a bed, a set of drawers, a mirror, and a palm-frond roof that constantly shifted and murmured to itself in the night breeze. Unlike Cliff's hut, which retained a Spartan air, Betty had somehow made hers homey. She'd put a liana around the mirror, the garland of flowers from her shoot the previous day already wilting but still adding color and a faint scent of perfume to the room, and put a picture of her and Cliff on the top of the drawers. In the picture, they were both smiling at the photographer, Cliff's grin goofy and Betty's sexy as all get-out, and Cliff felt a sudden rush of love for her.

"Let's go out," he said, remembering Leonard's offer of a beer. "I'll take you to Charlie's."

"Charlie's?" asked Betty.

"The island's only bar," said Cliff.

"How do you know that?"

"I work for the government," he replied, grinning in what he hoped was a mysterious way.

Charlie's turned out to be a shack a quarter mile or so toward *Les Sept Veuves'* interior in what passed as the island's main street, a smattering of shops and businesses strung out along either side of the wide unpaved road that led back from the dock. Outside it hung a sign reading CHARLIE'S, and the door was wedged open with a lump of rock. The sound of voices emerged from the open doorway, but no music.

Inside, the room was dark and cool. There was no actual bar, just a table behind which sat the barman (*Charlie?* Cliff wondered), guarding bottled beer resting in ice buckets set on the floor under the table. A bottle of white and another of dark rum were perched

on one side of the table, and jugs of fresh fruit juice lined the other.
Cliff went to the man and got himself a beer and Betty a fruit juice;
then they went and sat at a smaller, scarred table at the side of the
room. There was no sign of Leonard.

"You sure know how to show a girl a good time," said Betty,
leaning against him.

"There might be dancing later," said Cliff.

"You hate dancing."

"I said there *might* be, not that I'd join in," said Cliff, and it was
good to hear Betty laugh. This had been a longer and harder trip
than either of them expected, he thought. Betty was working every
day, fitting in film shoots between Jones's travelogue work whenever
they could, and she was tired most nights. They hopped from island
to island, and there was the constant nagging fear that they might
run into a stray Nazi ship. So far they hadn't, save for a distant shape
on the horizon one day earlier on. Jones kept insisting they were
quite safe, but the fear was there nonetheless, an ever-present dark
cloud in the distance. Fleets were gathering, and Cliff sensed the
war coming closer and closer, reaching out to ensnare them along
with the rest of the world.

Someone at the table a bit away from them rose, stumbled and
knocked against their own table, sending their drinks crashing to the
dirt floor. "Hey!" said Cliff, rising, but before he was fully up, the same
person turned and punched him in the chest. Cliff stumbled back.
Betty screamed. Cliff pushed himself off the wall, punching out, but
missed the attacker as the man staggered to the left and Cliff's fist
sailed over his bowed head. The man let out a long, pained groan,
going down first onto one knee and then pitching over onto his side.

"Cliff! No!" cried Betty.

"I never touched him," said Cliff. "Besides, he hit *me*, remember?"

A small crowd gathered quickly around the fallen man, pulling
him to his feet. Several of them turned to face Cliff, and at least one
was holding a machete. Another had a fishing gaff in his fist. Dark
faces glared at Cliff and Betty, menacing eyes like bright ivory in the
dim light. One of them said something in French, a long sentence
that Cliff had no chance of understanding, although he did catch
the name Claude somewhere in the middle of it.

"Hey," he said, keeping his eyes on the eyes of the man with the gaff and not looking at the gaff itself. "Is that Claude's brother? Have you had any news?"

It was the wrong thing to say. With a furious shout, the crowd surged forward. Cliff heard the words "Yankee" and something that might have been "salad" but was unlikely to be, and then the men were pushing against Cliff. He tried to protect Betty, shielding her with his body; then someone punched him in the side of the head, a glancing blow that stung his ear. Someone else grabbed at his wrist, and Cliff kicked out, feeling a satisfyingly meaty connection and hearing a groan. He lashed out with his free hand, his open palm slapping against something that felt like a nose.

Betty screamed again. Cliff shouted, trying to turn to her, but the press of bodies was too thick, and she was separated from him by a crowd of movement, muscle and skin. "Betty!" he called. She answered with a cry of her own. A hand grabbed at his face, and he slapped it away. It grabbed again, and then there was a gunshot, and a hole was punched into the shack's tin roof with a noise like a tin drum imploding.

"I apologize for my countrymen," said Leonard, moving through the stilled crowd. He muttered low, in French, and the men turned and went away like scolded children. Leonard was dressed in a policeman's uniform, short, blue-sleeved shirt and darker blue trousers. The shirt and trousers were both old and faded, the trousers shiny at the knee, and he was wearing leather sandals rather than shoes, but the gun he held was new and large, and its barrel exhaled wisps of smoke as he ushered Betty and Cliff outside.

"It is no excuse, but Claude was popular," said Leonard once they were outside. "His brother, Danny, looked up to him ever since their father died several years ago."

"That's no reason to attack us," said Cliff, who would have said more except Betty put her hand on his chest and hushed him.

"This is a difficult time on *Les Sept Veuves*," said Leonard. "The fishing harvests are down, people are struggling. I have worked to build links with the outside world and hoped that Jones and his travel film might be the start of something for our little home, but the fact is no one here really likes outsiders. They only seem to bring trouble."

"You know Jones?" asked Cliff.

"He and I are friends," said Leonard, walking Cliff and Betty back to their cabins. Cliff rubbed at his ear—it hurt, and he bet it would be red as beet by morning. *Damned drunken fools*, he thought sourly and wished Jones had been with them. Maybe the men could have beaten the photographer up. Hell, if that had happened, Cliff might have even joined in.

"*Les Sept Veuves* is usually quiet," continued Leonard. "As I said, we get few visitors, unfortunately. As mayor and chief of police, my role is mostly ceremonial and bureaucratic. Usually my duties are little more than to settle the occasional argument and roll the drinkers home safely. But now I am filled with worry. The events in Europe unsettle everything, and depending on how the winds of war blow, we might become strategically important, which would be a terrible thing. Whether or not that will ever happen, I do not know. We are 'off the beaten path,' as Americans say, but I *am* sure that at the very least the edges of the war will soon touch our shores, spoiling our waters, and endangering our livelihoods. I have asked Jones and his people not to shoot pictures of bloody whale carcasses or tell stories of missing fishermen, but there is little else I can do. One cannot control the wind, can one, Mister Secord?"

"No," said Cliff, "I suppose not. I don't envy you. I guess the sun and the sand sort of blinded me to your situation."

"May I ask something?" said Betty.

"Of course," said Leonard. They were at the door of Betty's cabin now, and Leonard turned to her. In moonlight, she looked stunning.

"What's the story behind *Les Sept Veuves*? Why are these islands called that, The Seven Widows? Jones said something about the wives of lost fishermen."

"Yes, that's the common story," said Leonard. "The seven smaller atolls that ring the main island are like weeping women. But there is a darker legend relating to the Widows, and that is another problem."

"Why? What do you mean?"

"It is a tragic story about loss and sadness. Most legends are, I suppose. Many islanders believe these stories, despite all my attempts to educate them. And with everything that's been

happening lately, they panic and say that the Widows are returned—
and will have their blood."

At first, no one would hire out a boat to Jones.

That morning the itinerant documentarian had sent Markham
and Swinney off, telling them to get good footage of the birds that
inhabited the tiny island's interior. ("Color, boys, we need color!") He
told Betty that she would be his for the day. *Over my dead body,*
thought Cliff and insisted that wherever she went, he come along.
Jones wasn't happy but eventually agreed. Betty tried to shoo him
away when Jones wasn't looking, so Cliff knew he'd pay for it later.
He pretended to mistake her increasingly desperate gestures for
friendly waves and simply waved back and smiled. Easier to beg
forgiveness after than gain permission now, he reasoned.

At the small dock, most of the fishermen were surly and uncom-
municative as Jones tried to hire one for the day. Cliff was pleased to
see one or two of the men who had been in the bar the previous
night looked the worse for wear. One had a swollen eye, and
although Cliff didn't actually remember punching anyone in the face
like that, it made him happy to think he might have. They avoided
his eyes and had the decency to at least act a little embarrassed.

The roll of American currency in Jones's hand became fatter
and fatter, but still no one would accept his job offer. Cliff knew this
was quite a statement for such a beleaguered island as this.

Finally, right at the end of the dock, they came to a tiny, oil-
smeared fishing boat whose deck was awash with old nets and
cutaway barrels and floats. The man on the deck was sitting on one
of the barrels, his head in his hands, and it was only when he raised
his face to them that Cliff saw it was Danny, Claude's brother. He
looked terrible, his eyes red-rimmed and his dark brown skin shiny
with sweat that looked sour and unhealthy.

"Will you take us out?" asked Jones, overly polite now, a hint of
desperation in his voice. "I need some shots of Betty swimming with
the beach in the background." He indicated Betty, who smiled at
Danny. Danny, apparently not noticing, rose unsteadily and took the
bundle of notes from Jones, thrusting it into his pocket, and then

began to untie the mooring ropes. Jones helped Betty down into the boat, leaving Cliff to fend for himself. *Limey bastard*, he thought as he clambered down, knowing that he'd have done the same himself.

Despite what appeared to be a crippling hangover, Danny easily guided the boat away from the wooden dock and out of the small harbor. There was little swell once they were past the harbor wall, and the ride around the island was relaxing. The boat smelled of oil and fish, but the scent was mild, thinned by a breeze that carried on its breath the tastes of palm and grass, coconut oil and clean brine.

Following Jones's instructions to find somewhere with "the beach in the background and lots of clear water," Danny took the boat around the island, to the opposite side from where their cabins stood. The sea was blue and clear and the bottom covered in rocks and patches of gently undulating weed and plants. There were few fish, Cliff noticed; he'd have expected to see more, but perhaps their boat had scared them away. Eventually, they anchored a couple of hundred feet from the shore, a stretch of sandy beach facing them and the largest of the Widows to their rear, a flat-topped upthrust of rock with what appeared to be openings dotted across its flank. Cliff had to admit that the spot was ideal for what Jones said he wanted.

Jones had an inflatable float as a prop for Betty to pose on. She could easily maneuver it just with her hands and feet, the water being so calm here. After she got in position, Jones started taking photographs, having Betty pose this way and that, then get in the water for some swimming shots, then back to the float to rest and touch up her hair and makeup from the small waterproof bag tied to the float where the camera wouldn't catch it. Then the routine would start all over.

It made Cliff realize all over again what a professional Betty was. She was really *working*! He finally had to tune Jones's annoying nasal voice out ("Slower, Betty, swim slower! Less splash, please!") and tried to read *Popular Mechanics* again but couldn't. Who cared about why nuts loosened if you shook them or how to stop it? Well, perhaps he could care if that nut was in his Gee Bee, but still...

"Sorry about last night," said Danny unexpectedly. He came and crouched by Cliff. He sounded genuine, and Cliff took the outstretched hand without needing to think about it.

◆

"Me, too," he said. "I didn't mean to offend you—I was just asking about your brother."

"*Oui*," said Danny. "I was drunk and upset, you know? He was my brother. With him gone, there is nothing left for me here."

Cliff didn't know what to say to this and tried to look sympathetic and understanding, respecting the man's grief. After another moment, Danny pointed at the Widow and said, "Those birds are new. The flock around the Widow, flying in and out of the caves, I think they nest inside. There are new fish in the waters. Attacking the whales but not eating them. Our catches are small, and sometimes at night the air is filled with voices that I cannot understand. I don't know the English word, but in French I am *inquiet*. *Les Sept Veuves* is changing."

"Why 'The Seven Widows'?" asked Cliff, more for something to say than anything else. Besides, knowing might give him something to talk to Betty about later, to stall the inevitable argument.

"The first French settlers here could catch nothing but black fish that walked on their fins across the seabed and made people sick when they were eaten. Eventually, the settlers made a deal with the gods of the sea to sacrifice the seven most beautiful wives in exchange for bounty. They promised their women a day of food and pleasure aboard their boats and took them around the island, and at seven points they threw a woman overboard, where she was taken by the gods and made into a stone ghost so that she might serve the sea forever. As the last changed, this one behind us, she called out that she and her fellow victims would return for revenge. Now they stand guard around the island, making entry to the harbor dangerous for outsiders, protecting the fishing for the few of us who live here. The story is that one day the Widows will wake and begin to talk, and their words will unleash a hell upon the island that will destroy our old masters. It is an old fishermen's tale, something to blame when the catches are low—that the Widows are whispering and scaring the fish away. Claude told me to ignore such superstitious nonsense. They are just rocks, the remains of volcanoes; they are not evil, so he tells us."

"Your English is very good," said Cliff, uncomfortably aware of his own inability to speak any other language.

"Leonard is a teacher as well as mayor and chief of police. He makes sure all the schoolchildren learn English, despite this being a French colony. He loves this place and has spent his life trying to make it better. He wants us to be educated, ready for the world when it finally comes here. For years he spoke about our little home making money, being an important fishing port, but nothing has ever come of it. We are too remote, too small and too well protected for anyone to be interested in us. The Widows want no visitors, it is said. They keep us all for themselves, in readiness for when they start to speak."

Danny was silent for a long time after that. Eventually Cliff rose and went to watch Jones. He found Betty off the float now, taking long, languid strokes as Jones "directed" her. "Smile, Betty, *smile*," his pale fingers stroking the sides of the long camera lens in a way Cliff really, *really* didn't like. He looked out at Betty, remembering that she was his gal, that she loved him and he trusted her, and trying to make his fists unclench.

There was something in the water.

Cliff saw its wake first, a long V-shaped wave whose point was angled at Betty, several hundred yards beyond her but approaching fast. "Betty!" he shouted, pushing Jones aside and ignoring the man's startled cry. "Betty, swim! Swim to the boat! *Now!*" Betty, mid-stroke, stopped and began to tread water, staring at him with an expression on her face somewhere between fury and disgust. *She thinks this is about Jones!* Cliff suddenly realized and shouted again. The V was closer to her, a gray shadow now visible in the water behind its point, the surface breaking over something smooth and long, longer than Betty.

"Betty, *swim! The float! Get to the float!*" Cliff screamed, starting to pull off his boots. Goddammit, there were too many laces, and his fingers had suddenly grown thick, unable to grasp. *Hell with it*, he thought and dashed to the rail, *I'll swim in the damn things*.

Oh Christ, there was another shape in the water.

This one was behind her as well, out of Betty's line of sight, on her other side. The two V's were moving fast, but at least Betty had started to swim toward the boat. But too slow, too damned slow! Danny shouted something, and then the vessel's tired engine was turning over, catching, and the bow was swinging around.

Jones shouted at Betty to swim for life, yet his camera was still at his face, the tiny *click* of the shutter audible even over the engine and their shouts. *I'm going to clobber that jerk*, thought Cliff. The distance between the boat and Betty was narrowing, but the shapes were moving faster now and, oh god, there was a third, further out but moving like an arrow through the water.

"Danny, faster!" shouted Cliff, leaning out over the side, thinking briefly, *This is why I hate the water; the air's far safer*, and stretching his arm out. Water leapt into his face, stinging his eyes, and for a moment he lost sight of his love, then he found her again, powering through the water toward him, her face showing real fear. Where were the shapes?

They were right behind her now, all three moving together in a pack, closing the distance fast. Cliff stretched and, as the first shape closed in on Betty, lunged out hard.

Overbalanced.

Cliff swung out too far over the rail and felt his feet leaving the deck. He knew he wouldn't be able to right himself and in that moment understood that he'd failed Betty, utterly.

"No!" shouted Danny. He grabbed Cliff's belt, hauling him back. As the boat swept past Betty, Cliff managed to plunge his arm into the sea and wrap it around her, and then he was dragging her aloft as the shape passed harmlessly below her. One of the other shapes banged into the vessel's hull, and there was a sound like a nail being torn from fresh wood before Betty and Cliff were collapsed on the deck and he had her in his arms.

"What the hell were they?" asked Cliff when his breath had returned and he'd made sure Betty was okay, secretly enjoying the way she clung to him and the promise of later reward that her kiss held.

"Sharks," said Jones.

"They didn't look like any shark I've seen before," said Danny.

"Trust me, I've filmed all sorts of creatures in my time, on land and in the sea, and they were sharks," said Jones, turning away and starting to fiddle with his camera again. But Cliff thought that Danny was right. They hadn't looked like sharks at all.

They had looked like men.

PART TWO: Incursions

Lord, but Betty's lips were warm and soft.

They had enjoyed, finally, a nice evening without arguments or the presence of Jones. Betty and he had taken some food down to the beach, sat far back from the surf and simply chatted. It was nice, simple, and reminded Cliff of a time before jet packs and governments and photographers and Nazis and secrets and gunshots. Afterward, he walked Betty back to her cabin. In the doorway, she took his hand and kissed him, long and deep and warm.

"Are you coming inside?" she asked him.

"You try to stop me," he grinned.

"Well, it *would* be a shame to let that fresh shave of yours go to waste," teased Betty. "I think you better kiss me again." And they went in to do just that.

And that was when the far part of the roof collapsed.

The lattice of palm fronds over the wooden beams burst downward with a horrible crash. The smell of the palms was suddenly thick in the room, accompanied by a great shriek, a chittering yowling unlike anything Cliff had ever heard. Betty cried out as something dark again punched down through the fronds, tearing them loose and scattering them across Betty's bed. The lantern went sideways, the flame going out in a gutter of shadow and smoke.

Betty clung to Cliff while the roof above them was torn open. For a brief moment Cliff saw stars, and then a shape blotted them out. Something gripped his hair, tangling it and yanking so that he stumbled backward. His knees hit the chair, and he sat unceremoniously down. Whatever was holding him yanked again, and this time its grip slipped and was lost. *Thank god for Brylcreem*, he thought, crouching low, pulling Betty toward the door.

Too late. The ceiling in front of the doorway buckled and then started to fall in, palms swaying and tumbling. "Stay low," Cliff told Betty quickly. As she dove to the floor, they heard more chittering, a shriek, and something that was almost a voice calling out things that might almost have been words. Cliff grabbed at the nearest thing to his hand, a shoe, and turned back to the door.

"Betty, get ready to run," he said carefully. "When you get out, run to anywhere that has light—and don't stop for anything. Understand?"

"Just say when, darling," she replied.

Cliff dashed forward just as more of the roof caved in under the weight of something that landed on Cliff's shoulders, knocking him to the floor. Rolling to the side, he struck out with Betty's shoe and felt a satisfyingly dense impact vibrate back up his arm. The thing yammered furiously, leaping off him, and he shouted, "Betty! Go!"

As Betty darted past him, the yammering thing jumped at her. Cliff tackled it, pinning it to the ground. Palm fronds thrashed as they rolled, the thing wiry and hairy and strong in Cliff's grip. It twisted loose and again jumped at Betty. Cliff lunged and caught a limb. He pulled it back and hit it with the heel of the Betty's shoe. She reached the door, flung it open and escaped into the night. Something crashed into the side of Cliff's head. Stars jumped and shimmied in his vision; then the shape broke loose again and, with a scream, was gone.

It was a moment before Cliff's starry visitors were gone, and another before the wave of dizziness and nausea that their visit had brought receded. He rolled onto his back and stared upward, seeing a dark shape rising steadily into the sky. He quickly sat up and climbed to his feet, using the bed for support. He found the lantern on the floor, righted it and lit it again. In its cheery light, the room was revealed as a mess. Torn greenery lay all over. The bed had been shoved away from the wall, and the drawers had somehow been knocked over, scattering Betty's toiletries. The picture of the two of them was on the floor amid shattered glass. One of the bottles of perfume had also broken, its smell—sharp, sweet and dense—filling the air. Looking up again, Cliff saw that the ceiling was torn open in three or four places.

"Cliff?" said Betty, peering from around the door.

"I thought I told you to run."

"Yes, but I had to come back," she said. "I was worried about you."

"No need to worry about me. I'm fine," Cliff said, sounding miffed but feeling secretly pleased. He walked carefully to her and pulled her into a hug. When he closed his eyes, a kind of weird secondary view was still imprinted on his eyelids, woozily pitching this way and that, that way and this. How hard had that thing hit him? Where had it gone?

What had it been, the thing in the sky? Nothing so big and heavy could possibly fly on its own.

"What happened here?" asked Jones from outside the cabin.

"We were attacked," said Betty as Cliff risked opening his eyes. Jones was framed in the light that fell from the room, a startled look upon his face, his damned camera hanging as ever around his neck.

"Attacked by what?"

"No telling," said Cliff. "Didn't get a good look at it."

"It?"

"It," agreed Betty. "Ugly sucker, too. I caught a glimpse of it as I ran out of the room—had a face like a prune turned inside out."

"A bird, maybe," said Jones. "Perhaps it landed on the roof and collapsed, got frightened and confused? Some of the birds round here are rather large and distinctly odd-looking."

"That," said Betty firmly, "was no bird. It had hands."

Betty spent the rest of the night in Cliff's bed, alone. When Cliff made hopeful eyes, she simply said, "No chance, buster," but her goodnight kiss was long and warm and spoke of promising futures. He spent most of the night awake, tossing and turning in the uncomfortable chair, wrapped in a sheet and trying not to look at his trunk in the corner of the room.

Trying not to think about what was hidden there.

He had promised Betty. "No funny stuff," she had told him before trip. "This is a vacation—for you. I'll be working during the day, and I need you to let me." He had agreed, of course, and meant it too. Bringing it with him was just to make sure nothing happened to it in his absence from Los Angeles. Why put that responsibility on Peevy, even though there were other working versions of the suit? Cliff wasn't going to actually use it. No.

Probably not.

Eventually, Cliff slept and dreamed of things with hands and faces like dried fruit peering at him from hiding places among the trees, of Betty and Jones and other things that shrieked and rose into the night sky and were lost among the stars.

"No," said Jones firmly the next morning. "Betty will be perfectly safe with me. Markham and Swinney are to accompany, and I won't let Betty get in the water this time. We're behind schedule, and you'll only get in the way."

"But—"

"No," said Jones again. And suddenly the little bastard didn't seem quite as wimpy. In fact he was surprisingly firm, and the still-silent Markham and Swinney formed a wall between him and Betty. Cliff looked at her, and she nodded, but Cliff could tell she was uneasy.

Jones had managed to hire a different boat today, a bigger one, thankfully. If the sharks came back, at least they wouldn't be able to sink the damned thing. Grudgingly, Cliff nodded his acceptance. Now he watched the boat chug out of the harbor and dwindle into the bright blue distance. Only when there was nothing to see did he turn and walk back into the village.

Although Charlie's was the only bar, there was also something that tried to pass itself off as a café. The High Tide was a shop-front that opened out from one of the shacks, with simple tables and chairs and drinks made in the kitchen behind a bead curtain. It was clearly a gathering spot for older islanders and hungry fishermen between trips. Although no one had ever spoken to Cliff when he'd visited over the last few days (save to take his order), he had never felt actively unwanted. Today the cafe was unusually quiet, empty except for Cliff, which was fine with him—he needed time to think.

The woman serving hardly emerged from the kitchen, thrust a mug of the local coffee at him without speaking, and retreated. Cliff left money on the table that passed for a counter, wedging it under the base of an ashtray, and took his java to a table near the entrance.

He drank slowly, drawing pictures with his toe in the thin coating of sand that covered the plank floor. *This was supposed to be a holiday*, he thought. It was supposed to be a break, a working one to be sure, but a break nonetheless, and yet it felt anything but restful. He and Betty hardly saw each other, and when they did, they argued as often as not. Things attacked them in the water; things attacked them at night in their cabin. *I mean*, he thought, *being attacked in the sea makes a sort of sense, I suppose, but in the cabin?* Could it have been a bird? The way it escaped certainly seemed to point that way, rising straight into the sky through the punctured roof. It hadn't taken any other exit, anyway. So, a bird? A *really* big bird?

But Betty said she had seen hands. Was she mistaken? Or was it some kind of damned monkey, not flying away but scampering away across the roof and into the trees without them seeing it clearly?

And what about the dead whales? Had they been killed and mutilated by the same "sharks" or whatever they were that had tried to attack Betty? Christ, but this was a real mystery, and Cliff didn't like it. He liked *action*, a clear goal, a defined enemy, not this brain-ache stuff.

It was frustrating, and a bore. Cliff had little to do but wait for Betty and keep watching, although for what, he didn't quite know. He tried to read the *Popular Mechanics* article again but gave up in disgust when he reached the phrase *lateral distribution of repeated pressures caused no significant loosening of tension in the Marbury Institute's new nut.*

"It still don't loosen when you shake it back and forth," he said, then wondered if he was going crazy. Wasn't talking to yourself the first sign? Did knowing you were crazy mean you weren't crazy? Maybe crazy people did know they were crazy but simply didn't care—because they were crazy?

If talking to yourself meant you were crazy, what did taking to the skies in an experimental rocket pack make you? Cliff knew the answer to that: a crazy test pilot.

"My head hurts," muttered Cliff.

"It hurts because the Widows are whispering," said a voice just over Cliff's shoulder, making him jump. He turned and saw Danny, looking just as terrible as he had the day before, his eyes heavy and the skin beneath them dark and bruised.

"Hi, Danny," said Cliff. "Glad to see you. What's that about the Widows?"

"Everyone is saying it," replied Danny. Cliff nodded at the chair next to his own, inviting Danny join him. He managed to get the woman in the kitchen's attention long enough to order a refill and a tea for Danny, who ignored the drink when it arrived.

"The fishermen haven't been out," Danny continued. "No one wants to leave their homes now."

So that's why it was so quiet in here, Cliff realized. It was not just the calm of a nearly empty dock and harbor but also the quiet of people hiding and staying away from the windows, retreating to the shadows and making themselves small.

"Not everyone," said Cliff, thinking of the boat owner who had taken Jones and Betty out that morning and the woman in the kitchen.

"Not everyone, no," agreed Danny. "There are outsiders here who have married into island families. They do not believe in the Widows, but if they stay long enough, they will."

"What about you? You came out today."

"What have I to be scared of?" said Danny. "I've already lost everything."

"Hey, fella," said Cliff reaching out to take Danny's hand and then pulling back. "Things aren't that bad, are they?"

"My brother was the only family I had. We worked together on the boat. Without him I will not be able to pay the French bank that loaned us the money to buy it. They will take the boat back, and I will have to find work on another, but with the fish leaving our waters, no one has need of an extra hand.

"Leonard wanted *Les Sept Veuves* to become a place of importance, but how can it? We will always be a tiny forgotten island with a dangerous harbor that nothing bigger than a fishing boat can enter safely. The Widows may only be rocks, but they do their job nonetheless, making the channels to the harbor practically impossible to navigate in anything bigger than a scow, and even then only if you know the rocks under the water well. Few come here, because there is nothing to come here for. Leonard made sure I could speak many languages, but I have no one to talk to with them. I still do not understand the Widows when I hear them, when their voices come from in the trees or from the air above me. This is a dying place, *mon ami*, and you would do best to leave it. Take your pinup girl away from the leering Britisher, and go."

"There's nothing I'd like better, but I don't captain the boat we're on," said Cliff. "If there was a plane around, I'd fly us out. Maybe in the next port." Danny rose and began to walk away. "You gonna be okay, my friend?" asked Cliff.

"No, I don't think I will," replied Danny without turning. "I don't think any of us will."

Cliff watched the man walk slowly out, shoulders drooped with sadness and fatalism. *Tough break*, Cliff thought. He looked down at his half-empty coffee cup, then took one last sip. He'd just swallowed the lukewarm brew when there was a loud, sharp sound, like tearing oilcloth, followed by a choked gasp. A shadow passed overhead, and Cliff rushed outside to see what the commotion was. All he saw was a shifting black patch silhouetted by the orange fire of the sun. *Another damned bird?*

He glanced up and down the unpaved street.

Something was different, changed, but at first Cliff couldn't tell what. Here was the same street, the same rutted road and shacks opposite, the dock visible in the distance. What was it?

Danny was gone.

Could he have disappeared into one of the shacks, or gone far enough down the street that he'd vanished from view? No, he hadn't had time. He'd just walked out the door onto the street, and now he was gone. Where? How?

Cliff scanned the sky, but the bird or whatever it was had also vanished. What in hell was going on?

"Cliff?" It was Leonard, now out of uniform.

"What?" said Cliff, still looking down the street for Danny. Should he say something about the man's strange disappearance?

"I have a message for you from Jones," said Leonard. "He says that their boat has engine trouble, and they have moored on the far side of the island. They are working on the problem but fear that they will be forced to stay the night and send out for a mechanic first thing in the morning. He says that all is well and that you should not worry."

"*What?!*" Cliff almost shrieked. "Betty on a boat at night with that lecherous creep? No goddamned way!"

"They will be quite safe, I assure you," said Leonard, placing a restraining hand on Cliff's arm. "Please, stay here in town. Perhaps join me for a beer? The sun will set soon."

Cliff shook off the man's hand. "Thanks, but no," he said, thinking of Danny, of sharks and dark shapes and wizened faces peering from out of the wreckage of ceilings and shrieks in the night. "I gotta go. Things to do."

"As you wish," said Leonard, "but please, try not to worry. I know your opinion of Jones, but he is not as bad as you think. Things will be fine."

But things were anything but fine. Dusk had fallen shortly after Cliff had left the sheriff, darkness coming quickly, as was typical of the tropics. During the run back to his cabin on the beach, Cliff heard two short screams, more of the animal shrieks, followed by a noise that could only be the flapping of wings.

Huge wings.

Although he could see nothing, he had the impression that all around him the night was full of movement, just beyond the edge of his vision. Well, that was fine; he *liked* movement, action. And he'd show them some, whoever *they* were.

Oh, how he'd missed this! Cliff soared into the night sky from behind his cabin, sensing the play of air around him, enjoying the feel of the leather rocket suit across his shoulders, the way the helmet distorted his vision at the edges, making the world seem to curl around him ever so slightly. He was *flying* again, with his Mauser strapped to his leg, flying to Betty. Except he didn't really know where she was, and only had limited fuel.

Fortunately, *Les Sept Veuves* wasn't very big. To conserve fuel, Cliff flew as slowly as he could along the coastline, letting the air current lift and drop him, using his shoulders to turn and climb and dip, navigating by moon- and starlight. The sea was a dancing silver ripple to his left, the land to his right, darker and inviting. He cursed himself for not getting more information from Leonard. Should he have flown over the island and started searching on the other side first? He wasn't even sure what direction the boat had gone after leaving the harbor. The exhilaration of flying was quickly turning to worry as he searched for signs of the stranded boat.

Were those lights out by one of the Widows?

Instinctively Cliff left the main island's shoreline and soared out over the water to investigate. If the jet pack conked out now, there would be no way for him to make it back to land.

There! A boat moored by the largest of the Widows, the shape of it black against the stars. It must be Jones. Cliff didn't want to announce his presence just yet, so he descended until he was just skimming over the water, spray from high waves streaking his helmet. Now he could see that no one was on deck, and no lights were showing from the galley. But it had to be them, didn't it?

Something large broke the water by the boat, curling out over a wave in a sleek arc before entering the water again. Another did the same, larger this time. *Sharks*, Cliff thought, but their shapes seemed wrong, too angular. As he passed over the boat, one of the creatures rose from the water and flopped over the vessel's rail, thrashing on the deck. Cliff didn't get a good view, only sensing that whatever the thing was was long and gray and strong; then he was out over the sea again and turning.

There were more shapes in the water all around the boat, discernible by the wakes they left, catching the moonlight in silver strings of bubbles and foam. He freed his Mauser, looping its strap around his wrist, and fired. The bullet made a small, weak plume of spray when it hit the water, and Cliff decided to save his ammo.

How could the people on the boat not be hearing him? Between the movement of the thing on the deck, the jet pack's loud, distinctive pitch and the crack of the gunshot, surely someone would come investigate. He hovered unsteadily over the boat and fired again, aiming for the still wriggling creature. Cliff heard a sharp cry and knew his shot had connected; lucky shots did happen sometimes. He quickly circled away, low again, not wanting to become a target himself against the night sky.

A cry? Could sharks make such a noise?

One of the creatures burst from the sea ahead of him, its triangular head streaming water, its mouth open, revealing rows of massive teeth the color of old linen. Cliff swerved, narrowly avoiding its maw, rising so that nothing from the ocean could reach him, but then something hard crashed into his back, and a hairy arm wrapped itself around his throat. Cliff fell upward as more shapes battered into him, knocking the wind out of him. His helmet was twisted off and his vision was blurring and, *Oh, Betty, I'm sorry I didn't find you*, and then he was gone.

PART THREE: Repeating Lateral Pressures

"Welcome," said a voice, and someone slapped him.

Cliff opened his eyes. If he wasn't in hell, then it was definitely a close approximation of it. The room was actually a large cavern, big as a church, with a domed ceiling that had a large portal in its center that was open to the sky. Cliff noted the complicated mechanism used to seal up the portal. (*To keep out the rain*, he guessed.) Whatever it had been in nature, it was now a giant lab. All around him there were worktables covered in beakers and Bunsen burners, a host of other equipment he didn't recognize. Most of the remaining space was filled with metal shelving and more lab tables, which were mostly empty, though one or two held shapes under sheets that were stained dark with what Cliff assumed was blood.

In the corner was a large still, festooned with copper tubing, a flame burning beneath it, its contents bubbling noisily, venting out through the opening in the ceiling. A large Nazi flag dominated one wall, and around it were things that clung to the walls and shuffled and chirruped quietly, making the shadows thick.

"What in God's name..." Cliff said, seeing the creatures more clearly as he adjusted to the light.

He guessed they'd been monkeys once, chimps maybe, or baboons, but now they were...what? Twisted homunculi, not monkeys nor anything else ever seen outside of a nightmare. They were bent and distorted, made into something new, something grotesque.

They had wings. *Living gargoyles*, thought Cliff. How could they exist?

Some were feathery, some were partly metal, thin steel struts impaled into flesh, while others were more bat-like, rustling as they moved. A few had folded their wings into neat arcs or had them stretched out behind them like fleshly fans. Most were dressed in green or black tunics and little leather shorts, hairy legs and arms emerging from the clothes like a parody of schoolchildren, their little feet clinging to rails that lined the walls, and they were staring at him with every sign of intelligence.

"They're beautiful, yes?" asked the voice, and without thinking, Cliff replied, "They're the ugliest little bastards I ever seen!" and someone hit him again.

It wasn't a hard blow, not enough to rattle his fillings, but it told him a couple of things—he was tied to a chair, and the monkeys' reaction to the blow meant they liked watching him be hit.

"They are the vanguard. The future of this war," said the voice as its owner walked into view. "They are made not in God's name, but in mine." The man was dressed in a long, stained doctor's coat, his body hunched and twisted, and he wore a surgical mask and cap so that only his eyes showed, large and blue and staring. "You see the first wave of the soldiers of the coming apocalypse, my friend, and soon you will understand their magnificence."

"Who the hell are you?" blurted Cliff.

"My name, for what it matters, is Doctor Edward Chadwick."

"A Nazi scientist," said Cliff—a statement, not a question.

"A scientist, yes," said Chadwick. "But I am no Nazi. I work for them because they give me the freedom I need. Of course, they are rabid nationalists with misguided racial theories and a messiah complex, but they do appreciate my work. The fools in the British government discontinued my experiments, refused to see their obvious value to mankind, even condemned them as 'morally repugnant'! Those sanctimonious fools drove me out, just like Moreau before me, another visionary exiled for attempting to expand the scope of mankind. The world is changing, and humanity must change with it.

"Fortunately the German Reich is not burdened by such Victorian-era hypocrisy. They believe in pure science, no matter the cost. It was an easy matter to come to a mutually beneficial arrangement with Herr Hitler and Herr Himmler. The Germans are experts in the construction of underground facilities; their Peenemünde rocket installation has an extensive bunker system. It was not difficult for them to adapt this cave system to house my own laboratories, provide me the total privacy I need to conduct my experiments and perfect my work. And in return, Germany will soon be able to end the war and bring about universal peace, fulfill their Aryan destiny as the world's caretakers for a grateful humanity."

"'A grateful humanity'? That's a hot one," said Cliff. *Keep him talking, keep him distracted*, he thought. He carefully tested his bonds, slowly rotating his wrists. Damn, they seemed solid. He looked down and saw that he was tied to what looked like a dentist's chair, capable of reclining, turning and being lowered and raised. Attached to one of its arms but out of his reach was a tray that held a variety of surgical instruments. Sharp and shiny. Cliff couldn't help but feel a little sick.

"Imagine," continued Chadwick, "battalions of soldiers with nearly human intellect and animal strength and speed—a natural cunning capable of unbridled savagery yet compelled to follow their masters' orders. First, the monkeys, some given wings from eagles, others augmented with sundered and stitched flesh. Then their intelligence boosted by a protein serum extracted from the glands of willing Aryan volunteers!"

He gestured at the still in the corner, his voice tinged with pride. "Then sharks, given an enriched, concentrated version of my serum, improved by the grafting on of limbs and implanting of lungs removed from prisoners or other enemies of the state. Now my creatures can hold weaponry and move about dry land! And after my small army of creatures shows its value, the next wave! Men, *soldiers*, enhanced by the same techniques, leading battalions of über-sharks on the shores, controlling the skies with squadrons of soaring monkeys. How terrified will Germany's enemies be in the face of these miracle fighters? And all created and controlled by my genius, and only I shall hold the key!"

"You're insane," barked Cliff, still pulling, still testing. There was no give in the bonds, even though the arm of the chair shifted very slightly.

"Insane? No, my friend, I am entirely sane. *Entirely!* After tonight, after my children have shown their worthiness, stage two begins. Your lovely girlfriend's pictures are already being distributed to the troops, showing her tanned and lovely body, such an alluring icon of American ideals. Such a morale-raiser! *This is why we fight*, the pictures say to all those desperate men in the mud and the dirt, to keep safe such willing flesh as this. *Fight harder*, your girlfriend says, for when you return home, girls like me will be waiting, all-American girls, ready to soothe and caress you with their gratitude and their lips.

"And then, such a tragedy when the second set of pictures emerge, of her body torn to pieces by the new German super-weapon! *You have failed*, those pictures will say, failed to protect the beauty, failed to protect the heart of America itself. And where better for this atrocity to occur than in the local police station, the very heart of law and order, the venue of her demise? A new and better plan, after the first attacks on her at the cabin and in the bay were thwarted by the meddling of her heroic but naive boyfriend!

"When my super-soldiers appear in Europe, flying above the trenches, taking over the rivers and coastlines, led by winged men with savage strength, what then? The rout will be inevitable. Men with wings, real angels of death, sent by the Aryan gods to purge the weak and aid the strong, to fight on the side of righteousness!"

"You are *completely* insane, Chadwick," said Cliff. "Lord, I hardly know where to begin."

The monkey-men chittered and shifted, growing restless. As they moved and turned, Cliff saw that each had thick twists of scar-ring across its scalp, ugly keloid ridges like graveyard worms, gleaming dully in the light from the torches and the flame under the still.

"It is time," said Doctor Chadwick. "My Death Guard—to your work! Begone, my winged warriors! Begone! Fly to *Les Sept Veuves* and destroy it! Return at my signal with evidence of your work!" Instantly, the monkeys became airborne, flapping and fluttering, rising up to the hole in the rock above them. The sound was like a terrible dark storm.

"The same thing is happening now with my seaborne Death Guard," the vivisectionist told Cliff. The man was suddenly much calmer, almost conversational. "There is only a small platoon of the monkey-men at the moment, and a mere squad of the über-sharks. So few perhaps, but oh so terrible. Once they destroy the village and I show the evidence to Berlin, then I will be able to make more, so many more. So, my American friend, whatever plan you had, it is already too late to use it. Oh, and your rocket pack? My superiors are very interested in that. I think they will reward Jones and I well for delivering it."

"Jones? He's in on this?" said Cliff. *God, that explains a lot,* he thought.

"Why of course," said Chadwick. "How else could we get such an American beauty to this remote backwater and then have the means to document in full color the unfortunate atrocities that will befall her? Beauty and its inevitable desecration—that is what animates Mister Jones. You really didn't think he just made travelogues and nature films, did you? Now, the time for talk is over. Please excuse me."

And as the monkeys disappeared through the open top of the Widow into the star-lit sky, all Cliff could think was *Jones, that limey traitor! I knew there was something more to him, the shifty bastard!*

After the winged monkeys had flown away, Chadwick acted as if Cliff was already dead and buried (or eaten), leaving without a backward glance. Cliff was now alone in the room, its smells of cordite and chemicals and blood and tropical heat hanging heavy all around him, and he still couldn't loosen his bonds—they stubbornly resisted his every effort, which only made him madder. He tried to rub the ropes against the edge of a nut that protruded from the joint in the chair's arm, but to no avail. It seemed hopeless, but Cliff knew better than to surrender to despair.

Hopeless? *No,* thought Cliff, and remembered: *the Marbury Institute.*

As hard and fast as he could, Cliff began to bang his arm back and forth, more and more, watching as the nut first began to twist, then rotated and, finally, after perhaps ten minutes of *repeated lateral pressure* (as Cliff told himself), fell off the thread completely. *Shoulda used a better nut, monkey-boys,* he noted as he tore the arm off the chair, then grabbed a large scalpel from the tray and slashed away the rest of the ropes.

Now what?

Cliff went to the exit that Chadwick had used and found that it opened into a short corridor fashioned from a natural fissure in the rock. He entered without hesitation, peering into various openings and hollows as he went. In one, there were sacks of grain and fruit; in another, rack upon rack of monkey-sized uniforms, all emblazoned with swastikas in tiny, precise stitching. *Monkey suits,* Cliff thought, and wished he had some matches on him.

The next opening contained equipment, metal shelves stocked with spares of things that Cliff didn't recognize: twists of metal and glass, vials and measuring tubes on trays, coils of tubing. How Chadwick and his Nazi pals had found this elaborate cave just off an isolated island no one cared about was anyone's guess, and Cliff almost regretted not having asked the mad scientist about it when he'd had the chance.

Hearing voices ahead of him, Cliff moved along the last few feet of the fissure cautiously, reaching another entrance. "Have you informed Berlin?" he heard the muffled voice of Chadwick ask. There was an answering grunt, then a familiar clicking sound that could only mean one thing: Morse code.

Cliff stuck his head around the doorframe. As expected, he found himself looking into a radio room, but he hadn't anticipated the two monkeys—wings retracted, leather shorts glinting—stationed in front of a massive shortwave radio setup. The oversized radio rig looked powerful enough to call the moon, let alone get a message to Berlin. Perched on a metal stool like some jungle bookkeeper, one monkey was throwing code with a straight-key telegraph, a pair of headphones over its ears and a look of intense concentration on its face. The other gargoyle stood near its partner, adjusting a group of dials while watching a row of jumping meters.

Hunched and lurching, Chadwick paused at a doorway in the far corner of the room, this one showing the scratch marks of having been created by man. *Or man-monkeys,* Cliff thought sourly. "You," the doctor barked at the creature on dial duty, "when you've sent that message, pack up the flying man's gear. Berlin will make the arrangements shortly." Then he turned and left, and Cliff saw his jet pack and flight suit in a pile on a small worktable opposite the radio.

It didn't take any thought, not really. Cliff hurled himself into the space, grabbing the dial jockey by its wings and spinning it violently into the wall. There was a crunch as its head connected with the rough stone, a wet splash as blood sprayed and its scars split. The code monkey shrieked and leapt into the air, wings furled, diving at Cliff—until the earphone cable reached full stretch, snapped taut and pulled it back. Cliff jumped on it, bashing it down from midair and trampling it down to the floor, cracking its wings and stamping on its head. It croaked in a voice well short of being human but making sounds that Cliff knew were words, understood only by Chadwick, he imagined. Then the creature passed out, or died like the other had.

There was no point in stealth now. Cliff sprinted over to his gear and to his surprise found his Mauser still in its holster, stuffed in his helmet. After he'd replaced the spent rounds and checked his fuel levels (another surprise, there was actually a decent amount of juice left), he pulled on his flight suit and slipped the helmet over his head.

The doorway Chadwick had disappeared into led into another short corridor, its walls more regular but still rough, propped here and there with large wooden beams. Cliff began to run down it, his breath loud in the confines of his helmet. Behind him he heard muffled shrieks and then a blaring alarm—the dead monkeys had been discovered. More sirens whooped, and a shot *wanged* along the corridor at his side, striking sparks as it ricocheted off the stone walls. There was a second shot, then a third. Cliff ran faster, zigzagging down the corridor, then saw daylight ahead of him. The corridor opened out, revealing a wide fragment of beautiful blue sky.

He tapped the ignition studs and lit the jet pack, the sound of skittering feet gaining behind him. Another shot passed near his shoulder. Taking a quick look backward, he was surprised to see just a single monkey with a pistol!

Cliff hit the ignition again, and the jet pack came alive, his feet left the floor, and then he soared out into the daylight as if shot from a cannon. Glancing back, he saw that he had emerged from a wide tunnel just above the waterline, a small dock below it, presumably where they unloaded supplies. It faced out toward the open ocean, keeping the dock and the lab's entrance a secret from *Les Sept Veuves*. *Smart*, Cliff thought as he wheeled around and headed toward the island, *smart Nazi bastards*.

Despite the urgency, Cliff savored being in the air. The feeling of speed, of weightlessness, of *freedom* was exhilarating. He angled his shoulders slightly, roaring across the sound to the main island, then along the coastline, heading back toward the town. Opening his hands slightly tilted him; closing them again straightened him— such tiny movements effecting such great change. *This*, he thought, *is definitely the life.*

But life was about to get very complicated.

The town was under attack, a full-on assault unfolding on the beach and main streets. Shark-troopers boiled out of the harbor, flying monkeys dotted the sky, Nazi gargoyles were bent on total destruction. Shrieks and cries, banshee-like and full of fury, shattered the island's natural tranquility. Chadwick's vile animal soldiers truly were the ultimate terror weapon.

Cliff arced high overhead, attempting to take it all in. So far the flying monkeys hadn't noticed him, which was fine with him. He saw them dropping into the trees away from the shore, falling on the shacks that lined the village's dusty tracks. Already the island's inhabitants were running in panic, the monkeys in pursuit, attacking from the air, the sound of their guns mixing with the screams of their victims.

In the harbor, just visible through the swarming flying simians, Cliff saw the shark-men climbing onto the docks and waterfront. Several had already caught fishermen and were tearing them apart, creating fans of blood.

Now the islanders were beginning to fight back against the monkeys. Cliff saw that one or two of the flying bastards had been downed and were being stomped and beaten, clubbed and cut with pikes and machetes. *Good for you*, he thought, and swooped down toward the invading sharks.

Up close, the shark-troopers were more grotesque than the monkeys. God knows what Chadwick had done to the original fish, but now the amphibious monsters on the beach had distorted limbs alongside their fins, bullet heads slashed by mouths filled with triangular teeth, spines twisting out into dorsal fins, and tails flapping between buckling legs that were pink and hairy. They dragged their heavy bodies across the piers' wooden planking, over the sand as they burst from the sea. The tops of their heads were tattooed with deep scars, sometimes still held together with thick black stitches and crusted with blood. *He's let them out too early*, thought Cliff as he fired his Mauser at the closest attacker. The bullet passed through its pectoral fin, causing the creature to stagger but not fall. At first clumsy on land, the shark-men soon learned to control their new limbs and move with lizard-like swiftness. Made of pure muscle and fueled by pain and anger, these snarling warriors didn't need weapons or encouragement to cut a bloody path through the islanders.

Cliff quickly saw that there were too many for him to simply shoot, and his bullets weren't very effective anyway. He'd have to find a more efficient way of fighting them, but the likelihood of a machine gun just lying around was remote.

Now the gun-toting gargoyles spotted Cliff, and several flew at him, but he was faster and easily dodged them. He also knew that he couldn't have much fuel left and that the monkeys' superior numbers would quickly outdo him if he slowed. Hoping for the best, he jetted back across the harbor, shooting along perhaps twenty feet above its surface.

More shark-men swarmed in the water around the fishing boats, destroying them, shattering planks and barrels, flinging shredded nets and sails into the sea. Their movements were smoother in the water but still jerky, their new arms and legs uncoordinated, as though they were unsure as to what to do with them. *Too early*, he thought again. *They aren't ready yet*. It was cold comfort but meant that Chadwick wasn't as prepared as he thought.

Cliff's flight had taken him out over the open water. He turned sharply, flying back toward the monkeys that were following him. Instead of using the Mauser, he simply barreled into the lead attacker like an airborne linebacker, knocking it aside much easier than expected. Then he was through the group and heading back to the island, flying as low as he dared, skimming the surface of the water, the chittering and shrieking from the chasing pack growing louder as they closed in from above.

As Cliff flew over the dock, he managed to snag the end of one of the fishing nets that lay coiled near the boats. As the net trailed out behind him, the flying monkeys began to grab at it, their weight slowing him more, testing the jet pack's power. Now he spun back around and headed for the dock, weaving in and out of the shark-men on the beach, entangling them in the nets, dropping the end when the weight threatened to slow him to a stop.

Back to the dock and another net.

It was like flypaper, the net catching monkeys as well as sharks, their shrieks crazed as they realized they were trapped. Some of the sharks, unable to move, the nets around them tight, began to snap their jaws at the monkeys ensnared alongside them. Soon they were fighting among themselves, tearing each other to pieces.

Then the jet pack coughed and shuddered. *Crap*, thought Cliff. He had to put down quickly or suffer the consequences. He quickly made for the small shipyard that serviced the fishing boats that had motors. He could get airborne again if he could find some kerosene. Though the rocket was tuned to run on the specially blended fuel Peevy concocted, Cliff knew that in a pinch, plain old kerosene would work, even turpentine or paint thinner, at least in theory. Regular gasoline would wreck the jet pack's motor, or explode, wrecking Cliff.

As he came in to land, the rocket motor quit entirely, and he fell about ten feet onto the roof a small warehouse. Luckily he was able to stop sliding before tumbling off the edge of the building. At least he was down safely, and from his vantage point, he could see several small machine shops close by.

By now the islanders had begun following Cliff's lead, stretching out nets and running between the shark-men, dodging monkeys, trying to snare as many of the creatures as they could before setting upon them with machetes and fishing gaffs. Soon the battle was, if not even, much less one-sided. One or two of the fishermen had guns and were sniping at the shark-men still in the water, crimson plumes appearing when their shots were accurate.

Other fishermen started casting their nets on the shark-troops surrounding their boats, and soon the sea was foaming as the creatures thrashed and struggled. Villagers brought more guns, and their close-range volleys began thinning the shark-men's ranks.

Cliff roared back into the air, his engine rougher but still strong. Islanders hiding in the buildings along the street had only been too happy to fill his canisters with kerosene and send him back into the fight. (So *now* they were friendly!) He saw the situation on the docks was resolving itself. Hadn't Chadwick said that there weren't that many shark-troopers? Just a squad, perhaps ten or twelve? Either Chadwick was lying out of habit or he was pulling out all the stops, sending in every creature he had, ready or not, because Cliff could see at least a dozen shark-men just on the beach, with five more caught in nets and two still loose on the main dock. All were being dealt with by well-armed fishermen. Clearly, the inhabitants of *Les Sept Veuves* were not allowing the easy victory Chadwick had counted on, so Cliff quickly turned his attention to finding Betty.

What had Chadwick said? Something about the police station being overrun? Rocketing high overhead, out-flying any winged assailants, Cliff located the island's largest building. From their earlier stops at other small islands, he knew it was common to house most civic functions in one location—from the mayor's office and the courts to the police headquarters and city jail. And there, at the center of town, up the road from the wharf, was a three-story French colonial structure fronting the dusty town square.

Dropping down again, Cliff zipped toward it, passing over groups of islanders and monkeys locked in fierce combat. Clusters of monkeys circled, gathered and then dived on the islanders, shrieking and chittering, firing their little guns, using their fists when their ammunition ran out. Having found their courage after the first onslaught of beast soldiers, the islanders were fighting back with equal ferocity. Some had guns; others threw rocks or used axes and pitchforks. Cliff saw one man with a harpoon gun firing it into the melee of winged fury in the sky, bringing one down, impaled through the chest by the barbed spear.

The monkeys' animal nature was showing through. As Cliff shot toward the buildings, he saw more and more monkeys discarding their weapons, most now useless anyway. Some were tearing their clothes off, and one, hovering ahead of Cliff, urinated down on the people below and then gathered a handful of its own feces to fling. As Cliff passed it, he caught the sharp stool smell, rich and pungent, reminding him of the zoos and circuses. How many left? Twenty? Fifteen? Still too many, but Cliff couldn't stay and fight; he'd already been delayed too long from finding Betty and stopping Chadwick.

Cliff made a running landing in the town square, feeling gravity catching him, hating the way he suddenly felt leaden and slow. The police station was to the right, a smaller French colonial building, with the jail extending along a side street. A pack of monkeys had followed him from the harbor, and now the ground was filled with wheeling shadows that grew larger as they approached. Cliff turned and shot the closest attacker with his Mauser, then ran toward the jail. The monkeys began returning fire. Their aim was lousy, but just one lucky shot could put him out of action. Man, oh man, gun-toting flying monkeys—like some stupid fever dream, only it was real. *How the hell did I get into this?* Cliff wondered, not for the first time, as he hightailed it to the building.

Inside the station, all was chaos. The doors and shutters had been torn from their hinges and the windows shattered, glass littering the floor. The booking desk had been overturned, and sheets of paper lay in drifts against the walls.

Cliff knew he had mere moments before his simian pursuers caught up with him. He saw Markham and Swinney lying dead in the center of the room, torn to pieces, their bodies arranged like offerings at some voodoo shrine. Swinney's microphone and tape machine were at his side, covered in blood, but there was no sign of Markham's camera, or of Jones. A single dead monkey lay on the far side of the room, a bloody bullet hole in its tunic, its eyes open and staring at Cliff.

Betty wasn't there.

Dropping from the air, monkeys appeared in the entrance but seemed wary of entering, having just seen Cliff's Mauser in action. A moment later, one came scuttling into the room. Cliff shot it, and the creature dropped, sending the rest back out into the sunlight, shrieking. They rose into the air and buzzing around the building like angry bees. Cliff had bought himself time, but not much.

"How did you escape?"

Cliff started, turning, ready to fire. "Jesus, Leonard," he said, seeing the older man, uniform bloodied and torn, "don't creep up on a man like that. You coulda got shot!"

"Yes," said Leonard and raised his gun, pointing it at Cliff. "Chadwick was supposed to kill you. Useless fool—him and Jones both—not doing what they were supposed to, Jones changing the plan, wanting Betty dead in the lab rather than here for added 'visual impact.' Idiot. The sooner this is done, the better."

"What?" asked Cliff, stunned. "Leonard, no. You can't be in on this!"

"Can't I? Are you so dim, American hero? How do you think Chadwick has been left to work for so long undisturbed? *Les Sept Veuves* is isolated, yes, the seas treacherous unless you know them and its poor people, but to hide an entire Nazi science lab, even a small one, without local help? Impossible. I'm tired of trying to change these people, so when my old friend Jones came to me with a proposal, I agreed. I keep the lab in the Widows safe, and when the time comes, I make sure the attack on the island goes smoothly. I get to never worry about money again, and Jones barely escapes with his life and becomes a hero, his word trusted. His remarkable footage of the attack causes a sensation. Living terror weapons, made in Nazi labs, ravaging an American pinup queen, desecrating this island paradise. The famous Rocketeer will perish as well, dying to protect his beautiful sweetheart. Such an unexpected bonus."

"How did you know?"

"About you?" said Leonard. "We didn't. Chadwick and I had no idea what the jet pack meant until Jones told us. That's why we let him restage the attack from night to day, so he could get footage of you in action. He'll reap a fortune spreading the message of the Nazis' fearsome superiority, sewing fear while reaping a fortune. Very American."

"Chadwick's monsters are scary, but they're not invincible," said Cliff. "The islanders are beating the hell out of them. They're winning."

"Don't be whimsical, Rocketeer. They're poor—and the poor will never win," said Leonard, and he fired. Cliff dove to the side, narrowly avoiding a bullet to the chest. Igniting his rocket as he hit the floor, he blasted across the room, Leonard firing again, then crashed into the sheriff and, carrying the man like a sack of potatoes, burst through the windows behind him. Screaming, Leonard took the brunt of the impact, and he kept screaming as they became airborne.

Slowed by the policeman's weight, the swarming monkeys soon caught up to Cliff and began clutching at him. Leonard stopped his screaming long enough to start yelling at Cliff.

"What do think you're doing, Secord?" he shouted. "You can't escape the Widows. Put me down, and I'll let you live."

The monkeys were all around them, grabbing and punching without regard to Leonard. They might've obeyed Chadwick, but they didn't seem to care about anyone else.

Cliff managed to punch one of the attackers, hitting it hard on top of its scarred head. It howled in pain, crashing into one of its comrades flying just below, and together they both tumbled out of the sky. But Cliff knew there were too many to fight and, with Leonard now holding on for dear life, there was no way to escape. It was definitely looking like grabbing the traitorous cop hadn't really been such a good idea.

"So, you'll let *me* live?" he growled at Leonard. "If these flying cheetahs obey you so well, then you have nothing to worry about."

More hairy fists battered at them, the air around them filling with shrieking black shapes. Cliff spun and hurled Leonard into the mass of flying attackers, then shot up into the sky. A moment later he looked back to see four monkeys supporting the struggling policeman—and then the rest began tearing him apart. Cliff turned away from this midair massacre and headed toward the Widow he had escaped from, or, as he now realized, had been allowed to escape from.

He had to find Betty.

PART FOUR: Filthy Monkey Scum

As Cliff rocketed across the water, he knew he had, at best, just a few minutes to come up with a plan.

The shark-men weren't the problem, although he saw a few suspicious gray shapes in the water as he neared the Widows, it was the monkeys. Them—and rescuing Betty, of course. How the hell was he supposed to stop an attack of Nazi flying monkeys, even if their numbers had been partially depleted?

By being a monkey, he suddenly realized. Despite all the surgeries and Chadwick's serums, the living gargoyles were still animals at heart, as their behavior during the attack clearly demonstrated. He just had to strike at their simian selves!

Cliff quickly reversed course and raced back toward the island battle zone. Monkeys and villagers were still battling, but in smaller groups now; whatever plan the monkeys had once followed had long been forgotten as their bloodlust took over.

He slowed, hovering roughly then flying a few loops, making sure he got their attention. "Hey, you filthy monkey scum!" Cliff yelled. "Look at me! I'm back, and I'm faster'n you, smarter'n you and a damn sight better-looking!" He barrel-rolled as he went, showing off, spreading his arms wide to make himself even more visible.

They were rising from the beaches, wharfs and rooftops, more and more of them, abandoning their human targets. Cliff tried to count, at least twenty, twenty-five, maybe more, all coming after him. Still shouting, spinning, dancing in the air, he stayed ahead of them easily—they were slow, clumsy, their flight growing irregular as they grew angrier, training and orders long forgotten. Cliff rose higher and saw that the howling cloud after his blood didn't like to fly too far from the ground, even in their rabid state. So as not to discourage them from following, he lowered his altitude and began heading back toward what he now thought of as Chadwick's Widow, the only one big enough to house the insanity that the man had created.

The monkeys pursued as best they could in the distance. They might have the wings of eagles, but they sure didn't fly like them. Cliff figured that fatigue was getting the best of their bloodlust, but by now there was no way they'd give up; they were heading home, and if they stopped flapping their tired wings, they'd fall into the sea and get eaten by man-sharks.

Cliff poured on the fuel, making for the cavern lab's rocky opening. He figured it wouldn't be sealed from inside, since Chadwick had ordered his flying death-apes to return there after attacking the town. Reaching the Widow, Cliff hovered briefly over the ragged hole, taking a look before descending. Even though he only had two rounds left, he drew his Mauser, just in case Chadwick—or something worse—was waiting for him.

Cliff landed quickly, not wanting to be an easy target any longer than necessary. He removed his helmet and held it in his left hand. As his eyes adjusted to the lab's comparative darkness after the bright sunlight outside, he saw there were two shining spotlights on stands in the far corner of the lab. No, not spotlights—*movie* lights, which Cliff recognized from the production gear Jones had brought. He moved to get a better look, his Mauser held at the ready. When he saw that the lights were shining on Betty, he almost cried out. Thank god she was alive, *but what the hell?* It was like a scene from a *Weird Tales* cover: the brunette beauty, bereft of clothes save for her bra and black lace panties, manacled to large iron rings set in the lab's rock wall, two burning torches on either side of her. And she was yelling her head off while struggling to get free.

Holy crap, it's a damn film set, realized Cliff. But whose? Then he saw Jones in the shadows, peering through a movie camera attached to a large wooden tripod ("sticks," Cliff remembered), filming Betty as she struggled and hurled threats and abuse at him. That he seemed totally unaware of Cliff entering the lab on a pillar of orange flame was a testament to the man's deep obsession with his subject matter.

"Cliff!" Betty yelled.

That made Jones look up. But he barely had time to register that someone was rushing at him when Cliff swung the Rocketeer helmet and conked Jones over the head with it. He went down in a heap. Cliff had put every bit of irritation and frustrations he'd felt over the previous weeks into that blow, filling it with every condescending comment he had borne, every little fragment of stress and anger and disgust, every memory of Jones eyeing Betty's legs and chest, staring lasciviously at her body.

"Get the key to these things!" called Betty, rattling the manacles for emphasis. "Try his right front pocket!"

Jones lay on the floor, groggy but not unconscious. Cliff put his helmet down and held the muzzle of his Mauser inches from Jones's head. "I've seen firsthand what those monsters can do to a man, specifically to your pal Leonard. And you were going to film them doing that to Betty? I can't think of one good reason why I shouldn't just shoot you now and be done with it."

"No, wait—I beg you, Mister Secord," pleaded Jones, rousing himself to the task. "Chadwick and Leonard forced me to make the films. They're for Himmler, for his propaganda machine. I'm English, sure, but I have family in Germany. Lots of Brits do. They'll be sent to the camps if I don't cooperate."

"Very convincing," said Cliff, not convinced. "Now cough up the handcuff key. Or I can take it off your dead body. Your choice." He prodded him with the Mauser.

"Okay, okay," said Jones. "Just take me back with you; I'll confess to everything. The films are proof. As good as anything Riefenstahl ever did. But please get me out of here. Chadwick's insane!" He began to reach into his coat pocket.

"Wait!" said Cliff sharply. "Let me help you." He reached into Jones's coat pocket with his free hand—and retrieved a small pistol. Jones looked sheepish, like he had no idea where *that* thing came from.

Cliff seethed with anger, electric and alive. He so felt the urge to pull the trigger on Jones that his hand shook with anticipation, quivering with the desire to send the traitor to hell. *If ever a man needed killing*, thought Cliff, it was this condescending Limey traitor.

"Cliff, hurry it up!" cried Betty. "We don't have all day."

"Okay, okay," he answered, then turned his attention back to Jones.

"Please, Mister Secord..."

Cliff hesitated for a moment. Jones might still be useful, and simply executing him—well, wasn't Cliff better than that? So he just kicked Jones in the head, knocking him unconscious. Then he found the key, dashed over to Betty and unshackled her.

"Are you okay?" he asked Betty after he had kissed her. "Did Jones...do anything?"

"I'm fine now," she said into his chest. "And you never had anything to worry about with Jones—his tastes lie elsewhere."

"Where are your clothes?" asked Cliff as he unlocked the manacles.

"Back on the boat," she said, then stepped past Cliff and kicked Jones hard in the balls. "I know it's not right to kick someone when they're down, but this is an exception."

"I won't tell anyone," said Cliff. He rolled Jones over, searching for more weapons. Finding nothing, he tugged off the man's coat to put around Betty.

The sounds of flapping wings and chittering simians began to fill the cavernous lab: the flying monkeys were coming home to roost. Cliff and Betty saw the surviving creatures starting to fly in through the ceiling entrance and collapsing onto their nesting perches set high up along the rocky walls. The creatures were in tatters, many showing bloody wounds, all with shredded uniforms—if they still had clothes at all. Their stench was terrible, thick and rich and sour, all animal sweat and excrement and blood and cordite.

Baskets of fruit had been hung near their nests, and the monkeys quickly fell to devouring it, all slurping and grunting, ignoring all else.

That was fine with Cliff. Now he could grab Betty and fly out of there while the monkeys were busy feasting. His vague plan had been to lead the creatures away from the villagers, back to Chad-wick's Widow, where he would most likely find Betty, since she hadn't been at the police station. Rescuing her was the main thing, but if he could wreck Chadwick's day at the same time, then all the better. Now that he'd freed Betty, the rest of the plan didn't seem so important. Escape and tell the military seemed the best course, and they could sure just fly right out of here.

Except now the lab's roof was moving, sealing up the opening to freedom. Cliff grabbed his helmet from the table next to Jones and jammed it on. "Come on, Betty. We gotta go!"

But it was too late. The roof was now sealed shut, throwing the lab into near darkness, the fire under the still and the movie lights being the main source of illumination now.

"Sorry to spoil your plans," said Chadwick. A set of lights rimming the lab walls came on as the doctor stepped out of the shadows from the far side of the lab. He wore a lab coat and surgical mask, both with fresh blood on them, evidence that he'd just finished working on another poor creature.

Cliff trained his gun on the man, who appeared unarmed and unconcerned. "Stay right there, Chadwick. There are other ways of getting out of here. Don't try to stop us."

"I'm not going to, Mister Rocketeer, but my Death Guard will. Now take off the rocket pack. Slowly."

The chittering and slurping from above had disappeared. Just past the glare of the lights, Cliff could see the surviving monkeys, now rested and fed, staring down like vengeful gods. Their eagerness to attack seemed to radiate from them like a physical force, yet Chadwick had complete control over them. *How does he do it?* thought Cliff as Betty shivered in his arms.

"Don't do it, Cliff," she whispered. Cliff knew his Mauser only had two rounds in it, but there was a reassuring shape in his pocket, Jones's gun.

"Okay, you win," he said, and tossed the Mauser so that it slid across the floor toward Chadwick.

The scientist walked to the center of the cavernous chamber, raising his arms like a country preacher giving a benediction.

"And next the flying suit. Jones was right to spare you for so long, but I do not need him or that broken-down policeman to further my studies now. My beautiful creatures will be improved by the knowledge that *you* have provided us." He pointed at Cliff and Betty, and his monkey troops shifted eagerly above them. "The proof of my genius will soon be dining on your livers."

"Dine on this, you bastard!" yelled Betty. She grabbed the nearest thing she could throw—a glass beaker—and hurled it at Chadwick. He stepped to the side, and it sailed by him harmlessly, crashing in the shadows behind him.

"So American, so brave," said Chadwick, his voice disgusted. Cliff noticed, however, that his eyes kept dropping to Betty's near-nakedness, watching her breasts rise and fall as she breathed.

"Distract him," he muttered out of the corner of his mouth.

"What?" asked Betty.

"Keep him occupied!" said Cliff. Betty, a confused look on her face but getting Cliff's drift, grabbed another beaker and flung it at Chadwick. He dodged easily, blue eyes wide and glaring at Betty.

Another beaker, another miss. "So American, so brave, so *pathetic,*" the man said, and began to laugh. It was a terrible sound, rising and joining the chittering of his mutant creations so that the room was filled with a shrieking that was nails-on-a-blackboard painful as Betty began to shout at him, cursing him. She tossed another beaker and then some piece of unidentifiable lab equipment, all cables and clips, at the capering figure. Cliff, waiting until he was sure Chadwick's attention was totally on Betty's shapely form, took out Jones's pistol and pointed it at the gas canister feeding the flame under the still. *Take your time; don't miss*, he thought, and fired.

The canister exploded with a sound that silenced everything else in the lab, a huge *crump* that was clothed in fire, the glare of it throwing gibbering shadows up the walls. The monkeys howled and shrieked, leaping off the rails and crashing into each other, blinded. One fell to the floor in front of Cliff, and he kicked it in the ribs, knocking it into the wall. He managed to fire several shots upward. Dead monkeys fell, others rose, trying to escape the flames that leapt up around the still. Blue fire rose from its top as the liquid within began to bubble.

One of the pipes exploded in a spray of steam, and then the serum gushed out, adding further fuel to the flames. Retorts on the shelves began to explode, spraying out chemicals that caught flame and glass fragments that glittered as they flew. In seconds, the room was a cauldron of fire, the heat rising sharply, the smell of burning chemicals sharp, catching in Cliff's throat. He grabbed Betty, pulling her close, shielding her. Burning monkeys, trying to fly, crashed into the walls in showers of soot and sparks and fell to the floor, where the flames ate them hungrily. The screams were terrible, so loud that they had an almost physical weight, and the stench of burning hair and roasting flesh was everywhere.

Cliff began backing toward the exit, pulling Betty along. Sirens sounded somewhere, running feet and shouts. Something exploded in the fire, sending a finger of flame upward to the cave's roof, catching more monkeys in its embrace and pulling them down.

On the far side of the room, Chadwick rose.

His lab coat was on fire, flames licking at his shoulders. His doctor's mask, the straps scorched, fell away to reveal a face that was partly fleshless, the jawbone replaced with metal, the skin peeled back. Great wings unfolded from his back, tearing the remains of his coat apart, beating the flames down as they flapped.

"I am the first," he uttered, his voice thick, "but I will not be the last." He flapped again, rising further above the flames. Cliff fumbled his gun up, tried to fire, but the heat was too great, and he was forced to back away.

"This place might be destroyed, but we can rebuild," said the thing that had been Chadwick. His coat was completely gone now, revealing a chest that had two extra arms grafted to it, emerging from just under the natural arms. They flexed and waved, and Cliff had the stupidest urge to wave back.

"I have created myself anew," said Chadwick, rising further. "I am the first human enhanced by science, the first truly über-man!"

"You're a goddamned monster," said Cliff, still retreating, the heat driving them back.

"No," said Chadwick, "I am not a monster—I am the father of monsters!" And, with that, he rose, flapping, circling around the capering flames, and then dropped, disappearing out of the cave along a corridor, followed by the few monkeys that were still able to fly.

"Come on," said Cliff, holding Betty to him. He grabbed Jones's unconscious form, draping him over his back, and then picked up the camera, evidence of everything that had happened. He started his rocket and jetted along the passage after Chadwick, heading for the light. He was slow, weighted down by his passengers, and could feel the heat of the burning lab through the soles of his boots. The walls of the tunnel flickered with orange and red light, dancing around them as they sputtered along. Cliff debated dropping Jones but knew he couldn't leave the man to die. No, the little limey prick needed to face justice.

They finally emerged into the sun, cooler than the flames within Chadwick's Widow, and struggled upward toward the clear blue sky. Cliff headed back to the land, skimming over the sea, taking one last look back as he did so.

Surely everything inside is destroyed, Cliff thought. *The lab and every-thing left in it—gone.*

Tongues of fire had started to emerge from around the edges of the lab's roof, the mechanism burning, smaller fingers of flame bursting through the exit they had just used. A single boat, aflame, drifted across the sea, the reflections of it glittering and jumping.

There was another explosion, this one far bigger, gouting fire, and then the top of the Widow fell in with a roar and a belch of dust and smoke.

That was enough for Cliff. Now he just had to find their way back to civilization. He turned back to the distant land and hoped like hell that his fuel would hold out, arms around Betty, and they flew.

And behind the curtain of billowing smoke and ash, Chadwick and the last of his Death Guard rose into the sky, silhouetted against the setting blood-red sun, and soon were gone.

THE
END

◆

SKY PIRATES OF RANGOON

by

CODY GOODFELLOW

October 1941

Dear Betty,

By now I guess you know I wasn't really filling in for the Benedetto brothers dusting oranges in Anaheim (which was a dumb idea and Peev's, by the way...I told him to tell you I had the mumps). Anyway, this little job came up and a chance to earn extra cash flying some parts and ordnance and such to some of our guys who've signed up with the Chinese army to fight against the Japs in Burma. They're called the American Volunteer Group, but they sound like they make out like bandits ($500 for every Zero!), or they will, once they get these guns...

But don't worry! No way I'm going to stick around after this one run. If the money's as good as promised, I should be able to fix the Gee Bee and still have enough left over to spend a weekend with my best girl on Catalina...

With luck, I should beat this letter back home, so wish me luc—

Cliff sat on his bunk behind the cockpit of the C-47 Skytrain scratching out his letter when the floor and the bulkhead of the cargo plane traded places. The "k" in "luck" ran right off the page.

Hanging onto the bunk like a raft in white water, he banged on the wall. "Wake up, Tex, you lemonhead!"

The cocky clod had only just relieved Cliff of pilot duty on this last leg of their flight across the Pacific. He ought to go give Tex a piece of his mind.

Suddenly, another plane that wasn't part of their group at all dropped into sight to pace them, doing a bit under 240 knots.

Definitely not a Jap job. He smiled at it, thinking it looked like a fugitive from a flying circus.

He was still smiling when a demon with bulging eyes and curling fangs from its grinning mouth crawled out onto the wing and flung a wreath of anchor chain into the props of the Skytrain's starboard engine.

Cliff was braced, but nothing could stay put when every one of the Pratt & Whitney's twelve hundred horses ran into a wall of pig iron.

The prop blades ripped free like flower petals. One of them slashed through the fuselage and came within an inch of giving Cliff his last haircut.

Tossed from the bunk, he bounced through the doorway into the cockpit as the big plane tilted alarmingly to take a good look at its options for final resting places.

Legs scissoring at the windshield, Cliff clung to the door, straining to pull himself up and away like there was somewhere safe to go. "Who the hell's out there? They sure don't look like Japs..."

Tex Veltum and the copilot—Birdwell, a yellow-eyed sourpuss with prematurely silver hair—fought to pull the crippled cargo plane out of its death spiral. "We ain't licked yet, Secord. Go aft and help us level off; now, there's a good log of deadwood."

"Yeah, kid," Birdwell added, "we'll let you know if a barn needs storming."

Lousy mop jockeys. Cliff hit the deck on both elbows when the plane righted itself, but they were listing badly over the gray emptiness of the wide South Pacific with no land in sight.

While Tex fought to hold onto their altitude, Cliff made his way aft. They were carrying three tons of cargo, including a mess of fifty-caliber aircraft machine guns and ammunition, but the C-47 Skytrain itself—really just a Douglas DC-3 with the seats ripped out—had no armaments.

Dumfries, the ground crew chief, slept in his jump seat near the tail. Some guys had all the luck.

Outside, over the erratic whine of their remaining engine, he heard the screams of several smaller planes passing over and under and all around them. His skin puckered with goose bumps. A real-life *dogfight*...

The plane wavered and shed a few hundred feet of altitude all at once, leaving Cliff's stomach way up above his belly. From a bit farther aft, he heard a strange sound that took some listening before he realized what it was. Someone was outside, maybe hanging on with hooks or a rope, but he followed them with his eyes as they crawled down to the hatch on the starboard flank of the plane.

Why does stuff like this always happen to me? Maybe, he thought, not for the first time, this kind of thing wouldn't happen at all if he just didn't bring the rocket with him...

He looked back at the cockpit, but the door was closed. The starboard windows showed only black smoke.

His duffel bag was stowed under the bunk. The helmet fit snugly, but the rocket straps balked going over the bulky leather jacket. Just as he turned, the hatch was *gone*—ripped off its hinges by hooks. The air was sucked out, and the C-47 became a tornado in a tube.

Suddenly, another bug-eyed demon swung into the open doorway, hanging from a chain like a spider. He started to climb in when he noticed Cliff. The demon's smile was just a mask, but it seemed to get wider when the invader pulled out a short, curved fighting machete.

Bombs away, Cliff thought, and ignited.

The Rocketeer came out of the plane like a bullet from a gun. The masked pirate folded over his shoulder like wet laundry. Before Cliff could shrug him off, a souped-up Tiger Moth dove into his flight path, and a snarling demon crouched behind the wings shot Cliff's kicking, screaming passenger full of holes with a fifty-caliber machine gun.

Cliff ducked the props and landing pontoons and came up under the wings. The gunner spun the machine gun on its bamboo tripod, searching frantically for the flying man. Cliff popped up over the wings and threw the perforated pirate at him. The gunner tumbled off the Tiger Moth to flail in the biplane's slipstream, still wrestling with his dead comrade. Cliff alit on the gun platform and made a grab for the fifty-caliber just as the pilot turned to deal with him.

The pilot wore a red balaclava hood, but the wind snatched the mask away when he pushed up his goggles. Cliff nearly tumbled off the deck.

Holy smokes, a dame!

And what a dame! From her glossy black hair and almond-shaped, jade-green eyes to the sly smile on her laughing coral lips, she was as pretty as any girl from the West...maybe even as pretty as Betty, if not for the deep, severe scar that ran from her hairline down the left side of her face to her chin, giving her delicate features a cruel twist.

For her part, the pilot seemed a lot less impressed with Cliff. Her enigmatic grin got downright nasty. She stood up in the cockpit holding some kind of silver ball on a shiny wire.

A yo-yo?

Cliff took hold of the machine gun's grips and tilted the barrel down at the fuselage, but he took one last little look before he could pull the trigger.

The yo-yo shot out of the pilot's hand to carom off Cliff's helmet, ringing it like a schoolhouse bell.

He flopped off the biplane's aft section like a side of beef. The sea and the sky swirled into a big blue mess, the sea racing to intercept him so fast, he knew he'd be dead before he got wet. Well, if he could fret about what was happening to him, he could do something about it, couldn't he?

Blood came rushing back to his head almost a second too late. He made a fist. The rocket sent him hurtling back up into the fiery sky.

Head swimming with altitude sickness, he had his hands full just trying not to get hit as he flew through the dogfight. The Tiger Moth was everywhere he looked. He felt her eyes targeting his tail whenever he couldn't see her. The biplane's sleek striped body and the mouth lined with dagger teeth painted under the nose made her look more like a tiger shark.

The convoy's six fighters were spread too thin, separated from the cargo planes by a baker's dozen of motley fighter planes. The pirates had everything from a Sopwith Camel to a couple of Hawker Hurricanes to things he didn't recognize and couldn't believe were capable of flight, all splattered with shark mouths and Chinese symbols and flying the same red banner.

The AVG's Tomahawks were faster, but the pirates' motley attack wing bristled with extra weapons and daredevil gunners, and their pilots flew like lunatics. Twice he saw a Tomahawk lock on the tail of the Tiger Moth, only to end up climbing and turning after her and stalling out when she went into an Immelmann or outside loop. One fighter tried to chase her all the way down to the frothy waves, spraying fire from the nose and wings but somehow never touching the dancing phantom. She pulled out of the dive just like her diabolical yo-yo, but the Tomahawk stalled and plunged into the sea.

Cliff stared down at the water instead of watching where he was going. A pirate biplane burst into flames close enough to scorch his boots. He nearly got tangled in the bailing pilot's hastily opened scarlet parachute.

The other, undamaged C-47 had climbed to Angels 12 to shake off the pirates, but Tex was listing badly and still falling, leaving a trail of black smoke. The coast began to spill into view below. An armada of junks anchored offshore opened up on the beleaguered convoy with Howitzers and machine guns.

Finally, a problem he could fix. Cliff drew his automatic and poured on thrust as he descended close enough to get spray on his helmet.

A volley of tracer fire surrounded him and made him double back upstairs to evade a rogue Hurricane with its wing guns chattering fiery red death everywhere he tried to go.

Now he was dodging gouts of hot lead from the Howitzers, too, navigating the crossfire the way a moth finds its way through a torrential rain. The Hurricane passed overhead, and Cliff rolled to fly just under its landing gear to hide from the anti-aircraft fire. The Hurricane executed a tight barrel roll. Cliff clung to the wing, ripped off the canopy and dropped into the cockpit. The masked pilot tried to stab him. Cliff caught his arm and helped him out of his plane. The junks underneath him ceased fire as he passed between them and the crippled convoy.

There was no time to try any of his standard heroics. Just enough, however, for a supremely stupid gesture. Climbing with the throttle wide open, Cliff charged the Hurricane's guns and pulled a reckless Immelmann that slewed through the staggered squadron of pirate fighters like a drunk on a crowded dance floor, then plunged in a screaming power dive toward the little flotilla of junks.

Training the pirate fighter's guns on the biggest and most heavily armed of the junks, he poured the remaining ammunition into the astonished pirates crowding the deck. He could just about see what each of them was wearing when he punched his thruster studs and launched into the sky. Just below him, the unmanned Hurricane smashed into the junk's crowded poop deck. A hot and deadly wind wafted him higher and singed his flying leathers. Somewhere in there must've been one hell of a powder magazine, for the explosion razed the pirate ship down to the waterline.

The crippled C-47 was within reach of the coast, but it looked like it wouldn't clear the riotous wall of palm trees just behind the white band of beach. Tex was getting everything the plane could give, but he wasn't going to make it with just one engine.

If only he knew where to find another one...

Slowing down and descending to pace the Skytrain, Cliff gingerly goosed his thrust until he was just underneath the wing and outside the gutted engine. Hoping the boys in the cockpit had too much on their minds to look out the window just now, he set his shoulders to the wing and tilted upward. He still didn't know more than ballpark how much horsepower the rocket delivered since the last time Peevy tinkered with it, but it certainly took the strain of lifting the cargo plane a lot smoother than his spine.

The first trees passed so close underneath, he could have picked a coconut if he had a free hand. The Skytrain bobbed upward on the coastal breeze, shaky but unbroken. The land was more or less flat, but nothing like a landing strip opened up in the sprawl of dense jungle. He was just starting to wonder if they could make it to Kyedaw airfield like this when the jungle vanished and a plain of drowned grassy fields opened under his nose. Beyond the rice paddies, the jungle loomed in a chain of hills that looked like the Himalayas from their desperate position.

Rice paddies it is, then, he thought. From the Skytrain's exhausted droop, he knew Tex agreed. He let go of the wing, applied his thumb to the thrust stud when the C-47 dipped, and banked hard to starboard.

The straining sound of its lone engine was suddenly buried under the howling whine of the Tiger Moth. Infernal red tracers punched right through the wing's aluminum skin all around him. The wing slammed into his back and sent him careening to earth. The muddy brown water doused the flame of the rocket. The impact took care of the rest.

Waking up in a strange place in a foreign land is no picnic at the best of times. Waking up on your back, neck-deep in mud in the middle of a shooting war is something else, again.

Immediately, he tried to stand and realized he'd forgotten how. The sun was halfway to noon and drumming on his head like Gene Krupa. The blazing blue sky was clear and empty.

He wobbled on his second attempt, but nothing gave out or fell off. The rocket was a hot, dripping mess, but he'd dunked it in worse. The Skytrain had it a lot rougher.

It was nosed up on the levee at the far end of the ruined rice paddy, at the end of a trail of wing, tail and landing gear.

Stumbling through the mud, he approached the plane, calling out to the crew before it occurred to him to take off his helmet. He'd have enough to explain without going into how he survived jumping out of the plane without a parachute.

No need to worry there, though. Tex and Birdwell and even that slumberjack Dumfries were all gone. Likewise the six thousand pounds of guns, ordnance and aircraft parts they'd been paid to deliver.

Tracks from at least a couple of trucks cut up the mud from the plane crash to a narrow trail that vanished into the jungle like a green snake.

Just when he was coming up with the suitable curse for such an occasion, he heard planes overhead, the ominous telltale drone of the Tomahawks, and his poor aching head really commenced spinning.

He could take off after the crew or he could try to find his way to Kyedaw airfield at Toungoo, but there'd be a lot of questions he'd rather not answer, like, *How'd you get all the way up here without a plane?*

Another option came to him a moment later. Before he could think twice about it, he crawled under his bunk and pulled a couple of empty jerrycans and blankets and junk in on top of him.

I bet this never happened to the Spirit, he thought...

It was a lot harder to talk about what happened after than it'd been to actually live through it. It was one thing to do a dozen impossible things at once. It was quite another to have to lie about the whole thing when people smarter than you were asking the questions.

His side of the story was supposed to be pretty simple, but the Old Man behind the desk wasn't having it. "So you were napping the whole time," he said around a crooked cigarette.

"I'd just got done flying all the way from Hawaii, Colonel Chennault, and, well...I was sound asleep when they attacked us." He pointed to the goose egg on his eyebrow and tried to put on a suitably solemn face.

The little man behind the CO's desk leaned forward and ejected a question mark of smoke from his sour, scowling mouth. His dapper little moustache; active, agile hands; and puzzling uniform—vintage WWI Army Air Corps dress decked out with weird insignia that could only be Chinese—all failed to distract from his cold, hard eyes. Even Cliff had heard of this man, spoken of with the same reverence as Mitchell and Rickenbacker—aces of the Great War. It was an honor to meet him, and it smarted to pretend to be a glass-jawed washout for his benefit.

"And you figure they must've just missed you when they cleaned out the plane."

Before Cliff could stammer out an answer, the big man behind him punched his shoulder. "Like hell, Colonel," Captain "Goose" Gorman sneered. "This goldbrick must've hid when the spit hit the griddle. Hell, maybe he's even a collaborator."

Colonel Chennault smiled, leaning back in his chair. His makeshift HQ sat alongside the barracks at the head of the Xshaped jungle track they kiddingly called an airfield. "I hardly think Mister Secord needs to deny collaborating with pirates."

"Begging your pardon, sir," said Cliff, "but I don't even rightly know what you guys are doing out here. I just answered an ad in the *LA Times* to fly that plane out here for that CAMCO outfit. Nobody said anything about pirates."

"Goose, why don't you go get the other recruits sorted out and then see about raising the Limeys up at Mingaladon? See what they know about these raiders."

The big man scowled fit to turn milk, but he and the other pilots turned and left Cliff alone facing the commander.

"D'you have any air combat experience, son? Aside from, uh... what happened today?"

Brother, if you only knew, Cliff thought. Gritting his teeth, he said, "Well, I've flown just about anything with wings, but...well, it depends on what you mean by combat. Does flying for the movies count?"

Stubbing out his cigarette, the Old Man held up his hands in a simple pantomime of a dogfight. "It's simple, son. Have you ever flown a plane while someone was shooting at you, and maybe shot back at them? With real bullets?"

Boy, the stories he could tell. But then again...*Damn it all!* "Well... not as such, no."

"It's not like the circus, son. No amount of stunt flying will substitute for real combat experience. Why did you come all the way out here, anyway?"

"Need money, like everybody else..."

"Did you come to fight, son?"

Cliff looked around the bare office, out the window at a Tomahawk taking off. "I guess I just came out here to do the one job. My girl would kill me if she knew."

"Secord, you know war is coming, yeah?"

"Sure, that's what everybody says, but America's clear on the other side of the world. They wouldn't dare start a scrap with the US of A."

The colonel lit a fresh cigarette, watching the fire burn down the paper match. "Not for long, son. The Japs have been eating up this part of the world just like the Germans are eating up Europe.

Japan's resources are exhausted, so they've chosen to conquer to get what they don't have. Right now, they need oil, and we're the only thing standing in their way.

"General Kai-shek has gotten Roosevelt to prop him up against the Japs, and lend-lease supplies are moving up to Chongqing through Burma. The Chinese are paying the American Volunteer Group to protect Rangoon and the Burma Road, and we need pilots."

"Well sure, sir, and the money's real good, but..."

"But maybe Goose was a little bit right about you—there's no shame in admitting it. We still need a couple good civilian ferry pilots..."

"What the hell kind of crack is that?" Cliff leaned across the desk like he meant to pick it up and throw it. "I'm not in any man's army, Colonel, but if you don't want to eat that cigarette along with those words—"

The little man cocked his bushy eyebrows but merely nodded and puffed his smoke. "Relax, Secord. We believe your story. But a lot of strange things happened today. Those pirates were a surprise but shouldn't have been, what with all the loot flowing into Burma. There've been pirates operating in these waters for thousands of years. About a century back, Shi Xianggu, the most successful pirate in the history of the world, commanded a fleet of eight hundred ships and eighty thousand men."

"That's a lotta pirates for one guy to keep track of..."

"But apparently not for a woman." Chennault pushed his chair back. "The pirates make sense, but that other story...that fellow who flew without any plane..."

"I wouldn't know, sir, I was..." Pointing to the lump on his head again, Cliff shrugged. "Begging the colonel's pardon..."

Chennault waved a hand at Cliff like a bad smell without looking up from his maps. "Sure, Secord. Dismissed."

Cliff was about to leave when he whirled around, thinking maybe he could fit *both* feet in his mouth this time. "One more thing, sir...I was wondering what you were going to do about, uh..."

"I imagine the pirates will demand some kind of ransom, if they don't just kill them outright. Even free in the countryside, I wouldn't give much for their chances. Most Burmese peasants have never seen a white man and treat our boys and the Japs alike as foreign devils."

Cliff swallowed hard. "Well, maybe you oughta pin notes to your pilots in Chinese or whatever, so they don't get strung up by the people they're here to save."

Chennault shook his head wonderingly but scribbled something down on a notepad and stashed it away.

"Well, if there's anything I can—"

"No, son. This calls for men who've faced the fire before. I can't ask, and in any case, I can't spare a plane for another sightseer. The bursar will cut you a voucher and a check payable from the Bank of America for your, ah, services. Dismissed."

"Well, okee, then," Cliff said, and dismissed himself.

Cliff had to help himself to the questionable grub at the mess hall, because he was invisible. Even the ground crewmen and the pilot who belly-flopped in the ocean chasing the Tiger Moth looked pointedly through him. If these bums knew what he could do, what he had done today. It was all he could do not to go drag the helmet out of the duffel bag, just to stop those rolling eyes and wagging tongues. That would shut them up for sure, he figured, because the guys he flew over with—all of who had signed up with the AVG— were all talking about the Rocketeer.

"Lucky that human bottle rocket showed up when he did, or it'd be curtains for the whole lot of us," somebody said.

"Yeah," said another, "some coincidence. The last we saw him, he was latched onto that cargo plane that went down. For all we know, that flying fruit cup was the real ringleader."

"Aw, horse feathers," Cliff blurted out. "The Rocketeer's a straight-shooter. He's done plenty of good stuff. Why—"

"Sure, listen to Sleeping Beauty…"

"How much can a guy be worth, if pirates can't be bothered to steal him?"

"Alright, that's it…" Cliff started to get up when a heavy hand forced him back into his chair. The other pilots laughed and ambled off to go drinking in the officers' club.

Cliff whirled on the man who'd stopped him. "Gimme one good reason—"

"You don't sit down and shut up, I'll give you all five of them at once."

Cliff tensed and glared at the stranger. He was wearing a leather flying jacket and the undecorated khaki uniform all the former Army fliers around here favored. He was almost as old as the Old Man, though not so worn down. A mild but scarcely soft or foolish face studied him with eyes sharp as Peev's. He felt like he was telling those eyes all kinds of secrets without opening his mouth. "What gives with you, Mister?"

The other man smiled ruefully as he lit his pipe. "So, you thought you'd be something hot around here, did you?"

"I don't have to prove anything to these mugs...or you, either, buddy."

"No need to bite my head off. I'm on your side. The colonel is a brilliant wing commander, but these boys are an unruly outfit. Money and glory are the worst reasons for a man to take up arms. Most of them got a pass to leave active service in the Navy and Air Corps to come over here and pick off some Japs for a nice fat bonus. They've got no skin in it yet. But those fellows who got snatched along with the cargo, weren't they friends of yours?"

Cliff thought of Tex and shook his head. "Just met them last week, and they were anything but friendly. Buncha loudmouth Army guys..."

"You've never been in the service, then."

Again, he felt those eyes taking his measure. "No, sir, but I can fly and fight as good as any man here."

"I don't doubt it. Some men join up for the money, some for the adventure, but some do it because they know what's in the wind, and they give a damn about doing the right thing. Sure, some only care about glory, but those guys don't last long, unless they're dumb enough to rate staff promotions. No, when you're out there with your ass in the wind, it's the guy next to you that you'd do anything for, because you know he'd do the same for you. It's what you do when there's nobody watching that matters."

Cliff bit his tongue, but it was no use. "Seems to me it's more what people think you do that matters, even if you didn't really do it."

Giving up an indulgent chuckle, the other man smiled wistfully as something else occurred to him. "I heard the pilots talking about that flying man. Whoever he was, he didn't hesitate to stick his neck in it to save those planes, or it would've been a whole lot worse. And he didn't stick around to collect a reward."

"Who *are* you, anyway? You don't have enough Chinese razzle-dazzle on your uniform to keep up with the Old Man."

"I'm not with the AVG. I'm a major in the United States Army. We're trying to convince Colonel Chennault to turn the AVG into a regular Army unit. It'd be easier for him to get planes and equipment, but he doesn't like it. The Old Man came out here to fight a war his way, and he's not about to knuckle under now."

"Well, their problems won't be solved if the regular Army takes over. Those pirates could teach these clowns a thing or two about maneuvering." Noticing the older man staring at him, he added, "At least, that's what I heard."

Smiling, the major tapped out his pipe. Ash spilled on his sleeve, and an ember burned a hole in his cuff, but he didn't notice, for looking up at the sky. "It's an exciting thing to know a man can fly without an airplane. I saw a newsreel feature about that Rocketeer fellow foiling a Nazi saboteur ring in Los Angeles a few years back. You're from California, aren't you?"

Cliff blushed and looked away. "I don't recollect hearing about anything like that. It was probably some phony Hollywood thing."

"Well, I know a thing or two about 'phony Hollywood things,' and if he was to come see me after the war, he might get all the attention he felt he deserved."

Cliff took the man's card. "Well, like I said, I don't know nothing about it—"

A ground crewman with a big, cheesy mustache came running into the mess hall. "Hey, you guys, listen to this!"

They moved onto the overgrown parade ground near the airstrip, where the rusty cone speakers for the control tower's PA sprayed static over a woman's syrupy voice. She had a soft English accent that only put the polish to a husky, brazen Oriental lilt. At least half of the AVG's three squadrons of fighter pilots gathered to hear the news.

"...If these three Americans matter to you, then you will deliver
the one we want by sunrise tomorrow..."

"What do they want?" Cliff asked, but even now, they didn't
deign to notice him until somebody else repeated the question.

"They want the rocket man!"

Cliff turned to the major, but he was gone.

Hollywood! Well, nuts to you, Cliff thought, flicking the card away
as soon as he'd read it. *Nuts to you, Merian C. Cooper...*

Cliff felt eyes following him as he paced around the ramshackle
hangars, but everyone was too busy to notice him at all. Planes were
being patched up and fueled for a night raid. The only casualties so
far in this outfit died in aerial maneuvers, trying to master Chennault's unorthodox aerial combat tactics. They would be taking a
terrible risk just to save a few guys they'd never met.

Why'd it have to be like this? He was no glory-hog, but he
enjoyed the attention his stunt flying brought, and the fame of the
Rocketeer was no bitter pill. But keeping the secret had cost him so
much, when just taking off the helmet might've made him rich and
famous. Now, it'd made him look worse than a nobody: he looked
like a washout and a coward.

The only way out of the doghouse was to try to rescue those guys.
The pirates must figure he'd fly out there and get snared in some kind
of trap. They couldn't expect him to just turn himself over. Well, he'd
give them all the rocket man they could handle and then some.

Nobody looked at him as he strolled out of the airfield grounds
and into the jungle. Almost immediately, the sounds of rushing men
and their machines were drowned out by the sounds of a hundred
strange birds, monkeys and bugs the size of birds, and the heady
perfumed rot of the jungle. Looking around one last time, Cliff knelt
and took his helmet out of his duffel bag, then strapped on his rocket.

Checking the control grips, he lifted his helmet and looked up at the
moon. He'd remembered everything—a compass, map, extra clips for his
automatic—and then he forgot it all at the sound of a hunter's voice.

"Holy hell, how'd a dope like you ever keep your identity a
secret for so long?"

Cliff spun around, clapping the helmet on too late. "Damn it all,
Cooper!"

"Just what were you planning to do, exactly?"

"Going to find those pirates and...bust Tex and those other mugs out, I guess."

"Congratulations, Secord. That sentence actually had more dumb ideas than words in it."

A fingernail of full moon peered out from behind stacks of clouds to light up the waves marching eastward across Martaban Bay, and he followed them as if he knew where the hell he was going.

Cooper catching him before he went off half-cocked proved to be a mixed blessing. The old pilot briefed Cliff on the lay of the land and gave him a map showing the coordinates the pirates' mouthpiece had given: an islet off the coast of Tenasserim, which was a disputed province of neighboring Thailand. The rest of that unhappy country belonged to the Japs, who launched regular bombing raids on Burma from bases just over the border.

"The pirates must operate out of these island chains between Moulmein and Tavoy," Cooper told him. "The RAF is losing badly from Rangoon to Singapore, and not just to the Japs. Even back at the Pentagon, we'd heard about Chinese bandits in stolen British planes in Hong Kong, extorting protection from shipping lines and even governments. Chiang Kai-Shek wouldn't play ball, so Chennault figured there'd be trouble. But he never saw anywhere they could take off or land."

Recalling the pontoons on the Tiger Moth, he said, "They don't need a runway if they're fitted up to land on the water."

Cooper nodded and made Cliff feel less stupid than he had all day. "Sharp observation, Secord. It's a safe bet they'd try to take you somewhere close to home. That only leaves about two hundred little islands..."

Cooper packed him a satchel and told him what to do when he found the missing men. As plans went, it wasn't much brighter than Cliff's, but at least this way, somebody was sure to know where to locate his remains.

And he took Cliff's letter to Betty, into which he'd hastily scribbled out his heart, in case he didn't come back.

Now, he passed high over the island where he was supposed to trade himself for those three guys, and saw no sign of anyone. The meeting spot was little more than a pillar of barren rock sticking up out of the lazy waves.

From high above, he heard the lopsided roar of an unsynchronized engine and saw a plane drop out of the clouds like a bird of prey swooping down from its perch.

Cliff bobbed and weaved and climbed to get out from under the blazing tracers of the Tiger Moth. She sported at least four wing-mounted fifty-calibers now, no doubt liberated from the C-47's stolen cargo. The big eight-hundred-horsepower Allison engine, somehow grafted onto the fragile old canvas-winged body, made it go like a paper plane in a cyclone.

Streams of white-hot fire herded him across the sky and into a thick coastal mist. Twice he thought he'd lost her, only to realize he'd lost himself and nearly hit an island or a wave. He came to find the tracers almost a welcome beacon in the dark.

Over a bay filled with soupy silver fog, he saw a towering island like a skyscraper, a colossal limestone fang just large enough to wear a patch of jungle for a hat.

Out of caverns bored into the sheer cliff face, a pair of Hawker Hurricanes sprang out and came clawing up the sky like vampire bats. Cliff couldn't believe his eyes. The planes had been launched from catapults out of caverns in the hollow island.

Before he could change course, he was boxed in by the Hurricanes. The Tiger Moth came roaring at him from above, circling for the kill. Somehow, his heart beat even faster when he looked up at the smiling maw filled with murderous teeth painted under the biplane's tapered snout. Drawing his automatic, he reversed and charged the Tiger Moth, flying just below the crossfire of its guns. No way could she outmaneuver a man with a rocket—

He flew into the net before he saw it. The Tiger Moth barrel-rolled as it passed overhead. The net unfurled out of the tandem cockpit like a parachute. Light as silk but tough as suspension bridge cable, it drew taut around him and dragged him down, but he stayed aloft until he hit the end of his leash.

The rocket screamed, straining against its harness. The net drew tighter. It crushed him as he tried to play tug-of-war with a fighter plane. It was no use.

The Tiger Moth circled the island until she just seemed to be making Cliff dizzy, then suddenly dove and turned like she meant to fly straight into the face of the sheer limestone wall.

Cliff reversed course, hoping to fly ahead of the Tiger Moth and maybe snarl the cable in the plane's props. The pirate biplane lurched into a tumbling dive, and suddenly he was not flying, but skipping across the water like live bait.

The Tiger Moth settled on its skids and passed through a cloud of mist clinging to the wall and vanished, towing Cliff along after her.

Behind the wall of fog, the biplane glided to a stop on the sandy shore of a lagoon in a vast natural grotto inside the hollow island.

Cliff's landing wasn't as elegant or comfortable as hers. Three pirates with bug-eyed devil masks and short, curved swords came to drag him up from the shallow lagoon. He hid his pistol and raised his hands, but they pummeled him with the flats of their blades until a sharp command echoed through the cavern. The pirates froze but stood ready and eager to finish the job.

Beyond the menacing masked pirates, he saw a dozen more planes beached on the shore and parked in the cavern's mechanic pits. Against the far wall, a mountain of cargo piled up to the stalactite-studded ceiling. Much of it bore the CAMCO stamps and twelve-pointed star of the Chinese Air Force.

A mob of pirates poured into the grotto to surround the pirate queen as she climbed down from her biplane. The crowd parted to let the tall, green-eyed Chinese lady pilot approach Cliff where he sat in the sand, glowering at his captors. Her henchmen drew back not just in respect or admiration for their leader, but in real fear.

"My men fear you," she said in lightly accented English, "but I do not."

"You should, lady," he said, holding up the control studs for the rocket. "I press both these buttons at once, and this thing goes off like a bomb."

Nobody else in the cave seemed to speak English, but the only one who could didn't react at all the way he'd hoped.

Her laughter was musical and rich and made him feel about six inches tall. "If only you Americans had the courage to lay down your lives like that, you would be good for something, but no...I would have this toy of yours; if it's worth your life."

"It's worth all your lives, to me. You don't think I'd be stupid enough to just come in here and let you take it?"

"I am Fang Li, of the Red Brotherhood, masters of the China Sea. And you look more than stupid enough for my purposes."

"Where're the three pilots? And what about our cargo?"

"You forfeit the cargo, but you and the others may leave unharmed...once you've surrendered the rocket."

Cliff kicked off the last of the net and stood up. "You blamed idiot! That stuff is for our boys to fight the Japs. You want them to take over?"

"The Japanese empire or the British, it matters little to us." Her smile faltered. Her hand went to her scar, tracing the seam down the length of her beautiful face. "Many have tried to make us bow, but none have succeeded. All who would fly or sail through our territory must pay the Red Brotherhood."

"Now listen here," Cliff came forward until two pirates moved to block him. "Those pilots are Americans, dang it. You'd better let them go, or I wouldn't want to be you." Even as he barked at her, he found his voice going soft and low, sapped of its anger. A line from some corny Hollywood movie came to mind: 'twas beauty that killed the beast. Her eyes smoldered with a strange, beguiling fire. Was she hypnotizing him? He didn't know, but he liked it. His hands reached up to remove his helmet before he caught them.

"This game bores me." Fang Li tossed her long, serpentine braids and snapped orders in Chinese to her lackeys. Two of them ran out of the grotto. "One last chance, American, to give me the rocket."

"You couldn't handle it," he said, but even the peculiar acoustics of the helmet didn't make him sound like he believed it. "You know what'll happen if you try to take it."

"Then there's no point in talking—"

"Where'd you learn to talk English so good, anyway?"

"'So well.'" Looking sideways at her gang, she said, "I was born in Hong Kong and educated like a proper English lady. Someone took great pains very early on to secure a high price for me. When I came of age, a very powerful man—the viceroy, no less—made me his concubine and taught me to fly. His wife had no luck pleasing him, but she took every pain to spoil me for him."

Again, her hand touched the scar, but this time, it seemed to excite her. The light in her eyes was not hypnotic. It was more than a little insane. "After that, only a pirate warlord would have me for his concubine. I...succeeded him, and as leader of the Red Brotherhood, I taught others what I had learned of airplanes. I knew if we would survive and grow as strong as in the days of Shi Xianggu, we must master the tools of tomorrow. This rocket, for example. Is it one of a kind, or are there many more? Surely, it could be duplicated."

"Come and take it." Cliff stepped back, but one of the masked pirates pushed him into the circle. Fang Li sneered at him, cutting loose a giddy, musical laugh as she limbered up her yo-yo.

Suddenly, one of the men she'd sent away came running back to fall at her feet, gasping some unwelcome news and pleading for his life.

Fang Li screamed a command, and most of the pirates scattered, leaving five guards around him. Cliff wondered what had her so worked up. Maybe the AVG's Tomahawks had been sighted, and maybe the Marines and the Army were outside, with MacArthur leading the charge on horseback.

Fang Li turned on him with her lethal yo-yo in one hand. "Since your friends have escaped, you will have to take their place."

The nerve of those bums! Not even sticking around to get rescued. "They're not my friends—"

The yo-yo twirled on its glittering silver line. "I grow impatient. Give me the rocket now, or die."

The circle tightened around Cliff. One of the masked demons confiscated his Mauser. The others had knives, viciously curved *kris* blades and, in one lucky fellow's hands, a Thompson submachine gun. Cliff's eyes stayed on the yo-yo swinging like a hypnotist's pendant.

Suddenly, Fang Li whirled to confront a pirate who'd raised a throwing dagger to plant in her back. Her yo-yo whipped around his neck and circled it three times before it smashed into his face. The "string" was like piano wire and dug hideously into his flesh.

Defiantly, she stepped over the traitor's corpse to berate her terrified men in venomous Chinese.

Cliff gave the grotto one quick survey before he decided to jump. Assuming the rocket was dry enough to ignite, he could blast off and knock down the goon with the chopper, or he could take out the dragon lady, but he still had no idea what to do about the runaway prisoners. Dang, strategy was hard.

"For the last time," said Fang Li, "give me the rocket." Demons to either side of her raised their weapons.

Cliff crouched and held up the control grip as dramatically as he could. "Then let's all go to hell together," Cliff shouted.

A short, wiry pirate leapt at Cliff, ducked under his wild round-house punches and seemed to run right up his body to kick him in the face. Another one crouched behind him, so he tripped and landed flat on his back on top of the rocket. Still seeing double, Cliff woozily awaited the knockout punch.

The masked pirate with the Thompson fired a blast into the ceiling, then turned on Fang Li and brushed her back with the red-hot barrel. Two others faced down the rest of Fang Li's rogues' gallery with revolvers. Firing at their feet, they sent the pirate gang dancing right out of the grotto, leaving an immovable Fang Li standing alone.

Slipping the yo-yo into a pocket of her flying jacket, Fang Li stepped back, spitting curses in her native tongue.

"Wish I spoke Chinese, ma'am, I really do," the masked pirate said in a dull Texas drawl. He removed the mask and tossed it away. His two partners did the same—Tex, Dumfries and Birdwell.

Cliff bit his lip to keep from blurting out their names as he got up, still hugging his bruised ribs, and took back his Mauser from a pirate who barely came up to his chin, then went over to Fang Li and took the revolver from her belt. She scowled at him but said nothing.

"How did you figure to get us out of here?" Dumfries asked.

"I was about to ask you fellas the same question."

"Well, don't that beat all," Tex grumbled. To Birdwell, he said, "This clown is almost as useless as that washout, Secord."

"All right, shut up," Cliff barked. "I've got a plan. I just need to get outside, and we'll have help and plenty of it." Turning out his knap-sack, he dumped a small oxygen tank and some fireworks on the floor.

"Those oughta come in useful, ya idiot. We'll have us a Fourth of July show for Halloween."

Shaking his head and cussing under his breath, Cliff pulled the rubber lining out of the knapsack and plugged the protruding valve into the spigot of the oxygen tank.

"It's a weather balloon, ya dumb hick. Which one of these planes is the fastest?"

Fang Li said nothing, but her eyes went to the Tiger Moth. He pointed the gun at her, but could he pull the trigger? This woman could kill him just as dead as any man and clearly would as soon as it suited her. But even now, he found his grip weaken when he looked into those fiery green eyes.

"Stay with me," she purred. "Together, we could rule these fools and plunder the seas like the Scarlet Brotherhood of old!"

Cliff found himself staring and thanking his lucky stars he was wearing a helmet with a facemask. The yo-yo that ripped the revolver from his fingers by its barrel came like a fire alarm through the landscape of a beautiful daydream.

Suddenly, the grotto was filled with the roaring of pirates charging at them with weapons of every description.

Fang Li easily ducked under Birdwell and took his gun. She kicked him in the knee, breaking it badly. She shrugged off a poorly aimed shot from Dumfries, and then they were a heartbeat away from blowing each other's heads off.

"HEY! CUT IT OUT!"

Fang Li froze with her gun to Birdwell's heart, Dumfries with his aimed at her face. Her small army of bloodthirsty cutthroats stopped too, their guns and knives trained on Cliff, who stood with his hands up and his Mauser in his belt.

"Now listen, you...I'm sorry for whatever happened to you in Hong Kong, but this is a whole other ball of wax. I'll just bet you like flying and running things a lot more than you like being a pirate. The Japs are fixing to come in here and corner the market on killing and stealing, and nobody else has the power to stop it. You could have all the plunder you like *and* be on the side of the angels for once, if you'd just use your head."

For just a second, she looked at him and seemed to see the dreams his words painted in her bitter, broken mind. Her lips curled in an odd half smile. She sheathed her revolver and said something in Chinese very sweetly and very softly; but at the sound, her lackeys roared through knives in their gold teeth and came charging at them.

"Get in the Tiger Moth, and fly out of here!" Cliff shouted as they ran to take cover behind Fang Li's biplane.

"What, in this crop duster?" Tex shook his head. "Nothing doing, I can't...I'm just a cargo pilot."

"You have to! Birdwell's down, and Dumfries is a mechanic!"

Cliff kept the pirates' heads down while Dumfries ran to the Tiger Moth with Birdwell on his shoulder. Tex sprayed blindly at the crowd with the Thompson. After his first lucky burst hit a charging pirate with two swinging *krises*, the rest of the drum went into the ceiling.

"What the hell is your problem?" Cliff asked. "Can't you fly a fighter plane?"

His face ashen, Tex shrugged. "Pretty much no. Just those big twin-engine jobs; it's like driving a bus back home. I cracked up two trainers and washed out of fighter training. And I deserted, OK? I'm not proud of it...I just joined up with the AVG because I thought I could start over and heard it was easy money. I used another guy's papers."

Cliff wheeled on Tex and caught him by the jacket lapel. "You're not really from Texas?"

Tex shook his head. "Oklahoma. My real name's Huber...Dale Huber."

Cliff reloaded the Mauser, and "Tex" threw rocks to keep the pirates at bay. The horde emerged from cover and starting shooting up the Tiger Moth in earnest.

"Well, I'll tell you what," Cliff said, shrugging off the rocket. "Let's switch."

Tex's eyes bugged out. "What?"

"Sure, I'll fly the biplane, and you..." He pointed at the rocket.

"Mister, you're crazier than a sack of badgers," Tex said as he climbed into the cockpit.

Cliff shoved the Tiger Moth off the beach and primed the propeller while Dumfries helped Birdwell climb into the tandem cockpit.

While Tex tried to figure out the idling biplane, Cliff holstered his empty automatic and faced the onrushing crowd. "All right, you asked for it," he shouted, and hit his ignition.

He went low. Blinking as bullets pinged off his helmet, he plowed into a forest of legs. He broke through with three or four pirates clinging to him. All of them dropped off when he crashed into the wall of CAMCO crates. Shaking off the unconscious thugs, Cliff seized one of the fifty-caliber Browning machine guns that spilled out of a smashed crate. He shakily fed an ammo belt into the receiver and threw the bolt. Slinging the ammunition belt over his shoulder like a steel scarf, he braced the gun on a crate and sprayed the ceiling, sending a hail of shattered stalactites down on the pirates.

Hurtling over the astonished mob, Cliff hovered in place over the sputtering Tiger Moth, looking in vain for the exit.

She had to fly that plane in here somehow, he thought, but the far end of the lagoon was a dull gray limestone wall. But then Cliff thought of the catapults he'd seen flinging those Hurricanes out after him and how the sheer cliff wall had seemed to part like a cloud, or a curtain...

And then it was too late to do anything like try to stop. The canvas curtain parted, Cliff burst through it and suddenly he was flying into the black night sky.

Clutching the oxygen tank and the balloon, he turned as he climbed to see the biplane come buzzing out of the tunnel like a bumblebee out of a hornet's nest. They'd be scrambling all their planes as fast as they could. They couldn't catch Cliff, but they'd have no trouble reclaiming the Tiger Moth with Tex at the stick.

Maybe they won't have it so easy after all, he thought when he heard engines on the wind.

Cliff saw a whole fighter wing only a few miles off and barreling at them out of the north like they'd been looking for trouble all night.

He wouldn't need those tomfool fireworks, anyway. Waving his arms, he pointed down at the Tiger Moth and the pirate planes already buzzing out of their hidden lair.

Go get 'em, boys! Only then did the full moon roll out from behind the clouds to set the sky ablaze with its cool silver glow. Finally Cliff got the benefit of the hours he'd spent looking at those fighter plane recognition cards on the flight to Honolulu.

The planes coming at him weren't AVG Tomahawks or RAF Hurricanes. They were Nakajima Nates, ablaze with the red-orange sun of Imperial Japan. At least a dozen of them, flying top cover for six heavy twin-engine bombers.

The Tiger Moth turned northwest, engine screaming, high-tailing it back to Burma with the twin Hurricanes in hot pursuit. The rest of the motley pirate circus came roaring full-throttle out of the island just as two Jap fighters peeled off to investigate the flying man in their flight path.

Cliff rolled and dove through flurries of incendiary rounds. One plane he could probably outmaneuver, but the Japanese pilots worked in lethal teams that bounced him down so close to the water he thought they were trying to drown him. Rolling over on his back to face his pursuers, he braced the fifty-caliber against his hip and fired.

The burst from the mighty machine gun chopped the propeller off a fighter, but it nearly dislocated his leg and sent him into a kamikaze tailspin. Whipping his head around and throwing out his arms, he skipped like a stone off the water as he got back under control.

Cliff dropped the heavy gun into the sea. He reversed course to pass under the fixed landing gear of the oncoming fighters. Rolling and flipping a tight loop to come up under one fighter, he drew his automatic and took aim at the nearest Nate's tail stabilizer. Two well-placed shots severed the pilot's pitch control and sent the Nakajima spinning into the waves.

A third fighter came down on him like a winged anvil, lighting Cliff's way with a crazy halo of flaming lead. Climbing and rolling, he sought cover in the only place he could find it in the suddenly cloudless, crowded sky: among the delta wing formation of Japanese bombers.

He flew up behind them and hung in the slipstream of a Mitsubishi "Sally" heavy bomber for a blessed, peaceful split-second. The gunner in the "greenhouse" turret saw him and fired.

Cliff felt his whole left side go numb. He thought, *This is it, they got me, and I didn't even want the crummy thousand bucks' bounty...*

"Lousy Japs," he groaned. The words came out of his mouth with breath, not blood. The good news was he wasn't hit. The bullet was stopped by the satchel with Cooper's dumb helium balloon and all the fireworks in it. And being as they were on a bombing run, the gunner was packing incendiary ammo. Which explained why his satchel was on fire.

Blasting ahead of the bombers, Cliff ripped the satchel off and flung it high into the air just as the first of the fireworks exploded. Starbursts and showers of green and blue and red flame erupted in Cliff's wake like a dazzling thunderstorm of pure color. The bombers followed him through it unharmed, but immediately, two fighters swerved in a blind panic and collided like huge aluminum kites and plummeted in a screaming, burning tangle to the ocean far below.

The remaining fighters now seemed to converge on Cliff, who flipped and danced across the predawn sky as his head whipsawed back and forth and all around to track the storm of fireball-winged fighters that had trapped him in a flaming box in the sky.

When one of them burst into flames, and then another, he was nearly crushed by flying debris, but then he saw the sinister shark grin of a pirate fighter flash past and then another and then a Gladiator biplane, all flying the red flag of the Scarlet Brotherhood. Though she flew past too quickly for him to see her, he felt those razor-keen green eyes on him and saw the wag of her wings as she passed him by. He watched her rip open a bomber with her machine guns like a tin can with a blowtorch, and thought, for just a second, of what it would be like to be a pirate king of all Southeast Asia.

Nah...

Just then, he heard the roaring motors of the Tomahawks and saw all three squadrons of the American Volunteer Group come howling down from top cover to carve up the embattled Jap formation like a government cheese. The pirates faded into the background but didn't attack the Tomahawks.

Cliff beat a hasty retreat. In the middle of a battle like this, he wasn't a flying marvel. He was just a guy in a dogfight without a dog.

Reality didn't set in until he touched down behind the mess hall at Kyedaw airfield. The officers club was closed, and a lone ground crewman sat in a jeep with his headlights trained on the runway, watching for the Tomahawks. The whole place was eerily quiet.

But then he saw that glow of a pipe in the shadows, right where he'd left it. "You must've either busted out or drawn a high flush," Cooper said, coming out of the shadows and passing Cliff an un-mailed letter.

"Fat lot of good it did me," Cliff shot back as he took off his helmet. "Those ungrateful crumbums. They're liable to figure it out now on their own, and it still wouldn't matter."

"You don't do it to get your name out there, though, do you? Hot dog that you are, you have to keep it a secret, but a washout you're not—just to do the right thing."

"Yeah…" Turning over the helmet in his hands, he looked up into the sky. "I guess it's not such a bad racket."

"Well, if you ever get tired of toiling in anonymity, look me up."

Cliff didn't say anything, but this time, he kept the producer's card.

When sweltering tropical dawn broke to find the AVG squadrons landing at Kyedaw, all the ground crew came running out to meet the victorious veterans of the group's first successful engagement with the enemy. The mess hall served beer with break-fast. It was just noisy enough to wake up Cliff Secord.

Cliff rolled out of his bunk and checked his duffel bag to make sure the rocket was out of sight. Let them have their glory, their bonuses. Let them think whatever they want.

He came out just as the last plane was landing. Cliff whistled and shook his head, but he crossed his fingers behind his back as he watched the Tiger Moth come barreling in. Its pontoons touched down on the red clay runway, and for a moment it skated gracefully as a dragonfly toward the control tower. But then cruel physics stepped in. The skids broke off, and the biplane came slewing in sideways on its belly to slam into the side of a jeep just in front of the barracks.

Cliff rubbed his eyes and tried to look like he'd gotten some sleep. "What'd I miss?"

"Go back to bed, washout," Tex said as he climbed down from the wrecked Tiger Moth. His voice was steady and bored as ever, though his legs were shaking.

Chennault and Cooper stood beside the Tiger Moth. The colonel pinched out his cigarette, nodding at the shark's mouth on the nose. "Looks mean as hell," he said. "Gives me an idea."

Cliff was headed back to the barracks when the speakers crackled and filled the tropical morning air with Fang Li's seductive voice.

"To the foreigners who have come to defend China and the Burma Road, we grant safe passage in their campaign against the murderous and despicable Empire of Nippon—"

"Against who?" Cliff asked under his breath.

"The Japs, dummy," Cooper said.

"You who have demonstrated the honor of great warriors and the ferocity of flying tigers, have no cause to fear the Red Brotherhood."

"Well, that's a relief," somebody grumbled.

"Flying tigers," somebody else said. "That's us all over!"

"But as for the Rocketeer...we will meet again. And all that is yours...*will* be mine."

Feeling an unseasonable chill, Cliff faded into the background when he heard Tex holding court with the other pilots.

"Yeah, that Rocketeer sure was a candy-ass when the chips were down. I had to pull his ass out of the..."

Shaking his head, he figured he'd stick around for a few minutes and wait for...

"Mail call!" Captain Gorman stood on a barrel and waved a mail pouch at the press of eager fliers. As he called out each recipient's name, they came up to get his package or letter. Tex kept running his mouth until even he noticed that Goose Gorman was repeating the same name over and over, with no reply.

"*Huber*! Sergeant Dale Huber? Anybody know a Dale Huber?"

Tex blushed and looked around, but pretended not to notice right up until Gorman tapped him on the shoulder. "Didn't they teach you how to address a postcard in Texas, Veltum?"

"Sir, I don't rightly understand..."

"I'll say you don't. You addressed this postcard all wrong. *Your* name goes in the corner, and this other guy, Dale Huber of Fort Sill, Oklahoma? He's the recipient, so his name goes in the middle, see?

I'm sure your friend Dale would love to hear about how many planes you've wrecked since you've been here."

Stealing a glance at Tex's gray, waxen face, Cliff strolled by with his duffel bag on his shoulder and his head down. Not until he was seated in the cockpit of a C-47 headed over the Hump to India and pointed west did he allow himself to bust a gut laughing.

ROCKETS TO HELL

by

NANCY HOLDER

February 7, 1941
Pasadena, California

Suicide Bridge.
She was standing on it.
She was really going to do it.

And the baby in her arms—her little Jean—began to cry.

Her husband had left her, and she couldn't find work. She was half starved, the baby needed medicine and she had gone for a walk in the night air to clear her head. The Colorado Street Bridge glittered around the bend like a fairyland, and it was so beautiful with its lacy lights and curving pedestrian walkway. It had reminded her that there was still good in the world, even if he had left them.

She had stepped onto the bridge. And the next thing she knew, she'd found herself standing on the railing and staring down into the darkness of the forest at shadowy traces of the dry riverbed, one hundred fifty feet below.

Come, a voice seemed to whisper. *Come down to me.*

Something was crawling up the bridge, beckoning, luring, enticing.

It will all be so much easier.

"No, I don't want to," she whispered.

But you do. And you will.

You will come to me.

She hiccupped a sob, kissed Jean's head, and stepped out into thin air.

One week later

"Hey, doll, happy Valentine's Day," Cliff Secord said as Betty sashayed over to him in her tropical sarong and flung her arms around his neck.

"Same to you, big boy," Betty said, mugging for the studio photographer who had been trailing her for past half hour. The sometimes model was an extra ("featured extra," she reminded Cliff, upon whom the distinction was mostly lost) in a two-reel "specialty" that had been filming for the last two days at the snazzy Vista del Arroyo Hotel in Pasadena. The twenty-minute "swim movie" was being shot in Technicolor, a first for Betty, and Cliff saw why she was being "featured"—her colorful sarong made her look like an exotic flower from the South Seas.

The hotel was a real high-class joint, commanding the eastern rim of the Arroyo Seco (Spanish for "dry gulch") canyon where its guests enjoyed a panoramic view of the San Gabriel Mountains and the Rose Bowl to the north, the ever-growing city of Los Angeles to the south and, of course, the majestic Colorado Street Bridge directly in front, connecting Pasadena with Eagle Rock and Glendale to the west.

As a publicity stunt, the movie studio was throwing a Valentine's pool party at the hotel, with the film's "Aquanettes" being the featured attraction. Dames in flower-patterned bathing suits and alluring thigh-slit sarongs were posing around the swimming pool, fluttering their lashes and tossing their hair in hopes of a close-up from the small mob of studio photographers and cameramen. Betty had gotten Cliff invited to the party, and as he was an occasional Hollywood stunt pilot (at least before Pearl Harbor) as well as one of Howard Hughes's few real flying buddies, his presence brought a bit of shine to the festivities (according the studio publicist assigned to the film; Cliff didn't believe it for a second).

"You smell just like a tropical flower and look even better," Cliff told Betty in a rare burst of romantic inspiration. She was the prettiest girl there, he thought, and her smile was a hundred percent come-hither. Oh yeah, there would be smooching with his girl when the sun went down. And maybe a little hubba-hubba when the moon came up...

A bright evening moon was sparkling in her eyes as they parked beneath the Colorado Street Bridge. Fog swirled and danced around Cliff's jalopy, while high above them, the distinctive globes of the bridge's lights cast a gauzy glow. Betty loved her pretty, new heart-shaped necklace, which Cliff had purchased from his paycheck working at the Grand Central Flying School. He had to admit that getting a regular paycheck for a change had its benefits, even if he and Peevy had basically been assigned to their civilian jobs, training pilots and putting the Fairchild PT-19 trainers and big-boy P-38s back together as fast as the wet-eared flyboys were wrecking 'em.

In what little time off they had (Cliff had heard it would take the military over a year to get its own flight instructors trained and in place), he and Peevy (mostly Peevy) were working out a few modifications on the rocket pack. That was the deal for being able to keep using it. Now they were trying to make it fly quieter and farther, turning it into something that might possibly be of use in the war effort. ("It'll never happen," Peevy declared. "They ain't got no vision. Only reason they keep us on it 'cause the Germans are trying to do the same thing.") It was all hush-hush, of course, which caused a certain amount of frustration. But that was the deal, and Cliff was committed to it.

Betty shivered, bringing Cliff back to the here and now. "Chilly?" he asked.

She thought a moment, narrowing her eyes, then shrugged and shook her head. "No, I..." She cocked her head thoughtfully. "What's that saying, 'someone just walked over my grave'?" She glanced out the passenger-side window. "I have goose bumps all over."

It was no wonder she had the heebie-jeebies. Ever since Pearl Harbor, everybody had been braced for the Japs to attack the California coast. Los Angeles was on its last nerve.

"Hey, Betty, everything is swell," he promised, but as he drew her face back toward his to plant a comforting kiss on her luscious red lips, an icy finger tickled his spine. Something had just walked over *his* grave, too.

Then Betty thrust her finger toward the windshield. "Cliff, oh my god! Someone's about to jump off the bridge!"

Death.

The beaux-arts gingerbread arches of the Colorado Street Bridge rose high above the trees of the dusty Arroyo Seco riverbed some one hundred forty feet below. Concealed in shadow from the necking couple it had just tried to ensnare, a strange black miasma crawled up the columns, billowing like smoke, searching for victims. A living, evil creature, it called to the lonely, the desperate, the helpless. It lured them to the railings. It promised them an end to their torment. And after they jumped...

...it feasted on their terror.

The bridge was cursed, people said. Haunted by the angry spirits of the men who had died building it.

They were right.

Fog settled like a shroud around the shoulders of two young lovers as they trembled in each other's arms at the bridge railing. Nineteen-year-old Jenny was California royalty—the daughter of Jackson Alexander Covington, one of the wealthiest tycoons in the country. Bobby Garcia was a twenty-one-year-old Mexican, a poet whose works inspired the migrant fruit-pickers—the *braceros*—to demand equal rights and lives with dignity. Her father's field boss had brought home Bobby's poetry, and Jenny had fallen in love from afar with the romantic rebel. They met with the help of Araceli, one of the house-maids, who believed in the cause. They passed notes; they met again.

And again.

And Jenny gave her heart to Bobby, born of a race her father considered subhuman. She knew Jackson Covington would never

consent to her marriage to Bobby, but she couldn't imagine life
without him. Jenny's father had ruined business rivals in the most
destructive ways he could devise. He nursed grudges. He plotted
revenge. He loved dealing out pain. She wasn't supposed to know about
the mangled bodies and ruined families, but she did. He wouldn't hesitate to do those things to the "Poet of the Grape Fields" if he could.

She also knew her father would rather see her dead than
married to a *bracero*.

But she couldn't live without Bobby.

Loyal and brave, Araceli had helped Jenny plan her escape from
the family's Pasadena estate. Jenny raced to Bobby, and then they
were on their way out of Pasadena to meet up with a sympathetic
Catholic priest in downtown Los Angeles to be married.

But they had made a fatal mistake: they had taken Bobby's
uncle's truck rather than her luxurious Packard, which would be
recognized in an instant. And just as they had reached the Colorado
Street Bridge, the old truck had broken down. Bobby had had just
enough warning to steer it off the road to avoid an accident.

Hand in hand, the two young lovers began to run across the
bridge, with plans to catch the Red Line on Figueroa in Eagle Rock
only a mile farther on. From there, wedded bliss and transport south
from sympathetic pickers, then across the Mexican border to safety.

Except that now, somehow, they were no longer running.

They were standing on the railing, teetering back and forth. An
odd, dark fog obscured the underpass; she thought she could see
something move within it.

"What is happening?" Jenny whispered.

"I don't know." Bobby held her tight. "How did we get here?"

The ravenous ebony shadow crept closer, sending forth icy
tendrils of temptation. *Come to me. Come now*, it whispered. *It will be
better if you jump.*

Eagerly.

"We'll never make it," Jenny whispered. "By now my father
knows I'm gone."

"The truck, the stupid truck," Bobby groaned. "We are cursed."

Leap. Jump, the evil specter beckoned. Around it billowed murky
obsidian ether, camouflage to cover its approach.

"My love," Jenny said, tears rolling down her cheeks. "It's too late. We can't go on. This is the only way we can be together."

"Sí. Yes. I know, *mi amor*." He kissed her long and passionately, their last kiss on earth.

"Stop! Stop!" Betty shouted at the couple as she burst from the car.

Cliff looked up as he got out. Sure enough, two people were perched on the railing of the bridge, and Cliff could tell they meant business. One false move and they'd be getting measured for wings and halos. He popped the trunk and grabbed the rocket pack and his helmet, suiting up as fast as he could. Then he hit the thrust button and shot into the sky, quickly turning and spiraling downward toward the couple. Sure enough, they had stepped off the rail and were plummeting toward the ground. Some kind of crazy smoke swirled over the bridge like an ocean wave, and he lost sight of them for a few seconds.

He didn't have a few seconds.

They had both almost hit the ground. The girl was closer; he grabbed her up in his arms and tried to catch the boy, too. But it was too late.

As Cliff landed, the girl pushed herself out of his arms and tumbled to the ground. She threw herself on top of the boy and screamed, "Bobby! No! Bobby!"

Cliff dropped down beside her. The young man's body was swathed in shadow, and something black ballooned around it like a parachute. Blood? Huntington Hospital was close by.

Then he felt a horrible, icy chill, and he shuddered. When Betty touched his shoulder, he jumped a mile, and she looked at him with a face as dead white as a ghost's.

Cliff said to Betty, "Get her to the hospital. I'll take him there and meet you."

"Got it," Betty said. Her voice shook, but his girl was fighting to stay calm in the face of a catastrophe.

"Miss Covington!" someone yelled from the bridge. "Are you down there?"

The girl—Miss Covington—covered her mouth with both her hands and wildly shook her head. She ducked beneath the arch of the bridge, and Cliff and Betty followed after. Miss Covington looked terrified as flashlight beams danced in the dirt.

"Found the Mexican's car!" another man shouted. "They must be around here somewhere!"

"Don't let them get us!" the girl begged Cliff. She threw herself around him. "Please!"

Jeepers, Cliff thought.

Something as cold as the grave crawled up his back again, then seemed to drench him like a wave of frigid water. He was so startled he hit the ignition key and was instantly soaring into the night sky with the girl clutching at him. He looked down long enough to see Betty bent down beside the boy, looking up at Cliff and shaking her head. Then she got behind the wheel and tore out of there. Later she told Cliff that the only reason she left was to keep the Rocketeer out of it. He knew she felt guilty over abandoning the poor boy. Cliff did his best to convince her that they'd done all they could, and Peevy said the same thing, but still, the image of the broken body on the ground haunted him just as much as it did Betty.

Rage.

That was almost all that was left of Bobby Garcia. The black fog puddled around the human who was for all intents and purposes dead and soaked up the boiling emotion. The cruelty, and the prejudice, yes, but more than that, *Jenny*. She was the one good thing that had ever happened to him. The one miracle. But she had been torn from his arms by that flying man, and she would go on to live a life without him while he…he…

Jenny. The boy's brain sparked with the word. It was all that was keeping him alive. He had to get to Jenny. Be with Jenny.

The flying man had taken her from him.

Rage.

The creature that lived under the bridge—it had no name for itself—covered the boy's body with its crackling cold and sucked the life force from him. It had never experienced such intense hatred before. It was exhilarating.

I will find him. I will kill him, Bobby thought. Then he died.

And the creature moved away from his body, drunk on wrath. And thirsty for more.

Glendale, California
February 24, 1942

"I knew it would happen, I knew it," Peevy said. "I knew the Japs were on their way."

He and Cliff were holed up in their hangar at Grand Central Flight School, and the military pilots in training there were about to bust. The night before, at nineteen hundred hours, a Jap submarine had risen off the coast about a hundred miles to the north and shot thirteen shells into an oil field in the town of Ellwood. They didn't hit anything important, but someone had signaled them from shore, and now civilians were terrified, fearing an imminent invasion. Grand Central's pilots were itching to bomb that sub down the hatch to Davey Jones. But everybody was grounded, and they were furious.

Then one of the flyboys made a crack about Cliff dodging real duty by working as an instructor: "You'll still be stateside when I'm risking my life doing a *real* man's job," the blowhard said, and his words were like a punch to Cliff's jaw.

Cliff's temper ignited. "It's the training you're getting from me that's going to keep you in one piece, hotshot. On second thought, maybe I'll just skip a few lessons with you."

That shut him up, but Cliff had to bite his tongue so he wouldn't go on to tell this ignorant moron that last night after the attack, the Rocketeer had met with Mister Hughes and some nameless, out-of-uniform "powers that be" about sending him out on solo recon missions, all the more reason for Peevy and Cliff to finish their long-range flight modifications.

Boiling over, Cliff clanged his wrench against the concrete floor. He was so angry he could spit nails.

"Hey, kid, easy," Peevy cautioned him. "That 'real man' is just blowing off steam. He don't even know what he don't know. Now, listen, I think I've got the reconfigured specs for the rocket pack figured out, and I drew up some new blueprints. The CO is going to do a thorough inspection of the entire base in about an hour on account of last night, and Mister Hughes is up to his eyeballs in meetings, so the best place for my new blueprints is with you. Take 'em, and drift. Go on to that big party Betty called about, and we'll set up a test with Mister Hughes ASAP."

Cliff cooled down a little. Betty had left a message with Peevy about attending a big, fancy party at Johnny Weissmuller's mansion in tony Bel Air. The world-famous movie star had spotted the "featured Aquanette" in a photograph from the Vista del Arroyo Hotel pool party. Now she was going to be in the former Olympian's next Tarzan picture!

Cliff was thrilled, his anger vanishing in an instant. He and Betty both loved those Tarzan movies. In fact, they'd gone to see *Tarzan's Secret Treasure* three days before Pearl Harbor was attacked.

The prospect of meeting a *real* star, not some Hollywood type, soothed Cliff some. Weissmuller had won slews of gold medals swimming at the Olympics before he'd found more gold in Tinseltown, and he made it a point to perform his own stunts (the ones in the water, that is; aerialists did the vine work). Cliff took a peek at the blueprints. "Circumference of Cliff's head," read one line beside a sketch of his noggin. Peev was always trying to make his helmet more aerodynamic, shaving off every extra inch he could. Cliff hoped he'd remember to include the jut of his nose!

He folded up the blueprints, put them in a plain, oversized envelope and placed them in his glove box. Then he drove home, put on his best duds, and tootled on up to Hollywoodland. He started to cheer up as he drove past a dozen fancy houses, some as big as castles. Then he reached a tree-lined boulevard bordered by Bentleys and Rolls-Royces. Beyond a stone wall rose a Spanish-style, white-washed mansion with a sloping red-tiled roof. Standing in the street behind a sawhorse, a man in a suit and tie was holding a clipboard. He politely motioned Cliff to come forward.

"May I help you, sir?" he asked through Cliff's open window.

"My girl invited me to Mister Weissmuller's party," Cliff said. "She's going to be in his next picture."

The man nodded. "You came just in time. Mister Weissmuller is ending the party at sundown, on account of the attack last night. Lights out. He almost canceled it. May I have your name?" he asked.

Cliff gave it. The man scanned the pages on his clipboard twice, then shook his head.

"I'm afraid you're not on the list," he reported.

Cliff gave him Betty's name. "She can vouch for me."

"Sir, there is no vouching," the man replied, not unkindly. "This is Mister Weissmuller's party, not your girl's."

"She didn't know I could come," Cliff insisted. "I'm in the war effort, but we had to shut down early today," he added with an air of importance.

The man looked apologetic. "I wish I could let you in, but I can't."

Cliff opened his mouth to protest, but as he gazed up at the tall wall and the palm tree drooping over it, he had an idea. He just smiled and said, "I savvy. I'll make sure I'm on the list next time."

He made a U-turn and trundled back the way he had come, disappearing around the side of the compound. Then he flicked open his glove box and got out the extra pair of leather flying gloves he always kept there. It was only then that he saw that he had accidentally left one of the three pages of blueprints in the box when he'd gone home to change. *Lunkhead!* Blowing air of out his cheeks in frustration at his own carelessness, he folded the blueprint into a square and stuffed it into his trouser pocket. It would be safer with him than in the car, that was for sure.

He slipped on his gloves; then, with the ease of a stuntman, he clambered onto the roof of his car, executed a good, tall jump, and grabbed onto the end of the dropping palm leaf. He pulled himself up and grasped the palm hand over hand until soon enough he was perched at the crown of the tree. He looked down into the movie star's compound. What he saw below made his eyes pop. An artificial river complete with a waterfall meandered over the grounds of the mansion, and the big man himself, Johnny Weissmuller, was swimming alongside a girl.

Then the girl next to Tarzan flopped over on her back. It was Betty! *And she didn't have on any clothes!*

Cliff was so shocked he nearly fell out of the tree. Instead, he slid down the trunk just like Tarzan himself. Then he stomped past some awfully famous faces, ignoring them all...just as Weissmuller popped out of the pool in his swim trunks, him with his movie-star hair and muscles, then bent back down and offered his hand to Betty.

"Hey, Tarzan!" Cliff shouted, furious. "Keep your big ape paws off my girl!"

Weissmuller was already lifting Betty out of the pool like she weighed as much as an exotic orchid. As she landed beside the towering King of the Jungle, Cliff realized that she was wearing a skin-colored one-piece bathing suit that was actually pretty modest, even if it did hug her hourglass curves in all the right places. It just made her *look* naked.

"Cliff!" Betty cried, and boy, did *she* look steamed. "What are *you* doing here?"

Heads turned in Cliff's direction. Lots of heads. Famous heads. Then a couple of men in black trousers and white shirts headed Cliff's way.

Weissmuller looked from Cliff to Betty and smiled. He raised a hand at the two men and said, "It's fine."

Cliff was abashed. Betty's cheeks were so red they could stop traffic. She reached for a towel from a stack on a wrought-iron table. Weissmuller got it first, unfurled it like a matador, and handed it to her. She forced a smile on her face.

"Thank you, Mister Weissmuller," she said.

"Johnny, remember?" he replied. The man had white teeth as big as his muscles.

They both looked expectantly at Cliff, who was getting a little hot under the collar again. He didn't like the way Johnny Weissmuller was leering at his girl.

"Hiya, Betty," he began, but at the same time, a man wearing riding jodhpurs, a white shirt, a red cravat, and a pith helmet approached, and Betty and *Johnny* gave him their full attention.

"You're right, Johnny. She's perfect for the queen of Atlantis," the man announced. He beamed at Betty. "Kid, you've got the featured role!"

"Oh!" Betty cried. She flung herself into Mister Weissmuller's arms, her chest smashing against his flat washboard abdomen. "Thank you!"

Cliff's mouth dropped open. He knew all about Hollywood. How pretty girls got starring roles. The words "casting couch" pulsated in his brain to the tune of air-raid Klaxons.

"Did you hear that, Cliff?" Betty cried. "I'm going to be the queen of Atlantis!"

Just then, Betty's snoopy reporter pal Dahlia Danvers hustled on over. That meant *she'd* been on the list. But not him?

"Mister Weissmuller, Mister Seidel," she said, "this is exciting news! I'm a reporter and—"

"Wonderful, wonderful," said the man with the monocle, in a tone that suggested to Cliff that he was only humoring Dahlia. Dahlia had been trying for some time to get a chance to cover important news, not just column inches about Hollywood celebrities and fashion. "Come with me."

Weissmuller looked from Betty to Cliff and said, "Betty, why don't you change? I'll give Cliff a tour."

"Sure thing, Mister...Johnny," Betty said brightly. She flashed Cliff her patented *don't ruin this for me, you big mook* expression and darted away.

Cliff had to take big steps to match the towering man's stride. It was on the tip of his tongue to apologize, but he wasn't sure what to say. Truth be told, he was kind of starstruck.

Cliff's shoes clacked on the marble floor as they entered the mansion and he gazed up at fancy oil paintings of the African jungle. Framed photos of Johnny Weissmuller and the dozens of famous people he had met were everywhere.

"Don't worry about Betty," Johnny assured him. "I'll look out for her while we're shooting the picture. This could be her big break, but she won't break your heart. You just have to stand back a little so she can shine."

Cliff was flustered. He was getting romance advice from Tarzan.

"You in the business, or do you make an honest living?" Weissmuller asked him. Cliff knew he meant the movies, the only "business" that seemed to matter in this town.

Cliff squared his shoulders. "I used to be an exhibition pilot, working the air race circuit mostly, but I did stunt work in the pictures, too. Now I'm training pilots for Uncle Sam and doing some test flying for Mister Hughes."

Weissmuller's brows shot up. He looked like a big, excited kid. "No kidding? A real test pilot, that's great! And an instructor, too, like Robert Taylor. After I retired from competitive swimming I thought about becoming a private pilot. I even got an offer from a flight school for free lessons. Always regretted not taking them."

Wow. "I'd be happy to take you up, show you the ropes," Cliff said brightly. "I've done private sessions before." His experiences with Zane Grey on Catalina quickly came to mind.

Weissmuller sighed and shook his head. "Can't. The studio. I'm no longer at MGM now, but RKO is no different, at least in that respect. If they won't even let me swing on a vine now and then, they sure aren't going to okay flying lessons. Wallace Beery could get away with it, not me."

Cliff knew that the great character actor used to have it in his contract that he'd be paid one dollar more than any other star, ensuring that he'd always be the highest-paid performer in the world. Scoop had told them that. But Cliff had actually met the actor several times at Grand Central since Beery had kept his planes there before the war. It was common knowledge that MGM had always been having conniptions over the actor's passion for the wild blue yonder. Heck, even his house had an aviation motif, and up until the war, he bought a new plane almost every year.

"Perhaps they don't need to know," Cliff blurted, making Weissmuller chuckle.

"You have a point there. But I'm kind of hard to disguise, being so tall."

"I'm good at disguises," Cliff said, and immediately wanted to kick himself. *What* was he saying? His identity as the Rocketeer was a secret, and he had to keep it that way.

"I am, too," Weissmuller replied enigmatically. "I've never felt as free as when I'm swimming. I always thought flying my own plane would be like swimming in the air."

"It is. It's just like that," Cliff said, vigorously nodding his head.

"Except that you're surrounded by metal. By a machine," Weissmuller said. "Unless you're the Rocketeer, I suppose." He chuckled. "Now *that's* one man I really envy. I'd give anything to fly through the air like he does."

"You *would?*" Cliff said, mentally strangling himself to keep from saying anything more. He had to keep his big yap shut. But the temptation to spill his secret to the great Johnny Weissmuller was almost more than he could withstand. "I mean, I would, too." He looked away.

They returned to the party, where a small cluster of super-famous movie stars was gathered around Betty and Dahlia. Betty had changed out of her suit and was all dolled up in a sexy Hawaiian-style cocktail dress. A fresh stab of jealousy pierced Cliff, and then he saw that attention was focused on Dahlia, not Betty. As he and Johnny drew closer, he could hear what the reporter was saying:

"And I suspect that at least half the suicides on that bridge have been kept out of the papers. To prevent copycats or avoid scandal. Why, Jackson Covington's own daughter was allegedly involved in a suicide pact with her Mexican lover. They both jumped on Valentine's Day after a quickie wedding—she lived, he didn't. And you'll never guess how she survived: the Rocketeer caught her on the way down! Guests at the big hotel there swear they saw it. But was it in the papers? No. Covington had it suppressed. I wonder if the Rocketeer was there by chance or had been hired to tail them."

Cliff stumbled but made himself keep walking. Betty turned her head and gave him her biggest, brightest smile. In return, he gave her a panicked headshake. She couldn't do or say anything about it, especially with Dahlia there.

Then he realized that Betty wasn't smiling at him. She was beaming at Johnny Weissmuller.

Ignition! Jealousy rushed through him, and then he fought it back down. He felt like he was wrestling an alligator, he was so piqued.

"I'd rather cover the war, of course," Dahlia went on. "If I can wrap this suicide bridge story up in a way that'll sell papers, my editor has promised me an exclusive interview with an eye witness to the bombardment last night."

"Maybe the Rocketeer will let you interview him," said a man with heavy eyebrows and big mustache. Holy smokes, it was Groucho Marx.

"Maybe he will," she replied enigmatically. Then she looked at Cliff. "Hey," she said. "You two were at the Vista del Arroyo Hotel that day, weren't you? The Aquanette party, right? Did you happen to see the Rocketeer making a daring rescue?"

He was saved from answering when Weissmuller said, "Thanks to all of you for coming. I'm afraid we're closing up shop now. What with the attack last night..."

"Whatever you say, *Johnny*," Betty said dreamily. "Cliff, can you take me home?" She didn't even look at him when she spoke to him!

"Sure thing, Betty," he managed.

Weissmuller himself began walking them toward the gate to the road. Cliff stuck his hand in his pocket to retrieve his keys. He froze. The blueprint wasn't there! He felt in his other pocket. Not there, either. He had dropped it somewhere!

Nosy reporter Dahlia stuck to Betty and Johnny like glue. The movie star was being really nice, saying all kinds of great things about Betty's natural aquatic abilities and how the camera loved her. Dahlia was taking notes. Then he thanked them all again, and the trio stood outside the tall walls of the mansion. A valet went to fetch Dahlia's car, and a lightbulb went on over Cliff's head.

Cliff said, "Jeepers, Betty, I don't have my car keys. I must have dropped them somewhere. I need to go back in and look for them."

But Betty reached her hand into his trouser pocket and seductively murmured, "No, they're right here. I noticed the extra bulge as soon as I saw you."

As she pulled out the keys, Cliff went as hot as a tin roof on a summer's day and as cold as the showers at the YMCA—hot for Betty, cold for the fix he was in.

"Oh, yeah, swell. Thanks, doll," he said, trying to sound enthusiastic.

Dahlia gave Cliff a suspicious look. Let her look. All they had to do was outwait her and get back in. But all the party guests swirled out at once, and the gate clanged shut decisively.

Dahlia's car came, and she drove away. Cliff and Betty had turned the corner en route to his car from the house when Cliff said to Betty, "I have to get back into Johnny's place. I dropped Peevy's new specs for the you-know-what in his yard!"

"What? Jeez!" she cried.

"Had to climb over the wall. I wasn't on the list!"

She gave her foot a stomp and crossed her arms. "I can't believe you!"

"Wait right here," he told her.

He trotted back around the corner and grabbed the end of a vine hanging from a palm tree. He yanked on it, and it came off in his hand.

Then the gate opened as if by magic. Johnny Weissmuller himself stepped out. Cliff took a deep breath. Tarzan was holding a very familiar folded square of paper.

He looked at Cliff and held it out to him. "I believe you forgot something, Mister Secord."

"Oh yeah," Cliff blurted, flustered. He stared at the paper without taking it. Maybe the actor didn't know what it was.

"No one else saw it," Weissmuller assured him. "I'm fairly certain, anyway—*Rocketeer*."

Cliff shut his eyes tightly. He was such a dolt! He should have left the blasted thing in the glove box!

"Mister...Johnny," he said urgently.

"Relax, Cliff. I know what it's like to have a secret, and I sure won't spill yours. Maybe someday, you can show me what it's like to swim through the air."

Cliff wondered what Weissmuller's secret was, but he figured most movie stars had at least one.

"Sure, Johnny," he promised, and then Tarzan shut the gate with a smile.

Cliff turned tail and roared down the path, nearly barreling into Betty, who had taken off her sandals and was making her way barefoot up the drive.

She saw the blueprint in his hand. "So fast?"

Betty had always been swell about keeping his Rocketeer activities to herself, but Cliff was plenty nervous that it was getting around. He said, "Piece of cake," and left it at that.

After Cliff and Betty "celebrated" (and not with cake!) he met up with Peevy, who told him that the Rocketeer had been cleared to test the rocket pack with a quick flyby in an open field down the road once the civilian population had gone to bed. Meanwhile, Peevy was on full alert. He had volunteered to be an air warden. A civilian serving sentry duty, Peevy watched the skies with his radio, binoculars, and a plane recognition card at the ready. It was on the tip of Cliff's tongue to tell him that Johnny Weissmuller knew his big secret, but as Peevy's shift ended and they trundled to the field for the test, he could tell that Peevy was already bursting with anxiety and exhaustion. It was three in the morning, and Cliff's pal had been up for nearly twenty-four hours.

They got to the field, and he soared high into the sky, startled by the lack of back-blast and the engine roar that usually accompanied it. Pleased, he climbed higher, mulling over the events of the day— Betty's big break and Johnny Weissmuller's discovery of his big secret—when suddenly, a dark shape blotted out his view of the moon. It was an enormous oval, and it hung in the air like a spider dangling from its web. He was too far away to make out any details. What was it, a blimp?

Cliff "hovered" as best he could and squinted but saw no seams that would indicate doors or entry points. Then the thing moved toward him, fast. He jerked, hard, nearly sending himself into a tail-spin. He took a deep breath and flew forward to meet it. Moonlight bounced off its smooth metallic surface.

Far below, air-raid sirens began wailing, and powerful search-lights blasted on. As he tried to blink away the blinding *pop-pop-pop* of bright white light, the entire sky lit up with fireworks. No, not fireworks—fire*power*! Shells burst around him. Some pinged and exploded against the object. *None* of them so much as left a scratch!

Just as Cliff blasted away, something ricocheted off his jet pack and he suddenly lost altitude. Tumbling end over end into a storm of bullets, he let out a yell that of course no one could possibly hear, not even him. Then he fought to level out and pressed his thrust stud, crossing his fingers that he could make it to land before he got shot or drowned. Surely someone would see the Rocketeer and summon help!

But he careened downward behind a billboard atop an old brick building, effectively blocking all sight of his entry. Slam! He crashed headfirst into a towering pile of fish guts. No stars or tweeting birdies circled his head. One minute he was sliding into slimy stink, and the next...

The sun had risen, the seagulls were cawing, and a cat was purring against the small of his back. His head was as hot as a baked apple; he jerked his helmet off and took a deep breath, expecting to find a crowd gathered around him. But he was alone. Above him, no monstrous contraption hovered in the sky. Around him, pelicans honked and the tide rolled out.

After confirming that there was a bullet-sized hole in the bullet-shaped housing of the rocket pack, he grabbed a sticky burlap sack off his garbage tower and wrapped up his gear. He stumbled along for what seemed like forever, moving through block after block of abandoned industrial buildings. Finally locating a pay phone, Cliff called Peevy, who told him that Betty had completely fallen apart. After last night's "Battle of Los Angeles," RKO wanted Tarzan in a more patriotic story, meaning that America was in and Atlantis was out—and Betty's title role along with it. Plus she was worried to death about Cliff. And on top of it all, Dahlia "Scoop" Danvers had been *very* suspicious about Cliff's whereabouts. With a citywide blackout going on, why couldn't he come to the phone to reassure his girl? She wasn't buying Peevy's "he was at the field keeping the cadets calm" line of hooey.

"Betty suspects that Dahlia dame's got it figured out," Peevy finished. "The mystery we don't want solved."

"Great," Cliff said, exhaling. "That's why they call her Scoop. What am I going to do, Peev?"

"We'll cross that bridge when we come to it," Peevy said, and Cliff's mind was jerked back to that awful scene on the Colorado Street Bridge. The boy, the blood, the blackness. Then the image faded. "We got more immediate problems. I already tried to talk to the mucky-mucks about last night." Peevy sounded frustrated. "There's something hinky going on. I'll tell you all about it when I get you."

Peevy arrived in his truck to collect one thirsty, hurting Cliff. The fallen flier clambered in, slurping down coffee and gobbling up the ham sandwich Peevy brought him. After that, he scanned the morning newspapers Peevy had. Cliff was astounded. Secretary of the Navy Frank Knox was calling the whole thing a false alarm! *False alarm, my hiney*, Cliff thought, furrowing his brow. *If Knox had been up topside in the clouds, he'd have seen that was no hoax!* Then General George Marshall of the Army claimed that the only thing in the sky had been twenty-five commercial aircraft brought in for psychological warfare—in other words, to create panic. "Are they admitting to causing the whole thing themselves?" Cliff asked Peevy. "Make Los Angeles go nuts—and for nothing? That doesn't make any kind of sense. People were killed."

Cliff's head hurt just thinking about it. It could not be denied that well over a thousand rounds of anti-aircraft ammo had been lobbed at the invader(s) and nothing was shot down! And two million people were pretty darned panicked, that was for certain! Cliff had to assume that at least a few shells hit their mark, so what did that make the thing he saw up there? How could a low-altitude balloon withstand a concentrated ack-ack barrage?

"Peev, the brass has gotta know this is a bunch of baloney. I should tell 'em what I saw."

"They *do* know," Peevy bit off, frowning at the sky as the truck bumped along. "I saw that thing up there too, Cliff. And get this: those glorified doughboys claim that the object must have drifted on a trajectory originating near Malibu. But they've got the wind currents all wrong. I triangulated, and I figure it had to come in from the desert. Somewhere up near Boron, most likely. If it *was* drifting, that is."

"Sure seemed that way to me," said Cliff. "Like some kind of metal balloon, but flimsy." He'd been relieved that it hadn't been one of those strange bell-shaped craft he'd encountered before. He'd been told that he'd forget his encounter with them, but he'd been able to retain some details and images, such as the face of a woman growing suddenly old before his eyes.

Peevy blew air out of his cheeks as he downshifted the old truck. "That's good to hear, I guess; though there hasn't been a metal dirigible around here since Slate Aircraft in Glendale tried back in '29. Anyway, I used my radio phone to tell 'em all about it, and I got five return calls, including two on the house phone, and damned if each time I wasn't ordered to mind my own business! And when I got hot and told 'em I'd go to the civilians—meaning Mister Hughes and his friends—and tell *them* what I saw, then just like that some colonel is on the horn sayin' I better shut my yap if I knew what was good for me. That's a threat if I ever heard one."

"But why? If the military already knew what it was, why try to shoot it down?" Cliff asked, bewildered.

"Beats me, though it wouldn't be the first time the Army didn't know what the Air Force was up to. Maybe it's just one big snafu and they're just covering their butts; still, no reason to threaten a man like that. So of course I put a call into Mister Hughes right away. I ain't heard back yet. In the meantime I figure we'd better do some investigating on our own, PDQ."

"Roger that. So, I'll go look in the desert around Boron."

"And we'll keep it on the QT," Peevy reminded him. "Don't even tell Betty. Wouldn't want to worry her, right?"

Cliff spared a moment to think about Betty's luscious lips. Was Peevy worried that if she knew, she might inadvertently tell one of her girlfriends? He let that thought go as he trailed after Peevy into the mechanic's house and went immediately to the phone to call his girl. She was in tears with worry. After reports of the Rocketeer being seen during last night's barrage and then not hearing from Cliff—it had shaken her badly. The Battle of Los Angeles had lobbed a hand grenade onto her dreams of stardom, dreams that seemed less important just now. He promised his brokenhearted baby a swell night on the town as soon as he could cash his paycheck. In return, she confirmed that yes, Scoop was asking *way* too many questions about Cliff's whereabouts during the recent Rocketeer sightings.

He showered while Peevy began putting together a fresh rocket pack, taking parts from the several he had in various states of repair or analysis and adding his new modifications. By the time Cliff was cleaned up and had some more grub, Peevy's work was done and he'd laid out a course for Cliff into the desert.

Two hours later, Cliff was aloft in one of the PT-19 trainers from Grand Central. Luckily it had sustained some damage from falling shrapnel the night before, and Peevy told the base CO that Cliff was taking it out to test the repair job.

Cliff headed for the western edge of the Mojave Desert. Despite last night's crisis, there was no restriction on flying. For most of the afternoon, he guided the aircraft easily through rocky canyons and long, blistering tracks of sand and scrub. But of any kind of possible weapon launch site, there was no sign. He banked up for one last circuit before beginning the flight back to Glendale.

At the very last second, something glinted in the sunlight. He flew in for a closer look and spotted a decrepit square of wood about thirty feet a side, built into a hillock of rock and sand rising from the desert floor. It looked like an abandoned mine.

Cliff set down close by. He figured that if there was anyone inside, they'd already heard the Fairchild in the air. He left his Rock-eteer gear in the aircraft, slipped a flashlight into his leather jacket, and climbed down, then walked cautiously but steadily toward the mine entrance.

There was a door, but it was padlocked. The cause of the lucky glint, maybe. For a second he was stumped. Then he shrugged and once, twice called out, "Hello?"

Nothing.

He debated with himself about breaking the law for all of two seconds before he went back to the plane, grabbed a crowbar, and started working at the hasp. This was wartime. Cliff was tired, but he was strong, and he made short work of the Skid Row security system. The door squealed on thirsty hinges as he forced it open. A terrible stench met his nostrils, a staggering blast of raw corruption. Cliff swallowed down a gulp of fear. Something had died inside this place. He hoped it was a simple desert critter, but it smelled bigger than that.

Sunlight filtered in, and fresh air diluted the stink somewhat. He heard the buzzing of flies. Another bad sign.

Cliff turned on his flashlight and entered a barren square space with dusty wood paneling and a single, equally dusty metal desk. His flashlight beam revealed several sets of tracks in the grit on the floor, coming and going, leading to another door on the other side of the room.

It was a little more difficult to open that door. Hot and sweaty, Cliff worked at the metal for quite a long time, watching the slant of the sunshine as it moved across the wall. He wasn't about to let a stupid bunch of wood get the better of *him*. He started throwing his weight against it in a determined rhythm, but the lock held. Finally he took the crowbar to the door, hacking until the wood splintered and broke, then discovered that the wall had been reinforced with slats of steel. Those took a lot more effort, but finally he was able to step through.

He gaped. The faded wood walls were covered with blueprints and maps of California, Arizona, and Mexico. Three trestle tables were spaced apart on a black-and-white marble floor, and each was crammed with scientific equipment, books and unfolded diagrams and blueprints. The middle table held a mad-scientist setup of beakers, test tubes and curling glass pipettes that dripped glowing liquid into a vat, lots of strange, shiny tools, a welding helmet and gloves, and several stacks of notebooks and leather-bound volumes. He stared at the elaborate glassware setup, then drew closer to the back wall. He scanned the charts and blueprints, some of which were in German, and others in Spanish. The blueprints were for buildings, not aircraft. In fact, there was no evidence anywhere of aviation activity. It seemed unlikely that the "weather balloon" had come from the mine. But something sure was up!

Cliff opened one of the notebooks. His elbow nudged a coffee cup, and he caught it as it fell. Pungent, cold coffee splashed over his hand. He knew what happened to coffee that sat around more than a couple days—a crusty mold formed on the surface. So this stuff was pretty fresh. He inhaled the aroma to mask the stink of rotting flesh, but it didn't do any good. The flies were still whining in the background like miniature buzzards.

As he set the cup back down on the table, he thought he heard a long, low moan. Someone in pain. His hair stood on end as he scanned the room and peered into the shadows. Holding his breath, he crept forward toward the wall of blueprints.

Another moan. Someone *behind* the wall was in big trouble.

"Hello?" he called out, then wondered if it had been a bad idea to announce his presence so close to the reek of death. Yes, he decided, it was. But he'd already done it. So he did it again. "Hello?"

Cliff gave the wall an experimental push. Nothing. He felt everywhere for a crease as another moan, this one more desperate, teased his eardrums. Then he realized that the sound was coming from the *base* of the wall.

He glanced cautiously over his shoulder, then hefted his crowbar in his right hand and squatted on his haunches, feeling along the base of the wall. He kept going...until he felt a blast of cold air against his fingertips. The smell was worse, and he recoiled. Then he stiffened his backbone and pushed again. Part of the wall swung open, revealing a set of wooden stairs leading into another space slightly below the room.

He crept down the stairs to find himself inside a mineshaft illuminated with kerosene lanterns. It had been cleverly concealed from view by the makeshift wall.

"*Help,*" someone whispered, the faint plea echoing off the craggy rock faces of the tunnel. Cliff moved forward. His silhouette blossomed and then shrank as he kept going. He had advanced a few feet when a metal door blocked his progress. He grimaced, and then he reached out to touch it, jerking back his hand with a cry. The metal was white-hot. Visions of a fire made him hesitate for a fraction of a second, but only that—someone was behind that door, trapped or hurt or both.

By the stench and the flies, someone else was already dead.

He bent down and grabbed a large rock, then used it to push against the door, forcing it open with brute strength.

"Look out!" the voice croaked, and as Cliff ducked to one side, a pencil-thin red beam of light blasted from out of the darkness and zapped the door. An odor, like welding, mingled with the foulness radiated from a glowing circle of scarlet rapidly turning white-hot.

The beam of light vanished.

"Now it's safe. Safer," the same voice said. Cliff raised his flashlight; this second room was easily four times as big as the first. The gauzy glow from his beam caught the glitter of metal everywhere. His attention was seized by a strange, boxy brass-and-steel contraption that looked like a gun turret. Half standing, hunched over, a silhouette was hanging on to the corner of the machine. The man raised his head. Cliff saw a vast, bloody landscape of bruises and cuts. The man's left eye was swollen shut.

"What the hell?" Cliff blurted. He darted forward and slung his arm around the man. "Who are you? What's going on?"

"Venden," the man mumbled. "Dohl Venden. Stop him. He-he... dangerous. Insane."

"Keep talking," Cliff said, glancing around.

"He kidnapped us. Scientists, like him, working for the government. Secret projects. He forced us to reveal...everything. So many projects. The Bell...the ray. His wife, scientist too, died of radiation poisoning. Horrible death. Government sacrificed her. Drove him insane..."

Cliff nodded, horrified by what he was hearing. "Okay. I'm going to get you out of here."

The man resisted. "No. Wait. There are others." Then his knees buckled, and Cliff lowered him to the floor with care.

"Next room," the man whispered. "Keep going. Horrors. Prepare yourself." He clutched Cliff's forearm, his grip surprisingly strong. Then his hand relaxed. Cliff feared the worst, but a check of the man's wrist revealed a pulse. He was still alive.

"I'll come back," Cliff promised.

Head down, he crouched past the turret, then moved through the room, trying to make sense of all the odd things he saw—what looked like ray guns from *Flash Gordon* and huge, cannon-like things and bronze boxes with wires curly-cuing out of them.

The opposite side of the room shrank down to a tunnel that curved at a steep decline. Next Cliff entered an enormous, illuminated cavern at least twenty feet high crammed with even larger, weirder contraptions all along the walls. They were humming and buzzing; the floor of the cavern vibrated through his boots. On the rock walls hung ten-foot-long banners that read SURVIVAL! NO MERCY TO OUR ENEMIES! THE FUTURE OF THE HUMAN RACE IS IN OUR HANDS! ALL GOVERNMENTS LIE! Hideous photographs of people who looked like they had been dipped in acid were arranged beneath one of the banners. In a gold frame, there was also an oil painting of a lovely woman with a hand-painted sign below it that read ARABELLA VENDEN RIP. YOU SHALL BE AVENGED.

Rumors were rampant that the Germans were planning to invade along the border. That they had zeppelins and bombers already in Mexico for a coordinated two-pronged attack with the Japanese. Could this Venden be in on it?

◆

Cliff searched for answers. But what he found were "the others" that the wounded man had told him about—three dead men, so badly tortured Cliff had to cover his mouth with both hands to keep from losing his ham sandwich. One was bound to a chair with thin wire that had cut into his flesh. The top of his skull had been cut away, and wires were connected to sections of his brain. The other two were dangling by bloody wrists from spiked manacles attached to the stone wall of the cavern. One of the men was missing all his internal organs.

The other one was in even worse shape.

What kind of monster does things like this?

Then Cliff heard footfalls in the tunnel. Someone was coming! He darted away from the three savaged corpses and hid himself among towers of boxes. He was shaking, with both anger and fear. He had to stop this madman—hopefully without getting butchered in the process.

"Show yourself," said a man's voice. It sounded surprisingly young. "If you're one of us, you have nothing to fear."

Cliff grimaced. He had made no effort to cover his tracks, and he had plenty to fear. There was no way for this fruitcake to know Cliff was inside this big room unless there was no other place to go. Which meant there was only one way out—the way he had come. Where the madman was. With his red-hot light beam and who knew what else.

Cliff didn't even breathe. If he crouched down here much longer, fear was going to get the best of him. And *nothing* got the best of Cliff Secord!

Still breathless, Cliff waited for the man to speak again so he could get a better sense of his location. He heard footfalls. And then a blazing light came on overhead. Cliff squatted as low as he could, but suddenly, a grate opened in the cavern floor, and the tower of crates he was hiding behind fell inside. A hail of gunfire sailed right at him as he zigzagged his way behind another tower, only to watch it collapse below the ground as well. More bullets zinged his way, hordes of them, and all Cliff could do was dash into the darkest recesses of the cavern. He dropped down beneath a stalagmite, but of course he was a sitting duck.

Then he caught sight of Venden—young, as he had sounded, very tall and lanky in a long black coat and brown leather boots, with curly black hair shot through with streaks of white. Venden's eyes were so deeply sunk into his sockets that Cliff couldn't even see them, giving the man's face a skull-like appearance. His teeth were enormous, and his nose was hooked.

"Stand still! I'm going to kill you, and I don't want to damage any of my equipment in the process!" he called. He raised a Mauser and pointed it straight at Cliff.

He knows exactly where I am, Cliff realized grimly.

"I'll give you to the count of three," Venden said. "One...two..."

Cliff looked around for something, anything, that he could use as a weapon. Two large pieces of brass atop one of the strange machines were way too far away to grab. He tried to break off the top of the stalagmite, but it was no go. *Ka-zing!* A bullet missed his index finger by less than an inch!

Without warning, all the machines in the cave began to hum like jet engines revving up. Venden yelled and spun around in a circle, dashing to the nearest machine and placing the gun on top, grabbing and whirling two knobs on its face. Cliff took the opportunity to rush him headlong, throwing his arms around him and pushing him to the ground. Venden started yelling and pounding on Cliff's head with both his hands. Smoke poured from the backs of the machines, and a stalactite above the two grappling men crashed to the ground.

"It must be Bastick! He's still alive! He's set the place to self-destruct!" Venden shouted. "He must be stopped!"

That had to be the name of the man who had passed out, Cliff concluded as he got in a good roundhouse that snapped Venden's head backward. Cliff staggered to his feet and was about to hoist Venden off the ground when the mad scientist surprised him with a leg sweep that landed Cliff on his behind. While he was scrabbling to get back up, Venden jackrabbited to his feet and tore out of the cavern—leaving Cliff in his dust.

But once Cliff was on his feet, he followed after, dodging a lantern, then a chair, as Venden threw each object in Cliff's path. Soon Cliff was racing along on an obstacle course, falling to one knee at the spot where he had placed the unconscious man. He was no longer there.

"Go, run!" someone called from the shadows, and Cliff remembered his flashlight. He pulled it out of his jacket and shined it in the direction of the voice. It was indeed the scientist Venden had beaten. Bastick. Cliff charged over to him.

"Leave me. Get him," Bastick protested as Cliff draped him fireman-style across his back. Venden might get away, but there was no way Cliff Secord would leave an innocent man to die.

Explosions ripped through the mine, and the walls and ceiling began to crumble and disintegrate. Just as Cliff began to cross the threshold into the front room, the one with the metal desk, the ceiling collapsed. *Cave-in!* Cliff threw the man to the ground and covered him with his own body, hands protecting his head. Rocks punched Cliff's back like the fists of a drunk in a bar brawl. Cliff pushed himself up on his hands and knees and gripped the man by the collar, dragging him inch by inch over the debris field to the relative shelter of the desk.

Finally the rock fall subsided. Cliff's head was ringing, his vision blurry. He looked down at the man, who was still breathing, then poked out his head and groaned at the stacks of rocks piled up against the entry door. There must be dozens of fist-sized rocks. Hundreds! But they weren't going to move themselves, so he pushed his way back out of the shelter to a standing position and started clearing them away.

He wished he had water. And a doctor for his injured companion. And a phone to call the police. More than that, he wished he could catch up to Venden and stop him. But as Peevy liked to say, "If wishes were horses, beggars would ride." Well, as soon as he got out of here, he was riding that Fairchild straight down Venden's throat!

He didn't know how many hours he labored. He stopped a number of times to check on his newfound pal, although there was nothing he could do for him except to tell him not to give up. They were sucking in stink and dust, and that couldn't be good for someone whose breathing was so slow.

Cliff kept going, pushing himself at a relentless pace, refusing to give up even though every cell of his body was screaming for rest, and for water, and for someone else to take over. But it wasn't in Cliff to quit until the job was done.

At last he touched the wood of the door, and the slivers of light where the rocks had made holes caused him to blink. He quickened his pace, and the battered remains of the door fell outward at his push. It was only then, as he sucked in the dry but fresh desert air, that he realized the mine was filling with smoke. Venden's ungodly hideout was burning to the ground!

He went back for the scientist and lurched across the sand toward the PT-19. Cliff managed to hoist the man into the rear seat; then he spun the prop and cranked the engine. He began to taxi on the dry desert ground, the moon and stars lighting his way. Faster he went, faster, until he could pull back on the stick and take to the air!

Behind him, the mine went up in a huge ball of fire. Cliff didn't look back. He kept his nose pointed forward, bracing himself for the shockwave. It rocked the PT-19, but Cliff kept her trim. The Fairchild could reach speeds at one hundred fifteen knots an hour—a hundred thirty-two miles. His rocket pack was faster, but Cliff had no idea how far ahead of him Venden had managed to get. He followed the ribbon of road across the desert for about an hour, and then he finally zeroed in on his nemesis. Venden was driving a Jeep, which Cliff knew could only get up to fifty miles an hour. Once he closed up the distance, Venden would be his.

Just as he flashed a triumphant grin, something green and lumi-nescent billowed around the aircraft. The Fairchild sputtered and wobbled. Cliff peered through the emerald haze to see that Venden had stopped the Jeep and was standing on the front seat with the same kind of oversized, shiny gun Cliff had seen in the madman's lair. A second green blast hit the plane, and the engine stopped dead. The PT-19 began to go down.

Cliff swore, but just as quickly, the Fairchild righted and flew straight and true. They barreled along the desert, he above, Venden below, as the sun went down, past the blacked-out small desert towns and then, finally, the tall buildings of Los Angeles. He was gaining!

But a third pulse sent the aircraft jittering down, and this time Cliff reluctantly surrendered. He expertly glided the stalled plane to a safe landing on a handy high school ball field.

Cliff was astonished to recognize that they were in Pasadena! Had they really come that far so quickly? Without missing a beat, Cliff reached into the cockpit, grabbed up his helmet and the rocket pack and took off after Venden.

Peevy had worked a miracle, and Cliff knew he was going faster than he ever had before. But he could congratulate Peevy later; he couldn't let this monster get away.

The scientist had sped on ahead again, and Cliff poured on the fuel.

Then the distinctive grounds of the Vista del Arroyo Hotel came into view. They reached the Pasadena side of Colorado Street Bridge. Suicide Bridge. Cliff remembered the screaming girl in his arms and the boy he'd failed to save. He vowed that Venden would not cross this bridge a free man.

Cars were jostling out of the way. Fingers were pointing upward at the Rocketeer.

Then the green light blossomed around Cliff again, and the Rocketeer plummeted earthward. Cliff depressed his thrust stud, and with that last burst of speed, he hovered just above the Jeep.

Bing! Jing! Jing! Bullets sang past Cliff's helmet as he slammed hard onto the hood! Dazed, he hurtled himself over the windshield and flung himself at Venden. Cliff grabbed the steering wheel. Flesh met flesh; the Jeep began to swerve.

Somehow Venden managed to shove Cliff so hard that he almost flew into the street. "Die, demon, die!" screamed the deranged scientist.

Cliff clung to the left side of the vehicle as Venden cranked the wheel and headed for the rail, obviously with the plan of crushing Cliff against it. Cliff thumbed the thrust stud.

Nothing happened.

He did it again.

Still nothing!

He was about to be crushed!

Then the icy sensation that had crept over him when he saved Jenny Covington thoroughly engulfed him, and he thought he heard a voice whispering to him: *Come with me now. Come.*

For a moment, Cliff had no will of his own. His muscles loosened, and he didn't care if he fell. It would be all right, really, to end it here...

Then he roused himself. "WHAT THE HELL?!" Cliff shouted.

He jammed down on the thruster stud as hard as he could, soaring skyward—just as an oncoming truck slammed into the right front bumper of the Jeep. The vehicle went spinning across lanes before jumping the curb and crashing through the cement wall.

"Holy smokes!" Cliff stared down at the car as he hovered above the bridge. The truck driver jumped out, unhurt, and ran over to the breached wall. He and Cliff both looked down, Cliff from thirty feet above the astonished man. A huge black cloud boiled up from below the bridge and engulfed the Jeep as it fell. It looked almost like a giant hand clutching the car, smoking fingers holding it in a viselike grip. Cliff swan-dived after Venden, feeling the coldness seep into him, the siren call to turn off his thruster, but once again, he pulled himself together. He reached Venden and began to pull him from behind the steering wheel. For a moment, he thought he had him, but Venden aimed his gun straight into his face. Cliff backed off.

Impact! The Jeep burst into flames.

Rage.

The bonfire blazed, and Venden boiled with fury that alas, the government would win again. He had no doubt that the rocket-pack man was a tool of the United States government, a spy sent to shut him down. Just when Mexico and safety were within his grasp. He thought of the Brotherhood, his followers, waiting for him...all their dreams. Their weapons, their technology...

No, he thought. *No, I won't die. I won't let them win.*

Arabella's face blossomed in his mind. Her face as it had been, and then, after the radiation had eaten her alive—the experiment that had gone so wrong, that they had *guessed* might go wrong, and they had done it anyway, playing the odds—

Daring the gods—

Hatred roiled through him, for the men with power who could do such things. The men no one said no to. The warmongering, bloodthirsty men who could ruin innocent lives with a signature on a requisition form. Innocents like—

"Jenny," he whispered, and suddenly he wasn't exactly himself anymore. He was also someone named Bobby. And someone who had despaired of life and leaped with baby Jean in her arms. Something cold and black was climbing inside him. Down his throat and up his nose and into his ears and eye sockets; something that was made of icy fury that had been seething, starving. It began to feed. To grow. To live.

Down in the underpass, hidden by the ebony balloon of ether, it moved his arms, and his blistered fingers pushed open the Jeep door. It pushed his charred shoes to the ground, and he stood up on bones and leathery sinews.

It made his blackened heart beat: Lub-dub, *I hate, I kill, I avenge.* Lub-dub.

He looked through the inferno beyond a canopy of black smoke to the rocket-pack man—the Rocketeer—hovering in the air. He could tell that the flying bastard couldn't see him, didn't know.

I live.

He was Bobby Garcia, and he was Dohl Venden, and he was... something else.

We live.

And we will destroy the Rocketeer.

A day later...

"I'll be a star if it's the last thing I do," Betty said to Cliff, grinning. "Johnny promised me that the next suitable role in one of his pictures is mine."

"I'm sure it's a promise he'll keep," Cliff said. After all, Tarzan owed Cliff a favor.

Cliff and Betty were standing outside one of the sound stages on the Paramount Pictures lot. A huge banner on the side of the building showed Uncle Sam pointing his finger and looking stern. BUY WAR BONDS! read a caption at the bottom of the poser. SHOW YOUR FIGHTING SPIRIT!

Like three-dozen other girls, Betty was dressed in a clinging, red sequined leotard, a blue cutaway jacket, a curly white wig and a silver tricorne hat that matched her sparkly tap shoes. Cliff had watched the rehearsal. Betty was Patri-ette Number One. Her job was to wave a flag when Bob Hope appeared in a skit about George Washington. Then all the girls would cut a catchy rug in their tap shoes to "Yankee Doodle." It was pretty swell. And Betty was the most beautiful of all the Patri-ettes. She wasn't the queen of Atlantis, but she sure was Cliff's American dream.

Beside her, Dahlia "Scoop" Danvers had out her reporter's notebook and cocked her head at Cliff. Betty had invited Dahlia onto the lot *supposedly* to meet Bob Hope, but Betty and Cliff had a little something else planned for Betty's inquisitive friend.

"Betty tried to reach you the night before last, when that flying saucer was threatening the city," Dahlia said. "Where were you?"

"Oh, look!" Betty cried. She pointed to the sky. "It's the Rocketeer!"

"Wow, it is!" said a buxom, green-eyed beauty as she began to wave both arms over her head. "Hey, Mister Rocketeer! Swoop down here, honey! Show me your patriotism, and I'll show you mine!"

All the girls began laughing and jumping up and down, catcalling and whooping at the flying man in the sky. Dahlia pursed her lips and grunted in what sounded like frustration.

"Will wonders never cease," she muttered to herself. She turned to the studio photographer who'd been assigned to her. "Take some pictures!" she bellowed at him. "Good enough for front page!"

"Look how he moves," the green-eyed girl said dreamily. "Like he's swimming through the air."

Cliff watched with satisfaction. He had coached Johnny Weissmuller about this and the graceful, athletic actor was keeping well away from treetops and buildings, so no one would realize that today the Rocketeer was much taller than usual.

Betty and Cliff traded secretive grins. "Looks like that's exactly what he's doing," Cliff said. "And it also looks like he's having the time of his life." He winked at Betty and added under his breath, "So he'll be *grateful*."

"Oh, Cliff, thank you," Betty whispered back. "Sometimes you make me feel like I'm *floating* on air." Then she kissed him.

Victory!

THE
END

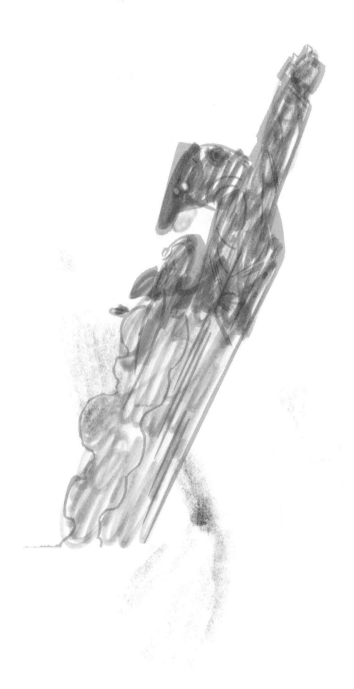

CODENAME: ECSTASY

by

NANCY A. COLLINS

June 1942

Ambrose Peabody, better known to his friends and some enemies as Peevy, was elbows-deep in an engine block when his friend and occasional partner in crime Cliff Secord entered the mechanic's workshop.

The pilot was in his late twenties, with tousled brown hair, handsomely chiseled features and an athletic build, and he seemed considerably more agitated than the last time Peevy talked to him.

"I can't believe that buzzard!" Secord fumed, waving a piece of opened mail in the mechanic's general direction. "Chaplin Airdrome just got bought out, and now the new landlord is raisin' the rent on the hangar! I'm having a hard enough time trying to make ends meet without some booshwah jerk throwing another monkey wrench in the works!"

"I thought you moved your planes over to Glendale?"

"Yeah, but I *live* out of Chaplin, and it's my base of operations for the Rocketeer. Besides, that hangar is the closest thing I've had to a real home since I lit out from the old neighborhood," Cliff sighed, running a hand though his tousled hair.

"Well, just be glad the owners didn't sell out to Uncle Sam, like they did Chandler Airfield over in Fresno," the older man sighed around the cigarette that seemed to always dangle from his lips. "If they had, you'd be out on your ear. So who's the new landlord?"

"Some real-estate tycoon called Dudley Sterling."

"I heard about him," Peevy grunted without looking up from his work. "He's been buyin' up private airfields all over the West Coast—even down into Mexico. Word on the street is that he's tryin' to build a network for airline service. But if you ask me, he's snatchin' up properties so when the dam finally breaks and we end up goin' to war, he can sell 'em to the government for training bases."

"That's the problem—finding a place that's not in danger of being snapped up by that jerk," Cliff grumbled. "The problem with Glendale is that it's too busy. The last thing I need is someone figuring out I'm the Rocketeer when I'm not skywriting over Pacific Park to pay the bills."

"You can always make good money doin' stunt work for the studios," Peevy pointed out. "Betty should be able to put the word in for you..."

"I'm not gonna let my girl wheedle me a job," Cliff said heatedly. "Besides, you *know* how I feel about those Hollywood types—they rub me the wrong way."

"And you return the favor," Peevy chuckled. "What was the name of that director you decked?"

"Aw, who cares? Besides, the louse had it coming, calling Betty a no-talent floozy! He's lucky all he got was a shiner."

"I'm just sayin', that's all," Peevy grunted, flicking the ash off his cigarette. "If you'd rather choke than swallow that pride of yours, that's your call. But it ain't like Chaplin's the only private airfield left. Why don't you ask around at the Bulldog?"

"You've got a point, there."

"That's why I always wear a cap," the mechanic laughed, touching its brim with an oil-stained finger.

The Bulldog Café was made from concrete and stucco and shaped to resemble its namesake—a goggle-eyed black-and-white bulldog. Assuming bulldogs smoked corncob pipes. The house specialties—tamales and ice cream—were printed in block letters on the café's forelegs, and a door was set into its broad chest.

Since it was located across the street from the front gate of the Chaplin Airdrome and his hangar lacked a kitchen, the Bulldog was where Cliff took most of his meals. It was also a hangout for a lot of the other pilots and mechanics for the same reasons.

As he approached the café, he spotted the owner's brown and white English bulldog sprawled on the doorstep. The dog lifted his massive head and licked his chops in welcome at the sight of the pilot.

"Hey, Butchy," Cliff said morosely, rubbing the mass of wrinkles that passed for the bulldog's head. "Looks like I won't be stopping by as often as I used to."

Millie, a middle-aged widow with a head of bright red curls, was standing behind the counter. A handful of regulars perched on the stools in what passed for the dining room.

"What can I get you, hon?" she asked, plucking the ever-present pencil from behind her ear.

"The usual, Millie," he sighed.

The café owner turned and yelled through the service window at the cook working the flat-top. "We got a Secord Special! Burn one, drag it through the garden, and pin a rose on it!" She then pulled a bottle of Ballantine's from the cooler and handed it to her customer. "You look down in the mouth. What's the matter, hon?" she frowned. "Betty givin' you girl trouble again?"

"I wish," he sighed, resting his chin on his fist. "Chaplin's changing hands. I need to look for new digs."

"Say it ain't so, Cliffy!" Millie exclaimed. "You're my best customer!"

Suddenly there was a tap on Secord's shoulder. He turned to see Jimmy Swenson, who was once a racer like himself but now flew the daily excursions to Catalina.

"If you're lookin' for a good price on a hangar, a buddy of mine runs a little airfield out in the Valley, just off the Camino Real."

"Thanks, Jimmy!"

Just then Millie slid the plate with his burger on it in front of him, and Cliff quickly dug in, his spirits considerably lifted.

Cliff looked out the window of his coupe at the eucalyptus trees lining the Camino Real. The Valley was a little Farmer Brown for a city boy like himself, but maybe some isolation wouldn't be so bad for the Rocketeer.

He had spent the Great Depression making his living weaving his racing plane between pylons like a basket maker, but none of that compared to the craziness he routinely found himself in since he found that stolen experimental rocket pack hidden in his hangar.

What had started off as an attempt to make some extra dough to woo his way into Betty's favor had snowballed into a part-time career as a high-flying mystery-man who smashed spy rings, battled crazed killers, and rescued damsels in distress—most of whom also happened to be his girl, Betty. And while he'd won a certain amount of fame as the helmet-headed Rocketeer, he still hadn't figured out a way to make a living at it. So far he had been lucky enough to keep his true identity from being splashed all over the papers. Being rich and famous was one thing; being infamous and broke was another.

He double-checked the address Jimmy had given him and turned onto a narrow side-road that cut through row after orderly row of citrus-laden trees. Eventually the orchards stopped, revealing a large, flat grassy field with a cluster of hangars and outbuildings.

A large wooden sign that said Valley Airfield was partially obscured by a banner draped over it: *Coming Soon: Silver Eagle Sky Port, Another Sterling Property. No Trespassing.*

Cliff groaned and leaned his forehead against the steering wheel: so much for escaping the grasping hand of Dudley Sterling. He must have made Jimmy's pal an offer too tempting to refuse. Although why Sterling would want a Podunk airfield with a single grass landing strip and no tower was a puzzler.

Well, since he'd come all the way out to the Valley, only to end up with a big fat goose egg, the least he could do was steal some fruit to make the trip worthwhile.

Ignoring the signage, he pulled his coupe behind an outlying hangar and disappeared into the orchard that encircled the tiny airstrip on all sides.

As he reemerged with an armload of purloined citrus, he spotted a green Buick estate wagon with wooden side panels approaching the "sky port." Fearful it might be the orchard's owner, he tossed his ill-gotten haul onto the ground and pressed himself against the wall of the hangar.

Peering around the corner, he saw two men step out of the car. They were dressed in matching light-gray shirts, blood-red ties and blue corduroy pants tucked into black jackboots. They also wore high-crowned campaign hats, similar to a park ranger's. He recognized their getup as the "uniform" of a private fraternal organization called the Silver Eagles that promoted itself as a grown-up version of the Boy Scouts.

"Is Schädel really bringing the Aryan Giant with him?" The younger of the two asked.

"That was his wrestling name," the older man said. "Now that he's in the SS, he goes by Parsifal."

"Do you think they can make the inventor talk?"

"*Hauptsturmführer* Schädel is known for his interrogation techniques. If anyone can do it, it's him."

Cliff quickly ducked back behind the corner of the hangar, mentally cursing his luck. *Nazis!* Damn it, why did it *always* have to be Nazis? Ever since he found the rocket, it seemed like he was constantly bumping into those goose-stepping jerks.

There came the drone of approaching propellers, and Secord looked up to see an unmarked Lockheed Model 9 Orion coming in for a landing. As the two men walked out to greet the plane, Cliff leaned out as far he dared to get a peek at this *Hasenpfeffer* Schädel.

The door on the Orion's fuselage opened, and out stepped the biggest man he had seen since that love-crazed maniac Lothar met his fiery doom in Atlantic City. Standing nearly seven feet tall, with close-cropped hair the color of summer wheat and shoulders like an ox-yoke, the ex-wrestler wore a dark suit that seemed in constant danger of busting at the seams.

The giant unfolded a stepladder and then stepped back, clicking his heels as he came to full attention. The Silver Eagles did the same, their right arms shooting out in an unmistakable Nazi salute as a dark-haired man dressed in a nattily tailored pinstripe suit exited the plane.

Having rid itself of its passengers, the unmarked plane taxied around and took off, its departure drowning out most of the conversation between the Silver Eagles and the Nazi in the snooty suit.

"—regrets he couldn't be here to greet you himself, *Hauptsturmführer* Schädel. But we should have Ecstasy's invention in the hands of the fatherland in no time."

"Where are your men holding the traitor?" Schädel asked, speaking in flawless English.

"Not far from here. You'll be able to interrogate without interference."

"Very good," the SS officer said.

Cliff watched as the Nazis piled into the estate wagon, the man-mountain Parsifal literally squeezing himself into the backseat. From what little he'd overheard, some kind of inventor or scientist code-named Ecstasy had been kidnapped and was going to be tortured for information.

Once the Buick was gone, he ran to his car to retrieve his Rocketeer uniform from the rumble seat. He'd discovered the hard way that it paid to be prepared, and he now carried the rocket pack and helmet wherever he went.

Upon slipping the finned helmet onto his head, he depressed the control buttons fitted into the flight gauntlets and shot a hundred feet into the California sky.

Even though he had flown as the Rocketeer dozens of times, he still felt the same thrill he had the very first time he'd been propelled into the wild blue yonder. Flying a plane was nothing compared to winging through the air like a bird. It was the greatest thing in the world, second only to the feeling he got whenever he kissed his girl.

From his vantage point, it didn't take long to spot the Buick full of Nazis. If the Silver Eagles and their passengers noticed a man-shaped speck following them from above, they showed no signs of it.

Eventually the estate wagon pulled off at a small roadside motor court, the sign for which was covered by a banner that said, "Coming Soon: The Silver Eagle Motor-Hotel, Another Sterling Property."

Schädel and his escorts went into the cottage set farthest from the road, leaving the former wrestler to stand guard. Cliff landed in a clearing behind the motor court and, drawing his Mauser, he crept up on the cottage, positioning himself so he could look through the back window.

In the middle of the room was a woman tied to a chair, her head covered by a pillowcase. Four Silver Eagles—the two from the airfield, plus two Cliff had not seen before—and Schädel stood hovering around her. But what were a bunch of Nazis doing with a dame? Weren't they after some kind of top-secret weapon? Maybe she was the inventor's secretary, or perhaps his daughter?

"So, Ecstasy—I regret that we meet under such circumstances," Schädel said as he studied the medical instruments and hand tools arrayed atop the nearby dresser. "I was an admirer of your earlier... works." He picked up a scalpel, turning it to study the blade. "I'm afraid that once we begin our little...chat, you'll no longer be suited for your profession. But I have been told Herr Mandl will take you back regardless." He turned to the senior Silver Eagle. "You are *certain* I will not be disturbed?"

"The place is deserted. You can do whatever you want to her, and no one will hear a thing."

Cliff had seen all he needed. If there was anything that made his blood boil worse that Nazis, it was jerks who threatened to hurt women. It was time for the Rocketeer to make his move.

The giant called Parsifal raised his head as he heard a strange whistling sound, not unlike a bomb hurtling to earth. His cornflower-blue eyes widened at the sight of a man-shaped rocket swooping down from the sky toward the cabin. He lunged forward, trying to put himself between the human projectile and the picture window that looked out onto the courtyard, but it was too late.

"*Drop the knife!*" the Rocketeer shouted as he came through the window. The stunned fascists stared, openmouthed, at the fantastical figure that had literally crashed their little torture party. "*Step away from the girl!*" he commanded, gesturing with the Mauser for emphasis.

"Who are *you* to give me orders?" Schädel snarled.

"He's that rocket guy!" one of the younger Silver Eagles explained excitedly. "I seen him in the news reels!"

Cliff fumbled with the woman's restraints while trying to keep the others covered. Just as the last knot gave way, the door of the cottage exploded off its hinges as the hulking Parsifal charged into the room like an enraged gorilla.

The Rocketeer fired his Mauser at the rampaging giant, the bullet grazing Parsifal's bulging brow without slowing him down in the slightest. It was like throwing a rock at an oncoming freight train.

"Hold on tight, lady! And whatever you do, *don't* let go!" he shouted. With a mighty *whoosh* the Rocketeer shot back through the broken window, quickly leaving the Nazis behind.

Even with the added burden of a passenger, there was enough fuel in the rocket pack to fly back to the city. However, he had left his vehicle—along with his registration and other identification—back at the future home of the Silver Eagle Sky Port. If Schädel and his buddies decided to return to the deserted airfield, the car would lead them right to his doorstep.

As he swooped down beside the coupe, he flicked the gyrostabilizer on the jet pack so he could make a two-point landing without going ass-over-tea kettle. "There you go, ma'am, safe and sound, courtesy of the Rocketeer!" he said as he deposited his passenger onto terra firma. It was only then that he realized he had neglected to remove the pillowcase covering her head.

"Get this *verdammten* thing off me!" his passenger exclaimed, her accent surprisingly similar to that of her would-be interrogator.

"I'm sorry, ma'am," Cliff apologized as he removed the hood.

"Thank you!" Ecstasy said, shaking out her ebony curls. "And thank you for saving me from those *Schweine!*"

"Holy smokes!" Cliff gasped, his eyes widening in surprise as he saw the face of the woman he had just saved. "You're—"

"Hedwig Eva Maria Kiesler," the woman called Ecstasy said. "Better known as Hedy Lamarr."

"I don't get it," Cliff said as he drove them back into the city. Although he normally went out of his way to protect his "secret identity," he had removed his Rocketeer gear and returned it to the rumble seat, as driving with the helmet on was as dangerous as it was obvious. "What does Hitler want with *you?*"

"It's not Hitler so much as Göring," Hedy replied. "He wants to get his fat hands on my invention." She was slouched down in the passenger seat so as not to be recognized, not only by potential kidnappers, but by random fans, as well. Although Cliff still thought his Betty was the most beautiful woman in the world, Hedy Lamarr certainly gave her a run for her money.

"So *you* are the inventor they were talking about?"

"You find that hard to believe, simply because I'm a woman?" she asked with a humorless laugh. "You'd be surprised what hides behind a pretty face, Mister Secord."

"My girl Betty's proof of that," he admitted. "But who's this Mandl fellow he was talking about?"

"My first husband," she replied bitterly. "He is one of the richest men in Austria, if not Europe. I should have *known* he was still spying on me! I caught my maid going through the papers in my office a couple of weeks ago. I thought she was looking for tittle-tattle to sell to Hedda Hopper, but now I realize she was working for Mandl. I fired her on the spot, but the damage was done. I doubt she understood the nature of what she found, but my ex-husband is another story. No doubt he took the papers to Göring, hoping he might overlook the fact he is half-*jüdischen* and give him another munitions contract."

"Your old hubby sounds like a real peach."

"He is a ruthless businessman accustomed to arranging every-thing in his life as it suits him—including me. I fled our marriage because I could no longer stand how he thought he could buy everyone."

"Sounds like you and me share some pet peeves," Cliff smiled crookedly. "But why did Schädel and his pals call you Ecstasy?"

"I assume it is their code name for me," she replied vaguely. "It's the title of the movie that made me famous."

"That's the one where you, uh, chase the horse in the, uh..." Cliff trailed off, and his cheeks turned red.

"Nude?" Hedy finished with an amused smile. "You are a very brave and resourceful man, Mister Secord. Would you be interested in acting as my bodyguard for the next day or so? I will pay handsomely for your services."

"I don't work alone," he explained. "I've got a partner, of sorts. I may fly around with a super-scientific rocket strapped to my back, but I'm not really much of a nuts-and-bolts guy. However, my partner is pretty handy when it comes that stuff."

Hedy raised an immaculately sculpted eyebrow. "I'd love to meet him. I'm always interested in talking to fellow inventors."

"*Jumpin' Jehoshaphat!*" Peevy exclaimed as Cliff and his new client strolled into his workshop, his cigarette actually falling from its perch. "*Hedy Lamarr!*"

"And *you* must be the Mister Peabody I've heard so much about," the actress smiled graciously. "Your partner speaks most highly of you."

"He does, eh?" Peevy turned to give Cliff a quizzical stare. "Where in tarnation did you find *her*? Last I heard you were out scoutin' for a new hangar."

"The Rocketeer kind of stumbled into a Nazi plot to kidnap Miss Lamarr and steal a secret weapon."

"Nazis? *Again?*" the mechanic groaned. "I thought we sprayed for those."

"Do you mind telling me what you are working on?" Hedy asked, eyeing the engine seated on the workbench.

"I'm re-toolin' a Duesy engine so it'll fit in Cliff's coupe," he explained. "It should help him make a clean getaway, should the need arise."

"Most interesting," Hedy said as she studied the tools and equipment scattered about the machine shop. "I invent as a hobby, but I lack the skill and training to bring my ideas to life. I must find engineers and technicians to collaborate with, like my friend Mister Hughes. That's how I met George Antheil, my partner on the frequency hopper."

"The what-hopper?" Peevy frowned, scratching his head.

"A secret communication system that can't be detected or jammed," she explained.

Cliff gave a low whistle. "I can see why Göring would want to get his mitts on something like that. And I know firsthand just how determined Nazis can be when it comes to stealing secret technology."

"I devised the frequency hopper to pilot torpedoes via wireless remote control," Hedy said, warming to the subject. "I got the idea from a Philco II6RX console radio that was given to me. It has a wireless remote control that allows me to change the stations from across the room. The control is basically a one-tube radio that communicates on a fixed frequency with the console, which has a matching fixed-frequency accessory receiver inside the cabinet. That, in and of itself, is simple enough. But the problem is that radio signals are easy to locate and even easier to jam.

"Then it came to me: what if a radio transmitter and its receiver were synchronized to change their tuning at the same time, hopping together at random from frequency to frequency? It would make the radio signal not only 'invisible,' but also virtually impossible to interfere with.

"I explained the basics of the idea to a friend of mine, a brilliant experimental composer and pianist who is also an expert on making machines talk to each other. George succeeded in synchronizing four player pianos at the Carnegie Hall performance of his *Ballet Mécanique* back in 1927. That's where we got the idea of using identical rolls of paper in both the transmitter and receiver, with slots cut to encode the changes in frequency. When the slots roll over a control head, they trigger a vacuum mechanism similar to that in a player piano, except that instead of a pushrod moving a piano action, it closes a series of switches. Closing a specific switch connects one of several differently tuned condensers to an oscillator that generates a continually changing carrier wave. Each different condenser involves a different frequency on the carrier waves. With the signal hopping all over the radio spectrum in an arbitrary fashion, the transmission is impossible to jam. Even better: anyone monitoring a single frequency would not even realize a signal was being sent."

"That is truly ingenious, Miss Lamarr," Peevy said appreciatively. "Assumin' it works."

"Of *course* it works!" she replied, a bit testily. "A prototype has already been built, courtesy of Mister Hughes. That's what Schädel wants to bring back to his masters. But he doesn't know that the Navy already has it in their possession. In fact, I'm scheduled to demonstrate it to Pentagon officials tomorrow at the Long Beach Naval Station. That's why I need your help, Mister Secord."

"That reminds me," Cliff said, "I need to call Betty. Can I borrow your phone, Peev?"

"Knock yourself out," Peevy replied, nodding toward the wall-mounted telephone. "I'll keep Miss Lamarr company, assumin' she doesn't mind talkin' to an old coot."

"Of course I don't mind," Hedy said, eagerly pulling up a stool next to his workbench. "I *love* to talk shop."

Betty arrived dressed in a black pencil skirt and tight-fitting red sweater that accentuated her curves, as well as a pair of wedges that showed off her calves.

"That's my girl!" Cliff said as he kissed her hello. "Did you bring your theatrical makeup case?"

"Yes," she replied, "But what do you want it for?"

"You'll see," he said with a cryptic smile.

As Betty stepped into the workshop, her eyes widened at the sight of the raven-haired beauty talking to Peevy. "*Holy Toledo!*" she gasped. "What is *she* doing here?"

"Lying low from Nazis sent to kidnap her," Cliff explained.

"Nazis? *Again?*" Betty groaned, rolling her beautiful blue eyes in exasperation.

Hedy got up and approached Betty, studying her as if she were a statue up for auction. "Did I mention how I escaped my first husband's clutches?" she asked thoughtfully. "I exchanged clothes with my maid, who was the same size as me and had the same color hair. We could do the same thing, with your girlfriend. She's a bit short—but that can be fixed with the right pair of shoes. I'd have to completely redo her hair, but it *is* the right color..."

"*Excuse* me?" Betty said indignantly.

"Whoa! Hold on a second!" Cliff exclaimed. "I had Betty come over so we could use her makeup kit to give you a disguise, not use her as a decoy!"

"In my line of business, we would call her a 'stand-in,'" Hedy replied. "And it would only be for a couple of hours."

"A couple of potentially *dangerous* hours," Betty pointed out.

"A director friend of mine is going to be shooting a picture for Fox with Ida Lupino and Jean Gabin in a couple of weeks," Hedy replied. "I could introduce you..."

"Uh-uh! Absolutely not!" Secord said as he saw a familiar gleam appear in his girlfriend's big blue eyes. "No way!"

"Cliff, this is between me and Miss Lamarr," Betty said, silencing his protests with a stern looks. "Now, about this director friend of yours..."

Later that evening, a late-model sedan drove up the long, curving driveway that led to an L-shaped ranch house located near the top of Benedict Canyon. It pulled into the three-car garage, parking alongside a brand-new Cadillac convertible.

Four people exited the vehicle, one of whom was the famed Austrian actress who owned the house. She was accompanied by a dashing young man with tousled brown hair, an older man wearing a cap and wire-rim spectacles, and an elderly woman dressed in a frumpy frock with a wide-brimmed hat.

"Do you think we fooled 'em?" Peevy asked once the door was safely shut.

"If nothing else, we've got them scratching their pointy little heads," Cliff laughed.

"Can I take this stuff off?" Betty grumbled, fidgeting with the gray wig covering her hair.

"Make sure all the drapes are closed," Cliff replied.

"What makes you so sure they're watching the house?" Betty asked. "It's pretty isolated around here."

"This house may sit on six and a half acres, but that doesn't mean someone hiding in the hills with a pair of binoculars can't keep tabs on me," the movie star explained as she closed the curtains on the bay window that looked out onto the swimming pool and tennis court.

"How did they snatch you in the first place?" Betty asked.

"They forced my car off the road last night. I was returning from a party at Jimmy Cagney's place on Coldwater Canyon," the movie star explained. "One minute I was on the road, the next I was in a ditch and these dreadful men were dragging me from behind the wheel. They must have chloroformed me, because the next thing I knew, I was in that horrible little cottage." She visibly shuddered at the memory, only to swiftly collect herself. "Well, since you're staying overnight, I better show you to the guest rooms."

The trio followed the movie star down a hallway lined with framed photographs taken at different stages of her life. Here was Hedy signing her contract with MGM, skiing in the Alps, posed with co-star Charles Boyer on the set of *Algiers*, boating with her family on the Danube, having tea with co-star Peter Lorre on a German soundstage, taking her bows on the stage in Vienna and Berlin, playing with dolls under her father's desk.

"Here you go," their hostess said, gesturing to side-by-side doors. "They each have their own bathroom. One has two beds, the other only one. I'm no prude: I'll leave you three to decide who sleeps where and with whom. Come with me, Betty. If you're going to serve as my stand-in, we need to fix your hair and find something in my closet that will fit you."

Betty stared in amazement at the array of expensive cosmetics and French perfumes lined up along the vanity table.

"How long have you and Mister Secord been together?" the movie star asked as she casually combed out Betty's raven tresses.

"We met on the set of a serial in '37. I was an extra with a line or two, and Cliff was working as a stunt flier. We clicked, and we've been dating ever since."

"That's a long time to be together, by Hollywood standards," Hedy exclaimed with a laugh. "I've been divorced, married, and divorced again in the same amount of time!"

"Miss Lamarr...do you mind if I ask you a question?"

"Of course not."

"Do you ever regret doing that nude scene? I'm asking because I, uh, sometimes do some modeling—pinups, that kind of stuff."

"I *see*," Hedy said sagely. "I do regret the fact I did not warn my parents before they went with me to the premiere. Things between my father and I were never quite the same after that. But I am not ashamed, either. My advice is to keep as many clothes on as possible if you want to move out of pinups to something better."

"But Grable does pinups," Betty protested.

"Yes, but Grable keeps her bathing suit *on*," Hedy replied as she parted Betty's hair down the middle. "What does Cliff think about you posing for pinups?"

"He doesn't like it," Betty admitted. "And he gets really jealous sometimes."

"Whenever my first husband and I argued, he would always throw my nude scene in my face, even though that was what drew him to me in the first place."

"Why do guys act like that, Miss Lamarr?"

"Because they are men," Hedy replied. "And it is a man's world. And no matter our position in life, we are just women. Now hand me that curling iron."

Cliff was stretched out in the guest room with the solitary bed, his hands laced behind his head, when Betty entered sporting her new hairstyle—now wavier and parted down the middle—and a smart sweater and skirt set that belonged to Hedy.

"What do you think?" she asked as she modeled her new look.

"I think you're gorgeous, no matter what," he replied. "But I like you better with the bangs."

"I do, too," she agreed, sitting down beside him. "And this cardigan and skirt is a tad snug..."

"You don't hear *me* complaining. Say—what's that smell?" he asked, sniffing the air like a hunting dog.

"You like it? It's Chanel No. 5. Hedy let me try some of hers. She's got a *huge* bottle of the stuff—it must cost five hundred bucks!"

"No, that's not it." Cliff said. "Holy cow! Someone's cooking steak!" He sprang to his feet and bounded out of the room, leaving a nonplussed Betty sitting alone on the bed. "So long, Meatless Tuesday!" he crowed. "You know, a guy could get used to this Hollywood bodyguard business!"

The next morning the elderly couple exited the home of movie star Hedy Lamarr. The bespectacled older man, dressed in a cardigan sweater with patched elbows and wearing a flat cap, helped his frail companion down the sidewalk to the garage.

Hidden by the brush of the surrounding hills, a solitary figure armed with a pair of field glasses watched the old couple climb into the sedan and head down the long curving driveway toward the main road. Once they were gone, he pensively puffed on his ivory cigarette holder and adjusted the monocle in his left eye before resuming his vigil.

"It looks like we made a clean getaway," Cliff said as he checked the rearview mirror.

"Thank goodness!" Hedy sighed in relief, yanking off the hat and wig and throwing them into the back seat of the sedan. "I was about to suffocate!" She quickly wriggled out of the baggy, matronly dress, revealing a stylish skirt-and-jacket set underneath.

"I had no idea being Peevy would be this uncomfortable," Cliff agreed as he peeled off his own wig and hat. As he reached up to remove the wire-rims, he paused to scratch his nose through the empty eyepiece. "We should reach Long Beach in an hour or so— plenty of time before your demonstration."

"Good; I'll need it to spruce myself up," Hedy said, kicking off the unattractive low-heeled shoes that had been part of her disguise. She reached into the large handbag she'd brought with her and pulled out a pair of strappy high-heels. "These men from the Pentagon may be coming to see my invention, but they're *also* expecting to see a movie star."

"I hope Cliff comes back soon," Betty said as she opened the drapes.

"Me, too. I feel like a damned fool." Peevy reached up, out of habit, to give the brim of his cap a tug, only to nearly unseat the brown wig he was wearing. He also had exchanged his cardigan for Cliff's flight jacket, but that was as much of a disguise as he was willing to wear. He refused to shed his wire-rims because, damn it, how was he supposed to see?

He got up from his chair and walked across to room to the fireplace, resting his arm on the carved mantelpiece. As he reached into the front pocket of Cliff's jacket for a pack of matches to light his cigarette, his fingers brushed against the oiled metal of the .38 Hedy had given him before she left. Although its weight was reassuring, he wasn't in a big hurry to use it.

"Look at the time!" Betty exclaimed. "My stories are about to come on!" She went over to the Philco radio console in the living room and turned it on. There was a squawk of static as she fiddled with the dial. "I don't want to miss *The Goldbergs!*"

"Turn that thing off, will ya?" Peevy snapped.

"But I want to hear Molly say 'Yoo-hoo'!" Betty protested.

"Just do as I say, girl!" Peevy said, pulling the gun from his pocket as he peered out the window.

Betty shut off the radio. "Is something wrong?"

"I'm not sure," he replied, heading toward the kitchen. "I thought I heard something..."

There was a loud crash as the back door was kicked off its hinges. A second later an enormous, blond-headed man with fists the size of cured hams entered the kitchen.

Peevy raised his gun, but the Aryan Giant was already upon him, clamping a hand big enough to hide a bible about the mechanic's throat. Betty screamed as Parsifal lifted Peevy off the floor, hurling him aside like a rag doll. As she turned to flee, the front door flew open, and armed men in jackboots and light-gray shirts poured into the house.

"*Let go of me, you rat!*" she yelled as one of the Silver Eagles grabbed her, driving a high-heel spike into his instep. Suddenly a cloth smelling of ether was clamped over her nose. Her vision instantly went from color to black and white, and her knees buckled.

The last thing she saw, before the darkness claimed her, was the giant lifting Peevy off the floor and slinging him over his shoulder like a sack of grain.

Cliff was on U.S. 6, about fifteen minutes from the Long Beach Naval Station, when Hedy's handbag started to buzz like a cicada trapped in a tin can.

"*Holy crow!*" he yelped in surprise. "What have you got in there?"

The movie star did not reply, but instead pulled a handie-talkie out from her seemingly bottomless handbag. "This is Ecstasy," she said, speaking into the mouthpiece. "Come in, Mabuse. Over." Her brow furrowed as she listened to whoever was on the other end, then gasped. "Betty and Peevy have been taken captive!"

"*What!?!*" Cliff shouted, causing the sedan to abruptly swerve into another lane.

"Roger that, Mabuse," Hedy said grimly into the handie-talkie. "Alert M and The Count. I'll contact Lola and Pepe. Ecstasy out."

"What's going on? Why did you call yourself Ecstasy?" Cliff asked in confusion. "And who were you talking to?"

"That is the code name I go by in a certain club I belong to," she replied. "I asked one of the other members to keep an eye on my house. I also gave him instructions to contact me should anything happen. I left him with a working prototype of a modified handie-talkie that uses frequency hopping."

"I thought you needed a player piano to make that work?"

"The player piano is merely an *example* of the theory, *not* the device itself," Hedy replied with an exasperated roll of her eyes. "We've already succeeded in reducing the frequency hopper to the size of a pocket watch."

"Did this Mabuse fella say if Betty and Peevy were okay?"

"He said they seemed to be alive and in one piece—but who knows how long that will last once Schädel realizes he's been duped? However, he *did* overhear them talk about the Silver Eagle's 'nest.'"

"I know where it is. The Silver Eagles have been on our, uh, club's list for some time. It's off Sunset Boulevard, near Will Rogers's ranch. I can give you the map coordinates..."

"'List'? Code names? I take it this club ain't the Ladies Auxiliary!"

"You've done your job, as far as I'm concerned. I can drive myself the rest of the way," she replied. "You go save your friends."

Cliff left the highway and pulled onto a secluded street. He jumped out of the sedan and removed his Rocketeer gear from the trunk.

"Good luck, Cliff," Hedy said, leaning out the driver's side window. "And good luck to your friends."

"Thanks. We're all going to need it," he said as he shot off into the sky.

Thanks to the rocket pack, he could literally travel as the crow flies, cutting across the bay toward the Santa Monica Mountains. The map coordinates Hedy had given him, with the help of his navigator's wristwatch, was enough for him to find the secret hideout. Whether he arrived in time to save his girl and his best friend was another story.

As the Rocketeer zipped past first Redondo, then Manhattan Beach, he was too preoccupied to notice the sunbathers below, shouting in alarm. It did not cross his mind that in a country made uneasy by the rumblings of an approaching World War that he might be mistaken for an incoming missile. He was too busy worrying about Betty and what that Nazi rat bastard Schädel might be doing to her at that very moment.

When Betty opened her eyes, all she could see was darkness. At first she was afraid that she had been blinded, but then she realized there was a pillowcase over her head.

"As you can see, Herr Schädel," she heard a man's voice say, "my Silver Eagles have made good on my promise. Hedy Lamarr is now yours."

The hood covering Betty's head was roughly yanked away. She looked around and saw the great room of a hunting lodge, complete with dead animals mounted on the walls. She was tied to a chair, and next to her was Peevy, also trussed up like a holiday turkey, his brown wig askew. Although the mechanic's lower lip was swollen and his face bruised, he seemed otherwise unharmed.

Standing before them were two men. One wore the uniform of a German SS officer, while the other looked like a park ranger. A third man lounged in the background, smoking a cigar as he leaned against the stone fireplace. Hanging above the mantel was a large Nazi flag. The third man wore a silver pin in the shape of an American eagle on the lapel of his expensive suit.

"Finally! What do you think I am? A birdcage?" Betty snapped, trying to sound braver than she felt.

"*Was ist das?*" the Nazi officer yelled, pointing at Betty with a trembling finger. "That is *not* Hedy Lamarr!"

"B-but she was in the house—there was no other woman in there," the Silver Eagle stammered. "Who else *could* it be?"

"*Scheißekopf!*" Schädel shrieked, spittle flying from his lips as his face turned an intense shade of purple. "Don't you ever go to the cinema?"

"Only when they run Gene Autry pictures," the Silver Eagle replied sullenly.

"Thank you, Henry," the man with the cigar said, as if speaking to a not-particularly-bright child. "You may rejoin the others."

"Yes, General Sterling," the Silver Shirt replied, clicking his heels and lifting his arm in salute.

Schädel turned to glare at the man with the cigar. "You expect to overthrow the country from within with *that* kind of material?" he exclaimed in frustrated disbelief.

"My men are raw recruits, still in the early stages of training," Sterling replied evenly. "What they lack in finesse they more than make up for in loyalty. And funding. They all come from very wealthy families and are happy to pay for the privilege of serving the Führer and the fatherland. How else do you think I can buy up airfields and create training facilities throughout the country in anticipation of our glorious uprising? *Reichsführer* Himmel has assured me that if the Silver Eagles prove their usefulness in this matter, there will be a steady stream of SS troops arriving via Mexico to help turn my men into true storm troopers."

"You're that real-estate wheeler-dealer, Dudley Sterling, ain't you?" Peevy scowled. "The one that's been buyin' up all the airfields and jackin' up the rent."

"That is *one* of the identities I go by," Sterling replied icily. "However, I'm afraid that bit of cleverness on your part means you and the young lady won't be leaving here alive."

"I kind of took that as a given, anyway," Peevy said with a shrug.

Schädel snatched the wig from the mechanic's head, holding it aloft like a freshly claimed scalp. "I'll peel the *real* one off next, old man, if you don't tell me where the Jewess is!"

"Juice? Hell, son, you're in California!" Peevy replied sardonically. "There's plenty of orange juice to go around!"

"Then perhaps I should ask your lady friend instead, *jah?*" Schädel said, favoring Betty with a sly, cruel smile.

"Hold on a minute, bub—!" Although he tried to sound tough, Peevy's fear for the young woman was visible in his eyes.

Betty's mouth went dry with dread. She was used to men looking at her in a certain way—but not like a butcher sizing up a side of beef.

Schädel snapped his fingers, and the giant who had forced his way into Hedy's house appeared as if summoned from the ether. "Parsifal—start a fire in the grate. Perhaps a judiciously applied red-hot poker will jog our guests' memories..."

To anyone on the ground, the Silver Eagles' "nest" was invisible. It was safely hidden away from prying eyes at the bottom of a two-hundred-foot-deep box canyon. It was only accessible via a winding dirt road that led down from the surrounding mountain range or a set of steep concrete steps that connected to the hiking trail along the ridgeline above.

At the mouth of the canyon was a flagstone wall with a wrought-iron gate that was left over from when the property had been a hunting lodge for the wealthy. Hanging from the gate's cross-piece was a sign that read, STERLING RANCH. A pair of Silver Eagles armed with rifles patrolled the entrance. Past the gate was a dirt road that cut through thick stands of ponderosa pine, bougainvillea and overhanging eucalyptus, beyond which stood an oversized Swiss chalet surrounded by smaller outbuildings, including a large water tank.

From the air, Cliff could see the steep slopes of the canyon had been terraced and irrigated and were thick with nut, fruit and olive trees. There was also, ironically, a "victory" vegetable garden.

Maintaining a high enough altitude to keep the sound of the rocket pack from calling attention to him, Secord was able to count at least two dozen Silver Eagles armed with rifles and small sidearms milling about the grounds.

His attention was caught by a solitary guard ambling about on the far side of the orchard, looking more bored than attentive. Seeing his chance, the Rocketeer swooped down on the unwary Silver Eagle like a hawk going after a rabbit.

"What the hell—?!" the startled guard hollered as he stared in disbelief at the treetops beneath his flailing jackboots.

"The girl and the old man—where are they?"

"They're in the chalet!" the terrified Silver Eagle wailed. "Just put me down!"

"Have it your way, bub," the Rocketeer replied, letting go of his reluctant passenger.

The Silver Eagle plummeted twenty feet into the open water tank, landing with a mighty splash that raised a column of water ten feet high.

The giant Parsifal prodded at the fire burning in the hearth with a poker, then thrust the tool deep into the heart of the flames. Once its tip turned cherry red, he handed the poker to Schädel, who accepted it as casually as he would a drink at a cocktail party. Betty struggled against her bonds as the Nazi approached her, unable to take her terrified eyes away from the glowing iron he held in his hand.

"You must understand, *Fräulein*," the SS officer said, waving the poker in the air like a conductor's baton. "I take no pleasure in this. This is merely my duty, nothing more, nothing less. I was sent to this country to capture the Jewess code-named Ecstasy—you know her as Hedy Lamarr—and return her to Berlin. Failing that, I am to dispose of her. Her celebrity will not save her. My superiors are not very understanding when it comes to failure. And, as "General" Sterling so kindly pointed out, neither of you will be leaving this place alive, anyway. But if you tell me what I want to know, you *will* at least be able to have an open casket at your funeral…"

Suddenly there was the sound of breaking glass. Schädel automatically looked up at the skylight overhead, only to see the soles of a pair of boots rushing toward his face. The force of the Rocketeer's landing carried the Nazi to the floor and sent the glowing poker flying from his hand.

With a wordless bellow, Parsifal charged like a bull going for a matador's cape. Cliff snatched up the fallen poker and swung it at his attacker, only to have Parsifal catch it in mid-arc. Every muscle in Secord's arm and shoulder screamed as he tried to wrest the weapon free, but the Aryan Giant's grip was as unbreakable as it had been in the wrestling ring.

When immovable objects meet with irresistible force, something has always got to give, and as it turned out, that something was the poker, which began to bend in the direction of the Rocketeer before finally snapping in two.

As Parsifal surged forward, Cliff threw a roundhouse at the ex-wrestler's head. The Nazi absorbed the blow as if it were a love tap. The Aryan Giant threw his powerful arms around the Rocketeer in a bear hug and began to squeeze the breath from his opponent.

Cliff tried to go for the Mauser on his belt, but it was impossible to move. It was like he was a rabbit caught in the crushing coils of a python.

"Let go of him, you big ape!" Betty shouted, kicking at Parsifal's shin with an untied leg. The former wrestler did not so much as flinch, and merely gave her a contemptuous side-glance.

The diversion of Parsifal's attention barely lasted three seconds, but it was enough for Cliff to press the thumb studs fitted into his flight gauntlets.

With a thunderous *whoosh*, the Rocketeer shot toward the roof, a startled Parsifal in tow, driving the Nazi's skull into the crossbeam of the roof.

Cliff cut the thrusters the moment he felt Parsifal go limp, allowing the unconscious Nazi to drop like a stone, while he used the rocket pack's built in gyro control to land safely.

The moment his boots hit the floor, the sound of men shouting in alarm, followed by the unmistakable chatter of submachine gunfire, erupted from outside. A moment later, a panic-stricken Silver Eagle ran into the chalet.

"General Sterling! The main gate has been breached, and the perimeter guards have been neutralized! We're under attack! What do we do?"

As if to underscore this statement, a metal canister came crashing through the front window, spewing clouds of thick, dark smoke. The leader of the Silver Legion tossed aside his cigar, pulled a handkerchief from his breast pocket and, using it to cover his nose and mouth, ran from the room.

"Sterling! Come back here, you *Schweinehund!*" Schädel shouted as he got back onto his feet. "*Ach!* I should have expected as much from a man who would betray his own country!" Pulling a knife from his belt, the SS officer sliced away Betty's restraints and yanked her to her feet, holding her in front of him as a human shield.

"Surrender, Schädel—it's all over!" Cliff said as he pointed his Mauser at the Nazi. "Your mission is a failure, no matter what! Hedy's demonstrating her invention to the Pentagon bigwigs even as we speak!"

"*Nein!*" Schädel spat. "I refuse to surrender to a...a...flying *hood ornament!*" As the Nazi backed toward the door, dragging a frightened Betty along with him, Cliff glimpsed what looked like a pair of figures moving stealthily through the smoke filling the room.

"I don't think you have a choice, buddy," the Rocketeer said.

"There is *always* a choice," Schädel replied, pressing his knife against Betty's neck. "You can choose to let me go, or I can choose to slit her throat. It's up to you which; will it b—*urk!*"

The Nazi's eyes widened, as if he had just remembered something important. He then loudly coughed, sending forth a spray of bright red blood. Stunned, Schädel let go of his captive and placed a trembling hand to his dripping mouth. He stared dumbly for a moment at the scarlet staining his fingers before dropping to the floor.

Betty turned to see what had become of her captor, only to find herself staring down at a short, slight man with curly hair and bulging eyes.

"Hello," the little man smiled as he cleaned the blood from his switchblade knife with a handkerchief.

Betty gasped and spun back around, searching for her boyfriend in the rising smoke, only to find a strange, menacing figure dressed in a long black cape stalking toward her.

Although the lower half of the strange man's face was hidden, she could see his eyes peering over his raised forearm, burning like those of the damned. Overcome by smoke and shock, she gave a tiny scream and fell into a swoon. The man in the opera cape quickly moved forward to catch her before she could hit the ground.

"Why ees it no one is *ever* happy to see us, Count?" the little man with the big eyes sighed wistfully as he cut the ropes binding Peevy.

"*Typecasting*, my dear M," his companion replied with an even thicker accent. "It vill be the death of us all!"

"*I'll* take over now, if you don't mind, Dracula," Cliff said, stepping forward to claim Betty, only to freeze upon seeing the caped man's unnaturally pallid—and familiar—face.

"Don't be afraid, young man," The Count said with a sardonic smile. "I von't bite."

"Cliff, I haven't gone nuts, have I?" Peevy asked as he got to his feet, staring at the macabre duo before them.

"If you have, then I'm right along with you, buddy," Secord replied. "Help me get Betty outside—she needs some fresh air."

Just then the front door of the chalet was kicked open, revealing a slender, middle-aged woman with softly curled blond hair, dressed in a man's suit and carrying a submachine gun.

"Sorry I'm late, darlink."

"Eet's about time you showed up, Lola!" the man called M chided.

"I vas just seeing vhat the boys in the backroom vere haffing!" she replied with a throaty laugh.

As Cliff and Peevy escorted the half-conscious Betty out onto the front porch, they were greeted by yet another familiar face, this one belonging to a certain Gallic matinee idol famous for inviting beautiful young women to the Kasbah. Like Lola, he was toting a recently fired tommy gun.

"The young lady—is she hurt?" the matinee idol asked as Cliff lowered the woozy Betty onto the front porch stairs.

"She's just dazed, that's all," he replied, quickly putting himself between his girlfriend and the French heartthrob.

"Where is Schädel?" the leading man asked, looking about anxiously. "Did he escape?"

"Only to hell," M said, spitting on the ground for emphasis. "Did the Silver Eagles geeve you any trouble, Pepe?"

"They all ran like rabbits the moment Lola and I opened fire!" Pepe laughed. "These Yankee-Doodle Nazis do not have the belly for fighting, n'est-ce pas?"

"Of course!" M snorted in disgust. "They're a bunch of eed-iotic cowards! Why else would they be here?"

"Where's that overgrown wrestler?" Pepe asked, looking about cautiously.

"He's laid out on the floor of the chalet, colder than last night's supper," Cliff said as he removed his helmet. "Last time I looked, he was still breathing, but you better tie him up before he comes to."

"I'll handle that," Lola said. "I learned a few rope tricks shooting that cowboy movie vith Jimmy."

Now that she was exposed to some fresh air, Betty's eyelids began to flutter, and she suddenly started to cough. "Where am I?" she moaned. "How did I get outside?"

"Are you okay, my dear?" The Count asked solicitously.

"She vill be, if you and M aren't the first things she sees," Lola growled, pushing the horror-movie actor aside. The famous cabaret singer removed a flask from the man's jacket she was wearing and handed it to the young starlet. "Haff a snort, dahlink. A little schnapps is good for vhat ails you."

"Thank you," Betty said. She tilted back the flask, only to nearly choke on its contents when Lola gave her a knowing wink.

"I don't mean for this to sound ungrateful," Cliff said, addressing the strangest cavalcade of Hollywood stars he'd ever seen. "I mean, I *know* who all of you are—but *what* the hell are you *doing* here?"

"We are the Hollywood Resistance, Mister Secord," an unfamiliar voice replied. Cliff turned and saw a distinguished-looking middle-aged man wearing a monocle and smoking an ivory cigarette holder standing behind him.

"Say—ain't you that von Stroheim fella?" Peevy asked.

"*Unglaublich*," the man with the cigarette holder groaned, catching his monocle as it dropped from its perch. "Allow me to introduce myself—I am called Mabuse; I am the director of our little underground commando unit. You have already met our gadget master and communications officer, Ecstasy, and now you have met M, Pepe, Lola and, of course, The Count. Most of us knew and worked with one another back in Europe, before Hitler and his henchmen poisoned the hearts and minds of our countrymen. Had we remained in our respective homelands, we would have lost not only our livelihoods, but our lives, as well. In my case, I lost my own wife to Hitler's siren song.

"One by one, we fled Europe to Hollywood to escape the Nazis, *ja*? But imagine our astonishment where we arrived and found the fascists *here* as well. Some, like the German American Bund, were simple enough to identify. But others, like the Silver Eagles, hid their agenda while playing at being patriots. You Americans tend to view men like Dudley Sterling as eccentric or dismiss them as crackpots, especially in California, but we who saw the Nazis rise to power know them for what they truly are: fascist snakes in the grass, waiting for the moment strike.

"We watched our homelands succumb to this cancer—and we have sworn an oath not to allow our new homeland to fall as well. Mostly we keep an eye on those we suspect of being Nazi sympathizers." Mabuse scowled and readjusted his monocle. "Speaking of which—where is our self-appointed General Sterling?"

"He took a powder the minute he heard the gunfire," Cliff explained.

"Do you theenk we've seen the last of him and the Silver Legion?" M asked.

"I wouldn't bet on it," Peevy replied. "He was braggin' to his Nazi pal about havin' other camps like this, scattered all over the country. He was plannin' some kind of overthrow, with direct help from

Himmler. I also got the impression that Dudley Sterling might not be his real moniker."

"Whatever his true identity and plans, should he resurface in Los Angeles, he will find the Hollywood Resistance waiting for him," Mabuse said grimly. "But come—we must get out of here. We are not, shall we say, kosher with the local authorities."

"But what do we do with Parsifal?" Pepe asked.

"Leave that to me," Cliff said with a crooked grim. "I know a guy called Doc who's big on rehabilitation through applied brain surgery. If it works on criminals, it should work on Nazis, too."

Cliff Secord sat in his office of his hangar at Chaplin Aero-drome, staring at the drift of bills piled atop his desk. At least he no longer had to worry about a rent hike. Turns out the check Dudley Sterling used to buy the Chaplin Airdrome bounced higher than a rubber ball, and now the deal was off, Sterling was nowhere to be found, and the old landlords were back in charge. But Nazis, Hollywood commandos and secret weapons aside, he was still no closer to making ends meet than we was before the whole mess started.

"There he is! See, I told you we'd find him here!"

Cliff looked up to see Betty and Hedy standing in the doorway "Miss Lamarr! What a surprise!" he said, rising from his chair. "How did your meeting go?"

"It would seem that the Pentagon considers me far more useful selling war bonds than making weapons," the movie star replied.

"You mean they're not going to use your frequency hopper?" Cliff exclaimed in disbelief.

"I'm afraid not," she sighed. "Although the government says they will grant me a patent."

"Still, what a lousy thing to do, after all the trouble you went through—!"

"That is always the risk an inventor faces—resistance to the new," the actress replied sanguinely. "And this is not the first time I have been valued more for my beauty than my brains."

"Boy, do I know how *that* feels!" Betty agreed.

"But, who knows?" Hedy shrugged. "Maybe some day, after this terrible war is over, my frequency hopper will be used for what it was designed—exchanging data wirelessly via mobile devices. Anything is possible.

"But the real reason I came looking for you, Cliff, was to pay you what I owe you for your services as bodyguard," she said, handing him a cashier's check. "I trust this is enough?"

Cliff stared, openmouthed, at the zeroes in front of the decimal point. "This is *more* than generous, Miss Lamarr!"

"It's only fair," Hedy replied with a shrug. "None of this would have happened if I had been more careful with my correspondence with Mabuse about the prototype. And you and your friends went above and beyond on my behalf. I do not take such things lightly. And I'll be sure to recommend you in the future, should anyone I know need your...unique services.

"And as for you," Hedy said, turning to face Betty, "take this note to the casting office at Fox. Mabuse, I mean, Fritz will be expecting you on the set."

"Thank you, Miss Lamarr," Betty said humbly.

"Just call me Ecstasy," she said with a wink.

"What a remarkable woman," Betty sighed in admiration as she watched the movie star leave the hangar. "It's a crying shame the Pentagon decided not to use her invention."

"Yeah, she's really something," Cliff agreed, slipping his arm about Betty's waist. "But to be honest, I can't see what possible use it might have during peacetime. I mean—who would want to carry a walkie-talkie everywhere they go?"

THE
END

FLYING DEATH

by

ROBERT HOOD

October 28, 1943. Morning. The Mountains Behind Santa Barbara

As he dragged himself from the tangle of twigs and leaves he'd crashed into, the first thing Cliff Secord thought was: "Peevy's gonna kill me!"

The second thing was "What the heck *was* that?"

Everything had gone swimmingly at first. Peev's modifications to his jet pack had worked like a charm. Extra speed, upgraded maneuverability and, best of all, greatly extended flight time had been the aim, and the engineer had hit the target spot-on. He might be a grouchy old coot, but he knew his stuff. Cliff had flown all the way from L.A., over Santa Barbara and into the Santa Ynez Mountains before he realized he might've gone too far.

Mountains, valleys and rugged forest spread out for miles in every direction. Looking down on it, streaking through the open sky, Cliff actually felt like the hero the newsreels sometimes made him out to be. What a glorious sensation! Made him feel in control of his life. He wasn't just some reckless pilot with a rocket pack and an overactive imagination. For a while, at least, he was the genuine article. He'd lost himself in the moment.

Big mistake!

From this height, he had a clear view into a long, deep valley otherwise hidden by rugged mountain terrain. And rising from the valley through a rolling green fog was a dirigible!

"Holy Hannah!" he muttered. It had to be Nazis. He'd heard about the Germans using airships to drop bombs, though he'd also heard that after the Hindenburg disaster they'd stopped. Reportedly Göring had ordered the entire zeppelin fleet destroyed a few years back, but maybe they'd developed something new…

Cliff banked and flew toward the airship. It wasn't a huge one, nowhere near the size of Herr Zeppelin's behemoths, but clearly it had a rigid frame. Very stylish—and well armed, too. *A battle-zeppelin?* thought Cliff. It rose fast, though not faster than him. In no time, he drew close enough to see the face of the pilot through the airship's observation window. The man didn't see him. Cliff waved, giving the mustachioed ponce a one-finger salute.

Bullets shrieked past, some of them flashing in the sunlight. Cliff jerked at the realization. A couple of slugs came straight toward him, too late to evade, but somehow they missed. Lucky, and way too close for comfort. The near-hit dampened Cliff's high spirits. He began to veer away. Then something turned the world into swirling chaos.

Cliff saw it first out of the corner of his eye—a shimmering green wave rushing over the mountains from the east. Was it the same green mist the dirigible had appeared through? As he glanced around, it hit him, and his mind shrank to a white dot. The wave pushed him into a tumble, snuffing out his rockets. He began to fall, his arms and legs flapping like a tossed doll's as he tried to get oriented and restart the jet pack before it was too late.

Then he saw an impossible sight: the sky filled with rocket-men, squadrons of them, flying in formation high above. They were translucent, illusory. But even through the rush of the air around him, Cliff could hear the roar of their twin-jet engines (different from his single-jet rocket pack, he noted) and smell the burn-off of their fuel. They wore helmets similar to his own. On the chest plate of their militaristic uniforms, however, each bore the insignia of the Third Reich. And there! A spaceship of the kind that appeared on the covers of pulp magazines. A genuine flying saucer! What the hell was going on?

Before he could think of an answer, he collided with something—and the world, rocket squads and all, swirled around him in a flurry of light and dark.

A hunk of broken wood pressed into his back. Cliff pushed it aside. As he shifted his elbow, it squished into a soft but bony object. The thing groaned. Cliff rolled away, desperately trying to control his dizziness. Instinctively he knew he was still aloft, in some sort of craft.

He saw he'd landed on a man in a pilot's uniform, which was torn now and speckled with blood, punctured by shards of glass and splintered wood. From his mustache, Cliff recognized the man as the pilot of the airship. He was conscious enough to register discomfort, but little else. He groaned again. "Sorry," Cliff muttered. Obviously he'd crashed through a window of the dirigible's observation deck, taking out the pilot in the process. The whole cabin was tilted at a 45-degree angle.

"*Wir gehen unter!*" someone yelled. "*Achten Sie auf den Berg!*"

Two crewmen grappled with the steering wheel and the balance mechanisms—but to little avail. Beyond them, through a window on the downward side of the cabin, Cliff could see the rapidly approaching mountains—a jagged rock-face they weren't going to avoid.

"You! Rebel dog!"

One of the crewmen had gained enough composure to turn a handgun on Cliff.

"You haft done this!"

"Not me!" Cliff held his hands out in a placating manner. "Didn't you see it? The green wave!"

"*Sterben, Amerikanischen Hund!*" the man growled. He fired the gun.

But as he did so, the entire airship shimmered, time seemed to stretch and slow and then, in an instant, the dirigible disappeared. Cliff had the impression of seeing the bullet with his name on it begin to fade before it reached his chest. He thought he felt it move through him—a vibrating sensation that ached momentarily and then was gone. Surely such a thing was impossible.

Impossible or not, the disappearance of the dirigible meant he now had no solid floor beneath him. As time sped up again, he realized he was tumbling earthward. The rugged ground rushed toward him, fast. Fighting the wind, Cliff pressed down on the ignition stud under his thumb, praying the jet pack would work. With a loud bang and burst of intense heat, the rocket on his back roared back to life—except he was still heading downward.

"No!" he screamed as the ground came at him even faster. He released the right-hand button and angled his finned helmet, swerving away. The top of a pine tree scraped against his boots. His jet engine spluttered.

He looked upward into a clear blue sky. No sign of dirigibles, flying saucers or squadrons of rocketeers.

Then his rocket engine gave one last gasp and cut out altogether, and he crashed back into the trees.

It took him two full days to trudge, scramble, and stagger across the rugged mountain landscape, carrying his jet pack and a massive headache.

He'd been lucky. No broken bones. Just an abundance of bruises and scratches. He hadn't been able to get the damn jet pack to work again. It'd splutter and cough and complain before pushing clouds of smoke out into the crisp mountain air. Without any proper tools at hand, Cliff soon concluded that no amount of finger-fiddling was going to get him airborne. And as no one knew where he was, walking out was his only option.

He'd quickly come to accept that the squadrons of flying Nazis, the dirigible and the flying saucer had all been some sort of hallucination, perhaps caused by fuel fumes from the jet pack. Why not? Made more sense than what he thought he'd experienced. A dirigible he might have believed. But squadrons of rocketeers? And that flying saucer? It was pure *Looney Tunes*.

He figured he still had enough fuel to get home, if only he could work out what was wrong with the jet pack.

Yeah, Peevy was gonna kill him, all right. He would've been mad enough even if Cliff hadn't smashed up his baby. He'd told Cliff not to go out by himself to test the modifications he'd made. "I'll shadow ya in the car, boy!" he'd said. "We do things right, okay? Not in the boneheaded way you seem to prefer!"

But when Peev had been called away to make emergency repairs to some goofball's stunt plane, and at a premium rate, no less, Cliff had gotten impatient and headed out on his lonesome. He didn't need a nanny watching over him. How long would it take to fly to Santa Barbara and back, anyway?

Night in the Santa Ynez Mountains was bone-chillingly cold. Luckily his Rocketeer gear gave decent protection against it, especially as he was wearing overalls over the top. He held out in a shallow cave, once he'd checked it was unoccupied, and set off westward again the next morning. No breakfast. But he came across a small creek with fresh-looking water—running freely, so he figured it'd be safe enough to keep him going. After a second night, though, he was starving.

It was pure luck that he stumbled across a track that looked frequently used. No one decided to use it while he was there, but it did lead him to a bigger road. After a while, a park ranger happened along in a jeep. Cliff endured some tense and rather suspicious questioning until the ranger realized who he was.

"Can't be too careful," the ranger said. "Since the Ellwood Oil Field got bombarded last year by that Jap U-boat, folks've been a tad nervy."

Cliff nodded. Could there be a connection between U-boat activity along the coast and the hallucinations he'd experienced?

"Turned out to be nothin' much," the ranger said. "But ya never can tell, eh? Bad times."

After a long drive that required him to entertain the ranger with tales of derring-do—most of them duly fictionalized—as well as a solemn promise not to reveal his true identity (he'd been quick enough to give a false name anyway), Cliff found himself deposited outside a dump reputed to be the habitat of a local "mechanic." "Ol' Sam'll be able to help ya!" said the ranger through his ill-groomed mustache.

◆

Thankfully the helpful ranger had been able to give him an old duffel bag to store his gear in; his overalls still looked presentable, though he knew he could use a bath, badly. Cliff thanked him, but before shutting the door decided to ask the question that had been rattling around in his mind for much of the trip.

"Um," Cliff said, "You heard of any reports about strange stuff happenin'?"

"Strange stuff?" The ranger frowned.

"Objects in the sky. Weird planes. Things like that."

The ranger scowled. "The folks round here are pretty down-to-earth, Mister Rocket Man. Don't go in for all that flyin' saucer nonsense like they do down in Los Angeles."

"Right. Of course." Cliff shut the door and waved him off.

The ramshackle buildings might have been a gas station once. He doubted it would've attracted much passing trade even in better times. It was too far from anywhere, and there was only one rather dusty pump. Still, it probably supplied locals with supplies for their tractors and the like. A larger structure with big doors was no doubt the workshop, rising as it did from a mass of old tires and rusty metal. Next to it was a smaller building that appeared to be residential as well as functioning as a shop front.

As Cliff trudged over in the direction of the workshop, a lanky guy who looked about fifty came striding out from whatever hidey-hole he'd been napping in. Like Cliff, he was dressed in overalls, but his were similar to the ones Peevy wore when engaged in really messy work, only much worse. Like the ranger, the man radiated suspicion. Seeing Cliff bathed in the fading light, the attendant stopped short, eyes narrowed, thin arms crossed defensively.

"Hi," said Cliff. "I need assistance. The ranger said you were the man around here could fix anything with a motor."

"Yeah?" the man said, brightening a bit.

Cliff opened the duffel bag and held up his jet pack. "This thing's not working. I need a skilled mechanic to take a look."

The man squinted at it.

"It's a sort of jet engine," Cliff offered. "I'm a stunt pilot, and I was testing it. In secret like, before putting it in my act, you understand?"

The mechanic looked doubtful, but Cliff could tell he was curious and willing to accept the explanation.

He ploughed on. "I've had a bit of an accident while...um, while practicing. Got a bit off course. Had some other problems."

More squinting, this time directly at Cliff.

"You look like that Rocketeer guy I seen in the papers."

"That's right. I'm trying to work out how he does it. For my act. Figure I could just about join any circus around if I could fly like the Rocketeer."

The mechanic smoothed his tangled hair. He looked less doubtful now.

"Reckon you could." He took the jet pack from Cliff and turned it over in his hand. "What's wrong with it?"

"Just stopped working. Still got fuel, so it ain't that. I didn't build it myself. Partners with a guy works at Hughes. Weekend inventor, but he's smart enough to stay on the ground."

The man turned it over, giving it a more careful inspection. "Might take me awhile, but I think I can get the measure of it," he said. "You can use the phone in the office if ya need to...phone your buddy or anythin'. I'll add it to your bill. Every call is long-distance out here."

"Thanks. Hey, there ain't anywhere I can clean up a bit before I go traipsing into your place, is there?"

"Out back of the workshop. Ain't much, but I use it meself. Daughter gets a mite tetchy if I come in covered in grease. Could be a clean towel under the sink if ya lucky."

"Thanks."

"Once you're decent, ya can have a snack while ya waitin'. My Mary makes great apple pie. You look kinda beat, you don't mind my sayin'."

Ol' Sam was right about the washroom. So pokey it was hard to turn around in, with a basin not much bigger than a soup bowl. After lots of twisting and balancing on one leg, scrubbing with a thin bar of soap, a not-too-filthy cloth and lots of icy cold water, Cliff didn't feel as much like a hobo as he had. He even managed to spruce up his overalls and boots a bit.

He headed over to the shop front. Mary of great-apple-pie fame turned out to be a very cute blonde with big eyes and a flirtatious attitude. Ol' Sam must've warned her he was coming. The girl showed no surprise as he stuck his head around the door, and the way she asked if he wanted coffee suggested something more than apple pie might be on offer.

"Coffee, no milk. And a slice o' pie. Make that several slices. I'm starvin.' Mind if I use the phone?"

She checked him out, her big, bright eyes scanning up and down. Cliff was conscious that even cleaned up he probably looked rather down at the heel. But she smiled sweetly and nodded him toward the office.

As it happened, neither Peevy nor Betty answered his call. It was about seven o'clock, and Betty at least should've been home. No doubt she was out on the town. He tried several times, without result.

Mary had his order carefully laid out on a table by the time he came back out. She gave him that smile again—and he suppressed the urge to flirt with her. Betty was his girl, wasn't she? Okay, she resisted long-term commitment, always yabberin' on about establishing her career and stuff. Yet despite that, he couldn't just let her go. One day soon, he'd learn what the heck she really wanted him to be. He'd win her over. Or find a way to forget her. Right now, though, givin' in to some boondocks bobbysoxer wouldn't be good form.

After mediocre coffee, four large slices of decent pie and lots of coy staring from Mary, he rang Betty's number again. This time someone answered. It was a woman's voice, though not one he recognized.

"Who's this?" he snapped.

"I think I get to ask that question first, buster," the woman on the other end snapped back at him.

"I'm looking for Betty. This *is* her number, ain't it? Who are you?"

"Edith. A friend of hers."

Right. Edith was Betty's new project, but Cliff hadn't met her yet. She was a secretary, or trying to be. Got laid off and kicked out of her digs when she missed a rent payment. Betty was letting her stay over for a while.

"So can I speak to Betty?"

"Who's asking?"

Cliff frowned. "Cliff. Her boyfriend."

"Sure you are." Sassy skepticism.

"I am!"

"If you were Cliff, you'd know where she was 'cause she'd be with you right now."

"What?"

"They went out of town. Together. So you can take a long walk off a short pier, jerk. And don't call back!"

She hung up.

Cliff rang back, twice, but both times no one answered. What the hell was that all about? How could Betty be out of town with her "boyfriend" when he was right here trying to call her? The Edith woman was clearly demented. Either that or...Cliff punched the wall. Another guy? How could that be possible?

He had to speak to Peevy, who was surely wondering where he'd gone. Peevy'd know what was goin' on. He tried ringing him again. No go.

Cliff slammed the receiver down and left the office. From behind the counter the girl looked at him hopefully.

"Sorry, miss," Cliff said. "Duty calls and all that! I'll better go check how the old guy's doin."

"That's Sam. My father."

Cliff smiled and stood. To his surprise the main door suddenly opened. Ol' Sam was standing there, still wearing that suspicious look on his mug and carrying the jet pack.

"Fixed," he said. He put it down on the floor.

"What? Already?"

"Carby needed adjustment—a bit out of alignment, that's all. Tightened a few other parts, too. Seein' how banged up it is, I'd say you're some lucky feller."

"Yeah, I guess I am, all right. So, it was just an adjustment?"

Ol' Sam shrugged. "Yep—helps to know what ya doin."

Cliff grinned. "That's what Peevy always says."

"Well, yer friend ain't wrong."

"That's fantastic. What do I owe—?" But Ol' Sam had turned away and was gone.

Cliff looked at Mary. "So what do I owe ya?"

"Nothing, sir," she said coyly. "We like to help those in need." Her smile nearly made him change his mind. If Betty could two-time on him, why couldn't he do the same back at her?

"Look, I'm just some guy, and I'm not broke." He handed the girl all the dollars he had. "Keep the change."

As usual, the light was on in Peevy's workshop. He'd still be tinkering away at the exhaust system he'd been tinkering with before Cliff left. Persistence was his middle name.

"Hey, Peev!" Cliff yelled as he strode through the door. "I'm back!"

Peevy's glance in his direction could have lowered the temperature of a Popsicle.

"Again?"

"What d'ya mean 'again'? I just got back."

The mechanic's eyes narrowed behind his spectacles.

Cliff moved closer. "What's the deal, Peev? You're actin' like I got leprosy or sumthin'. Sorry for takin' so long. I had an accident. What sorta welcome home is this?"

"Welcome home?" Peev growled. "What about yesterday's homecoming, ace? What d'ya call that bit a theater then?"

"I dunno what you're talkin' about, Peev." Cliff raised his voice as his impatience threatened to spiral out of control. "Look, I'm sorry I took off without ya. But I ain't got time to play dumb games, you old goose. I wanta know what's going on with Betty."

"We've been through that once already!"

Cliff clenched his fists in frustration. "You're outa ya flippin' mind, Peev."

"Gonna hit me now?"

"I might. Knock some sense into ya."

Low growling from the shadows distracted him. Crouched in the corner among some tool boxes was Butch, his canine pal, big eyes staring from a face taut with attitude.

"Hey, Butch! Give us a hug!"

Butch growled some more.

"What's up with Butch?"

"What d'ya expect? Ya kicked him pretty hard!"

"Bull, I did!"

Peevy came close, gesturing with a wrench. "You got some nerve, boy. Ya turn up actin' like a goddamn fascist, abuse Butch, threaten me and demand info ya already know. Now ya plead ignorance. What a load of—"

"When was this?"

"Last night, of course. Geez—"

"Yesterday I was still in the damn mountains, freezin' my bum off!"

"I'm not stupid, Secord!"

Confusion had bled the knee-jerk anger Cliff had been feeling. "Tell me this ain't some kind of joke?"

"It was no flamin' joke, boy."

Peevy glared. A muscle in one side of his cheek began to twitch.

Cliff turned to Butch. Dogs were way more intuitive than people. Whatever had happened last night, he'd recognize Cliff as the real thing and not some imposter going around besmirching his good name. He crouched and extended a hand toward Butch, who was still lurking in the shadows. At least he'd stopped growling.

"It's me, Butch. The real me. You can tell the difference, can't ya? Better than my so-called friends!" Cliff glanced at Peevy but got no response. "Come on, boy. Show the knucklehead here you're a better judge of character than he is!"

For a few moments, Butch did nothing. A hesitant whimper emerged from deep in his chest.

"It's Cliff, Butchie. Honest to God, it is."

Butch made a tentative movement toward him. Ears back, sniffing the air, he approached Cliff's outstretched fingers. When he got close, his nostrils flared, sucking in whatever telltale Secordish scents were being exuded by Cliff's skin. Then, with a yelp, Butch leapt. Cliff tensed, but it was a huge tongue that slapped across his cheek, not canine fangs.

"Atta boy!"

The dog yapped excitedly as Cliff hugged him. Butch's floppy jowls looked like they were grinning now.

"See?" said Cliff, turning to Peevy.

Peevy grunted. "If he weren't you," the mechanic said, still frowning, "he dang well looked like he was!"

Cliff patted Butch's head and stood. "Did you get a good look? Was this imposter an exact match?"

"Exact?"

"Come on, Peev. I rang Betty earlier, and that Edith that's stayin' with her reckoned she'd gone off with me. But she couldn't have. Someone's impersonating me—and I think Betty might have fallen for it."

Doubt crept over Peevy's features. He pulled off his grease-stained cap and rubbed his free hand through his hair. "Yeah, he was an exact match...'cept now you mention it, he had this scar—an old one—here." He tapped the left side of his face, under his ear. "On top o' that, his hair was cut tidy-like. Lot tidier 'n yours."

"Otherwise he was just like me?"

"Well, he was better spoken. Didn't sound like an uneducated slob." Peevy grinned.

"And none of this twigged ya to the *possibility* that this fake wasn't me at all?"

The mechanic shrugged. "Geez, Cliff, he looked like ya. He sounded like ya. Cliff Secord is what he called himself. He knew me...he knew Betty. What was I supposed ta think?"

Cliff grabbed Peevy's shoulders. "Wait! What'd he say about Betty?"

"Nuthin' much. Wanted to know where she lived?"

"Where she lived! For god's sake, Peev, why would I ask that? Just tell me what the dickens happened!"

"...so I sez, *What's with the Nazi crap?* 'E laughs and sez, *Ya might have to get used to it?*

"And with that he took off like a bat outa hell." As he finished the story, Peevy shook his head. "That jet pack of his...much faster than yours, even with the upgrade. Incredibly powerful. I wonder how he manages to—"

"So he asked where Betty lives?" Cliff clenched his fists. "And you told him? Cripes, Peev. What were you thinking?"

"I was thinking you were havin' some sorta brain seizure!"

"I've gotta go." Cliff began fumbling with his jet pack and Rocketeer gear. "I think Betty might be in trouble."

"Ya don't know anything about this guy." Peevy grabbed Cliff's arm. "What is he? A spy? Some damn look-alike Silver Shirt? Maybe I was just hallucinating."

"So was Edith then. And Betty!" Cliff shook off Peevy's grip. "Doesn't matter! I'm going."

"It's crazy. Just call the cops."

"Sure. Some doppelgänger is goin' around pretending to be me. They'd love that! They already think I'm a whack-job. I'm—"

"*Look out!*"

Peevy's sudden warning put him off balance. Cliff managed to turn in time to see a burst of flame break through the shattered main door, which splintered across the workroom. A moment later, what remained of the wooden framework gave way to more fire and a dark jet-pack-wearing figure that landed mere feet from Cliff. His stance was strong and unyielding. Smoke and wisps of dying flame swirled around him.

"That's the guy!" cried Peevy, backing away.

Cliff managed to keep his feet, though the shock and the impact had made him drop the jet pack. His helmet clattered across the floor.

"So you do exist," the newcomer said over the fading echoes of his entry. His voice sounded weirdly familiar. "A weak, pitiful masquerade."

"Who the deuce ya think you are?"

The new arrival laughed. "I? I'm the warrior you'll never be. The Cliff Secord you might have been if you weren't such an inconsequential fool. I am your true self, Cliff Secord, and there can be only one."

He took off his helmet. If not for the scar under his ear and the short-cut hair, Cliff could've been staring into a mirror. For a moment, he felt drained, unable to move. He stared. His own eyes stared back at him. But the man's smirk flirted with arrogance and disdain, and his eyes seethed with emotions so foreign, seeing into them broke the illusion for Cliff. With that, something snapped. He leapt. His strike was fast and unexpected, yet his fist merely glanced off the man's turning cheek. The stranger elbowed Cliff hard on the chin, grabbed his arm and swept him over his hip. Cliff crashed to the ground. Before he could regain his composure and while he struggled to stand, the stranger's fist smashed into his jaw and then into his gut. Winded, coughing and spluttering, Cliff collapsed.

"So undisciplined," the stranger growled.

Cliff pushed himself up. The man's boot collected him in the ribs and spun him onto his back. He was looking straight up the barrel of a gun—a Walther like his own but modified in ways he hadn't seen before.

"This may be your world, Secord," the man said. "And you may think Betty is yours—but I won't let you take her from me again."

Again?

The man's finger tightened on the trigger. Cliff shut his eyes. No way out of this!

Moments passed, and nothing happened. He opened one eye. The man, the gun, both were still where he'd left them, but there was a different look on the stranger's face, one that Cliff knew well: doubt.

Thanks to this hesitation, Peevy had found time to fetch a shotgun. He pointed it straight at Cliff's assailant. The man showed no sign of caring. Butch circled, growls rumbling from his throat.

"Put the gun down," Peevy demanded.

The man sneered, eyes only on Cliff. "Shoot and he dies," he said. "Two Cliff Secords depart this world in the same instant."

"Just lower the gun."

"That wouldn't be in my best interests, now would it?" He smiled grimly at Cliff. "You've got friends, I see."

"What if we promise Peevy won't plug you?" Cliff managed. "Whatever the hell's goin' on here, we should talk about it."

"There's nothing to talk about, Secord," the man who looked like him said. "I had Betty once. We were engaged and about to be married. I loved her more than I've loved anyone, even myself. But—" He paused, licking his lips. "She was taken from me. Now, by some miracle, I have her back. If you try to take her from me again, I'll kill you. I swear it."

"What d'ya mean she was taken from you? Who the hell are ya?"

"Our worlds have collided, Secord. Our lives have gotten all tangled up. One way or another, I'm keeping Betty for myself, whatever the consequences."

"Over my dead body."

"If necessary."

With his gun trained on Cliff, he backed toward the shattered door. "Careful, Peabody," he growled at Peevy, who was looking as if he might pull the trigger any second. "Don't do anything Cliff here will regret. I'm younger, smarter and better-trained than you. I could probably get you both without too much trouble. You'd be surprised what this gun is capable of."

Peevy grunted. Butch growled.

The man laughed cynically. "I swear they'd die to save you, Secord. Impressive. There must be more to you than meets the eye."

He used his free hand to put on his helmet. "Maybe we can sort this out. But not here. Not now."

"Where then?"

"Philadelphia."

"Philadelphia? Why—?"

"There or nowhere."

"It's a big place. How am I supposed to find ya?"

"You won't. I'll find you."

He stepped backward into the night. "Hey! Wait!" As Cliff, Peevy and Butch rushed through the shattered door after him, the interloper's rockets ignited, burning the darkness with a blinding light. When ordinary gloom returned, there he was, high above them, trailing fire as he shot skyward. Peevy raised his gun.

"No!" Cliff pushed the barrel downward. "We don't know what he's done with Betty. I'll deal with him. In Philly."

"Don't be stupid. It's a trap."

"So?"

Peevy huffed in frustration. "Think, blast ya! *His* jet pack might be able to get him across the country, but yours sure as hell won't!"

Cliff raised one quizzical eyebrow. "That's why I'll need to take the Bulldog."

Cliff Secord considered himself a lot of things, but a fool wasn't one of them. Yet as his trusty yellow and blue Granville Model Z racer skimmed through the dawn light, he mulled over his actions to date. Was he making the right decisions? This imposter, whoever he was, had caught them all off guard, and even now, little of what he'd said made sense or gave a real hint as to what he was up to. He'd threatened Cliff but failed to act on the threat. He had weaponry and flying gear that to Cliff's knowledge shouldn't exist. And most significantly, he looked uncannily like Cliff and yet was so different—a man without honor or an apparent sense of humor. He wore a uniform that bore the emblem of the Third Reich, though his motivations seemed to center more on Betty than on some act of political subversion. Was Philadelphia the key? Dragging Cliff to the City of Brotherly Love was obviously some sort of scheme, but what sort? Did it have something to do with the naval shipyard there? That seemed more than possible.

It made his mind spin. But Cliff had no intention of going off half-cocked. While Peevy had readied the Bulldog, Cliff visited Edith, and in person he'd managed to convince her he was who he said he was and that Betty was in real danger. He spun an account of what had happened that played up indications of Nazi subversion. "This is a matter of national security," he'd declared with more authority than he actually felt.

Overwhelmed, Edith explained that Betty had left with the "other" Cliff two days before and hadn't returned. As she went, though, she'd whispered to Edith that Philadelphia was their destination and that she'd be back soon. "I think Cliff is going to propose at last," she'd said.

"Why Philadelphia?" Edith had asked.

"I think he might have been offered a job with the naval air force," Betty had replied, adding that Cliff was being rather "cagey" about the whole thing. Anyway, he was certainly sounding more serious about their future than he'd ever been before. He'd even mentioned staying at the Ritterhouse.

Cliff ground his teeth. First job security and now the Ritterhouse! The other Cliff obviously knew how to win Betty's heart. He rang the hotel and asked to speak to "Cliff Secord." No one was registered under that name. Did he have a room number? Of course he didn't. By then it all sounded so suspicious it finally raised issues of confidentiality. He'd hung up.

Feeling desperate, Cliff had rung the only person he knew in Philly, an old friend, Sam Chiodo, who used to work as a pilot at the naval base, and hopefully still did. With a bit of encouragement, he might be willing to duck over and check up on Betty. When Chiodo didn't answer his home phone, Cliff tried the naval base. However, the base's receptionist fobbed him off, informing him the entire shipyard was locked down in an emergency drill. No communications allowed.

This "drill" had to be connected to the imposter's presence in the city. Cliff considered calling the FBI; after all, hadn't Betty been kidnapped, even if she'd gone along willingly?

But he'd rejected that option for now, so there was only one thing he could do: go to Philadelphia and face the fascist rat who was playing games with his life. At least this way he wouldn't have to wait for the imposter to make the first move. Cliff would go to the Ritterhouse. He'd find Betty—and free her.

And if she wasn't there...? Or if she was but she didn't want to be freed? What then...?

His speculations died abruptly, knocked on the head by the view through the cockpit window.

Directly in his path, something hovered, suspended in place. It was silhouetted by the sun but clearly human. Translucent clouds swirled about the figure's boots, while steady jets of flame punctuated by short, stabilizing bursts allowed him to remain in the one spot, an impressive display of aerial precision that Cliff had never managed himself. Cliff was in awe of this rocketeer, fraud or not— for a moment anyway.

Then the man's apparent arrogance set loose Cliff's seething anger once more, and he accelerated the Gee Bee straight toward the floating figure. Wanted a game of chicken, did he? Okay, let him have it.

The Bulldog drew closer. Still the man didn't move. Cliff was so near now that he could make out the fool's defiant posture and the superior tilt of his head. He figured Cliff wouldn't cut him down. Well, he figured wrong! "Get out of my flight path, idiot!" Cliff growled. "Give it up."

The imposter didn't give it up. He simply stared Cliff's way from behind his helmet (or so Cliff imagined), stance unrepentant. He held his rather slight body rigid...Wait! *His* body? Only now that Cliff could see the figure more clearly did he notice the figure's shape. "What the—?" he muttered. This wasn't his imposter at all. This rocket-man was a woman!

"Damn it!" Cliff muttered. In the last few seconds before impact, he pulled on the Gee Bee's yoke and slammed down the rudder pedals. The plane veered sharply, even as the rocket-woman shot away, fast. Despite her amazing speed, she mightn't have made it, but knife-edge turns were what the Gee Bee was good at. Cliff lost sight of the woman then, cursing his own better nature.

At the same time, he realized it had all been a distraction. Rock-eteers had appeared all around him, weapons in hand—maybe half a dozen of them, moving in a breakaway pattern that would get them close enough to put a few holes in his fuselage—or maybe in him. A bullet hit his plane's prop, sparked and disappeared. Another cracked the windscreen. This was bad.

He'd have to outrun them. He had no other choice. He'd brought a gun with him, but his chances of using it effectively—even of getting the cabin open without losing control—were nonexistent. Speed was his only friend right now. The other problem, of course, was fuel. He'd stopped once already to re-fuel, but it was awhile back. He had enough to reach Philly—maybe—but only if he didn't push too hard. Right now, pushing too hard was mandatory.

His attackers closed in. He felt the impact of bullets hitting the Gee Bee's body. So far they hadn't managed to do the sort of damage that would ground him. But it was only a matter of time.

The Bulldog shuddered as he pushed it to the limit, until every joint, every rivet shook and rattled. No use. The Gee Bee had a maximum speed of about 294 mph. The Nazi rocket squad, with their obviously superior jet packs, kept up with him more easily than he'd hoped. One of them appeared beside him, close. The woman. She was wielding some sort of automatic weapon. He didn't recognize the design. Light flared from it, sending out nuggets of energy that riddled the area of the fuselage and tore into the plane's wings. Long ribbons of black smoke snaked out from around the propeller mount. The woman waved, pointed downward and veered away.

In construction, the Gee Bee was little more than a Pratt & Whitney R-1340 engine with some accessories attached—such as wings. It was this that gave the plane its peculiar bulbous shape. The Gee Bee was far from ideal in an air battle, despite its speed and maneuverability. Too physically vulnerable. Bullets did damage, real damage. It stood no hope against whatever weapon this woman was using.

A cloud of smoke rolled up and over the windscreen. Clouds of smoke didn't bode well! Cliff felt the carburetor cough. The Bulldog's thrust weakened. The engine could cut out any second, he thought—or worse, burst into flames.

He was going down.

The landing was rough, but it didn't kill or disable him. And any landing you can walk away from is a good one, right?

The Bulldog had taken a beating but probably wasn't beyond salvage. Cliff didn't have time to inspect it now, for behind the grinding of the Pratt & Whitney's final death rattle, he could hear the rocket squad's jet packs coming closer. Smoke and dust obscured sight of them, but they were there, and what cover the cloud offered would quickly dissipate. *Run, you goofball!* he muttered, dragging his duffel bag from the downed plane. It contained his jet pack and helmet. No way he was leaving those behind.

Where was he? Hard to say. He'd done his best to avoid the trees he'd spotted as the ground zoomed closer, and since he wasn't hanging dead in their branches, clearly he'd managed it. He thought he'd seen a building through the smoke, a barn perhaps. It should be to his right. He ran hard in that direction, carrying the duffel bag before him like a shield and hoping for the best.

Cliff emerged from the haze maybe twenty yards from the barn and stopped to look around for the Nazi rocketeers. There! Three of them. Had they seen him? He couldn't tell.

"Hey, you! Over here!"

An older man with a beard and a shotgun gestured toward him from a small door in the side of the barn. "Hurry, damn it! They're comin."

Cliff didn't even hesitate.

"Name's Joe," whispered the farmer after he shut and locked the door behind them. "This is my place."

"Sorry about the mess."

"Saw 'em attackin' ya." He grunted. "They got the mark of the devil on 'em." He sketched a swastika in the air. "Whatcha got in that bag, eh? Holdin' it like it's gold or sumthin'. That what they're after?"

Before Cliff could get his head clear enough to stop him, the man had pulled open the bag and seen what was in it. "Hey, you're the Rocketeer guy, ain't ya? Seen ya in a newsreel 'bout that UFO ruckus in Los Angeles last year. Ya nearly got blowed up."

Cliff jerked the bag back instinctively, though he could tell the man didn't mean him any harm. He didn't know what to say to him.

"It's okay, fella. Ya secret's safe with me. Don't even tell me your real name. Hell..." The man thumbed toward the door. "'Splains a lot. Adolf's gone and got hisself his own rocket-men, eh? Now he wants you outa the way. In my book, that makes you a four-star goldanged American hero—"

Something hit hard against the larger barn doors, causing the structure to rattle. The man's face scrunched up like a used napkin. "Uh-oh!" he muttered.

At first Cliff had accepted that hiding in the barn was a good plan, or at least a reasonable alternative to one. But of course it wasn't much of either. The bad guys would know that's where he was, even if they hadn't seen him scramble through the door.

More banging. More bullets gouging into the wood. Flames and smoke licking through gaps. The barn door was sturdier than the door of Peevy's workshop but wouldn't last. It would burn through or come off its hinges before too long.

"Follow me!" growled Joe.

He led Cliff toward the back of the barn, negotiating a maze of old machinery, discarded cattle fodder, dried-out animal droppings and a big tractor that had seen better days. In the shadows behind a pile of broken crates, low to the ground, he indicated an anomaly in the wooden surface of the wall. "Loose board!" he whispered. "Crawl through. There's cover. Go! Quickly."

"Okay, thanks."

"With a bit of luck, they won't see ya. I'll distract 'em here."

"What? No, you come, too."

The farmer laughed. "They're not int'rested in me. Scoot!"

Unconvinced but accepting the farmer would be in serious danger if found in his presence, Cliff slipped the loose board aside and squeezed through with his duffel bag. He emerged into long grass and weeds.

"Good luck, son!" whispered Joe, and dragged the board back over the gap.

"You, too," said Cliff to no one.

Cautiously he raised his head through the grass. Just over the paddock beyond was a grove of trees. Plenty of cover to get lost in there. He could hear the Nazis working on the door at the other end of the barn. One, obviously scouting for him from the air, flew over the roof. Once he was out of sight, Cliff ran.

To his own amazement, he made it into the trees without being spotted. He peered out from a clump of low foliage in time to see two rocket-men appear around the corner of the barn, on foot. They glanced about then kept walking to the far side and disappeared at a run. The aerial surveillance guy circled overhead for a moment before swooping lower and, like his ground-level comrades, returning to the front of the building.

Quickly, Cliff put on his jet pack and helmet, sick of carrying it and thinking he'd probably need to fly sooner or later. He turned to race along the line of cover while they were distracted.

An explosion roared through the country stillness. Cliff glanced back as a plume of smoke rose from the other side of the barn. Fearful for Joe, he moved around, so he got a partial view of the area in front of the barn without breaking cover.

It was enough. After a moment, the old farmer staggered into the open, shoved and jostled by the goons. They were yelling at him—though Cliff couldn't hear what they were saying. No doubt they were demanding to know where Cliff had gone. One of them waved the others to silence and continued the interrogation. It was the woman who'd buzzed him and shot out the Gee Bee's engine. Was she their leader? Seemed like it. Joe yelled back, gesticulating wildly. This went on, backward and forward, for a while. The whole time three of the Nazis kept their weapons on him.

Minutes later two more appeared from inside the barn. They spoke to the leader, who waved them away and turned to the farmer. She seemed calm enough. Cliff was tense, contemplating what he should do. He was unwilling to leave Joe to their dubious mercies, but his options were limited. He was outnumbered and didn't even have a gun. Nevertheless, if he had to he'd rush them—

No, it was okay. The woman gestured for the farmer to go. Slowly the old man stood, turned and began to walk away, heading for his house. Cliff breathed a sigh of relief.

The leader nodded to her men. One of them raised his weapon and sent a spark of hard light through the back of Joe's head.

Shock galvanized Cliff for a moment as he watched Joe's body fall forward into the dirt. The rocket-goon stepped closer—and shot him again at point-blank range.

"Bastards!" Cliff muttered. It took a Herculean effort not to rush toward the killer, screaming for blood. Though he knew it would be a futile gesture, he might have done so, but he heard the farmer's voice—"a four-star goldanged American hero"—and he knew that real heroes didn't get themselves killed over nothing. The man's sacrifice would be in vain if Cliff tried to avenge him now.

Hating himself for involving the old man in this and feeling like a coward nevertheless, Cliff ran off through the trees. The time for revenge would come.

It didn't take long to get to Philadelphia. Once he felt it was safe to do so, he gave up walking and took to the air, keeping low and watching for enemy eyes. At the edge of the more built-up areas of Philadelphia's outskirts, he landed, stowed the jet pack and helmet in his duffel, and travelled by train. No need to draw undue attention.

Now, slouching behind bushes in Rittenhouse Square, he watched the entrance to the hotel for a sign of his doppelgänger or any of the Nazi rocketeers. Or Betty. Yes, please, let it be Betty!

But there were only ordinary folk...well, ordinary *rich* folk. A big woman in a mink coat, carrying a poodle. Two dandies in tuxedos, sporting bowler hats and fancy, gold-topped walking sticks. A group of rowdy conventioneers. Lots of couples—but not his impersonator with Betty in tow. None of the women were a patch on Betty.

After what seemed like an eternity, but was more like ten minutes, Cliff headed over the road to the hotel's posh entrance. The doorman in fancy duds looked him up and down suspiciously, no doubt taking disdainful note of his somewhat grubby jodhpurs and leather flight jacket.

"Can I help you, sir?" The words slithered from the man's thin lips, as if reluctant to make Cliff's acquaintance.

"No thanks, Jeeves. Just headin' to my room to change out of this stuff. Tough game of polo, don't ya know."

The man frowned, and Cliff barreled through into the reception area. Still no obvious Nazis, though there were several young men in casual clothes that he eyeballed for signs of recognition. None of them even looked his way. The receptionist, a thin-mustached stereotype, gave him a tight smile as he approached. With head slightly cocked, he said, "Ah, Mister Zircon, can I help you?"

"Zircon? Um...sure." Weird name, but Cliff decided to play along with it. "May I have my key, please?"

"The young lady is already up there, sir..."

"What? In my room?"

"Certainly not. The adjoining room, sir, as you requested."

"Of course. My key?"

"Certainly." The receptionist turned to the key rack and reached toward a pigeonhole marked "420."

"Any messages?" asked Cliff, on the off chance.

"No, sir." The man handed Cliff a key with a fancy label attached, being careful not to make actual skin contact.

"Thanks," Cliff muttered and headed for the elevator. So far, so good.

Apparently no one spent much time in Room 420. No bags, no scattered clothes, nothing. He growled deep in his throat.

Leaning his ear against the interconnecting door, he listened for sounds of movement. Seemed quiet. It was locked, but the room key fit. He opened the door a crack.

He could hear the shower running now and smell the soapy fragrance of a woman. Had to be Betty, hopefully alone.

Quietly he eased himself through the door, dumped the duffel bag with his rocket gear on the carpet and crept toward the bathroom. The sound of water cut off. He waited, standing in the middle of the room feeling awkward. Should he sit down and try to look casual? Cough lightly to signal his presence? Before he could decide either way, Betty emerged. She was rubbing her hair with a towel, but was otherwise in the altogether. At first she didn't notice him.

"Um, Betty?" he began.

She shrieked and tried rather ineffectually to cover herself.

"Cliff?" Her beautiful face scowled fiercely. Cliff realized how much he'd missed that. "What on earth are you doing sneaking in on me like this?" She adjusted the towel. "I told you I'd meet you in the foyer when I was ready."

"The foyer?"

"The foyer. I'm not here to do a private peepshow."

Cliff felt his blood rise. No doubt he flushed bright red.

"You look a mess," she said. "Turn around while I get dressed. Or better still, go back to your own room and clean yourself up. What have you been up to?"

"Crazy things have been happening, Betty."

"You don't say."

"Betty, I need to explain—"

"Stop gawping at me! Just turn around, for Pete's sake!"

He did and listened for a moment as she dressed, imagining the process.

"Look, I'm sorry," he said finally. "But there's—well, a problem."

"I knew it was too good to be true. With you, there's always a *problem.*"

"I have to tell you something. Something important."

"Oh? Is tonight off then?"

Cliff spun around. "Tonight? What was gonna happen tonight?"

She was in her lacy underwear and stockings, but hadn't yet made it into the stylish blood-red dress that was draped on the bed. The sight made Cliff pause, breathless.

"You've forgotten already?" She narrowed her eyes at him. "Honestly, Cliff, now you're starting to act more and more like..." She sighed.

"More like what?"

She turned away and put on the dress. "Never mind."

"Come on, Betty. Like what?" Cliff insisted.

"I don't want to argue—"

"More like what?"

"More like your old self!" she snapped.

Cliff didn't know whether to be angry or relieved. "That's just the problem." He stepped closer. "I haven't *been* myself! The guy you ran off to Philadelphia with wasn't me at all. He's an imposter!"

Betty's eyes widened, and she froze in place.

"I only just got back from a test flight up the coast—"

"The one you took despite Peevy telling you to wait?"

"Yeah." He shrugged. "Seemed like a good idea at the time."

"And it took two days?"

"I had an accident." He held out his hand in appeal. "It was crazy, Betty. Peev wouldn't speak to me 'cause he reckoned I'd been actin' weird and had kicked Butch in the head. Me, kick Butch? I wasn't even in Los Angeles at the time. Then we get attacked by this other Rocketeer who looks a lot like me, even uses my name. Threatens to kill me, almost does, then just flies off. And Edith—"

While he blathered on, Betty's expression went from annoyance to bemusement to something that, if he'd been paying closer attention, Cliff would have recognized as revelation. What he registered instead was the fact she hadn't said anything for several long minutes. She was staring at him, eyes wide.

"Betty, I'm telling you the truth, honest. I know it sounds daffy, but there's a Nazi agent around who's pretending to be me. I swear it!"

"Cliff—"

"He's even got a Rocketeer outfit like mine." He went to his bag and part exposed the helmet. "Well, not much like mine actually. It's more...I don't know, more military. You've got to believe me—"

"I do, Cliff."

"Please, Betty, it's vital ya—" He stared at her. "What?"

"I believe you, Cliff."

"Really?"

She came close, taking his head in her hands and studying his face. Then she kissed him. Cliff felt his legs go limp. She patted the side of his face.

"No scar," she said. "I didn't think anything of it at first. He has one under his ear. An old one. I'd never noticed it on you before, but assumed my memory had gone wonky." She took Cliff's hand in hers. "But it's not just his appearance that makes me believe you..."

"What then?" Cliff felt a sliver of doubt cut into his relief.

"The way he acted. He was *different*, cold to others, but so thoughtful to me. Look what you...what *he* bought me." She held out her left hand. A huge diamond ring decorated the fourth finger. "And he got me beautiful outfits, like this one. You never buy me nice things!"

"Betty, I—"

At that moment there was a firm knock on the main door. Cliff spun around, ready to fight—and tripped over his duffel.

"Betty?" said his voice from beyond the door. "Betty? Are you all right?"

"It's him," Betty whispered to Cliff.

Cliff was back on his feet in a flash, nudging her aside. "Good! I'll pummel the jerk until he's a smear on the carpet!"

She grabbed him. "No, Cliff, don't be a goose. He'll kill you."

He glared at her. "So not only is he better-lookin' and more *thoughtful* than me, but he's a better fighter, eh? Just as well you've got his damned ring already."

"Cliff, don't be an ass!"

"I'm an ass? What about—?" It was probably lucky his next words were lost in the turmoil as the door flew open and the flailing form of an angry pseudo-Secord came hurtling into the room. Before Cliff could utter more than a few incoherent mono-syllables of protest, the imposter's fist connected with his jaw. He stumbled back, staggered against Betty's bed and steadied himself in time to get a fist in his gut. Winded, he tried to regain some advantage—if not dignity—by grabbing at his attacker's coat.

It didn't work. Fake Secord hit him in the side of the head and he lost his grip as he crashed to the floor.

"You were a fool to come here, Secord," the man snarled. "I told you what would happen."

He leaned down and struck Cliff again. Cliff tried to reply, but the blood in his mouth made him cough and splutter. The imposter muttered, "Pathetic!" and raised his fist to hit Cliff again.

That's when Betty clobbered him with a vase.

By the time the fake Cliff became conscious enough to raise his head and look at them, he was tied up with torn sheets and one of Betty's belts. He blinked and groaned, "Betty...you hit me."

"Yes."

"Why?"

"Why?" Betty stood over him, staring fiercely. "You've been lying to me all along."

"I said I loved you, and I meant it! That was no lie!"

Cliff stepped toward him, face red and fists clenched. "You stay away from her!" he growled.

Betty grabbed his arm.

"Don't, Cliff!"

The imposter smirked. "I told you before, Secord—she's mine. It's shameful how you don't treat her as she deserves."

"I dunno who the hell you are, but she's definitely not yours. Not now, not ever. She's mine and always will be."

Betty, annoyed, stepped between them. "For god's sake, Cliff. I don't belong to either of you. Don't talk about me like I'm some sort of kewpie doll—"

"But—"

She shushed him and turned to the imposter. "As for you, just tell us who you are."

"Your fiancé."

"Not anymore, you're not."

Cliff glared at her. "Fiancé?"

Betty shrugged, taking his hand. "I thought he was you. Sorry."

Cliff pulled his hand out of her grip, his face reddening even more and his lips pulled back over clenched teeth. "I'll kill him!"

Betty grabbed his arm. "No, you won't. Calm down, Cliff! Please."

Cliff huffed.

"We need to find out who he is."

Cliff nodded. He turned to the imposter, whose expression was blank.

"Answer her question!" Cliff yelled. "Who the hell are ya?"

The man's lips twitched into a weak smile. "I've already told you. I'm you. A better version, admittedly—"

Cliff growled and moved toward him. "I'll *better version* you, ya—"

"Don't, Cliff." Betty held him tighter. "No more violence, please. You're a better man than him. I know that. Act like it."

Cliff looked into her eyes for a long moment. The tension drained out of him. "Okay, okay. But he tried to kill me."

"I wanted to, sure." Fake Cliff's blue eyes held him in their grasp. "Maybe I should have. But I didn't. That must count for something."

"Yeah? What about your rocket squad? You sent them to kill me on the way here."

"What?" The imposter shook his whole body against the restraints. His face had become a savage mask. Cliff knew the makeshift bindings wouldn't hold long against too much of that, but the imposter didn't continue. Instead he stopped and looked Cliff in the eyes again. This time his stare was demanding, but not threatening. "Tell me. What did they do?"

As Cliff told him the story, the imposter broke eye contact. "I didn't tell them about you. Or Betty. I gave them direct orders—no killing. They were supposed to be discreet—"

"They were far from that, I can tell you. What're they up to?"

"I will resolve this. It's my responsibility."

Cliff turned to Betty. "This is pointless. They're obviously a bunch of spies. I'm gonna call the FBI, let them do the 'resolving.'"

"No!" The man glared at them and to Cliff's surprise what he could see in the imposter's face was resignation tinged with fear. "If the *Fliegan Tod* find out what I've been doing, it will be worse for Betty, and for your world."

"*Fliegan Tod?*"

"The Flying Death. My squadron of rocketeers. Please. I'll tell you everything, I promise."

"Everything?"

He nodded. "But I warn you now...there'll be much you'll find hard to swallow."

"Go on!" said Cliff coldly.

"I don't suppose you would consider untying me?"

"You'd be right."

"Okay, listen to me. I'm from another world—"

"Another world? You mean like Mars? You gotta be kiddin' me."

"Not Mars. That's not what I mean. It's more a reflection of this world—*like* this one, only different. Have you ever heard of quantum mechanics?"

Cliff shrugged.

"It's a way of understanding the atomic structures of the universe, a theory developed by a German physicist named Max Planck, along with some others—most recently Werner Heisenberg and his collaborator Albert Einstein."

"I've heard of Einstein. We have one of those."

"One aspect of particular interest to the latter pair is the until-now theoretical notion that there is not one but multiple universes that have been spawned since the big bang by breakaway shifts in the space-time continuum. These universes are copies of each other—but copies that, while similar in their basics, have undergone divergent changes due to the near-infinite possibilities that exist in every decision."

"Are you a physicist?"

"An amateur only. But I did several years of it in college. Didn't you?"

Cliff shrugged. "More carnival than college."

"Then I'll forego the details. Let's just say that many believe it is possible that ruptures could occur in the membranes separating each world from the others. In fact, they believe that such ruptures *have* occurred. One such event took place on October 28. I know this from direct experience. On that day my *Fliegan Tod* and I were swept out of our world and deposited here, in yours."

Cliff vividly recalled the strange visions he'd had on the 28th—visions of zeppelins, flying saucers and rocket squads, a reality that wasn't this one. Had that been part of it?

"You're saying you come from a break-off version of our world?"

"From your viewpoint, yes. Exactly. In the brief time I've been here, I've seen how this world both diverges from and parallels ours. Once I realized this, all I wanted to do was find out if Betty existed in this one."

"Why on earth would that be your first priority?" Betty asked.

The man turned to her, his eyes wet. "Why? As I've said already, I love you, Betty—or if you prefer, I loved the Betty from my world. Loved her more than anything. And something happened, something that affected not only my life, but also, I've come to realize, the world itself, in ways I now deeply regret."

"What was it? What happened?"

He studied them doubtfully for a moment before answering.

April 12, 1938. Mid-morning. Chaplin Airfield, Los Angeles. Another World.

"This was a wonderful idea, Cliff," whispered Betty, her breath teasing against his ear.

Cliff Secord grinned.

Chaplin Airfield was abuzz with excitement, the intense good-humored excitement of people happy to be with friends and loved ones, watching pilots and their crews perform spectacular stunts in airplanes of all shapes and sizes. It was the lure of flight, the fulfillment of mankind's oldest dream that made the adrenalin rush of the machines such a profoundly joyous experience. The war was still distant in this place.

A biplane passed overhead, low to the stands, women dressed in red, white and blue swimsuits standing upright on each wing. Secord knew they were safely strapped onto the plane, but it was nevertheless a thrilling sight.

"Wow!" exclaimed Betty.

"You haven't seen anything yet," Secord replied.

His job as a naval pilot trainer had given him insider knowledge regarding a most extraordinary event to take place at the Chaplin Field Air Show—an event heralded in publicity with the claim "SEE THE FUTURE TODAY!" Secord knew what it was they were to see—he'd been part of its development.

"What is it, Cliff? Tell me!"

"Wait and see!"

"Does it involve girls prettier than me?"

"No girls are prettier than you!"

Betty snuggled against him. "You know, Cliff Secord," she whispered, "if you talk like that more often, I might have to go through with this wedding thing after all."

"You'd better," Secord replied.

They waited out the standard air-show events with intense anticipation—the daredevils, the showgirls, the clowns, a display of aircraft both past and present, stunt acts of the usual kind. No sign of the future, though. As the sound of three of the new Curtiss YP-37 fighters flying in close formation above them faded into the distance and the buzz of the crowd took over, the announcer's melodramatic voice reverberated across the field. This was it!

"And now, ladies and gents, if you cast your eyes to the east and ready yourselves for astonishment, you'll see a sight that no one has seen before in all of recorded history. Thrilling! Exciting! Unbelievable! Man has mastered flight but hitherto only using clumsy machines. *That* is about to change thanks to the ultimate advancement in rocket construction! Witness now the first man to fly...*without* an airplane!"

A lone figure appeared with a roar over the roof of the main hanger, trailing blue fire and a haze of smoke. The crowd gasped. No plane. No wires. No possibility of a trick. Just a man dressed in orange overalls and some sort of padded jacket, his head sporting a winged helmet. Strapped on his back was the jet pack that gave him the gift of flight. It was a prototype and had barely been tested; Secord had argued that it was too soon to unveil it. But Chief Engineer Hughes had insisted there was nothing to worry about. Secord glanced at Betty and was pleased to see the wonder on her face. As the figure shot skyward, then managed a tight turn that swept him back toward the field (slightly inelegantly, Secord noted), the emcee's voice screeched: "Give a big welcome to *the Rocketeer!*"

The crowd burst into applause, cheering as the Rocketeer zoomed low over them, waving one hand triumphantly. It appeared the chief engineer had been on the money—this public test was looking like a great success.

At the speed the Rocketeer was going, it would only take one slip, one glitch in the mechanism, for the whole thing to go awry.

Drunk with the adulation of the crowd, the Rocketeer flew around the field, spiraling toward the stands where Secord and Betty were watching his approach. Now the flying wonder was on an even lower trajectory than before.

As he came closer, Secord heard a splutter in one of the rocket motors. Something flew off behind the Rocketeer. He looked around, the movement destabilizing him even further. One of the engines spewed smoke and sparks. Even from this distance, Secord could hear a high-pitched whine. Sounded like something was jammed up and screaming in agony. The Rocketeer shouted. Secord couldn't hear his words, but it was obvious he was going out of control. Flames licked around his torso, igniting his coat. Secord leapt to his feet.

"What's happening, Cliff?" Betty grabbed his arm.

The Rocketeer headed straight toward the crowd. Straight at Secord and Betty. The scream from the engine Dopplered into a cry for help.

"Run!" he yelled.

Too late.

The fuel tank exploded, raining shrapnel and flames across the bleachers. Something struck Secord on the side of the head. He was picked up by a rush of heat and sound and tossed backward.

"Betty!" he screamed.

Smoke and fire. Broken wood and screams. Chaos engulfed him in that instant. As the swirling darkness overtook him, he tried to locate Betty. A burning body lay to his right, obscured by smoke and falling debris. He could make out a red dress, torn and burning. A dark stain spread around the body. Blood.

Not her. No. Surely not her.

Deep inside, he knew better.

"You killed her!" he heard himself screaming. "You bastards killed her!"

Then oblivion dragged him into silence.

"That's awful," said Betty, her features displaying her horror.

"It sounds like pure guff," Cliff added.

The fake Cliff ignored him. "I was so angry, angry with everyone,

angry with America itself. I blamed the military, the government...
and it made me vulnerable. I did things—"

"You became a traitor?"

He nodded. "And so much more. I see this world now, and it
makes me realize the importance of every decision, every action. I
changed my world...and not for the better."

Neither spoke, waiting for him to continue.

"More than anything, I'm sorry for lying to you." Cliff's double
looked to Betty for forgiveness. "I was so caught up in the *possibility*
of what it might mean if you were alive, I could barely think of
anything else. When I found out you were still alive and I realized
there might be another Clifford Secord to take you away from me
again, I...I went a bit crazy, I guess."

"You expect us to believe all this?" said Cliff.

The intensity in his double's eyes sent out invisible fingers that
gripped his attention. "You must. The Flying Death has a plan. I'll
need your help to stop them. The fate of your world depends on it."

"Sounds a bit melodramatic."

"It's the plain truth." He looked away from them, staring at the
outside world like he'd never seen it before. "In my world, much of
this country has already fallen. Rocket squads, dozens of them, act
as 'peacekeepers'; the *Fliegen Tod* is just one of many. I helped establish them, and as a result, the East Coast is a land of peace. But it's a
Pax Romana, a peace imposed by force, by fear and insecurity. My
senior officer, Flight Lieutenant Melitta Schenk Gräfin von Stauffenberg, wants to return to our world and bring back an army, set up
a wider network of crossover points. And she will do it, too, even
though I've attempted to delay her. I know she distrusts me, believes
I've gone soft, and maybe I have in some ways. But listen to what I
am telling you: when they come, you won't stand a chance. Your
world is unprepared, and they have very powerful weapons. They'll
take this country of freedom for themselves, and then the world."

Major Clifford Secord, squadron leader of the *Fliegen Tod*,
stared up at his double, wondering how things would play out
from this point. Face to face, he'd found himself unable to dispose

of this other Clifford Secord—it felt too much like self-destruction. Perhaps that would have been the effect—in a situation such as this, who could say? So he'd pulled back. But he didn't totally give up on getting rid of him. Truth be told, he had planned to lure the man to Philadelphia so he could send him through the inter-world gateway he knew Gräfin von Stauffenberg and her pet physicist would be establishing. Then he would shut down the portal, hopefully forever, banishing his rival for Betty's affection and stopping whatever invading force his recalcitrant second in command might be able to muster from coming here. He knew he could never fully atone for the damage he had helped inflict on his own world, but at least he could try to prevent it from coming to this new one.

However, though he still held on to that plan, the past ten minutes had unsettled his resolve. Seeing how quickly Betty's loyalty had reverted to this other Cliff, he suddenly wondered if what he desired—a second chance at the life he'd striven for in his own world—was even possible. Small changes could have major reverberations, on a micro as well as a macro level. He might have fooled Betty into being with him for a little while, but now he was thinking that maybe this Betty simply wasn't *his* Betty, never had been and never could be. One way or another, he would have to find out.

Step one: he'd have to convince them to untie him.

"So, in your world, Hitler has already defeated us?" Betty asked. Fear burgeoned behind her words. Secord's awareness of her distress unsettled his resolve still further.

He shrugged. "Not exactly. In my world, the Führer is dead."

"Dead? So the Allies got him—"

"Not the Allies, his own lieutenants and commanders."

"You're kidding."

"They recognized the defeat of the Third Reich was certain with such a lunatic in charge and took the only logical course of action. Hitler's decisions had become extreme, erratic and self-destructive. A rebel movement grew within the ranks of the high command. In the end, they assassinated him and executed those who remained too enthusiastically loyal to his misguided ideals."

"Didn't happen here."

"No, and that is surprising. After all, the necessity is obvious. I suspect this failure to act will result in defeat for the Reich. In my world, Hitler's death gave renewed vigor to the regime, commanded henceforth by men with strong strategic abilities and a more clear-headed view of the world. They weren't blinded by myths about Aryan super-races."

His doppelgänger glared at him suspiciously. "And what's your part in all this?"

Secord adopted the sort of repentant air he suspected his double would respond to favorably. "I came late to the party, as you Americans say—at a time when news of the Führer's death had caused the fear of invasion to diminish and apathy to grow.

"Unfortunately, the United States' economy had already begun a downward spiral. Morale had plunged to its lowest level. When the air fleet and the flying squads appeared, carrying out a well-devised plan, many of your citizens welcomed the possibility for positive change. There was a period of resistance, of course, and much death, but the process did not take very long. With a veneer of self-determination in place to soothe their souls, the people were content to trade the chaos of so-called 'freedom' for security they could trust. The squads made all the difference—and I'm afraid I was the one who supplied the plans for the jet pack in the first place. The compact rocket plans allowed Nazi scientists to develop its technical complexity and effectiveness far beyond yours." He gestured at Cliff's bag with a careless flick of his hand.

"I ain't ever seen a weapon like the one your rocket squad used against me," said Cliff. "It shot out...I don't know...hard light."

The major nodded. "A reasonable description. The regime had already gained technological advantage through the back-engineering of an alien spaceship that crashed in Siberia in 1908, identified officially as an asteroid. Perhaps you saw pictures of the destruction, all the flattened trees. Did that happen here?"

Cliff nodded. "I think so."

"The Russians kept the truth secret for decades. Due to their own political struggles and general lack of scientific capability, they'd made little progress in understanding the alien craft's advanced technology or how to adapt it. Eventually the Germans became aware of this potential scientific wealth after a defecting scientist brought proof of its existence to Berlin. But Hitler's Aryan superstitions hindered the Reich from exploiting the knowledge, another key factor in the need for his removal. Immediately after Hitler's death, in fact, the Nazis invaded Russia, and a special SS team located the recovered technology. German scientists went to work on it. The advanced redesign of the jet packs was a direct result—along with new weaponry and advanced methods of power generation. They even made a version of the alien craft that could fly. Scientific progress happened quickly and—" He paused, head cocked. When Cliff went to speak, he shushed him urgently.

"Someone's coming."

"Here? To this room?"

"Yes, to this room. Untie me, quickly."

A rather forceful knock on the door startled Cliff and Betty. Major Secord merely scowled.

"Hurry," Secord whispered. "It's von Stauffenberg. I recognize her tread."

Cliff and Betty looked at each other.

"I won't give you away. I promise."

"*I know you're in there, Major. We need to talk.*"

Secord gave Cliff a dark look. Then turned to the door. "I am not trying to hide, *Oberleutnant.*" He raised his voice and projected it forcefully. "But I do not wish to be disturbed."

"*This is important.*"

"Important?"

"*Of course.*"

"It better be. Wait!"

Untie me now! he mouthed at Cliff. Betty nodded her agreement. Reluctantly, Cliff untied the bonds. When his hands were free, Secord ordered Betty to take off her dress and get into the bed. Cliff began to object, but Secord cut him off.

"Use your head, man." Secord leaned close. He smelt like leather permeated by rocket fumes. "I need a reason why I've been reluctant to let the flight lieutenant in. Besides, the room smells of Betty. You hide in the bathroom—*and be quiet.*"

"Just hide, Cliff," whispered Betty. "I'll be fine."

Secord watched as his double retreated to the bathroom and Betty, clad only in her underwear, climbed into the bed and messed it up. Leaving her back bare, she turned over and feigned sleep. Secord smiled at Cliff knowingly. He took off his coat and boots, ruffled his shirt and loosened his belt to suggest he'd just put his pants back on. Then he went to the door.

Okay, he thought. *Now it gets tricky.*

Through the narrow crack between the bathroom door and the frame, Cliff could see that von Stauffenberg was older than he'd expected. She had to be about forty. The harsh lines of her clothes, militarist though now stripped of military insignia, added years to her appearance. Her hair was short and her bearing rigid and dominating. Faced by Secord, she gave the Nazi salute by reflex. He waved it away.

"What is it, *Oberleutnant?*" he growled. "Can't you see I have business to attend to?"

Von Stauffenberg looked toward the shape of Betty in the bed and visibly suppressed a sneer.

"Is this appropriate, Herr Secord? We have urgent matters to attend to."

"I decide what is appropriate. At any rate, my presence has not been needed at this stage of preparation. You *are* competent to handle things, are you not?"

"*Jawohl*, sir. But—"

"There is a 'but'?"

The woman looked like she was holding back some foul-tasting gob of spittle.

"No, sir."

"Give me a report on our progress then. I assume your urgency reflects some measure of success."

She stiffened further, though Cliff had scarcely believed it possible. "The device will be completed within the allotted time frame, ready for activation soon."

"How soon?"

"We could begin within the hour, they say."

"I think not. Get the scientists to recheck everything. We'll only get one chance at this."

"But, sir, the more we delay, the greater the likelihood our plans will be discovered. We need the element of surprise. Should they realize—"

"The original experiment took place soon after dawn. That may be the optimal time."

"Or it may be irrelevant."

"Need we risk it?"

Von Stauffenberg took a deep, frustrated breath. "Sometimes I doubt your commitment to this course of action, Herr Secord."

"Be careful what you imply, Melitta. You may command some influence among the upper echelons in Germany, but here?"

Through his narrow peep space, even Cliff could see Secord's attempt to intimidate her hadn't worked. "Your grip on the Eastern States is tenuous, Herr Secord. Think what having access to this world's resources would mean. It might save your failing reputation."

"My reputation is not your concern, *Oberleutnant*. You overstep. Obey your orders. The test will take place when I say it will."

"Very well, sir."

With a curt nod, she turned to leave. At the door, she looked back at him. "I came to you out of respect for your position, sir. I can guarantee nothing if you ignore my advice." With that, she stepped out into the corridor.

"*Oberleutnant?*"

"Sir?"

"On the issue of obeying orders, is it true that you and those most loyal to you recently went on a search-and-destroy mission?"

Cliff gripped the knob on the bathroom door so tightly he nearly caused it to slam shut.

Von Stauffenberg said nothing.

"What was your objective?" Secord continued. "Did it perhaps have something to do with the probability there is another Cliff Secord, one native to this reality?"

The woman stared into his face, trying to determine what he knew. She glanced away. "Your influence on our North American victories was so...*significant*, sir, it seemed prudent to assume that this world's Cliff Secord might be a useful ally. Or a formidable foe."

"And did you find him?"

"*Nein.*"

"I see. You may go. But I repeat, no violence until I say so."

"Sir." She strode away.

Secord shut and locked the door.

Cliff emerged from the bathroom. "She lied to your face. They found me, all right—they just didn't succeed in killing me."

Secord glared at him.

"Yes. She plans to betray me. But can you understand what you will face if von Stauffenberg gets back with the knowledge of how to open a passageway between our two realities? They will listen to her, believe me. Her husband and her brother-in-law were leaders in the coup against Hitler. She must be stopped. I fear she knows I have sought you out."

"Does she really have the means to get back?" Cliff asked.

Secord shrugged. "You heard what she said. While I've been chasing you around the country, they've been working on a way to open the gate."

"What caused this to happen at all?" asked Betty as she put her dress back on.

"It began with an experiment undertaken by the military at the naval base here in Philadelphia. Operation Rainbow, I believe it was called. Our people were working on something similar—using electromagnetic and quantum-level gravitation field manipulation to render ships and aircraft invisible. Our best guess is that in both realities, at the same relative spatial coordinates, a similar test was initiated simultaneously. The synchronicity and the nature of the gravitational phenomena generated by the dual field generators caused effects that no one had anticipated—a multidimensional cross-tear. Apparently the aircraft carrier USS Eldridge disappeared—we assume transported to our reality briefly. My *Fliegen Tod* appeared here.

"When the machine was shut down, the Eldridge reappeared in its original location, but the Squad didn't. Why? Maybe because we were in motion and had left the epicenter of the field by the time the interweaving of the two realities was disentangled, thus breaking the connection."

Visions of a vast futuristic armada, with squadrons of rocket-men filling the sky, flashed through Cliff's mind. "Somethin' happened to me," he said. "Woulda been about the same time as this experiment with the Eldridge. Only I was over on the other side of the country. There was a green wave, and then these rocket squads appeared, dozens of 'em. A small zeppelin, too. And a flying saucer. They weren't just an illusion. For a moment they were physical enough to touch. Hell, I crashed right into the airship's control room, almost got shot dead."

Major Secord stared at him, wondering what this meant. Perhaps the effect had been more de-focused than they thought, causing a ripple that momentarily tangled their two worlds in a line right across the continent.

"Do you think replicating the test will send you back?" Betty asked.

"With the right equipment. It seems that in the past few days the boffins have worked something out. The last time I paid any attention, they were making modifications to the existing field generator. Just on-the-fly stuff. I don't really understand the mechanics of it all. Too advanced for me."

"How has your team figured this out so quickly?" Betty responded. "Your people are soldiers, not scientists."

"One of our major quantum technicians is a man named Chiodo, and he was stationed in Philadelphia. I suggested we seek out his double in this world and get him to help."

Cliff jerked to attention. "Chiodo? Sam Chiodo?"

"You know him?"

"He's a pal from way back. But last I heard he was a pilot, not a physicist."

"So we discovered. However, not coincidentally, I'd suspect, he's been studying applied physics in his spare time, reading all of Albert Einstein's papers and lectures. He's been very useful."

"Sam'd never help Nazi spies."

"He thinks he's getting rid of us. Why wouldn't he help?" He paused. "Particularly with a gun to his head."

Cliff scowled.

"You, too, have a gun to your head," Major Secord continued.

"Help me stop the *Fliegen Tod*—or stand back and watch your country die."

They had little choice. That was Cliff's assessment. In his heart and mind, he fought it, convinced that, whatever the truth of the absurdities his double had told them, the man's motives still somehow centered around Betty. He might be willing to betray his own squadron to redeem the guilt he felt in betraying his country, but would he give up on Betty so readily?

"Well?" growled Major Secord. "What's it going to be?"

Cliff said nothing.

"I think we'll have to trust him." Betty took Cliff's hand. Her touch was warm and reassuring.

He remembered that touch and all that it meant to him as the three of them crouched in the shadows of a warehouse just outside the main periphery of the naval shipyards. Evening had passed into darker night, and it was very quiet—but this was a U.S. government military base during a time of war, and he felt no confidence they could slip in unchallenged.

"We'll be seen," he said. "The place is in lock-down. There's no way we can get in."

"I know a way," the major replied.

His "way" involved a convoluted series of backstreets and passageways, as well as a hole cut in a wire fence. Within the compound, they stumbled upon a corpse, carelessly hidden behind a pile of empty crates. It was wearing a U.S. naval uniform, with a burn-hole torn through the chest. Cliff shot Secord a foul glance, but the major was too preoccupied to respond.

The place was more deserted than Cliff had expected, though that could be accounted for by the out-of-the-way obscurity of the areas through which Secord led them. A few times he gestured them back, to hide while yard personnel wandered by. Once, Cliff heard a guard say to his companion, "...report of someone poking around the Eldridge. They lost 'em, though."

"Been tight security over there since that weird action last week. How could anyone—?"

"Dunno. Prob'ly just Ed bein' paranoid."

Then they were gone.

"Come on!" hissed Secord.

Eventually they found themselves in the main corridor of what looked like a research lab. It was dark and empty, shut down for the night. Secord guided them to a solid steel door marked "AUTHO-RIZED PERSONNEL ONLY."

"Okay," he said. "This is it. I don't think there'll be more than one or two of the Squad here. I'll deal with them. We grab the gizmo they've been working on and get the hell out."

Without waiting for a response, he tapped a combination of numbers on the door's keypad and slid the door open very gently. No presence was immediately obvious in the room, so he opened it further and they went inside. The lab was quiet and still—empty, except for a single figure tied to a chair against the far wall.

"Chiodo?" blurted Cliff.

The man looked up. His mouth was gagged with cloth. He mumbled incomprehensibly. Cliff rushed over and removed the gag.

"Stay away from me, Secord," Chiodo growled. Then he noticed Major Secord behind Cliff. "What the hell—?"

"Yeah," growled Cliff, "there's two of us." He gestured at Secord. "He's the bad guy. I'm the good one. It's a long story."

As he untied Chiodo, Cliff began to give him a quick rundown on events. His friend cut him off. "I know—they're from an alternate world. Quantum reflection and all that. I thought he was you though. You vouched for their good intentions. Only reason I helped 'em."

"Well, it was him, and he lied. There were no good intentions."

"But he's—"

"Cooperating with us now, Sam. Just go with it."

Secord shoved Cliff aside and grabbed at Chiodo's collar. "Enough of this. Where's the field generator?"

"They took it."

"They?"

"The female officer and her rocket-men. She said she didn't have time to wait. That it had to be done now."

"Will it work?"

"It worked once already, but it's a lot more powerful since I modified it to link into the residual energy that's still active around the Eldridge. Should make a hole big enough for them all to go through."

Secord frowned. "Worked once? What do you mean?"

"She...the leader. She went back—" He gestured at Secord. "—to your world. Two days ago, as a test run. The field was weak, connecting via coordinate traces in the vortex, so the link was very erratic. One-sided. She could only stay a few minutes. The fields need to be activated on both sides to open a stable-enough bridge to their own reality."

"I don't understand—"

"I figure objects from each reality are constructed using different quantum markers—structural signatures unique to their own worlds. These signatures can be used within the field generator to better control universal spatial orientation—even more so if we'd been able to complete a full modeling of the key subatomic structures. Tying like to like, you might say."

"But that also means they could facilitate movement backward and forward between the worlds, assuming they could activate fields on both sides according to a pre-arranged timetable."

"Sure, but why would they—"? Chiodo slammed his fist back against the wall. "Oh, god! I should have realized."

"Realized what?" snapped Cliff.

Major Secord's tone was icy. "What *was* an accident can now be controlled. Without a doubt, von Stauffenberg has already arranged with the other world to prepare an invasion force—and to activate a copy of the field generator on that side as she activates the one here. When the worlds cross over this time, the invasion will begin."

He stared at Cliff. "We have to go. *Now.*"

They'd barely left the labs and begun the trek to the wharf where the Eldridge was located when a massive rumble vibrated through the ground and into Cliff's bones.

"What was that?" Betty grabbed at him.

"It's started," said Chiodo.

Major Secord stopped, staring into the darkness. Cliff noticed his clenched fists. The man turned. "I was hoping we'd get to her before she acted. No such luck. So my options have been narrowed." He put on his jet pack, which he'd fetched from a storage cupboard in the lab.

"What are ya doing?" asked Cliff.

"What I must," he said. "I'm sorry."

With that he hit Cliff, hard. Betty gasped. "Cliff!"

The Rocketeer felt his brain slap against the inside of his skull as he collapsed, dazed. For a long moment the world was a mass of shifting shadows. The swirling darkness tried to take shape but failed to find an acceptable form. Cliff was aware of Major Secord grabbing Betty.

"Come on," he said.

"Let me go!"

"There's no time for this—"

Light flared, and Cliff was struck by a wave of heat and a roaring sound. Time passed. It might have been a second or an hour—he couldn't tell. He blinked and was conscious of pain throbbing in the side of his head. Someone shook him. One of the shadows surrounding him coalesced into a familiar face.

"Chiodo?" he groaned. "What happened?"

"The bastard slugged you."

"Where's Betty?"

"He took her and flew off."

"Where?"

"Toward the Eldridge. I guess he wants to get back to his own world before the two spaces are disentangled again."

"The invasion?"

Chiodo said nothing, but Cliff didn't need a response. Across the tops of the buildings, over toward the main wharves and the Delaware River, the sky was hemorrhaging a thick cloud of green light. In that light hovered the specters of armored zeppelins and seemingly endless squadrons of rocket-men. They were shimmering and translucent as yet, but their potential filled Cliff with rock-solid terror.

He dragged himself up. His legs felt wobbly. "I've gotta go after him. Gotta stop this."

"How?" Chiodo fussed anxiously with his coat. "They've activated the field generator and obviously established a connection with one on the other side. The nexus of the two is generating a lot of power, and the process is too far along to be turned off."

"What if we blow it up?"

"Blow it up?" Chiodo looked confused.

"Yeah. Kaboom! What would happen?"

Chiodo considered the idea.

"Well?"

"I...I don't know. It might cause massive feedback that'll destroy the other generator and drag all nearby foreign matter back to its native universe. Or—"

"Or?"

"It might blow everyone to Kingdom Come."

Cliff strapped on his own jet pack. "I have to get Betty. Then we'll deal with the invasion fleet. Do what you can here."

And with that, he zoomed into the night sky.

Air stained green swirled around Betty. When Cliff's double had first grabbed her, she'd struggled against him with vigor. But now, high above the naval buildings, convincing him to let her go held much less appeal. Ahead, a gaping wound had opened in the sky, while all around them the phantom shapes of otherworldly rocket-men and Nazi airships shimmered toward solidity.

"Cliff!" she yelled, not wanting to use the name to refer to this man but unable to think of a viable alternative. "Please! What are you doing?"

"I won't let anything happen to you," he yelled through the wind and the growing roar of rocket thrusters. "But I won't lose you again."

"Take me back. Please."

"That's exactly what I'm doing."

They were heading straight toward a huge stain in the night—a vast maelstrom of intermingled images, fragments of each reality mixed together as they cross-shifted to opposing coordinates. Beyond the surface level of the stain, Betty could see the Philadelphia naval yards as they were in the shadow world—similar to this one, but with more and different warships, most of them flying flags of the Third Reich.

"Please. If you love me, don't do this!"

Before he could respond, the roar of his jet pack was caught up in a bigger, multiplied roar—and three members of his Flying Death appeared in front of them. Their weapons pointed straight at him. He pulled up and hovered in place.

"What is the meaning of this?" he yelled. His voice was so strong Betty wondered if he wore some kind of amplification device.

One of the Squadmen moved closer. As he did, his reply came through an intercom in Secord's helmet. Betty could hear words trickling out into the wind, audible if faint. Not that it made any difference to her—they spoke in German.

"What did he say?" Betty asked.

"Seems I've been relieved of duty. They're placing me under arrest."

"Are you going to go with them?

He smiled grimly. His reply, sent in German now, cut through the ambient noise like a sword blade.

Another warning whispered through the intercom. Secord laughed and gunned his jet pack, heading straight for the nearest rocketeer. Was he calling their bluff? The Squadman fired, his weapon releasing a sharp, electric crack. A spark of solid light struck Secord in the chest. He jerked to the side. As he did, Betty felt his grip on her loosen. She began to slide into open air. The ground was so very far away.

Major Secord yelled, spun around and down and grabbed her. She could see his pain as he strained against the tug of gravity. Blood leaked out of his jacket into the wind.

"I'm sorry," he whispered.

The entire Squad trained their weapons on him.

In that instant, Betty was aware of something sweeping over them from behind. Ordinary pistol shots cut through the din, and one of the Squad members cried out and fired blind. The bullet went wide, and the man's jet pack reacted to a sudden lack of control by carrying him away into the distance. The attacker was moving so fast at such close quarters, the others couldn't get a proper bead on him. In that hiatus, he bore down on one of the men, boots pounding into his head from above and to the side. The man lost control, and the Rocketeer, the real Cliff Secord, put a bullet into the main engine of the man's pack from close quarters. The jet spluttered and failed, and the man tumbled downward. Without missing a beat, Cliff made a quick turn and shot at the third Squadman. The gun flew from his hand, and as Cliff roared toward him, the Nazi turned and accelerated away.

Cliff let him go and continued toward his double and Betty.

"Give her to—" he began.

Before he could finish, Secord thrust Betty into his reaching arms.

"He'll be back with more men," Secord said, breathing erratically. "Get Betty to safety!"

Cliff was too surprised to speak.

"What about you?" Betty managed.

"I'll stop them. I'll stop them all. I was foolish to think I could rebuild the past." He looked at Betty. "You don't belong with me. And they don't belong here."

"How will you stop them?" Cliff swerved backward and forward awkwardly, his jet pack ill suited to hovering.

"I'll think of something. Just get away. Both of you. Live the life I cannot."

Betty saw a softening of emotions in Cliff's face. "Chiodo thinks," Cliff said, "if we can blow up the field generator on this side, there's a chance it'll destroy the one on the other. Send everyone back where they came from."

"I'll keep that in mind." Secord smiled through his pain.

"Don't have any explosives to give ya."

"I'll improvise. Just get her to safety. Now."

Secord revved up his engines and was gone in an instant, following a trajectory that would lead him to the wharves. For a moment, Cliff and Betty watched him disappear into the green fog. Then Betty noticed that around them the vast otherworld armada had solidified. "We should get out of here," she said.

"Reckon we can trust him?"

"At this point, there's only one thing he can regain."

"What's that?"

"His pride."

Cliff scowled, but headed away from the invasion fleet.

Major Secord knew exactly what he would do. He knew where von Stauffenberg had determined to place the generator, and he knew the rest of the Squad would be there to protect it. But his plan involved a frontal assault, so fast and uncontrolled that whatever measures they tried to take, they would not be able to stop him. There was a certain irony to the whole business, and that pleased him. In a way, this had begun with an out-of-control Rocketeer— and now it would end the same way.

Hopefully.

As the wharves came into view, he spotted the members of the *Fliegan Tod*, gathered around a box-like device surmounted by something resembling a radar disk. That must have been a recent addition, for he'd never seen it before. Maybe it was intended to gather and re-direct the residual energies from the previous test that Chiodo had mentioned. Whatever it was, it didn't matter. Soon it would be junk.

He locked the jet pack's stabilizers so he'd soar straight at the device, whatever happened. Then he reached back and manually adjusted the exhaust controls. These had failed on April 12, 1938, at Chaplin Airfield when the first public demonstration of the prototype jet pack had ended so disastrously. As he shut them down now, a shrill screaming cry built within the jets. It grew exponentially as he accelerated, until within seconds it had become loud enough to be heard right across the naval yards. Secord was barely conscious of the men below, looking up, crying out warnings, the bullets and light shards that went past in slow motion, the projectiles that hit him and tore into his flesh. None of it mattered. In moments, it would be over.

He reached up and ran his fingers over the scar under his left ear.

"I'm coming, Betty," he whispered. He hoped fleetingly that this world's Cliff Secord and the Betty he now knew belonged with him would be safely out of the way.

Then his jet pack exploded, and the world erupted into fury.

Cliff passed over the yards' outer fences before he landed, arms tightly wrapped around Betty. They hadn't spoken since parting from the other Cliff, aware only of the conflict that had broken out across the whole area and the apocalyptic potential it brought with it.

"Do you think—?" Betty began. But a booming explosion engulfed her words. It shook the ground, blew out windows in nearby buildings and created a shock wave that made them stagger. They clutched each other for support. Looking back through the wire fence, Cliff saw the green cloud being sucked away, absorbed into the spatial bruise that dominated the sky. The mist spiraled in like water down a plughole—and then suddenly it was gone. So were the dirigibles, the rocket squads and all the other strange aircraft that the field generator had summoned into being. The gray bruise had gone, too. All that was left were bewildered soldiers and a few columns of smoke from fires that had been ignited during the brief conflict.

"They're all gone," said Betty, clinging to his arm as if he were still flying her to safety. She stared out across the buildings toward the unseen Delaware, saying nothing.

Cliff settled his arm around her shoulders. "Looks like Major Secord did what he said he'd do."

"What do you think happened to him?"

"Who knows? Probably went back where he belonged."

Betty's pellucid eyes turned to him. "I hope he's all right."

Cliff nodded doubtfully. It had been a *big* explosion. "For someone who was supposed to be me, he wasn't much like me, was he? A Nazi traitor, and an over-educated prig. Bit of a nutter, too."

Betty smiled wistfully. "There's a chance he sacrificed himself to save us. That sounds like you."

Cliff thought about that then grunted. "Tell me, though. Did ya really like him better than me—even only for a while?"

Betty extricated herself from his arms. She looked up at him, patted his cheek and began to walk away. "Come on!" she said. "I want to go home."

THE
END

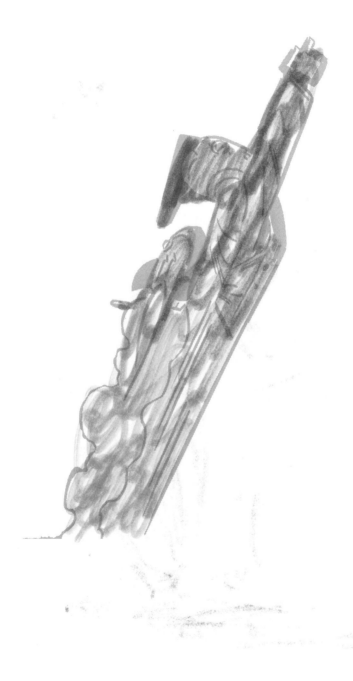

THE MASK OF THE PHARAOH

by

NICHOLAS KAUFMANN

1943. Hollywood, California

1.

"Scream, lady." The hulking man with the angry scar on his cheek cocked the pistol pointed at Betty's head. "Scream like your life depends on it. Because it just might."

Trembling, Betty stared down the barrel of the gun and let loose a soul-rending scream.

The scarred man winced at the sound of it. He lowered the gun and glanced to the other side of the room, where another man sat behind a messy, paper-strewn desk. "What do you think, Mister Rogell? Need it again?"

The second man leaned forward in his desk chair. "Not on your life. I think we've found our leading lady. Congratulations, young lady. You're about to become a star."

Betty jumped and clapped with joy. "Oh, thank you, Mister Rogell! I'm so excited to make this picture with you!"

Cliff smiled to himself. Sitting in the reception room of film producer Karl S. Rogell's Hollywood headquarters, he watched Betty's audition through the open doorway to Rogell's small office.

The reception room wasn't much larger—just a couple of old, uncomfortable wooden chairs and the desk where Rogell's secretary read a magazine and watched the phone not ring. A standing fan in the corner rattled as it blew the hot summer air around the room.

While it was true Rogell was a movie producer, technically, he wasn't with one of the big studios like Paramount or RKO just down the street. Instead, Rogell had his own "studio," one Cliff had never heard of before: All Artists Alliance—or AAA, as it said in gold stencil on the office door, which looked so flimsy a hard sneeze could probably blow a hole through it. But then, everything in Gower Gulch felt a little cheap and flimsy. Once you ventured north of Melrose and into the Gower Street/Sunset Boulevard area, you left behind the Hollywood most people knew and entered a world of low-budget cheapies, one-week wonders, eight-day miracles and ten-day terrors, all churned out on a breakneck schedule by independent producers and no-name "studios" on soundstages rented by the day. If Hollywood was a glamorous stretch limo, Gower Gulch was a grimy city bus.

Cliff would never admit it, but most of the time he hated accompanying Betty on auditions. It wasn't that he wasn't supportive. Of course he was. He loved that crazy girl like...well, like crazy. When she was happy, he was happy. But more often than not, auditions had Betty screaming in terror or swooning over a handsome leading man, and Cliff didn't like seeing her do either. Sure, he knew the scar-faced thug menacing her in the next room was just a character actor running lines and the gun was a prop, but he'd seen Betty in real danger enough times that even this play-acting was putting him on edge.

But that wasn't all that had Cliff's hackles up. He couldn't stand the way Rogell was leering at Betty like she was an order of skirt steak from the Melrose Grotto, mentally undressing her with his eyes. Not that this was anything new. It happened at every audition Betty went on. It didn't seem to bother her, or if it did, she never said anything. The attention had even landed her a few parts in pictures, though most of the roles were what you might generously call "decorative," little more than a pretty face and a cocktail dress in a scene or two. But she was taking acting classes now, and with a helping hand from their friend Hedy Lamarr, Betty was starting to land small roles on a regular basis. Better roles. But the lecherous looks like the one currently on Rogell's face never changed. Cliff didn't like the idea of Betty being within arm's reach of this creep, let alone working with him on a picture, but she'd insisted. If she landed the role, it would be her biggest yet.

"That was one heck of a scream...Betty, was it?" Rogell stood up. He was a good thirty years older than Cliff, with a round stomach that drooped over his belt, big enough to put Santa Claus to shame. Rogell picked the smoldering stub of a cigar out of an ashtray on his desk and popped it in his mouth. "Where'd you learn to scream like that?"

"I've had experience," Betty said.

"On pictures?" Rogell asked.

"Sure, let's say that," she replied.

Rogell nodded, chewing on his cigar. "You've got moxie, kid. And with a pair of lungs like that..." Rogell's gaze dipped to Betty's chest, making Cliff's blood boil. "...you're perfect to play the reincarnation of Princess Nefertari of Luxor."

That was another thing. Rogell's picture was hardly destined to be the *Casablanca* of 1943. No, this masterpiece was called *The Mask of the Pharaoh* and was about a woman who goes to Egypt, discovers she's the reincarnation of an ancient Egyptian princess and gets chased by the mummy of the pharaoh Sekhemkhet as well as a gang of ruthless, mob-connected treasure hunters. Just a hokey, no-budget knockoff of Universal's mummy films and every other pyramid-plundering picture since.

The front door opened, and two men walked into the reception room, drawing Cliff's attention. The first was tall and dapper in a gray, three-piece suit. His dark hair was cut short, matching his neatly trimmed beard. The second was a round, short man in denim overalls with a cloud of white, puffy hair and an equally white, push-broom mustache that hid most of his mouth. The two of them were so different they didn't look like they belonged together. The taller man's polished shoes and manicured nails were the complete opposite of the shorter man's dirty work boots and rough hands covered in plaster and paint. The unlikely duo blew past the secretary's desk without a word, heading straight for Rogell's office.

The secretary dropped her magazine, jumped to her feet and followed after them, her brassy blond ringlets bouncing at her shoulders. "You can't go in there, Doctor Morlant! Mister Rogell is in the middle of an audition!"

The tall man—Doctor Morlant, Cliff presumed—smirked confidently. "Thank you, Yvonne, but Rogell will see *us*, I assure you."

Morlant glanced dismissively at Cliff, noting his presence without bothering to acknowledge it, as if Cliff wasn't worth his time. Jackasses were a dime a dozen in Hollywood—Cliff knew that all too well—but something about this guy got under his skin fast. Cliff forced himself to let it go. What else could he do? He was here as Betty's boyfriend, not as the Rocketeer. Besides, Betty would never forgive him if he made a scene at an audition—again.

At that moment, Rogell came strutting out of his office, intercepting the two visitors. Betty and the scar-faced actor followed at the producer's heels.

Rogell shook Morlant's hand eagerly. "Hang tight, Doc, I'll be right with you." Then he brazenly swatted his secretary, Yvonne, on the bottom and sent her back to her desk. "Get the paperwork started right away for Miss Betty, sweet cheeks. We found our Princess Nefertari!"

Cliff saw Yvonne's expression darken, though the secretary held her tongue. She went back to her desk and pulled a boilerplate contract out of the top drawer for Betty to sign.

The scar-faced actor's expression darkened, too, at Rogell's behavior. But the livelihood of a small-time character actor depended on not rocking the boat, so he hid his anger before Rogell noticed. He tipped his hat genially to Betty and said, "That's my cue to depart. Congratulations, miss. I'll see you on set."

"Yes, you definitely will!" she replied, her voice bubbling with excitement. As the actor left, Betty turned joyously to Cliff, her eyes as big as moons, and mouthed the words *on set* incredulously.

Cliff stood up and went over to her. "I knew you could do it, darling."

"Oh, Cliff, it's a dream come true! I can't wait to tell Hedy!" She threw her arms around him and hugged him tight.

Rogell gave Cliff the stink-eye. "Say, Betty, who is this fella?"

"Mister Rogell, this is my boyfriend, Cliff Secord, the famous pilot. Cliff, this is the producer—the *great* producer—Karl S. Rogell."

Cliff held out his hand, but Rogell didn't take it. Instead, he studied Cliff the way a cat studies a mouse. "A stick jockey, huh? Shouldn't you be out there shooting down Japs for Uncle Sam?"

Cliff let his hand drop back to his side, bristling at Rogell's tone. "I train men to do that very thing, Mister Rogell."

"Karl," Morlant interrupted. "A moment of your time, please. There are important matters we need to discuss."

"Sure, sure, I've got all the time in the world for you, you know that," Rogell said. "But first, Betty, I'd like to introduce you to Doctor Julian Kort Morlant, one of California's leading Egyptologists, if not the best in the whole darn US of A. He's been kind enough to lend his expertise to *The Mask of the Pharaoh* so the 'critics' can say we got everything right. Doctor Morlant's the real deal—writer, lecturer, collector, consultant for auction houses and museums. What we might lack budget-wise, we make up with integrity."

Cliff wondered how Rogell could say that with a straight face.

"Enchanted to make your acquaintance, miss." Morlant bent to kiss Betty's hand. As he did, Cliff noticed a gold ring in the shape of an Egyptian scarab flash on Morlant's finger. The man obviously took his work seriously. Like Rogell, though, he didn't bother shaking Cliff's hand or even introducing himself to him. Cliff was starting to feel like a third wheel. It didn't make him feel any better about Betty working with these people.

"Doctor Morlant was an assistant consultant for DeMille on *Cleopatra* back in '34," Rogell said. "He's been hooked on Hollywood ever since. Must have caught the bug when you saw Claudette Colbert film that scene in the milk bath, huh?"

He clapped Morlant on the back and chortled. Morlant flushed, looking distinctly uncomfortable.

Rogell gestured to the small, round man. "And this is Gionvanni Bortello, artisan extraordinaire. He came out to Hollywood after escaping the Nazis, and since then he's worked with the art department of every major studio in town. We're lucky enough to have him in charge of the most special props we'll be using in the picture."

"That's what we came to tell you, Karl," Bortello said with a slight German accent. "The props are ready for your inspection. They're waiting at the soundstage."

"Perfect timing," Rogell said, clapping his meaty hands together. "I'll take a look right now. Betty, come with us. I want you to see this."

Betty took Cliff's hand. "We're right behind you."

Rogell frowned. "Both of you, huh? What are you, joined at the hip or something?"

"Karl, please focus," Morlant said in an exasperated tone. "This is important."

Rogell sighed. "Fine. Sure, Betty, your boyfriend can come, but he has to agree to keep his trap shut about everything he sees. I'm handling the publicity myself, you understand? I've got a schedule worked out and everything. No leaks. You hear me, Clod?"

"It's Cliff," he replied, "and yes, I understand. Don't worry. I'm not a reporter. I don't even have a camera on me."

"Keep it that way," Rogell said.

The producer led the way out of the office, followed by Morlant in his dapper suit and Bortello in his work clothes. Betty paused a moment and squeezed Cliff's hand. Her eyes sparkled in a way he hadn't seen in a long time.

"Can you believe this? I'm going to be a movie star!"

"Of course I believe it," Cliff said. "I never had a doubt."

But he did have doubts. On some level, he knew Betty would never be as successful as Hedy Lamarr, not even with all the acting classes she was taking. It filled him with more guilt than he could bear, but sometimes he wished Betty would leave Hollywood behind and get a normal job, one where she wasn't treated like a slab of beef. Though apparently you didn't have to be an actress to be treated that way. He glanced at Yvonne sitting at her desk. She didn't meet his eye. Her face was still red with humiliation after Rogell had swatted her bottom. Cliff frowned.

"Come on," Betty said, squeezing his hand again. "We'd better catch up with the others. I don't want to miss anything!"

2.

The soundstage Rogell had rented was in a small lot just around the corner from his office building. When the five of them walked up to the front gate, Rogell showed his ID to the security guard stationed there. The guard waved them around the wooden barrier gate and onto the lot. There were only four soundstages here. Rogell led them to the farthest one, with the words STAGE 4 painted on its front wall. Bortello produced a key from his overalls pocket and unlocked the door, letting them inside. Rogell switched on the over-head lights, revealing a soundstage that Cliff guessed was roughly the same size as Peevy's hangar. It hadn't been set up for *The Mask of the Pharaoh* yet, so Cliff found himself walking through a mishmash of recycled sets and backdrops—the drawing room of a manor house, a Wild West sheriff's office, an Army barracks, the stone walls of a gothic castle.

"What do you think?" Rogell asked. He put his arm around Betty's shoulders in a way Cliff didn't like.

"It's swell," Betty said, gazing at it with wide eyes.

"Glad you like it," he said. "We're shooting on a tight, ten-day schedule, which means you're going to be seeing this place a lot more than your own home once we start. Think of it as your home away from home."

Betty grinned at Cliff like she thought that sounded great. Cliff smiled back thinly.

In the near corner of the soundstage was an enclosed prop workshop. Bortello unlocked it and led them inside. Cliff looked around. Tools hung on the walls. Dried splotches of paint and plaster decorated the cement floor. A heavy, wooden worktable stood on one side of the room. A huge, steel safe squatted in the corner, partially obscured by the four wooden transport crates in front of it. Bortello took a crowbar off the wall. He cracked open the crates and began assembling their contents on the worktable. Within moments, the table was overflowing with glittering Egyptian artifacts in impossibly perfect condition—chunky amulets of gold and precious stones, jewel-crusted jars with the sculpted heads of jackals and monkeys on their lids, papyrus scrolls, daggers, brooches, scarabs, necklaces and rings.

Cliff's mouth fell open. "Holy cow! Is this stuff real?"

Rogell laughed. "That's *exactly* the reaction I was hoping for! No, they're not real. Our good man Bortello has made reproductions of some of the most prized artifacts of Doctor Morlant's collection, specifically for our picture."

"It's certainly very convincing," Betty said, walking over to the table.

Rogell scoffed. "Convincing? That's like saying Rita Hayworth is a looker—it's the understatement of the century! Now you see why I'm keeping this under wraps until we're ready to start publicizing the picture."

Like a man hypnotized, Morlant zeroed in on a single item on the table. He walked over and picked it up. It was a gold and lapis funerary mask, similar to ones Cliff had seen on mummies in news-reels. A striped headdress bordered the face, while the emblems of a hooded python and a falcon head sat just above the forehead. A stylized, cylindrical beard hung off the chin. But there was something sinister about the mask's face, Cliff thought. The dark-lined eyes looked scheming, as if plotting something devious. Morlant stared into those eyes, completely captivated.

Rogell smiled around the stub of his cigar. "And that's the center-piece of our picture. The Mask of the Pharaoh itself!"

"Yes, the Mask of the Pharaoh..." Morlant muttered distantly. "It's...breathtaking."

"Put it down," Bortello said angrily. "Put it down before you ruin it!"

Morlant shot an angry look at him. "In a moment!"

Cliff watched, confused. Why was Morlant acting so enamored of this one piece? Wasn't it just a reproduction of something in his own collection? He was acting as if he'd never seen it before.

"Think of the publicity," Rogell continued. "A mummy picture featuring what everyone will believe to be authentic Egyptian arti-facts. I can see the ads now: 'Come see the mummy walk in its natural habitat! See the Tomb of the Pharaohs like you've never seen it before!' *The Mask of the Pharaoh* will put Universal's mummy pictures to shame." His face grew redder as he ranted. "To hell with those studio jerks! Blackball me, will they? I'll show 'em. I'll hit 'em where it hurts—right in the box office!"

Betty went over to the table and picked carefully through the jewelry, admiring piece after piece. She pulled out a clothes hanger. Pinned to it was a skimpy, jewel-covered, two-piece bathing suit.

"What is this?" she asked, arching an appreciative eyebrow.

"That's one of our, ah, less authentic pieces," Rogell explained. "What do you think?"

"It's gorgeous," Betty said.

"I'm glad you like it, sweetheart, because it's for you. That's one of Princess Nefertari's costumes."

"Really? Thank you! Holy smokes!"

Betty held the outfit against her body to get a feel for what it would look like on her. She loved it, but Cliff didn't. Far too much of Betty's blouse was showing through the gaps between the gemstones, he thought, and when she wore it for real, she wouldn't even have a blouse on under it. It would show too much of *her* instead.

"She's not wearing that in the film, is she?" he asked nervously.

"Oh, no, of course not," Rogell said.

Cliff relaxed, sighing with relief.

"It's for the publicity shots," Rogell continued. "Photos of our beautiful Princess Nefertari adorned with exotic Egyptian jewelry will run in every newspaper and magazine from California to New York. Every red-blooded American male who sees her will run to the theater to buy a ticket."

Cliff tensed again, silently fuming. He turned to Morlant, who was still studying the Mask of the Pharaoh with the glazed eyes of a zombie. "What do you think, Doctor Morlant? It's not exactly authentic Egyptian evening wear."

Morlant barely looked up from the mask. "Hmmm? Oh, it's fine, it's fine." He waved a hand dismissively.

So much for lending a "genuine authenticity" to the production, Cliff thought. Did Morlant even care about his reputation as a consultant? From the looks of it, he didn't care about anything but that stupid mask.

"Put it down, Doctor Morlant!" Bortello yelled again.

Morlant sighed and put the mask gently back on the table. "There. Are you happy now?"

Bortello stalked angrily to the table, grabbed the mask, and put it inside the open safe. "*Now* I'm happy, yes." He started taking other items off the table and putting them in the safe, too.

Betty picked up another two-piece costume. This one was adorned with red rubies. *Fake* rubies, Cliff had to remind himself. They looked so real. Astonishingly, this costume was even skimpier than the first. She held it against herself. It barely covered anything.

"The jewels may be fake, but they'll look great for the camera. I can tell," she said. "Oh, Cliff, won't the pictures be beautiful?"

He sighed. Every instinct was warning him to talk Betty out of doing this, but those same instincts told him she would never listen. Not when her first leading role in a Hollywood picture beckoned. Cliff looked at Rogell. The producer's lascivious leer was back on his face as he watched Betty model the costumes.

"I'll need you back here tomorrow morning for the photo shoot," Rogell said. "You can pick up the address from Yvonne in my office." Then he turned to Cliff, his eyes challenging him, warning him not to get in the way of whatever twisted fantasy was playing out in his imagination. "Don't worry, Clod. I'll get her back to you in time for dinner."

Cliff had no intention of backing down. "It's Cliff, and I'm not worried, Mister Rogell. Because I'll be here tomorrow, too."

Rogell cleared his throat and struggled to keep his voice sounding cheerful. "Sorry, but it's a closed set."

"I don't take up much space," Cliff said. He kept his tone friendly for Betty's sake, but he was sure Rogell was reading him loud and clear. "In fact, I wouldn't miss it for the world."

"Oh, but Cliff *has* to be there," Betty insisted. "He's my ride, and I'd hate to think of him sitting outside in the car all alone the whole time. He'll stay out of the way, I promise. Won't you, Cliff?"

"That's right," Cliff said, not breaking eye contact with Rogell. "I won't be in the way. I'll just be watching. Everything."

"Fine," Rogell grumbled. His forced smile drooped around his cigar.

If watching Betty merely hold the skimpy costumes against her body made Cliff feel overprotective, there was no word for how much worse he felt seeing her actually wear them at the shoot the next morning. The first costume was a sparkly gold, amethyst and jasper two-piece that left so little to the imagination it would have made Millie turn redder than her famous beet soup. The gold and jewels weren't real, of course, but even he had to admit they looked genuine. Bortello's handiwork was miles ahead of anything Cliff expected to see on a picture like this.

Rogell's crew had fixed up the soundstage for the shoot. They brought the gothic castle walls to the front and hid the rest of the backdrops in the rear. Leaning against the set was a papier-mâché Egyptian sarcophagus, its lid open. To one side was a big prop throne painted gold, decorated with glass jewels and inscribed with hieroglyphs. With the atmospheric lighting switched on and the fog machine activated, the set looked pretty darn spooky.

It was stiflingly hot in the soundstage. Cliff glanced at the big standing fans set up around the stage. He wiped the sweat off his forehead and hoped they would turn them on soon.

A professional photographer had been hired to take the publicity stills, although Rogell directed the shoot himself. While the photographer snapped pictures and his assistant monitored the lighting and prepared rolls of film, Rogell told Betty where to stand, what to do, how far to stick out her chest to "really show off the jewels." Despite the heat and being on her feet the whole time, Betty was a pro. She never complained once. She posed standing beside the sarcophagus, then bending forward (much too far for Cliff's liking) over the throne, then cringing in fear from a mummy-wrapped department-store mannequin Rogell claimed he'd "borrowed" from a store where his niece worked. The Mask of the Pharaoh had been placed over the fake mummy's head.

When Rogell finally told his crew to turn on the fans, they only turned them to a very low setting to keep the breeze from stirring up the fake fog too much. It was just enough to blow Betty's hair and the diaphanous material of her costume around her alluringly, but not enough to cool Cliff off. He wiped the sweat from his brow again. Maybe it wasn't just the summer weather heating him up, though. Betty did look pretty spectacular in that outfit. Everyone noticed, too. Rogell's crew and the photographer's assistant were busy adjusting the props and lighting equipment, but not too busy to sneak occasional peeks at Betty in her skimpy costume. When Rogell called for a costume change and Betty went into the makeshift dressing room, Cliff was relieved that at least the makeup and wardrobe people who went with her were women.

An angry hiss from the corner of the soundstage drew Cliff's attention. "Keep your voice down, blast it!"

It was Morlant. He was standing near the prop workshop, engaged in a heated discussion with Bortello. Cliff didn't know what they were arguing about, but it didn't look friendly. Bortello was shaking his head no, his cloud of white hair bouncing side to side like a clown wig, his mustache drooping with defiance.

"Do you think I'm afraid of a rich, spoiled academic like you?" Bortello demanded in a half whisper. "I stared down Nazis on the streets of Munich's Italian neighborhood before I came to America! You're nothing compared to them!"

Morlant noticed Cliff watching them. He escorted Bortello farther away and turned his back to Cliff. They resumed their argument, but Cliff couldn't hear what they were saying anymore. It occurred to him that Morlant and Bortello had been off in the corner arguing the whole time. Unlike everyone else, these two weren't the least bit interested in watching Betty prance around in her skin-baring costumes. Even when she came out again in a new outfit that seemed composed more of translucent veils than opaque cloth, they didn't look up from their argument. Morlant kept insisting on something in harsh whispers, while Bortello kept vehemently shaking his head.

Betty stood beside the throne, waiting to resume the shoot. A sparkling, jewel-handled dagger was sheathed at the mostly bare curve of her hip. The crew had seated the mummy in the throne and jokingly taped a pair of sunglasses over the mask's eyes, transforming the mummy into a lounging movie star on holiday.

"Get those stupid glasses off the mummy!" Rogell yelled. "Sekhemkhet is supposed to look frightening, not like something out of a Foster Grant ad!"

A crew member rushed to remove the sunglasses. Betty waved at Cliff. Cliff was about to wave back when Morlant stormed past him toward the soundstage door.

"You'll regret this decision, Bortello," Morlant snarled over his shoulder. "I don't have time to continue this now. I have to catch a flight to San Francisco. But this isn't over!"

The door slammed behind him as he left, but no one seemed to notice. All eyes were on Betty as she drew the dagger from her hip and leaned voluptuously over the throne again. The camera resumed snapping. Gionvanni Bortello turned with a smug look on his face and disappeared into his workshop.

4.

That night, Cliff sat with Betty on the living room couch in her boarding house. She'd fixed mugs of tea for both of them, but Cliff left his cooling on the coffee table. Part of him wished he had a beer instead. At least it would help steel him for the conversation he was about to have.

"So," he said. "Those costumes were something, huh?"

"Oh, I know," Betty said, sipping her tea. "Aren't they beautiful?"

"That's not exactly what I meant," Cliff said. "They're, um, kind of skimpy, don't you think?"

She smiled and arched a devilish eyebrow. "I've done shoots wearing less."

That didn't make him feel any better. But before he could say anything else, things that would probably only get him in trouble, the phone rang. Saved by the bell, he thought. He looked at the clock on the wall. It was 11:45 at night. Who was calling at this hour?

Betty got up off the couch and answered the phone. "Oh, hello, Mister Rogell," she chirped.

Cliff rolled his eyes. Of course it was Rogell. The letch was probably calling to invite himself over for a little scotch and sofa...

"Oh, my God, that's terrible!" Betty exclaimed. The color drained out of her face. She looked at Cliff with panicked eyes.

Cliff bolted to his feet. "Is everything all right?"

She didn't answer him. She listened to Rogell on the other end of the line for several long seconds, nodding mutely or murmuring in shock. Finally, when she hung up, Cliff rushed over to her. She threw herself into his arms.

"Oh, Cliff, it's horrible!" she said. "Gionvanni Bortello was murdered!"

"What?"

She looked up at him, tears streaming down her cheeks. "They—they found his body in the soundstage workshop. But that's not all. The Mask of the Pharaoh was stolen! Mister Rogell said the police are coming here tomorrow to ask me questions. You—you'll be here, too, won't you? Or do you have to work?"

"Of course I'll be here," Cliff said. "I'll get Peevy to cover my flight school classes. He's done it before. They know him there."

He led her over to the couch and gently sat her down. He sat next to her and held her hands.

"We're—we're not allowed to use that soundstage right now. It's a crime scene," she said, her voice trembling with worry. "Mister Rogell said it's going to take at least another couple of days before— before…" Her voice broke into sobs. Cliff put his arms around her. "Oh, Cliff, it's terrible! That poor man!"

That sealed it. Until now, Cliff thought he could handle Betty being in the middle of a Hollywood viper's nest, but now someone was dead. That changed everything.

"Please tell me you're not still thinking of doing this picture," he said.

She stopped crying. "What? Of course I am!"

He pulled back from her. "But Bortello's been *murdered*!"

She sniffled, lifting her chin defiantly. "Bortello was an artist. He died trying to make this picture something special. I won't let his death be in vain. I'm more committed to *The Mask of the Pharaoh* than ever," she said. Then she deflated a little. "Oh, Cliff, I know this isn't *How Green Was My Valley*. It's just a jumped-up horror picture that'll probably be forgotten a month after it comes out. And I know Mister Rogell only hired me for my looks. But it's my first leading role. I need this."

"Betty…"

"I keep thinking about Evelyn Keyes," she said. "She started off in adventure pictures, too, and then just a few years later she was in *Gone With the Wind*. I'm not saying the same thing will happen to me. The odds are against it. But if I don't keep trying, I'll never forgive myself."

"But what if the killer isn't finished?" he pressed. "What if he comes back?"

"You have to trust me, Cliff. I can take care of myself. You know I can. You've seen it." She leaned her head on his shoulder. "Besides, you'll be there, too. Mister Rogell can't object to that. Not now."

Unless Rogell was the murderer, Cliff thought gloomily. Then he and Betty would be walking right into his clutches.

5.

The next day, Cliff watched through the window as a chunky, mustard-yellow Oldsmobile parked in front of Betty's boarding house. The man who stepped out of it was tall and wide, a bruiser with a weathered face so craggy it looked like the surface of the moon. Judging by the turnip-like shape of his nose, he was no stranger to fistfights. Dressed in a rumpled suit, he looked like a thug, but the badge clipped to his belt identified him as a policeman. A second car, a sleek Chevrolet Blackout, came out of nowhere and pulled up next to him. Another man, skinny, in a tight suit and fedora, stepped out. As Cliff watched, the two of them started arguing.

A few minutes later, they both knocked on the door, their argument apparently resolved. Betty and Cliff opened it together. The big man spoke first. He unclipped his badge from his belt and held it up for them to see.

"I'm Lieutenant Max Argyle, Homicide Division."

"Hello," she said, nodding. "I'm Betty. And this is my boyfriend, Cliff Secord. It's okay if he stays, isn't it?"

Argyle looked Cliff up and down. "Is he your lawyer, too, or just your boyfriend?"

"Does she *need* a lawyer?" Cliff asked, worried.

"I suppose we're about to find out," Argyle said.

"Cliff Secord?" the second man interrupted. "I thought I recognized that name. You're the hotshot pilot, right? I saw your stunt show last Fourth of July. Impressive stuff."

"Thanks," Cliff said. "Are you with the police, too?"

"They should be so lucky," he said. He pulled out an ID card in a leather pouch.

Betty read the name on the card. "Lincoln Burton?"

"Call me Link. I'm an investigator with MacMurray & Keyes, the insurance company. All Artists Alliance hired us to underwrite its antique Egyptian jewelry."

All Artists Alliance? That was Rogell's production company. Cliff frowned. Why would a penny-pincher like Rogell spend the money to insure props that were just reproductions? The answer was so obvious it came to him immediately. It was all part of Rogell's publicity scheme. Rogell intended to fool the public into believing the jewels in *The Mask of the Pharaoh* were genuine by using the insurance policy as proof. He must have bribed someone at MacMurray & Keyes to fudge the appraisal and list the items as authentic.

Betty led them into the living room. She and Cliff sat on the couch. Argyle and Burton sat on two chairs facing them.

Argyle gave Burton the stink-eye. "I would rather do this alone, but it seems I don't have a choice."

Burton shrugged. "MacMurray & Keyes holds a lot of sway in this town. We've worked with the LAPD plenty of times. But I'm happy to let you begin, Lieutenant." He gestured graciously.

Argyle grunted in annoyance. "Fine. Miss, I take it you're aware Gionvanni Bortello was murdered last night?"

Betty nodded solemnly, taking Cliff's hand for support. "Karl Rogell told me. How did it happen?"

"Stabbed to death," Argyle said curtly. Betty winced. Argyle pulled a photograph out of the inside pocket of his blazer and put it down on the coffee table for them to see. It showed Bortello lying face down on the cement floor of the workshop. A pool of blood spread out near his chest. Cliff could see the safe was open in the background. Several of the props were scattered on the floor around Bortello's body, as if someone had been rummaging through the safe's contents.

Betty whimpered and buried her head in Cliff's shoulder.

"Apparently, he stayed late at the soundstage to make some last-minute alterations," Argyle said. "He was alone."

The lieutenant put another picture on the coffee table. This one was a close up of a jewel-handled dagger on the floor of the work-shop, its blade stained dark with blood.

"Do you recognize this dagger, Miss?" Argyle asked.

Betty looked at it and went as white as a sheet. "I—I do. It's the same dagger I posed with at the photo shoot yesterday. Is that...is that...?" She couldn't finish.

"The murder weapon? Yes, it is. We dusted it for prints. Only one set showed up. Yours."

"That's because I was holding it during the shoot; I just told you that," Betty insisted.

"When did you last see Mister Bortello?"

"When Cliff and I left the shoot together around six o'clock last evening," she said.

"Did you take the dagger with you after the photo shoot?"

"No, I gave it back to Mister Bortello when I was done with it," she insisted.

Argyle nodded. "How much is Karl Rogell paying you to be in this picture, miss?"

Betty balked, stunned. "What does that have to do with anything?"

"I'm thinking maybe he's not paying you all that much," Argyle said. "Or maybe it's just not enough for you. Maybe you saw something on set that you thought you could sell, and decided to steal it. Only, you never expected to find Bortello still there. You surprised him. One thing led to another—"

"You can't honestly think she killed him," Cliff interrupted.

Argyle ignored him, keeping his eyes on Betty. "Bortello was murdered with one of his own props. That tells me it was a weapon of convenience, not forethought. You didn't go there planning to kill anyone, did you, Betty? You just wanted to take the mask, but things got out of hand."

"That's absurd," Betty said. "I would never!"

"What about the security guards?" Cliff interjected. "The lot must have night watchmen."

"There's only one guard posted after hours," Argyle said. "He was knocked out cold. Never saw who snuck up on him. When he came to, he did his rounds to make sure nothing had been stolen. He's the one who found Bortello and called it in."

"Well, that settles it," Cliff said. "Does Betty look like someone who could knock out a security guard?"

Argyle squinted at him. "Maybe she didn't have to. Maybe she got her boyfriend to do it for her. Where were you last night around ten?"

"I was here, with Betty."

Argyle grunted. "Convenient. You're each other's alibis. Next you'll tell me you were here all night."

Burton grinned at Cliff. "Lucky man."

Cliff shot him a look. "You stay out of it."

"I'm afraid I can't," Burton said. "The lieutenant and I are both here on official business, though for different purposes. He wants to catch a killer. I want to find a missing Egyptian funerary mask."

"It's not even real," Betty said, crossing her arms. "None of the props are real."

"They're all reproductions," Cliff said. "Gionvanni Bortello made them for Karl Rogell's mummy picture."

Burton nodded. "I know. I figured that out the moment I saw the jewels at the crime scene. Bortello did a fantastic job. They're practically indistinguishable from genuine pieces. But to a trained eye like mine, I could tell. That said, I'm thinking whoever killed Bortello didn't know they were fakes. Someone thought his workshop was filled with priceless jewels, one of the cast or crew maybe, and they came to rob it. Like the lieutenant said, they probably figured no one would be there. Bortello surprised them and got killed for his trouble. Then the killer got scared. Bortello died with the safe still open, so the killer grabbed the biggest, most valuable-looking item in there—the mask—and ran out with it."

"You're full of it, Burton," Argyle said. "The safe's contents were all over the floor. The killer was looking for something in there. My gut tells me whoever did this was after the mask from the start. But I agree with you: Bortello was in the wrong place at the wrong time."

"But Cliff and I both knew the mask was fake," Betty insisted. "So why would we have stolen it?"

Argyle grunted again, but this time he nodded, too. Cliff took that as a good sign. Maybe he didn't consider them suspects anymore.

"Did you see anyone acting strangely on set?" Argyle asked.

Betty shook her head. "No. I was too busy with the photo shoot to notice anything."

"I did," Cliff said. "Betty, you remember how fixated Morlant was on that mask the moment he saw it, don't you?"

"Who's Morlant?" Argyle asked.

"Doctor Julian Kort Morlant," Betty said. "He's a consultant on the picture. And yes, he did seem very taken with the mask."

"That's not all," Cliff said. "Yesterday, during the photo shoot, I saw him arguing with Bortello."

Argyle leaned forward in his chair. "Any idea what they were arguing about?"

Cliff shook his head. "Only that Morlant was pushing hard for something and Bortello kept refusing. He thought Morlant was threatening him. Then Morlant stormed out and said Bortello would regret his decision. Whatever that meant."

"You think Morlant had something to do with Bortello's death?" Argyle asked.

Cliff shrugged. Morlant seemed like the most obvious suspect. Bortello's death right after their big argument couldn't be a coincidence, could it?

Link Burton took the opportunity to stand up and smooth his pants legs. "Well, I've got everything I need. Now that I know the stolen mask was as phony as the rest of the props, I'm done here. As far as MacMurray & Keyes is concerned, this case is closed."

Argyle looked up at him with disdain. "The case isn't closed until the murderer's behind bars, Burton."

"That's your job, Lieutenant," Burton said. "Cops catch killers. I'm just here about the mask. Thanks for your time, miss. You too, Mister Secord. Maybe I'll see you at the next stunt show."

He started toward the door, then stopped when he noticed something on top of an end table. It was a framed photograph of the Rocketeer with the inscription: *For Betty, my biggest fan. Yours truly, the Rocketeer.* Cliff had given it to her as a gag gift for her birthday, but much to his surprise, she loved it enough to put it out in the living room. With the blessings of the couple who ran the boarding house, of course. It helped that they thought having a boarder who was friends with the Rocketeer would drum up business. Burton lifted the photograph and studied it.

"You know the Rocketeer?" he asked.

"We've met once or twice," Betty said.

Burton nodded. "Don't suppose you know who's under the mask, huh?"

She shrugged. "Sorry." Cliff had to give her credit. She didn't even blink or cast an involuntary glance his way. Maybe he'd misjudged her acting abilities.

"It's just as well," Burton said. "You know what they say about men in masks, don't you? The masks don't hide their true faces. The masks *are* their true faces. Makes you wonder about the Rocketeer, doesn't it? What that says about him?"

Burton put the photograph back on the table, tipped his hat and took his leave.

Once Argyle heard the sound of Burton's car starting, he grumbled, "Nice to see some people don't change. Link Burton is still an insufferable jerk."

"You know him?" Cliff asked.

Argyle sighed. "Our paths have crossed before. He wasn't kidding when he said MacMurray & Keyes holds a lot of sway over the police department in this town. Too much sway, if you ask me, but these days the department bends over backward for anything involving Hollywood. As for Burton, let's just say he's not one of my favorite people."

It was hard for Cliff to imagine this curmudgeon having any favorite people.

"Tell me something, miss," Argyle said. "How well do you know Karl Rogell?"

Betty frowned. "Not very well. I only met him a couple of days ago, at my audition. Why?"

"So I take it you didn't know All Artists Alliance is his fourth production company in four years?"

"What?"

"Rogell's been using a tax loophole to create a series of one-picture corporations. I won't bore you with the legalese, but basically he's been setting up corporations on a film-by-film basis. As a result, he gets a tax break. A big one."

"But surely that's not illegal," Betty said.

"Illegal? No. Unethical, maybe. Especially with the war on, when everyone should be pitching in their fair share for Uncle Sam. Rogell is hardly the only independent producer doing it, but that's the point. Karl S. Rogell was never supposed to be an independent producer. Not so long ago, he was a studio producer at Universal, a real up-and-comer. Might have even become studio head one day. Then he ticked off the wrong people. Rogell had an affair with the wife of a Universal exec named Edwin Humler. When Humler found out, Rogell wasn't just out of a job—he was out of the game. Humler made sure Rogell was banned from all the major studios. If he wanted to keep making pictures, he would have to do it on his own, without studio backing. Hence the four different corporations in four years."

Cliff thought back to Rogell's rant about how his picture would show up "those studio jerks" at Universal. Now he understood. Rogell had been carrying around his resentment a long time and planned to use *The Mask of the Pharaoh* to beat his enemies at their own game.

"Wait, did you say Edwin Humler?" Betty asked, sitting bolt upright. "That's so strange. There's a character named Edwin Humler in *The Mask of the Pharaoh*. He's the mummy's final victim, and he gets it worse than any of the others."

Argyle chuckled. "Killing off his real-life enemies in a picture. Classic, but shortsighted. They'll run him out of town as soon as they find out."

"What if he's not just planning to kill them off in the picture?" Cliff suggested. "Bortello is already dead. What if Rogell is cleaning house? What if more people are on his list?"

"Nah, Rogell's got an alibi for last night. Some naive farmer's daughter just off the bus looking to make it as an actress. Don't get me started on wolves like Karl Rogell. He exploits young women looking to break into show business—no offense, miss—but he didn't kill Bortello. He needed Bortello's expertise to give his picture a leg up. I don't see why he would steal the mask, either. As the producer, he essentially owns it already."

"He could have done it for the insurance money," Cliff suggested.

Argyle shook his head. "And sink his own picture in the process? Unlikely. *The Mask of the Pharaoh* is too important to him, especially if he's planning to use it to show up his rivals at Universal. But there's no shortage of suspects who might have seen that mask at the sound-stage. The rest of the cast and crew. The photographer and his assistant. Bortello had an assistant who worked with him on the reproductions, a young man who happens to have a record for petty larceny. And then there are the film's investors. People who back independent producers like Rogell aren't always on the up-and-up. That's a lot of people to question. I've got my work cut out for me. But one of them killed Bortello because they wanted that mask. The question isn't just who, it's why. What's so special about that prop?"

"Are you going to talk to Doctor Morlant?" Cliff asked.

"Eventually," Argyle said. He flipped his notepad closed and stuffed it in his pocket.

"*Eventually?*" Cliff demanded. "I just told you he was obsessed with the mask and arguing with Bortello! Shouldn't that make him the prime suspect?"

"How about you leave the police work to the police, kid?" Argyle said, standing up. "I'll be in touch if I have any more questions. And if you remember anything you think might be important, call me at the precinct. The number's on the card." He tossed a business card on the coffee table. "Thanks for your time."

6.

Later that afternoon, while Betty was at a cast and crew meeting with Rogell to discuss how the picture would move forward, Cliff sat in his parked car on a street in the Hollywood Hills. He was still fuming about Argyle's attitude. There was a murderer running free, someone possibly involved in Betty's picture, and all the lieutenant had to say about questioning the most obvious suspect was *eventually*. Someone needed to flush out the killer before he struck again. If Argyle wasn't going to do it, then he would do it himself, before anyone else got hurt. Before *Betty* got hurt.

Cliff looked again the address he'd written down, then across the road at the big Frank Lloyd Wright mansion with a view of the city so breathtaking it must have added a few extra zeroes to the price. This was the right place. Morlant's home. Cliff had gotten the address over the phone from Rogell's secretary, Yvonne. He'd told her Betty was supposed to meet Doctor Morlant to discuss how to play an Egyptian princess as authentically as possible, but had lost his address. Yvonne had coughed it right up. Cliff took in the sprawling mansion and whistled. Morlant obviously came from money. Nobody could afford a house like this just from lecturing at universities and consulting on the occasional Hollywood picture.

A sudden tapping on the window made him jump. He turned to see Argyle standing outside his car, knocking on the glass. Cliff glanced in the rearview and saw the lieutenant's mustard-yellow Oldsmobile parked on the street behind him. He sighed. He'd been so lost in his own thoughts he hadn't even heard Argyle arrive.

Cliff opened the door and got out of the car.

"What are you doing here, Mister Secord?" Argyle asked.

"I was going to see Morlant," he admitted. "I didn't think you were interested in talking to him, so I was going to do it myself. I'm certain he's got something to do with Bortello's murder."

"I thought I told you to leave this to me," Argyle said. "Go home."

Argyle started walking toward Morlant's driveway. Cliff hurried after him.

"I'm coming with you," he said.

Argyle chuckled. "Is that so?"

"You bet it is," Cliff said. "The longer it takes you to catch the killer, the longer Betty's life is in danger. Not that you care. You still think she's a suspect, don't you?"

Argyle stopped and turned to him. "Not anymore. I had a hunch the killer wasn't a woman anyway. Bortello's stab wounds angle downward, which means he was murdered by someone taller than him. Betty's tall, but not that tall. The killer is most likely a man. I'm guessing his prints aren't on the dagger because he wore gloves."

The killer was taller than Bortello? That clinched it in Cliff's mind. It had to be Morlant.

"So why don't you go home and tell Betty the good news?" Argyle said. "Let me do my job."

He walked up the driveway. Cliff followed.

"I'm still going with you," he insisted.

"We've been over this. Am I going to have to stick you in a cell for obstructing justice?"

"Obstructing? I'm trying to help!"

"You can help by staying out of my way," Argyle said. "I have questions for Doctor Morlant, a lot of 'em, and the last thing I want is for him to clam up because some starlet's boyfriend thinks he's John Wayne."

"Look, if I have to call my friend Howard, I will," Cliff threatened.

Argyle stopped. "Howard?"

"Howard Hughes," he said. "He's a close personal friend. I could have him call your captain, or even the chief of police, and they would order you to let me come along. Or they would take you off the case entirely. But I hope it won't come to that."

Argyle squinted at him. "You're playing hardball, kid. Why's it so important to you?"

"Because if I just stood by without doing anything and something happened to Betty, I would never forgive myself," he said.

Argyle's stern, craggy face almost softened. Almost. "You love her that much, huh?"

"Take whatever you're thinking and multiply it by a thousand," Cliff said.

Argyle thought on it a moment. "Are you bluffing about Howard Hughes?"

"Nope."

He took a deep breath. "Fine. Just let me do the talking. And no flying off the handle. We do this by the book. Deal?"

"Deal," Cliff said.

They walked to the front door together. Argyle knocked. Cliff half expected a tuxedoed butler with an upturned nose to open the door, but Morlant opened it himself. He was surprised to see Argyle, but even more surprised to see Cliff with him.

Argyle flashed his badge. "I'm Lieutenant Max Argyle, Homicide Division. This is Cliff Secord."

"Yes, he and I have met," Morlant sneered. "May I ask what this is about?"

"I'd like to ask you some questions about the death of Gionvanni Bortello."

"*We'd* like to ask you some questions," Cliff corrected.

Argyle shot him a look.

Morlant gave a long sigh, as if they were wasting his valuable time, but he opened the door wider. "Very well. Come with me. Please don't touch anything. Most of the art pieces on display in my home are priceless antiquities. Priceless and fragile."

He led them through corridors lined with ancient busts, urns and vases on pedestals. As they passed a doorway, Cliff peeked through and saw a room filled with unrolled papyrus scrolls inside glass display cases. Finally, Morlant brought them into a study of dark, polished wood. The walls were lined with bookshelves cluttered with old books and delicate artifacts. Morlant sat in a plush leather chair behind an antique desk. Argyle and Cliff remained standing.

"Now, what can I help you with, Lieutenant?" Morlant asked.

"Like I said, just a few questions," Argyle said. "Can you account for your whereabouts last night, particularly between ten and eleven o'clock?"

"I was in San Francisco all afternoon and well into the evening yesterday," Morlant replied. "A gallery hired me to appraise its collection of Twentieth Dynasty statuary. I was there quite late. My flight landed in Los Angeles at ten o'clock, and I got back home around eleven. In the hour between, I'm afraid the most interesting thing I did was drive from the airport. If you like, you can confirm with my contact at the gallery that I was there." He passed Argyle a business card. "It should be easy enough for you to confirm my presence on the nighttime flight from San Francisco as well."

Cliff remembered now that Morlant had mentioned something about going to San Francisco when he'd stormed out of the soundstage, but in all the chaos afterward he'd forgotten. Did that mean Morlant *wasn't* the killer? He'd been so sure...

"You were seen arguing with Gionvanni Bortello that morning," Argyle went on. "What were you two arguing about?"

Morlant glared at Cliff. It was clear he knew who ratted him out.

"Yes, we argued," Morlant said. "I wanted to purchase one of his reproductions from him. He refused to sell it to me."

"Which piece?"

Morlant rubbed his forehead and sighed. The golden scarab ring on his finger glittered in the light.

"Which piece, Doctor Morlant?" Argyle pressed.

Morlant looked up at him sharply. "It was the mask, all right? The Mask of the Pharaoh. Look, I'm trying to cooperate, but I answered all these questions already when the other investigator was here."

Argyle looked surprised. "What other investigator? Who else was here?"

"His name was Chain, I think. Or Fence? Something like that. He had a movie star last name."

Cliff stiffened. "Burton?"

Morlant nodded. "That's it. Link Burton. He was here earlier, asking me the same questions you are. The three of you could really save time by comparing notes."

Cliff turned to Argyle. "What was Burton doing here? He said he was done with the case."

"Evidently not," Argyle said. "Doctor Morlant, why did you want to buy the mask? I was under the impression all of Bortello's props were reproductions of your own collection."

"Not that one," Morlant said. "The mask was commissioned specifically for the picture. I was quite taken with it. It was a perfect reproduction of the actual funerary mask of Sekhemkhet, a Third Dynasty pharaoh of the Old Kingdom—the same pharaoh whose name Rogell is using in the picture. Bortello must have done his homework. I asked him if I could buy the mask from him when the picture was wrapped, but he refused. He said it wasn't for sale. I offered that man a sum of money that would take your breath away, Lieutenant, but he only laughed at me."

"He didn't like you even touching the mask," Cliff said. "I saw him yell at you to put it down."

"Yes, well, Bortello was an eccentric man," Morlant said.

"That must have made you angry, him treating you like that," Argyle said.

"Yes, I was angry. Can you blame me? I'm the foremost Egyptologist in the state. That mask didn't belong with some filthy, paint-covered little peasant. It belonged with *me!*" He banged his fist angrily on the desk.

Cliff tensed, startled at the outburst, but Argyle didn't even flinch.

"Maybe you can clear something up for me," Argyle said. "Why not make a deal with Karl Rogell to buy the mask? As the producer, he's the one who actually owns it, right?"

Morlant remained silent, glaring at him.

"You were going behind his back, weren't you?" Cliff said. "You didn't want him to know you were making a deal for the mask. Why?"

Morlant squinted angrily at him. "If you're here to accuse me of something, just get to it."

"No one's accusing anyone of anything," Argyle said, shooting Cliff another angry glance. "But I do have a few more questions. For example, I'd be interested to know how exactly you were you planning to pay Bortello for the mask."

Morlant frowned. "What are you implying?"

"I didn't have to do a lot of digging to find out the Morlant fortune isn't what it used to," Argyle said. "You came from money. You inherited this house..."

"That's no secret," Morlant said stiffly.

Argyle pulled a bundle of mimeographed papers out of his coat pocked, unfolded them and put them in front of Morlant on the desk. Cliff saw they were copies of bank statements and financial papers.

Morlant raised an eyebrow. "How did you get these?"

"A warrant," Argyle said.

"Does that mean I'm a suspect?"

"Everyone is a suspect right now," Argyle said.

Morlant glared at Cliff. "Even him?"

"Not him. He and his girlfriend have been cleared."

"So why is he here?"

"Friends in high places, unfortunately," Argyle said. He tapped the papers to bring Morlant back to the topic at hand. "According to these statements, you've been selling off stocks at an alarming rate. You almost don't have any left. I'm guessing all the lectures and museum consults aren't keeping up with the bills. So I'll ask again: how were you going to pay Bortello for the mask?"

Morlant stuck out his chin defiantly. "Times have been difficult, yes, but that hardly makes me a murderer. Things are going to turn around for me soon. I stand to come into a great deal of money from a prior business arrangement. I could have paid Bortello handsomely for the mask. But murder, Lieutenant? Come now. If everyone who ever fell on hard times became a murderer, we would all be dead or in jail."

"Someone *is* dead," Cliff reminded him.

"I'm well aware of that, young man," Morlant sneered. "It's the only reason I'm allowing this vulgar interrogation to continue. But let me remind you I was in San Francisco yesterday, not skulking around the soundstage like Dracula looking for victims."

Argyle took the mimeographed papers off the desk and pocketed them again. "I appreciate your cooperation, Doctor Morlant. How well did you know Gionvanni Bortello?"

Morlant composed himself, running a hand through his hair. "Not very well. We'd never met before we started working together on the picture. We collaborated on the reproductions, of course, but not closely. He had access to the items in my collection, and photographs to work from. He would occasionally ask questions about one piece or another, but that was the extent of our communication. He didn't talk much about himself."

"I'm not surprised, given his history," Argyle said. "Bortello was a wanted man in Egypt."

"What?" Morlant demanded.

Argyle pulled a notepad out of his pocket and flipped through the pages until he found what he was looking for. "They have a warrant out for his arrest on charges of theft, but with no extradition treaty, Bortello was a free man here in the U.S. It seems he worked on a few of the German expeditions to Egypt back in the twenties, restoring and duplicating ancient jewelry for the National Museum and a few rich collectors. He became something of a self-taught expert. Unfortunately, he'd already left the country by the time the museum realized one of its most valuable artifacts had been stolen and replaced with an identical reproduction. Care to guess what that artifact was?"

Morlant remained silent.

"The funerary mask of the pharaoh Sekhemkhet," Argyle said.

Cliff's heart skipped a beat. "Holy smokes!"

Morlant leaned back in his chair, steepling his fingers under his chin. "Do you honestly expect me to believe Bortello brought Sekhemkhet's *real* funerary mask to the soundstage as a prop?"

"Whoever killed Bortello sure thought he did," Argyle said. "Any ideas why?"

Morlant stroked his trim beard. "Lieutenant, have you ever heard the legend of Sekhemkhet? No, I don't suppose you would have. Sekhemkhet wasn't just a pharaoh of the Third Dynasty. He was a magician. A sorcerer. Legend has it he never truly died. Instead, he stored his life essence—his soul—in his funerary mask, and there he waited for a new, suitable host body to present itself. It was said anyone who touched the mask was in turn touched by Sekhemkhet himself. They made contact with the great pharaoh's mind, even became a slave to it. Perhaps Bortello was already under Sekhemkhet's control. Maybe that's why he refused to sell the mask to me."

"Now you're the one pulling *my* leg, Doctor Morlant," Argyle said. "You think Bortello was under some dead pharaoh's influence?"

Morlant shrugged. "I offered him a lot of money, Lieutenant. He wouldn't have had to work another day in his life. Can you think of another reason he would have turned that down?"

"Maybe he knew you weren't as rich as you like people to think," Argyle said. "Maybe he thought you couldn't put your money where your mouth was."

To Cliff's surprise, Morlant didn't take offense. Instead, he smiled in an almost friendly manner. "Of course. I suppose that makes more sense. Sometimes I let my fascination with ancient Egyptian lore get the best of me. But I want to help you however I can." He tore a piece of paper off a pad on his desk and began writing on it. "This is a list of local antiquities dealers. If Bortello's killer is trying to sell the mask, these are the people he's likely to approach. You'll need to act fast if you want to catch him red-handed. The killer may already be trying to unload it."

Unless the killer was already taking the mask back to Egypt, Cliff thought. Was the Egyptian government involved? Did they kill Bortello in order to take back what he'd stolen from them? It was a plausible theory, but it didn't feel right. Bortello had been killed with a weapon of convenience, the bejeweled dagger from the photo shoot. Egyptian agents surely would have brought their own weapons with them. Guns, most likely. No, everything about this felt individual, not international. Someone wanted that mask, someone who knew it was real. But why? To sell to the highest bidder? Or to keep as part of a personal collection? Cliff only knew one person who collected ancient Egyptian artifacts: Doctor Morlant. But the Egyptologist was cooperating. Suddenly, he wasn't looking like the most obvious suspect anymore.

After they left Morlant and walked back to their cars, Cliff asked Argyle, "Do you believe his story about being in San Francisco?"

"I'll make some calls when I'm back at the precinct and check it out," he said. "In the meantime, I've got a whole list of antiquities dealers to contact."

"Is that our next step?"

Argyle rolled his eyes. "Give it a rest, Dick Tracy. I know you're concerned about your gal, but the best thing you can do for her is go home and be with her. Let me do my job."

"But—"

"You gotta trust me, kid," Argyle said. "I didn't become lieutenant of Homicide Division by sitting on my hands. I'm good at what I do. But not when I've got someone playing private dick under my feet all day. So go take care of Betty, and let me catch Bortello's killer."

Cliff sighed. "Fine. But will you at least keep us in the loop? Let us know what's going on?"

"You want me to tell you that you'll be the first person I call? You won't be. The truth is, you're so far down on my list of priorities you'd be lucky to be the tenth person I call. But that's the way it's supposed to be. My job is catch a killer, not hold your hand."

He knew Argyle was right. But he also knew the killer wasn't likely to approach any of the reputable antiquities dealers on Morlant's list. It was the surest way to get caught. Argyle was barking up the wrong tree. Cliff's gut told him *The Mask of the Pharaoh* was the key to solving this case. Someone involved in the picture had killed Bortello and stolen the mask. If Argyle didn't want him tagging along, that was fine with him. He had his own hunches to follow—on his own.

7.

Cliff wasn't surprised to hear Rogell had been playing up Bortello's murder and the theft of the mask for all the free ink it was worth. Bortello's body wasn't even cold, and the publicity-loving producer was already doing newspaper interviews about the "ancient Egyptian curse" haunting his picture. What did surprise him was that Betty had agreed to be roped into Rogell's new PR scheme. Rogell wanted her to do another photo session with those skimpy costumes and Bortello's jewelry, this time for members of the Hollywood press. And in the same soundstage where Bortello had died, no less. The police had gathered all the evidence they could, finally releasing it as a crime scene, and now Rogell was ghoulishly cashing in on the murder that had happened there. Cliff couldn't talk Betty out of it no matter how hard he tried. She was sure it would great publicity for the picture, and for her own career, too. Of course, Cliff knew who would get the real publicity payoff—Karl S. Rogell, the producer who bravely faced down an ancient Egyptian curse for the sake of his art. It was enough to make him wonder if maybe Rogell had murdered Bortello after all, just for the publicity.

Cliff was with Betty at the boarding house when Rogell picked her up the next day for the photo shoot. Cliff offered to go with her for protection in case the killer turned up again—and in case Rogell got too touchy-feely, too, though he kept that part to himself—but Betty refused.

"I'll be fine," she said. "You can pick me up at the soundstage when the shoot is over this evening."

"Yeah, no need to worry about your sweetheart, Clod," Rogell agreed around the stub of his cigar. "She'll be in good hands. Mine." He winked grotesquely.

Cliff flushed with anger as Rogell escorted Betty out the door and into his waiting car. He watched from the window as they drove away, then looked at his watch. It was almost time to go teach his classes at flight school. His heart sank. He ought to be with Betty, protecting her, not teaching a bunch of cadets how to do a barrel roll. Especially now, with Bortello's murder getting so much atten- tion. The killer had to be feeling the heat and thinking about tying up loose ends. And everyone involved in *The Mask of the Pharaoh* was a loose end, including Betty. What if something happened to her and he wasn't there?

No. He shook the thought out of his head. The best way to protect Betty was to find the killer before he had a chance to strike again. And to do that, he knew where he had to start.

8.

Cliff stood across the street from the building in Gower Gulch where Rogell had his production office. He wore big sunglasses and a hat to conceal his face. It wasn't the world's best disguise, but he'd been forced to improvise. The last thing he wanted was Yvonne, Rogell's secretary, recognizing him and tipping Rogell off.

Before leaving the house, he'd called Peevy and asked him to cover his flight school classes again. Peevy wasn't happy about it, but he agreed to do it. "I don't want anything to happen to Betty, either," he'd said. "Just don't make a habit out of this. I've got my own work to do, you know."

The front door of the office building opened, and Yvonne walked out on her lunch break. Rogell was with Betty at the photo shoot, so Cliff knew the office would be empty. He hurried across the street. There was no doorman in the building, just an intercom system. He rang every bell until someone buzzed him in. He climbed the steps to the third floor and tried the door marked AAA in gold stencil. It was locked. He looked up and down the hallway to make sure the coast was clear, then knelt down in front of the door. He pulled a couple of Betty's bobby pins out of his pocket. He fit them into the lock and picked it, just like he'd learned from the carny troupe when he was sixteen. The door swung open.

He hurried inside and closed it behind him. He didn't know how long Yvonne would be out of the office, so he would have to be quick. He just wished he knew exactly what he was looking for. If the killer was someone involved with *The Mask of the Pharaoh*, there was a good chance something in Rogell's files would tip him off to the culprit's identity. Something in a cast or crew member's past, maybe, or a connection no one else had noticed.

He took off his sunglasses and hat and rummaged through Yvonne's desk. He didn't find anything useful. He moved into Rogell's private office next. Three tall metal file cabinets stood against one wall. He opened a drawer and started looking through the files. There were a lot of headshots and résumés. More than two-thirds of them belonged to pretty, young actresses looking for their big break. Rogell had jotted down notes on the backs of some of the headshots, names like *Palomar* and numbers like *1205*. It took Cliff a moment to realize they were hotels and room numbers. He shook his head in disgust and kept looking.

He paused when he came across Betty's file. His heart pounded in his chest. If he turned her headshot around, would he find anything written there?

He heard Rogell's voice in his head again: *She'll be in good hands. Mine.*

But he heard Betty's voice, too: *You have to trust me, Cliff. I can take care of myself.*

He took a deep breath and put her file back in the drawer without looking. He was sure Betty would never cheat on him, not even for her career's sake. But thinking about her put a knot in his stomach again. He wished she were safe at home, or with Peevy, or at the Bulldog Café—anywhere but out in the open where the killer could find her if he wanted to.

The next drawer he opened held the corporate registration papers for All Artists Alliance, including documents confirming the production company's significantly lower capital gains tax rate. Just like Argyle had said. Another file held a partnership agreement in AAA. Cliff paused. Rogell had a business partner? It was the first he'd heard of it. He flipped to the signatures on the last page and saw Rogell's partner in All Artist Alliance was none other than Doctor Morlant.

So he wasn't just a consultant after all. Now that he thought about it, it made sense. Morlant was running out of money. He'd been struggling for years to maintain his collection and hold onto his family home. Taking advantage of the same tax loophole as Rogell had to lighten his load quite a bit. He could maintain the lifestyle he'd inherited and elevate his professional status at the same time. But what was in it for Rogell? Why would he agree to share the income from *The Mask of the Pharaoh* with Morlant when he could just as easily keep it all for himself?

In the next drawer, Cliff found a file of carbon-copy documents that appeared to be brokerage agreements from an establishment called Rodeo Drive Elite Jewels & Antiquities for the sale of numerous unspecified items. On the last page, on a line above the word SELLER, was the signature of Karl S. Rogell. Cliff frowned. That was strange. What was Rogell selling? He dug some more and found a letter guaranteeing all the pieces Rogell was selling were genuine and appraised for tens of thousands of dollars each. The letter was signed by Doctor Julian Kort Morlant.

Stranger and stranger. The only things Cliff could imagine them selling were pieces from Morlant's collection, but that didn't make sense. Morlant was working with Rogell on *The Mask of the Pharaoh* so he could hold onto his collection—not to mention his beautiful house in the Hollywood Hills—not sell them off. But even if he'd changed his mind about selling his collection, surely Morlant would sell it himself, wouldn't he? Yet the papers listed Rogell as the seller and Morlant merely as the appraising agent. Cliff sifted through the documents, trying to figure it out, but the sound of a woman's voice in the hallway outside caught his ear. Was Yvonne back already? He'd barely had time to look through Rogell's files. He certainly hadn't discovered anything that told him who the killer was.

But maybe he had what he needed after all, he thought as he closed the file cabinet drawer. At the very least, he knew where he had to go next.

He put on his sunglasses and hat and went to the front door. He opened it slowly and peeked out. Yvonne, holding a brown lunch bag, was standing at the far end of the hallway, talking with a woman from one of the other offices on the floor. Cliff stepped quietly out into the hallway, hoping neither of them saw him, and gently closed the door. Keeping his head down, he walked past them to the stair-well. Neither of them paid him any mind.

9.

Rodeo Drive Elite Jewels & Antiquities was located on the same street it was named for. Cliff had been expecting a storefront like the jewelers farther down the block, but it turned out to be a private office on the second floor of a commercial building, albeit with its own door to the sidewalk. Cliff was about to cross the street toward the door when it swung open from the inside. Link Burton stepped out onto the sidewalk.

Cliff ducked behind a street lamp. Burton didn't see him, continuing down the street toward his parked car. Cliff watched him drive off. What was Burton doing here? It couldn't be a coincidence. Something was going on, and Cliff was determined to find out what it was.

He crossed the street, opened the door and climbed the flight of stairs up to Rodeo Drive Elite Jewels & Antiquities' office. He found himself in a waiting room with framed pictures of gleaming gemstones and ancient artifacts on the walls. A small, round table had been set up in the middle of the room, stacked with color catalogues. An older man with a horseshoe of graying hair and a fine Italian suit was just getting up from the table with some papers when he spotted Cliff.

"Can I help you?" he asked. The badge on his blazer read GEORGE CARPENTER, VP OF MIDDLE EASTERN ACQUISITIONS.

"That man who was just here, what did he want?" Cliff asked.

Carpenter sneered at him. "I'm sorry, sir, but we keep all information confidential. Who might you be?"

Determined to find out everything he could, Cliff thought fast. "Link Burton, the man who was just here...we work together at MacMurray & Keyes. Maybe you've heard of us? There have been a few mix-ups at the office lately, and I just want to make sure we're not both here about the same case. Was he here about...a mask?"

Carpenter visibly relaxed. "Oh, I see. MacMurray & Keyes, of course. Yes, Mister Burton was here about an Egyptian funerary mask. He was asking if anyone had come by trying to sell it to us."

"And has anyone?"

"Sorry, no," he said. "As I told Mister Burton, I wish I could be more helpful."

"You might still be," Cliff said. "Is it true your company is entering into a business agreement with the film producer Karl S. Rogell?"

"Well, we don't really comment on such things," Carpenter said, "but seeing as how you're with MacMurray & Keyes, I don't see the harm. We signed with Mister Rogell just last week to broker the sale of quite a large number of pieces for him. I think it will be very lucrative for all parties involved. They're Egyptian antiquities, too, if I recall."

"But the mask wasn't among them?"

"No, Mister Rogell is selling amulets, brooches, and other jewelry along those lines. No masks."

It sure sounded like Morlant's collection. But why sell it under Rogell's name? Rogell clearly wasn't going behind Morlant's back. The Egyptologist had signed off as the appraising agent on the deal. But now that Cliff thought about it, that didn't make sense, either.

An establishment like this surely wouldn't allow someone to appraise his own collection. Unless...

Cliff's heart lurched in his chest. Unless it wasn't Morlant's collection they were selling. Not the genuine items, anyway. But what about the reproductions? Burton had said they were virtually indistinguishable from the real things. Rogell had already had them insured as if they were real. Maybe that wasn't just for publicity purposes. Maybe insuring them laid the groundwork for something more insidious, something he and Morlant were in on together. This, Cliff realized, was what Rogell had gotten in return for letting Morlant partner with him in the production company. Morlant's reputation would make it that much easier to sell the pieces without anyone knowing they were fakes.

This had to be Rogell's exit plan. He was about to burn all his bridges in Hollywood by killing off his old enemies as characters in *The Mask of Pharaoh*. Afterward, he would retire with the millions he expected to make selling forgeries to the rich and famous. That was what Morlant had meant when he said he would be coming into a great deal of money soon. Probably, it was also why Morlant had felt the need to go behind Rogell's back when he tried to buy the mask from Bortello. Rogell must have planned to sell the mask along with everything else. But did Rogell know it was real?

How did Bortello fit into all this? Had he discovered their plan to sell his reproductions and demanded a cut? Had Rogell and Morlant killed him so they wouldn't have to share the money with him, and then stole the mask to make it look like a robbery? It was a strong motive for murder. Unfortunately, there wasn't any evidence to back it up.

But one question still dogged him. Why on earth had Bortello used the authentic funerary mask of Sekhemkhet—a priceless relic he'd stolen from Egypt years ago—as a prop for a cheeseball horror picture?

The door behind Cliff opened. He turned to see Argyle walk into the waiting room. As soon as the lieutenant saw Cliff, his craggy face flushed with anger.

"What the blazes are you doing here, Secord? I thought we had an agreement!"

Cliff ignored the question. "Link Burton was just here, asking about the mask!"

Argyle stopped in his tracks. "Burton was *here?*"

"Yes, not ten minutes ago," Carpenter confirmed. "Are you from MacMurray & Keyes, too?"

Argyle grunted and looked at Cliff. "Outside. Now."

Cliff thanked Carpenter for his help, then followed Argyle down the stairs to the street. He was prepared to have his ear chewed off, but instead Argyle just sighed.

"This is the fifth dealer I've been to," the Lieutenant said. "They all said the same thing. No one's been by about the mask. It's obvious the killer isn't trying to sell it. I'm half ready to believe Morlant sent us on a wild goose chase."

He probably did, Cliff thought.

"Except I did learn something very interesting," Argyle went on. "A couple of the other dealers mentioned I wasn't the only one asking about the mask."

"Link Burton is still on its trail," Cliff said.

Argyle nodded. "He's been one step ahead of me this whole time. He went to see Morlant before I did. He must have gotten the same list of dealers Morlant gave me. The question is what's Burton's angle? Why is he after the mask?"

"Maybe he figured out the mask is real the same way you did," Cliff said. "And that means he has to recover it, or else MacMurray & Keyes will be forced to pay the insurance money."

"It's possible," Argyle said with another sigh. "Morlant's alibi checks out, by the way. He was in San Francisco and took the night flight home. I feel like I'm running up against a brick wall. There's something I'm not seeing. A connection I haven't made yet."

"There's more," Cliff said. "Before you showed up, Mister Carpenter was telling me they signed a deal with Rogell to broker the sale of ancient Egyptian artifacts and jewelry. Rogell stands to make a fortune. Except, I don't think he's selling the real stuff. I think he and Morlant are planning to sell Bortello's reproductions as if they're real."

Argyle narrowed his eyes at Cliff. "Fraud is a pretty serious accusation to make against someone. Do you have proof of this?"

"No," Cliff admitted.

"But Carpenter just coughed up confidential information about signing a deal with Rogell?"

"No, of course not. I had to ask him about it," Cliff said. He realized his mistake a split second too late.

"What exactly made you ask if a two-bit producer like Karl Rogell was getting mixed up in the jewelry trade?" Argyle pressed.

Cliff's palms went sweaty. He couldn't tell Argyle about the files he'd seen. That would be admitting to breaking and entering, and Argyle was definitely the kind of straight arrow cop who would arrest him for it.

"It was just a hunch, that's all," Cliff spluttered. "Something Morlant said about coming into money soon. But it makes me wonder if he and Rogell had something to do with Bortello's death after all. You know, to get him out of the way."

"That wasn't much of a hunch to go on, Mister Secord, but it sounds like it paid off," Argyle said. "Maybe Morlant wasn't cooperating as much as I thought he was. I'd say it's time for me to pay him another visit." He glared at Cliff. "Alone this time."

"Fine," Cliff said. "I have to pick up Betty at the soundstage anyway. She's doing another photo shoot—" He paused. "Oh, no. Betty. She's with Karl Rogell right now! If he was involved on Bortello's murder, then she's in danger! We have to get over there!"

Argyle cursed and yanked open the passenger door of his mustard-yellow Oldsmobile. "Get in!"

Argyle pulled out a dome-shaped portable police light, slapped it on top of his car and switched it on. They sped toward the lot in Gower Gulch, the siren parting traffic in front of them. When they got to the front gate, Argyle showed his badge to the guard, who lifted the wooden arm of the barrier gate and waved them through. The parking lot in front of Stage 4 was crowded with cars—not just Rogell's and his crew's; there were dozens of cars belonging to members of the Hollywood press. Argyle and Cliff managed to find a spot, got out and started toward the entrance.

A distressed moan coming from around the side of the soundstage stopped them in their tracks. They rushed around the corner and found a man sitting on the cement pavement. He was wearing white briefs, a white undershirt, socks and shoes, but nothing else. They helped him to his feet.

"What happened?" Argyle asked.

The man rubbed the back of his head. "I have a gig here, playing a mummy in a publicity shoot for a horror picture. We took a break, I came out for a smoke and someone clocked me on the head. I—I think I was only out for a few minutes." He looked down at himself, as if only just realizing he was in his briefs. "Holy cow, they took my mummy costume!"

Cliff looked at Argyle. "Why would Rogell do that?"

"This wasn't Rogell." Argyle squinted at the studio door. "This was someone else, someone who wanted to sneak inside undetected. Someone who wanted to get close to the action."

"Betty!" Cliff exclaimed.

Argyle drew his gun and ran into the soundstage, with Cliff right behind. Inside, it was wall-to-wall with press, the crush of bodies slowing them down. As they passed the prop workshop where Bortello had died, Cliff noticed it was blocked off with fake police tape marking it as a crime scene. All part of Rogell's show. Ahead, a platform had been set up in the middle of the soundstage, surrounded by four prop sarcophagi with their lids closed and new backdrops evoking ancient Egypt. Rogell had gone all out to make the production look like it had a higher budget than it really did. On stage, lit by colored lights and shrouded in a dry ice fog that clung to her ankles, was Betty. She posed for the flashing cameras in a skimpy, bejeweled two-piece.

Rogell stood in front of the stage, speaking into a bullhorn for all to hear. "No studio would dare to touch a dangerous picture like *The Mask of the Pharaoh*! Only I, Karl S. Rogell, had the courage to take it on! And yet the mummy's deadly curse has already doomed one member of the production to an untimely demise! Who's to say it won't claim another *this very day*?"

The sarcophagi on stage started to thump and shake. Their lids creaked open. Four big men covered head to toe in mummy wrappings emerged to menace Betty. They reached for her and swiped at her but never touched her, always maintaining a safe distance. The cameras kept flashing.

"They're coming for you, Betty!" Rogell shouted into the bull-horn. "The angry dead of ancient Egypt have come to drag you into the tomb! Whatever you do, Betty, don't faint! Don't faint, or they've got you!"

Just then, one of the mummies lunged forward and grabbed her. She played along for a moment, though Cliff—and probably *only* Cliff—could see how annoyed she was at being touched. But when the mummy lifted her off her feet and clamped one hand over her mouth, the realization dawned in her eyes for all to see—this wasn't part of the show!

Cliff and Argyle made their way toward the stage, shoving through the crowd of murmuring and confused members of the press. Up ahead, the mummy began to drag Betty away. She struggled and kicked, but no avail. The other mummies on the stage stood by awkwardly, unsure of what was happening. Betty reached up to the mummy's hand over her mouth and raked it with her nails, pulling away the cloth and briefly revealing pale, Caucasian fingers—fingers adorned with a familiar golden scarab ring. Angrily, the mummy threw something to the ground that exploded with a bright flash and filled the room with smoke. Cliff coughed and waved the smoke from his face, trying to see. He thought he heard Betty scream, but by now everyone in the room was screaming and blindly running into each other.

"Betty!" he shouted.

"Cliff!" she shouted back.

The smoke cleared quickly, but not quickly enough. By the time he could see again, Betty and the mummy were gone.

"There!" Argyle shouted, pointing at an open door in the side of the soundstage that was slowly swinging shut again.

Cliff and Argyle ran for the door and burst through it, finding themselves back outside. The sun was setting in the distance. A black car screeched away from the building. It smashed through the barrier gate and disappeared into the twilight. Cursing, Cliff turned back to Argyle.

"I saw the ring on the mummy's hand," he said. "It was a golden scarab—the same ring Doctor Morlant wears. He's got Betty!"

Argyle ran back to his car. Cliff followed, but Argyle stopped him from getting in. "You can't, Cliff. Not this time. It's too dangerous."

"But Morlant's got Betty!" Cliff shouted.

"I can't let you put your life in danger, too," Argyle insisted. He pushed Cliff away from the car and got in. A moment later, he squealed out of his parking spot, racing after Morlant's car.

All around the parking lot, mayhem unfolded. People were screaming and running out of the soundstage. Rogell waddled through the crowd in terror, his enormous belly jiggling, the stub of his cigar drooping from his gaping mouth. The fear in his eyes was real, Cliff saw. Whatever Morlant was up to, Rogell wasn't part of it. This had nothing to do with their jewelry scam. Following Rogell were the three other men dressed as mummies, running stiffly with their wrappings trailing behind them. Cliff would have thought it was comical if he weren't going out of his mind with worry.

He had to get to Betty. There was only one way to get to Morlant's house quickly. The rocket pack. But he was nowhere near home, and his car was still parked on Rodeo Drive. He ran to the nearest car in the lot. The door was unlocked. He found the key under the sun visor, started the engine and sped away. He'd already committed one crime today, he figured. What was one more, especially if Betty's life was at stake?

10.

Fifteen minutes later, wearing his jet pack, helmet, and rust-colored leather jacket, the Rocketeer flew toward the Hollywood hills. He prayed Betty was still okay.

Why had Morlant taken her? What did he want with her? She didn't have anything to do with Bortello, or the stolen mask, or the jewelry scam. The Rocketeer cursed himself for not staying with Betty this whole time and protecting her. He thumbed the ignition buttons on his handheld controllers as hard as he could, forcing the jet pack to go faster.

When he reached the sprawling mansion, he saw Morlant's black car and Argyle's mustard-yellow one both parked in front. There was no sign of either of them, or of Betty. The Rocketeer landed, cut the power to the jet pack and ran to the front door. It was open. He stepped cautiously inside, drawing his Mauser C96. The foyer was empty. The house was as quiet as a tomb. A grand staircase led up to the second floor. On top of the newel at the bottom of the stairs was a decorative, carved sphinx, only it was tipped off center. The Rocketeer touched it, and the sphinx shifted. With the loud churning of hidden gears, a large hatch opened in the stairs before him. Stone steps descended into darkness. He started down carefully. As he descended, his eyes adjusted, and he saw the warm glow of torchlight flickering below.

At the bottom of the steps, the Rocketeer paused, astonished at the sight before him. Deep beneath his mansion, Morlant had created a secret temple filled with ancient Egyptian antiquities. Burning torches lined the walls and illuminated an enormous chamber flanked by two giant statues—one a man with a hooded python's head, the other a man with a falcon's head. The same animal symbols that had adorned Sekhemkhet's mask.

Argyle's unconscious body sat slumped in the corner, secured with ropes. Morlant had tied Betty to an altar in the center of the temple. She screamed and struggled but couldn't break free of the thick ropes that bound her. Morlant stood with his back to the Rocketeer, still wearing the stolen mummy costume. He loomed over Betty with an ancient, jewel-handled dagger in his hands. It looked like the original ceremonial dagger on which Bortello had based his reproduction—the same reproduction that had been used to murder him. Now, Morlant held the blade over Betty's heart, preparing to murder again with the real thing.

The Rocketeer shot once into the air to get his attention. "Drop it, Doctor Morlant! Drop it, and let her go!"

Surprised, Morlant stiffened, but he didn't turn around. Instead, he lifted a large, bulky object off the altar beside Betty. It was the missing funerary mask of Sekhemkhet. Morlant put it on over his head, fitting it snugly against his mummy-wrapped shoulders. Only then did he turn to face the Rocketeer. The dagger glittered in his hand.

"I said put it down," the Rocketeer said, coming closer with the Mauser pointed at him.

"Fool!" Morlant shouted. "Don't you understand? I have spent a lifetime studying the legend of Sekhemkhet! The more I learned, the more I could feel him calling to me across the gulf of time. I knew that if I acquired the correct set of mystic articles and papyrus scrolls, I could bring him back. I could *become* Sekhemkhet!"

The Rocketeer inched closer.

Morlant spread his arms to indicate the artifacts all around his temple. "It was easy enough for a man in my position to smuggle what I needed out of Egypt, or to purchase them on the black market. I had all the pieces in place but the most important one of all—Sekhemkhet's funerary mask. And then I saw it, hiding in plain sight among Bortello's props. It called out to me even then. I knew it had come for me at last!"

The Rocketeer shuddered, recalling how he'd fixated on the mask the moment he saw it. Morlant had known it was real from the start.

"But the mystic artifacts aren't enough. Sekhemkhet demands a blood sacrifice," Morlant went on, pointing to Betty on the altar. "And this wretched city will hardly miss one struggling, unknown actress among the thousands who come here every year."

"You're insane," the Rocketeer said. He took another step closer, keeping the Mauser trained on Morlant. "What do you think all this is going to get you, besides a lifetime behind bars?"

"Power! Power beyond your feeble understanding!" Morlant cried. "Under Sekhemkhet's rule, ancient Egypt possessed technology the likes of which has never been seen since. That technology was lost when Sekhemkhet died. I can bring it back. I can use it to rule the world. A new dynasty with myself set on high as pharaoh. And I won't let you stop me!"

Morlant reeled back and threw the dagger like a pitcher sending a fastball across home plate. The Rocketeer had only a second to get out of the way before its sharp tip pierced his chest. He hit the jet pack's ignition and soared into the air. The dagger sliced through the spot where he'd been standing and landed harmlessly on the floor. The Rocketeer holstered the Mauser and launched himself forward, but Morlant dove to the floor before he could tackle him. The Rocketeer tried to turn, tried to brake, but there was no time. The jet pack drove him right into the python-headed statue.

The giant statue rocked precariously on its base. The Rocketeer tumbled to the floor, dazed. Above him, the statue started to fall forward. He scrambled out of the way. The falling statue narrowly missed the altar where Betty was tied, slamming to the floor and smashing apart into big chunks of stone. The Rocketeer let out a sigh of relief, then remembered they weren't out of danger yet. He looked around for Morlant—

—and saw him lying on the floor. The giant statue had fallen on top of the mad Egyptologist, pinning him. Only the mask, his shoulders, and a single arm were free from beneath the statue's rubble.

The Rocketeer picked up the sacrificial knife from the floor, ran to the altar, and cut Betty free from the ropes. She hugged him tight and sobbed into his shoulder, "Oh, thank God you're here! It was terrible!"

"I'll get you out of here as soon as I can," he said. "But first..."

The Rocketeer went over to Argyle's unconscious form and cut his ropes as well. As he did, Argyle regained consciousness, shaking his head groggily. The lieutenant looked at him in surprise.

"The Rocketeer?" he said. "What are you doing here? Where am I? The last thing I remember is following Morlant into his house..."

"You're safe," the Rocketeer said. "Believe it or not, you're underneath Morlant's house right now. He built his own temple down here."

Argyle stood up. He looked around in wide-eyed astonishment a moment before regaining his usual stoic composure. "Betty, are you okay?"

"I'm fine," Betty said, coming down off the altar. "But I don't think I can say the same for Doctor Morlant."

Argyle looked down at Morlant on the floor. The funerary mask over his head glittered in the torchlight. Somehow, miraculously, it was undamaged by the statue's collapse.

Argyle knelt down beside him. "That's the stolen mask."

"Morlant had it all along," the Rocketeer said. He and Betty knelt down on Morlant's other side. "I suspect he killed Gionvanni Bortello, too."

Betty reached down and pulled the mask off of Morlant's head. Beneath it, Morlant's face was hidden in the wrappings of his mummy costume. Betty pulled those away, too, finally revealing

Morlant's features. The Egyptologist was still conscious, blinking up at them in a daze. Blood dribbled from the corner of his mouth. Argyle raised his radio to call for an ambulance, but Morlant put his free hand on the lieutenant's sleeve to stop him.

"Don't," Morlant said. "They'll never...get here...in time. It's just as well."

"Why'd you do it, Doctor Morlant?" Argyle demanded. "Why kill Bortello and steal the mask?"

Morlant coughed up more blood. "At the first photo shoot... couldn't stand seeing the mask...used as a prop like that...like it was a joke, like it was nothing. I knew what it was. What power dwelled within it. Bortello knew, too. I could tell. I begged him to sell it to me...instead of allowing this desecration to continue...but he refused. He was adamant that the mask was not meant for me. When I returned from San Francisco, I drove straight to the sound-stage from the airport. I intended to steal the mask...but Bortello was there, the old fool. He tried to stop me..." Morlant's body convulsed with coughs. More blood trickled from his lips.

"I don't get it," Argyle said. "If Bortello knew the mask was real, why use it as a prop for the picture?"

"Don't you see?" Morlant said. His body was racked by a coughing fit. It was clear he didn't have much time left. "Sekhemkhet commanded him to bring the mask to the sound-stage...so it could be united with the great pharaoh's chosen host body."

Betty looked at the Rocketeer, alarmed. He shook his head. It was obvious Morlant was insane.

"Except, Sekhemkhet did not come to me," Morlant continued. "Bortello was right. It wasn't me Sekhemkhet wanted. I offered myself to him willingly, yet even after his five-thousand-year wait, Sekhemkhet rejected me. He did not find me worthy. He...chose... another..."

With a long sigh, Morlant's eyes closed. His cheek turned life-lessly to the floor. The Egyptologist was dead.

Argyle sighed and looked across the body at the Rocketeer and Betty. "What a waste. A brilliant scholar with a promising career, and he throws it all away for some superstitious ghost story—"

He was cut off by a portion of the ceiling high above them smashing inward, raining chunks of plaster and stone down into the temple. The Rocketeer grabbed Betty, shielding them both and diving out of the way. Argyle jumped back in the opposite direction. When the dust cleared, all three of them looked up at the hole in the ceiling.

And the man slowly descending through it.

He stood upon an oblong, metal disc inscribed with hieroglyphs and arcane symbols. Somehow, the disc was staying aloft without any visible means of propulsion and circling the temple without any visible means of steering. Either the man atop it was guiding it with subtle shifts in his balance, the Rocketeer thought, or...or he was doing it with his mind. But that was impossible, wasn't it?

As the strange craft glided down toward them, the pilot's features became clearer. He had used heavy kohl to draw two ankhs on his face, their top loops circling his eyes, the crosses on his cheeks. He had covered the rest of his face, neck and hands with other symbols, but even so, the Rocketeer recognized him.

"Burton!" he yelled.

"Not Burton—Sekhemkhet!" the pilot replied. "Link Burton is merely the shell that houses my consciousness. A consciousness that is now reborn!"

The Rocketeer reached for his Mauser, only to find it missing from its holster. It must have fallen out when he dove for cover with Betty, who was still clinging to him in terror. He glanced around the rubble-strewn floor and saw the pistol in the distance, too far away to reach.

"I'm here for what is rightfully mine," Burton said. "What I have been looking for all this time."

The craft hovered a few inches above the floor. Burton stepped off it and onto the rubble right next to Morlant's body. He picked up Sekhemkhet's mask and lowered it over his head, covering his face. Maybe it was an optical illusion, a trick of the light, but the Rocketeer could have sworn the mask's eyes seemed to glow subtly.

"It's just like my host body once told you, Miss *Betty*," Burton said. "The mask does not hide the true face. The mask *is* the true face!"

The Rocketeer slipped out of Betty's grasp and dove for the pistol. He snatched it off the floor and spun around. Before he could fire, Burton leapt onto his craft and flew quickly up through the hole in the ceiling. The Rocketeer blasted off after him, soaring up through the hole and into the night sky.

Burton was already several yards ahead of him, zooming over the Hollywood Hills and balancing on his flying disc like some hideous nightmare surfer. The Rocketeer squeezed off a shot, but Burton gracefully evaded the bullet on his strange craft. What was that thing? He thought of Morlant's story about Sekhemkhet's strange technological marvels. Could it be...? No, it was impossible. The legend of Sekhemkhet's soul entering a host body was just that—a legend, nothing more. It couldn't be true. It was Link Burton he was chasing, not a ghost from ancient Egypt.

Burton spun his flying disc around in a fast circle, coming up behind the Rocketeer. The Rocketeer tried to turn, but his jet pack wasn't as maneuverable as Burton's craft. Before he could loop around, he saw Burton throw something, a dark object that grew in size as it flew toward him. Too late, he realized it was a net.

It enveloped the Rocketeer, tangling him in its knots and ropes. He tumbled blindly through the air, unable to right himself. If he didn't do something quickly, he would crash full speed into a tree or someone's house. With no other choice, he cut the jet pack's engine and fell out of the sky like a rock. Fortunately, he landed on grass, although that only prevented him from breaking any bones, not from having the wind knocked out of him. He rolled down a steep hill for a few seconds before grabbing hold of a bush root and stop-ping himself.

Burton hovered over him, laughing. "I see you are already pros-trating yourself before your new pharaoh, Rocketeer. You learn quickly."

"You're insane, Burton," the Rocketeer shouted up at him. "You're not Sekhemkhet! You're not a pharaoh!"

"Aren't I? As soon as Link Burton touched the mask, he was mine. But beware, Rocketeer. Burton was not the only one who touched it. The woman, Betty—she touched the mask in the temple when she pulled it off Doctor Morlant. I have a bridge to Betty's mind now. I could take her as easily as I took Burton. And perhaps I will yet!"

With another diabolical laugh, Burton flew off into the night, leaving the Rocketeer in the dirt below.

11.

The jet pack had been damaged in the fall, forcing the Rocketeer to walk back to Morlant's house. When he got there, he found Betty and Argyle waiting for him in the temple. Argyle had found a blanket and put it around Betty's scantily clad form.

"The police are on their way," Argyle said.

"Burton got away," the Rocketeer reported.

Argyle sighed. "I'll put out an APB on Burton, or Sekhemkhet, or whatever he's calling himself. But between you and me, with that flying machine of his, he's long gone."

"He'll be back, you can count on that," the Rocketeer said. "He's only just getting started."

Argyle's radio squawked then. He excused himself, walked a few feet away and answered it.

"Are you okay, Cliff?" Betty asked, keeping her voice down so Argyle wouldn't hear.

"I'm all right. But there's still one thing I don't understand. Burton claimed Sekhemkhet possessed him after he touched the mask. But when did he touch it? Burton didn't show up until after Morlant had already stolen it."

"You don't know that," Betty said. "That's only the first time *we* saw him. It doesn't mean he didn't handle the mask before. He deals with antiques for MacMurray & Keyes all the time, doesn't he?"

The Rocketeer snapped his fingers. "Of course! Betty, you're a genius! *Burton* was the one Rogell bribed to appraise the reproductions as originals for the insurance! Only, Burton must have seen right away that the mask was real. I'd bet anything that if Morlant hadn't gotten to it first, Burton would have stolen the mask himself."

Argyle came back, looking happy for the first time since Cliff had met him. "I've got good news and bad news. The good news is that Karl Rogell has been arrested for fraud. It seems he was making secret arrangements to sell Bortello's copies as real jewelry. We suspected as much ever since we found out the jewels he insured were fake, but we didn't have any proof until now. According to my captain, we got everything we needed, including correspondence between Rogell and Morlant talking about their plans in detail, courtesy of a young woman named Yvonne Morris."

"Yvonne?" Betty asked. "Karl Rogell's secretary?"

"That's the one," Argyle said. "I guess that creep slapped her bottom one too many times, and she finally found a way to get back at him."

"Good for her," Betty said. "But if my producer is going to jail, I suppose I can guess what the bad news is."

"Sorry, miss," Argyle said. "They're shutting down production on *The Mask of the Pharaoh*."

Betty sighed. "I suppose it's just as well. I think I've had enough of mummies and pharaohs for one lifetime."

"You and me both," Argyle said. "This temple is giving me the heebie-jeebies. I'm going back upstairs to wait for the uniforms."

Argyle walked up the steps that led to Morlant's house. When he was gone, Cliff took off the Rocketeer helmet and put an arm around Betty's blanketed shoulders.

"Sorry," he said. "I know how much being in this picture meant to you."

She looked up at him and smiled. "It's all right. There'll be others."

Cliff shook his head. "If being an actress is always this dangerous, you'd be safer off as a lion tamer."

Betty slipped out of his arm, laughing, and started toward the steps. "Why, Cliff Secord, if I didn't know better, I'd think you cared about me."

"You're funny," Cliff said. "Maybe you should be in the next Marx Brothers picture."

He looked down at the Rocketeer mask in his hands, and the smile faded from his lips. He couldn't help remembering what Link Burton had said.

You know what they say about men in masks, don't you? The masks don't hide their true faces. The masks are their true faces.

Maybe that was how Burton felt about the mask he wore, but Cliff wasn't anything like him. Was he?

Something else Burton said had gotten under his skin, too. As crazy as it was, he couldn't shake it.

I have a bridge to Betty's mind now. I could take her as easily as I took Burton.

But it wasn't true. It couldn't be. So what if Betty had touched Sekhemkhet's mask? It was just an old piece of junk.

Wasn't it?

He looked up. Betty was standing at the bottom of the steps. She'd unrolled one of Morlant's ancient papyrus scrolls and was studying its hieroglyphs with an eerie intensity. After a moment, she noticed Cliff looking at her and smiled at him.

He hoped she couldn't see the worry in his eyes when he smiled back.

THE END

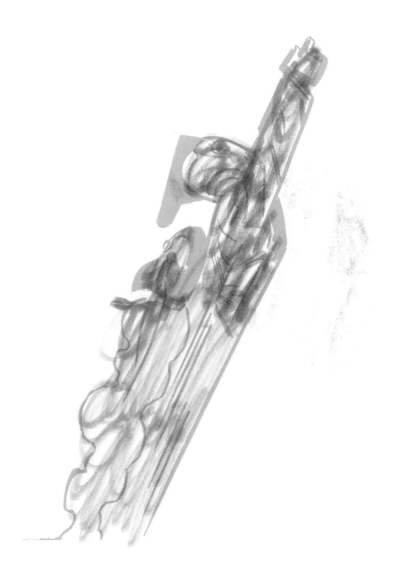

THE RIVET GANG

by

LISA MORTON

Summer 1945

"**G**ood afternoon, sir. May I park your car?"

Cliff Secord looked up at the smiling valet. "Look, friend, I prefer to do it myself. Just tell me where, okay?"

The valet's smile plummeted, and he pointed to a row of cars along both sides of the long drive that led back to the street. "Just pull up behind the last one."

"Thanks, buddy."

As Cliff backed up, he felt Betty's displeasure like a suffocating cloud. "Cliff, you promised to be on your best behavior tonight."

"What? C'mon, I don't want anyone else to touch my baby—or my car. What's wrong with that?"

Cliff eased his five-year-old Packard, with the dented fenders and fading paint job, behind a row of large black cars that seemed to radiate wealth and prestige. "Like anyone at this party would want to touch this hunk of junk," Betty laughed.

Nodding toward the trunk, Cliff countered, "Hey, it runs great. And besides, I've got...you know...*valuable* items in the trunk."

"Oh, Cliff, you didn't. You brought...*it*?"

Cliff shrugged. "Well...sure. Who knows? I might get bored while you're hobnobbing with the hoity-toity types."

Betty answered by opening her door and climbing out. Cliff followed, tugging nervously at his rented tuxedo—but he stopped dead when he saw Betty walking ahead of him. She wore a white satin designer gown slit to the thigh, stockings (*real* stockings, now that the war had ended) and a glittery jacket. Just the sight of her decked out like that made Cliff's heart pound as loud and fast as machine-gun fire.

Then he realized she was walking away from him toward the elegant two-story mansion, and he had to run to catch up. Now they could hear live music and voices. "So, the guy throwing this party..."

Betty sighed. "Robert E. Gross, the head of Lockheed. Remember?"

"Jeez, Betty, I know that. I'm just wondering how *exactly* you know him."

"Don't be silly, Cliff—I've never met him before today. My agent set this up." Betty relented and grabbed Cliff's arm, locking hers around it. "C'mon, you should like him—you've probably flown a lot of his planes."

"That doesn't make him anybody special. The real heroes are—"

Betty cut him off. "—the pilots. I know, you've said that a million times."

She gave him a peck on the cheek, instantly lightening his mood, and they stepped past the doorway and into the house.

Cliff had to force himself to not gape. He had no idea what the paintings and vases and silver were worth, but he knew any one piece would probably sell for many times more than he made in a year as a pilot and flight instructor. "Holy cow," he muttered. "Wonder how often stuff gets stolen here?"

"Don't even think it," Betty whispered.

"Think what? I'm one of the good guys, remember?"

Betty was about to respond when a voice called out, "Ah, it's our star!"

Cliff turned to see a middle-aged man in a tuxedo approaching. He had a friendly smile, and Cliff envied the ease with which he wore his monkey suit. The man stepped up to Betty and thrust out a hand. "I'm Robert Gross. I already thought you were the prettiest girl in pictures, but I must say, you're even lovelier in person."

Batting her eyelashes, Betty answered, "Oh, you're too kind, Mister Gross. It's a pleasure to meet you. This is my boyfriend, Cliff Secord. He's a test pilot."

Gross grabbed Cliff's hand and gave it a hearty shake. "A test pilot, eh? Well, Mister Secord, I always say the pilots are the real heroes of our industry!"

Cliff tried to ignore the smirk Betty shot at him.

Gross checked his watch and gestured broadly. "We've got about ninety minutes until we need you. Waiting for sunset, you know. The light's perfect in the library then, so please mingle and enjoy yourselves."

"Thank you, Mister Gross," Betty grinned. After he disappeared back into a throng of guests, the grin vanished, and she turned a warning look on Cliff. "Now you—*behave.*"

They made their way through the house and to the backyard, where a live orchestra played and a dance floor on a low platform had been set up at the end of a spacious pool. Couples swayed to a vocal number while waitresses circulated with trays of drinks and hors d'oeuvres. The late fall air of Los Angeles was a cool pleasure, especially given how hot Cliff's tux was.

He was about to snag a pair of drinks when he heard a voice call out, "Betty!"

Cliff spun to see Betty waving at another woman—Dahlia "Scoop" Danvers. Her often-lurid and sensational news stories had made her a name to be reckoned at the *Herald-Examiner*, especially after the yarn she'd written about the deranged scientist dying in a fiery crash right in the middle of Pasadena's infamous Suicide Bridge. Cliff saw her byline in the paper at least once a week. Scoop rushed up to give Betty a hug, then threw a playful salute out to Cliff.

"Dahlia, I haven't seen you in ages!"

"You're thinking in dog years."

"What are you doing here? There's no dead bodies or Nazi spies."

Scoop feigned shock. "Day's not over yet, kiddo. Besides, this is the social event of the *year*! It's like a coming-out party, except there's no debutante."

Cliff tugged at his suit collar. "Huh? Coming out of what? Betty wouldn't tell me the details."

"That's because I don't know them." Betty answered. "But Mister Gross is a major collector, like Hearst. Art, antiques—refined stuff like that. I was hired to help him show off a new treasure. I just heard that it's some sort of rare book."

"Wait a dang minute," said Cliff. "This whole black-tie garden party is about a *book*? I thought it was the crown jewels at least."

Betty slapped playfully at Cliff, then turned to Scoop. "You'll have to excuse him—the only books Cliff ever reads are airplane manuals."

"What? Lingerie catalogs don't count?" Betty slapped Cliff again, a bit harder this time.

"Would you two cut it out?" said Dahlia. "Betty's right. Gross has a museum-quality collection. If he's throwing a coming-out party for a new trinket of his, then it must be something really special, and I want to see it, even if it is a moldy old book."

Now the two women began chatting and catching up, leaving Cliff to content himself with watching the other attendees mill about. He was running a finger around the sweaty collar of his starched shirt when he heard a voice ask, "Care for a drink to cool down with?"

He turned, and the woman before him nearly made him do a double take. She was one of the waitresses, but there was something about her, something different from the other servers, something... *familiar*. She was pretty, without possessing Betty's charisma, and had short red hair and a small, wiry build.

"Excuse me, but...do I know you?" Even as the words left his mouth Cliff regretted them—they sounded like the oldest line in the book.

The woman smiled, shifted her drinks tray and stuck out her right hand. "No, but we can change that right now. Call me Rose."

Cliff accepted her hand and was surprised by the strength of her grip. "I'm Cliff. That's a heck of a grip you got there, Rose."

"Really? Must be from hoisting these trays."

Where do I know her from? Cliff couldn't take his eyes off her face, and finally she giggled, nervous under the examination. "You don't seem like the rest of these stuffed shirts."

"And you don't seem like somebody who carries trays for a living."

Rose ignored the comment and scrutinized him. "I'm thinking maybe a cop, or a...?"

"Not exactly. I'm a pilot."

Rose blinked for a moment, and Cliff wondered why she'd almost looked panicked. She hefted her tray, her warmth fading several degrees. "Nice talking to you, Cliff, but I need to get back work. Have fun now."

She strode off. Cliff watched her go, enjoying the sway of her compact rear beneath her short, tight black dress.

"See anything you like?"

Cliff's heart leapt, and he spun to see Betty standing behind him, hands on her hips, brow creased. "Betty! I thought you and Scoop were talking..."

He didn't miss the way her small, high-heel-clad foot tapped the ground rapidly. "We *were*."

Cliff pointed back toward Rose, stammering, "I know her—I mean, I *think* I know her, but I just can't remember where from, and I—uh—"

"Her ass is familiar, just can't place the face? Tough break."

Cliff clammed up, knowing that he'd strayed into a minefield.

Relenting, Betty took his arm again and led him to the dance floor. "C'mon, Mister Pilot, dance with me, and maybe I'll find it in my heart to forgive you."

"Yes, ma'am."

Having been born with two left feet, Cliff usually turned down requests to dance, but he owed it to Betty this time. They swayed slow and close as the band interpreted The Pied Pipers' "In the Moon Mist" and The Mills Brothers' "I Don't Know Enough About You." Cliff's confidence in his dancing ability was starting to multiply, so when the orchestra picked up the rhythm with Count Basie's "The Mad Boogie," Cliff let Betty spin him. He laughed, enjoying the sensation, feeling like the richest guy in the joint, flapping his free hand, moving recklessly—

As the sun began to hang low on the horizon, the bandleader stepped up to the microphone. "And now, Mister Gross has asked that you all join him in the library."

"Oh." Betty disengaged herself, leaving Cliff a little lightheaded. "That's my cue."

"Me, too." Scoop threw a little wave to Cliff. "See you later, handsome."

Cliff waved back halfheartedly, then joined the rest of the party as they made their way into the house, down a short hall, and into the library. When he arrived, Betty was already front and center with Gross, who stood beside a waist-high pillar draped in red velvet. Books in glass-fronted cases and framed illustrations on parchment and vellum lined the walls. The sunlight was perfect, Cliff noted, for the room was filled with warm orange glow, like a Maxfield Parrish painting.

Gross tapped a Champagne flute with a spoon to quiet the chatter. "Thank you, my friends, thank you for coming tonight. Most of you probably know of my weakness for fine books, and what I'm about to show you is so special that I felt it deserved its own coming-out party." Gross gestured to a middle-aged, bespectacled man on his right. "I've asked Don Hill, president of the esteemed group of bibliophiles known as the Zamorano Club, to help me make the introduction. And," as he gestured to Betty, "the lovely rising star of the silver screen will perform the unveiling."

The crowd applauded lightly, Betty glowed and Cliff tried not to glower.

Gross continued. "Don, would you talk a little about what we have tonight?"

Hill smiled and addressed the crowd. "Ladies and gentlemen, what you are about to see is one of only seven remaining copies of Joseph de la Vega's *Confusion of Confusions* in its original 1688 edition. Not only do many historians consider it to be the most important business book ever written, but the copy now in the possession of Mister Gross is particularly important because it contains annotations in the author's own hand."

The onlookers murmured appreciatively. Cliff hid a small snicker.

"Tell 'em what you paid for it, Bob," called a jovial voice from the back of the room.

Gross chuckled. "I paid three hundred thousand at auction, but it's since been valued at twice that."

Cliff's next snicker died in his throat. *Three hundred thousand for an old book? Holy crow!*

Another voice called out, "So what's to keep somebody from stealing it? I don't see any guards."

"I don't need any guards." Gross nodded at the shrouded pedestal as Betty stood behind it, awaiting her cue. "What you're about to see is a marvel of modern engineering unto itself. The case is made of acrylic glass, three inches thick and shatterproof. The pillar beneath is solid steel and has been secured directly to the foundation of the house. The final touch is a motion-detector system, the latest technology. An alarm will sound if any attempt is made to impact the case."

Cliff could hold his tongue no longer. "So how do you read it?"

The crowd laughed. Betty shot Cliff a look but instantly resumed her model's smile. Gross said, "I have cheap reprints for that purpose. In English, of course. A new translation. For my own annotations."

The crowd laughed louder, and Cliff tried to shrink into a small, unseen ball.

Gross let the sounds die down before adding, "In fact, the book has never gone out of print; de la Vega is still that influential. And now, ladies and gentlemen, presenting *Confusion of Confusions*."

Betty gripped the velvet covering, took a dramatic pause and then, with a flourish, whirled it aside to reveal—

An empty case.

Gross gave out a loud gasp, as did others in the crowd. Reporters fired off flashbulbs, and Betty stood frozen, still clutching the velvet cover.

Cliff pushed up to where he could see that a large hole had apparently been melted on one side of the top. The thieves had been careful enough not to have the dripping acrylic be directly over the book itself.

Gross looked close to tears. "The book...the case...there was no alarm, because they used solvents to dissolve the acrylic." He pounded a leg in fury and despair. "Damn!"

As the onlookers broke into whispering groups, Scoop pushed through up to the case and gave a practiced look at the partially liquefied display, noting every detail. "Mister Gross, when did the book and this case arrive?"

"It was all in place this afternoon. I placed the book there myself."

Scoop said, "Then this must have been done during the party."

Betty set the covering aside and moved from behind the dissolved case to join Cliff, speaking softly. "If this happened during the party, whoever did it can't have gotten very far away. I bet they'd be easy to spot...from *overhead*..."

"Right!"

Cliff started to leave, stopped, turned back, gave Betty a kiss, then made his way through the mystified audience and ran outside. Scoop looked up as he left, then glanced over at Betty, arching her eyebrow. Betty grinned and shrugged.

Cliff dashed to the valet, who stood next to a pegboard bedecked with keys. "Hey, who all's been through the gate in the last few minutes?"

The valet spoke without looking up. "Couple of guests...the caterers...ask the traffic cops they got outside."

"The caterers?"

"Sure. They left maybe ten minutes ago. Big white panel truck, their name on the side...RTR or something like that..."

Cliff passed a five to the valet. "Thanks, pal!"

The valet glanced at the bill and looked up in surprise. "Uh—thanks, mister!"

Cliff had already torn off his tuxedo jacket by the time he reached the Packard. He tossed it into the backseat, grabbed the duffel bag, looked around anxiously and ran off to the side of the garage. In a narrow, dark walkway between the garage wall and a line of tall junipers, he fumbled open the bag and donned the flight jacket and rocket pack. He could only hope that the guests were preoccupied by the stolen book and wouldn't see him as he shot off into the darkening sky.

As always, the exhilaration of hurtling heavenward set his senses reeling, but he soon remembered why he was up here. He leveled out and began inspecting the streets below him. Gross's home was in the Hancock Park area of Los Angeles, surrounded by quiet streets lined with impressive mansions set well back from the street. There was little traffic, so despite the tree-obstructed view, Cliff could quickly dismiss regular automobiles.

There...something big heading south on Rossmore.

Cliff tilted himself down and dove until he was flying parallel to and above the vehicle. It was a white GMC panel truck with a large logo painted on the sides: *RTR Caterers.*

Cliff grinned and started to move closer, dodging around palm trees and chimneys. He didn't like flying this close to the city streets, but he wasn't going to lose this truck now. Not with Betty counting on him.

The truck turned right onto Wilshire Boulevard, a busy thoroughfare on a Saturday evening, with steady traffic flowing in both directions. Cliff knew the eastbound traffic was heading for the popular mid-Wilshire District nightspots: Cocoanut Grove, Brown Derby, Slapsy Maxie's. But his quarry could be bound for the beach, up the Pacific Coast Highway, maybe even Mexico.

It was time to make his move—if only he knew what it was. Maybe if he could fly in front of them, startle them into stopping... or perhaps he could open the passenger door. By now Cliff was sure they were the robbers, but such criminals were often armed, and Cliff hadn't even brought his Mauser.

He had to risk it. He couldn't very well follow them all night, not on Wilshire, anyway. He veered closer to the truck, descending more, swooping and swerving to avoid light poles and buildings.

Then the passenger-side window opened, and a face hidden behind a gas mask looked up at him.

The insect-like mask was just enough to startle Cliff, who almost collided with a traffic light. He pulled up and over just in time but shot past the van, which had squealed to a halt. Cliff curved his entire body to pull a sharp U-turn just as the truck started forward again. He barely cleared the truck's top, then maneuvered another hairpin to get up even again with the side.

The passenger window was down now, and before Cliff could react, he saw the muzzle of an unfamiliar weapon thrust out. There was a rapid series of loud pops, not exactly like the sound of gunshots, but Cliff felt something impact him hard enough to set him spinning. He struggled to correct his spiral but was hit again, in the side; then the jet pack was struck hard. The rocket began to sputter, and now he was tumbling, helpless. Cliff knew a collision with the street's hard asphalt or the concrete side of a building would likely kill him. As he struggled to stop the corkscrewing, the jet gave one last burst and then quit entirely, sending Cliff into a wild tumble.

He hit something wet and sticky. His mad flight path drove him down for a few more feet before he stopped. Everything froze for a few seconds while Cliff tried to understand why he was still alive. But he couldn't move or see anything—was he blind? Paralyzed? He tried to push against whatever held him and felt some give, but the weight of the rocket pack was dragging him down. He shrugged out of the straps; he needed air badly now, his lungs were burning even as a strange smell filled his nose—

His head broke the surface of whatever he was in, and then he got his hand free. He lifted the helmet, sucked in precious air, and finally looked around: he was surrounded by black liquid, a pool rimmed by gently sloping grassy knolls and tall trees.

The La Brea Tar Pits.

At first Cliff was grateful—the place stank but had saved his life—until he realized he wasn't out of trouble yet. Like quicksand, the tar held him and wasn't about to let go easily. He struggled and twisted but was only dragged down more. He tried to reach back for the rocket pack and realized he would follow it down to his doom like some Ice Age mammal if he tried to retrieve it. Perhaps he could retrieve it later somehow—tar pits were only around 20 feet deep, and police divers sometimes looked for high-profile evidence in them—but for now he had to concentrate on not drowning in black sticky goo.

Okay, stay calm...move slow and careful...remember how Tarzan gets out of scrapes like this.

Cliff saw he wasn't far from the tar pool's edge. Maybe he was close enough to the bank to risk trying to walk out. *Hell, if the tar doesn't get me, the methane will*, he reasoned. Taking as big a gulp of air as he could, Cliff forced his legs down. He began to sink, and panic rose up in him. This would not be a good way to go...but then his toes found solid ground. *Thank God!* He pushed, each step exhausting, tar still threatening to bring him down to meet a woolly mammoth or giant sloth or dire wolf. Another two achingly cautious steps and he could easily stand upright. Then he was free up to his hips...his knees...calves...then he was staggering onto the solid ground, covered in black tar and drained, but alive.

Once Cliff had caught his breath, he assumed that the robbers were long gone, and he was lucky no one had discovered him yet, which frankly seemed incredible. He heard sirens in the distance—the police might be arriving any second, and he didn't want to explain how he'd wound up dipped in tar. He shrugged out of his flight jacket and pants and reluctantly cast them back into the tar, along with his boots. He took the helmet off and carried it under one arm, then, clad only in a white T-shirt and skivvies ran across the grass until he reached Wilshire. He could see the sirens now speeding toward him, and he frantically waved to flag down a cab. The cabbie eyed him, then said, "Where to?"

"Five-five-four Rossmore. And step on it!"

Cop cars arrived just as the cab pulled into traffic. The cabbie eyed Cliff in his rearview mirror, scowling. "What's with the half-naked routine? And is that tar on your face?"

Cliff ran his fingers across his jaw, and they came away black and sticky. "Oh, probably. I...uh...well, there was this girl, and uh... somehow I tripped and fell in the tar pit—"

The driver waved him to silence. "Save it for the priest. Just don't get any on my cab, okay? Upholstery ain't cheap, pal."

Glancing at the cracked and frayed leatherette around him, Cliff just nodded and assured the cabbie that it wouldn't happen. Besides, he had bigger things to worry about...like how bad Peevy was going to kill him when he found out that the rocket pack was now residing with the bones of prehistoric animals in the La Brea Tar Pits.

Cliff returned to the Gross estate and found Betty waiting for him by the Packard. There were police cars everywhere, and Betty scowled when he made her pay for the cab ride. Cliff had to stand half naked before an officer and endure questions about his lack of clothing (he fell in the pool) and a search of the Packard, to make sure he hadn't stolen the book (and, thank goodness, he didn't have the rocket pack to explain away). When he and Betty were finally cleared, they headed home, and Cliff told her about the chase and the crash.

Betty listened and then said, "Peevy's going to kill you. Slowly."

"Yeah, well, the tar would've done it for sure. I might have a chance with Peevy." But Cliff was thinking of other, more powerful interests who would also take a dim view of his losing the jet pack. A midnight fishing expedition back at the Tar Pits might have to be arranged. It was going to a sticky subject.

Cliff glanced over and saw Betty trying to hold the helmet up to the light. She used a handkerchief to wipe some tar away from the rear fin, and murmured, "Aha."

"What?"

They pulled up at a stoplight, and Betty held the helmet out for Cliff to see. "See that? I knew it would be there!"

Squinting, Cliff eyed the fin. It was slightly bent, and a small piece of metal seemed to be lodged in the middle. "What...what is that, a bullet?"

"Uh-uh." Betty put the helmet down and looked at Cliff excitedly. "It's a *rivet.*"

"A rivet? You mean those robbers fired *rivets* at me?"

Betty leaned forward, excitedly. "After you pulled the disappearing act, and before the cops came, Scoop did a little snooping and found a rivet near where the book had been. We went outside, and she leveled with me. It seems that our ace reporter wasn't there to cover a social event; she had a hunch that something like this would happen. She's been working this robbery gang story for a few months, while the cops have kept it quiet."

"What do you mean they want to keep it quiet?" said Cliff.

"According to Scoop, these robbers are called the Rivet Gang by the police," said Betty, "and this is their third big heist this year. Remember that First Pacific Bank robbery back in February? Over a hundred thousand snatched. That was them, and they always leave a chrome-plated rivet behind, as a kind of calling card."

"Oh, sure. I remember that." The truth was Cliff had no memory of it, but he didn't want to give Betty any more reason to mock his lack of interest in any news story that didn't involve flying...or Betty.

"Two months later it was some real estate tycoon's gold bars. They found a brass rivet in his empty safe."

Cliff frowned. "Who keeps gold bars in a home safe? And what kind of robbers leave clues like that? Ones who want to get caught?"

"No." Betty leaned forward, excited. "Ones who want to needle their victims. Wanna hear the best dirt? Dahlia says the cops have eyewitnesses who said at least a couple of these robbers are *women*."

"Women?" Cliff guffawed, as he steered the Packard around an old jalopy doing twenty on Santa Monica Boulevard. "That's the craziest thing I ever heard."

Betty sat back in her seat and glowered. "Oh, really? And why is that so crazy?"

"Well, because...women don't crash bank vaults." Cliff remembered the robber shooting the rivet gun at him. "Besides, I saw the person who shot at me, and that was no woman."

"I thought you said they wore gas masks."

"I did...I mean, they did, but...aw, c'mon, Betty, this guy blasted a souped-up *rivet* gun at me! Outside of a circus, what kind of dame could even pick one up, let alone turn it into a weapon?"

Betty was fuming now, and Cliff felt his gut clench. "How about the 'dames' who built all the planes and bombs during the war? Were they circus freaks?" she asked evenly. When she acted icy calm like this, Cliff knew she was fuming inside.

"No, I didn't mean..."

"While all you men were off fighting or training the other pilots and soldiers, women were building all the things they needed to fight with. And then the war finally ended and all the boys came home, and suddenly hundreds of thousands of women were out of work without so much as a thank-you note from Uncle Sam. Going from full-pay jobs to no-pay kitchen duty and baby wrangling."

"Oh, I get it—like Rosie the Riveter in the song, right? So that's why they're leaving the little shiny rivets?"

Betty stared heavenward. "The Quiz Kids got nothing on you, clearly."

"Okay, fine. So they're dames. Maybe. You don't have to be so sore about it."

But it was too late—Betty was already looking out the window, pointedly away from Cliff. It was almost as if she knew that he didn't really believe the rivet-shooting robber behind the gas mask had been a woman.

Peevy wasn't quite as mad at Cliff as Betty was. In fact, he'd been working on some improvements on the rocket pack and had a new, lighter and faster model ready to go. He told Cliff to come back tomorrow.

Cliff spent the day using gasoline to get the tar out of his hair and thinking about his argument with Betty. He knew she was free-spirited when it came to women in general and her own independence in particular. "There's something you need to understand about me, flyboy," Betty had told him on one of their first dates. "No man's ever going to tie me down."

But a gang of female criminals? A female heist mob? They were not only daring, but smart, too—they'd known how to dissolve Gross's acrylic glass with solvents, they'd figured out how bypass a custom-made security system and they'd turned a rivet gun into a mobile weapon.

During lunch at the Bulldog Café, Cliff grabbed a morning *Herald-Examiner*, intent on proving to Betty that he really *did* read the paper more than once a year. News of the book heist had made the front page, with a byline by Scoop Danvers. There was no mention of a chromed rivet or female robbers, just facts about the book's value and the daring nature of the crime. Cliff noted an unrelated item about the Rocketeer buzzing traffic on Wilshire for no good reason, but it wasn't featured. The last thing he wanted was Scoop suspecting him again.

After he'd finished lunch, Cliff tucked the paper under his arm and went to check in with Peevy at his workshop. He needed to talk to someone smart, someone who could tell him if it was really possible that the Rivet Gang were women. Dainty, delicate, beautiful, fragile *women*.

As Cliff approached the shop building, he noticed an unfamiliar sedan parked outside. He knew most of Peevy's visitors—mainly pilots looking for ways to boost engine performance—but he didn't recognize this car, and it was memorable. The shiny white Ford SuperDeluxe Tudor sedan looked like it had just been driven from a Beverly Hills showroom. He peeked in the windows, but his curiosity was left unsatisfied. Cliff wondered who Peevy knew who could afford a vehicle like that. Maybe it was a new promoter in town or a film producer.

Just to announce himself, Cliff knocked on the door as he entered. "Hey, Peevy, how's the—"

He broke off as he saw two things: one, Peevy was tied up to his working chair, gagged with a red handkerchief; and two, there were four men in black clothing and Halloween masks rummaging through the mechanic's things. One was holding the nearly finished latest rocket pack.

"Hey—!" Cliff started to call out, and immediately regretted the sound. One of the robbers wore a backpack that held canisters of air that were connected to a large, heavy rivet gun, now pointed at Cliff. He leapt to the side as it fired. *Thunk-thunk-thunk.* A line of rivets lodged into the door behind him.

The Rivet Gang. It had to be them.

"Let's go," shouted a voice, muffled by a rubber clown mask, but obviously female.

The one holding the rocket pack ran out first, followed by another one holding a bag, and then the rivet-gun wielder. The last robber held a satchel of tools, and Cliff impulsively dove as she tried to dash through the door. They collided and rolled to the ground, tussling, but the woman was stronger than Cliff had expected and managed to kick him off and leap to her feet. But Cliff was fast, too, and he snatched at her as she tried to make it out. She whirled and raised a fist that landed a powerhouse to Cliff's jaw. He flew back, dazed but still conscious, and looked up to see his opponent rubbing her knuckles and trying to get her breath. "Thanks for the rocket pack," she said, as the rivet-gun wielder moved up beside her.

Cliff asked, "How'd you figure out it was me?"

The women both laughed, and the one who'd hit him said, "You didn't really think nobody saw you take off from that house, did you, genius? C'mon, the Rocketeer shows up at a party where there's only one real pilot talked about in the society columns, beside Howard Hughes. Pretty smart for women, huh?"

Cliff nodded at the rivet gun. "So is this where you fill me full of rivets before you leave a chrome-plated one?"

The leader walked up to kneel before him, and there was something familiar about her voice. "We're not killers, Mister Secord. That shows lack of class and imagination. We want you in one piece for what comes next. You're going to enjoy it."

"That rocket pack wasn't finished, you know."

"It will be. Now say good night."

She pulled back her hand again, and before Cliff could react, her fist flew into his skull and turned out the lights.

Cliff awoke to the sight of two men standing over him. One was short and broad, with a low brow and red hair; the other was tall, slender and as elegant as any movie star.

"About time," said the ginger-haired man.

Cliff tried to sit up and was rewarded with a wave of lightheadedness and nausea that forced him back down to his pillow. "Where am I?"

"Hospital. Know your own name?" That was the dapper don, who eyed Cliff with an air of disdain that boded nothing good.

"'Course I know my name. Cliff Secord."

"Good. You didn't know that yesterday. The doctors say that's normal for a concussion."

The lightheadedness was passing quickly, replaced with alarm. "What do you mean, 'yesterday'? How long have I been here?"

"Two days," said the shorter, blocky man.

They were called Monk and Ham, and Cliff knew appearances were deceiving. Monk, despite his thuggish looks and manner, was a noted scientist, and though Ham might seem a slightly fey stage actor, he was in fact a brigadier general with a mind for deadly strategy. Both men worked for the rocket pack's elusive creator...and if they were there, Cliff knew the Big Boss wasn't happy.

"Look, if this is about losing the gizmo in the tar pits..."

The two men looked at each, Ham with one raised eyebrow, before Monk gazed down at Cliff. "See, we don't even know about that, bright boy. But I bet it somehow fits in with *this*."

Monk hurled a newspaper at Cliff. It bounced off his face, but Cliff buried the anger to focus on the front page—and his heart nearly thudded to a halt at the headline:

ROCKETEER JOINS RIVET GANG IN DARING ROBBERY

According to the story, the criminals had the Rocketeer track an armored car carrying a steel company's payroll. When the car had reached a quiet, industrial area just south of downtown L.A., the Rocketeer had swooped down, planted a bomb on the car's roof and flown off.

Cliff's tongue seemed to have stopped working properly. "Well, it's...it wasn't...I..."

Ham waved a manicured hand. "Relax, Secord, we know it wasn't you. You've been visiting Slumberland the whole time—which is what the Boss would've done to you anyway if he'd suspected for an instant that you were the flyboy in that story."

Throwing the paper aside, Cliff looked away, jaw working. "Damn that dame..."

"A dame?" Monk asked, incredulous. "You mean some *twist* did this to you?" He glanced at Ham, and both smirked broadly.

"Yeah, a dame conked me, okay? You happy now? Not only that, but she took the new rocket pack Peevy was fixing up after the tar pit crash."

"Mister Secord," Ham said, making no attempt to disguise his amusement, "haven't you always told me that only the very best pilots could handle the jet pack?"

A female voice interrupted. "So why can't the best pilot be a woman? Or a 'dame,' as you so quaintly put it?"

Betty stood in the doorway of Cliff's room, her arms crossed, ready for a fight. Usually Cliff wanted to climb into the nearest flying device and take off when she got in one of her fighting moods, but today he was glad to have her on his side.

Monk grinned at her, and it made his huge face look like a gorilla with cramps. "You ever gotten behind the controls of a plane, girly? It takes a real man to choke a throttle."

Ham rolled his eyes. Cliff practically saw steam erupt from Betty's ears. "Look, shorty," she said, walking up to Monk and stabbing a finger into his broad, heavy chest, "I still don't know who or what you are, but I do know this: you're an idiot if you think women can't fly planes or that rocket pack."

Monk's smile vanished, and his chest bulged outward as if to repel Betty's finger. "Look, I'm just sayin'—it takes a certain amount of strength to fly a plane. Frails just ain't got it, 'cept maybe for Sunday flyin'."

Betty wasn't backing down. "Ever spend twelve hours on an assembly line and then go home and cook dinner for your family?"

Monk turned away from Betty to Cliff, shoving a thumb over his shoulder. "This your girl, Secord? She's a looker but a handful, huh?"

Cliff wondered if he could crawl under the bed. He didn't seem to be connected to any IV tubes, so—

"Would you gentlemen mind," Betty said with barbed ice in her voice, "leaving us for a few minutes?"

Monk started for the door. "With pleasure."

Ham said, "Here's the dirt, Secord: the Big Man wants you to get that pack back. Whatever it takes. He's not very happy with you right now, and you've got one shot at making it right again. Are we clear?"

"Like crystal. I'll get it back—don't worry."

Ham started to follow Monk out but turned back at the doorway and gave Cliff a sarcastic salute. "Good luck with your girl—I think you're gonna need it."

The door closed behind them, and Betty softened. "Now that *they're* gone...how are you, Cliff? You've had me worried sick."

"Ah, I'm okay. Thanks, Betty."

"You said some crazy things yesterday, Cliff." Betty couldn't stifle a laugh.

"Oh no. What'd I say?"

"Something about woolly mammoths and redheads."

Cliff groaned. And not from any injury.

That evening when Cliff was released from the hospital, Betty handed him a fresh newspaper. "They did it again."

"RIVETEERS" ON CRIME SPREE

This time they'd broken into the office of a shipbuilding firm's owner and made off with a stash of war bonds. And somebody had gotten a picture of the Rocketeer, zooming into the sky with a burlap sack full of the loot.

"I think I feel sick again," Cliff said, scanning the article.

"Well, there's one bright side: Scoop's given up thinking you might be the Rocketeer."

Cliff looked up at Betty in irritation. "Aw cripes, does *everybody* think that now? Look, Betty, I'm sorry, 'cause I know how you feel about this gang, what with them being women and all, but—I gotta stop 'em."

"Cliff," Betty said, as she drove them away from the hospital, "make that 'we.' They may be women, but they're also criminals. And besides...nobody makes a monkey of *my* Rocketeer." Betty didn't turn to Cliff, but he knew she was smiling, and he suddenly felt his spirits soar without a rocket pack.

"So where do we start?"

"Well," Cliff said, forcing his mind to turn away from thoughts of Betty, "I had time to think in the hospital, and one big thing occurred to me: they've got to have somebody in the gang who understands science. They knew just what solvents to use on Gross's case, and they were able to finish putting together the rocket pack that Peevy hadn't quite finished."

"Right," Betty said, turning to Cliff excitedly as they pulled up at an intersection, "and because they're all women who presumably had a grudge, we're probably looking for a female scientist who worked in a Lockheed plant."

"Right. Unless the cops have already thought of that..."

Betty shook her head. "They haven't. Scoop tried to suggest to a friend on the force that the Rivet Gang might be *all* women, and they just laughed at her."

"Well, that's actually good for us, because I'd like to beat the cops to the rocket pack. Hey, speaking of Scoop...maybe she could pull some strings and find our gal for us."

"You mean check Lockheed employment records and all? I'll bet she could."

When they reached Cliff's place, Betty parked, leaned over and gave Cliff a kiss that left him flushed and shaking. "What was that for? Not that I object, mind you."

"That was for taking my side after all."

Cliff made a mental note to let Betty win all of their arguments in the future.

They met with Scoop the next day.

"I found exactly one woman who fits all your criteria," she said, passing a typed sheet of paper across the coffee-shop table to Cliff and Betty. "Her name is Doris McAuliffe, and she worked at Lockheed for three years. Get this: they employed her originally as a blocker on a rivet team, even though she had a degree in chemistry and was easily as smart as any of the men in Lockheed's research department."

"Well," Betty said, scanning the mimeographed employment application, "that'd give a girl a few thoughts about revenge, I'll bet."

Cliff grabbed the paper. "There's a home address here..." He looked up, practically bouncing in his seat. "Scoop, you're a lifesaver." He dug a few crumpled bills out of his pocket, slapped them on the table and stood up.

"Where do you think you're going?" Betty said.

"Where do you think? I'm going to pay a little social call on Doris McAuliffe."

Betty shimmied out from under the table and stood up. "Not without me, you're not. And no arguments about how this isn't a woman's place."

"And me." Scoop rose as well.

Cliff slapped his forehead, and even Betty frowned and said, "Scoop, this could be dangerous—"

"Then that's even less reason for me to sit back and wait for somebody else to grab the big story! Besides, if it's dangerous, then having a third man—or woman—might help."

Raising his hands in a gesture of surrender, Cliff turned to go. "Fine. At this point I don't care if the entire Women's Army Corps comes with me, as long as we get to that address."

They arrived twenty minutes later at a modest Craftsman bungalow in Pasadena, nestled on a side street between Colorado and Duarte. It was a Friday morning, and the neighborhood was quiet, just the distant ambience of traffic and a few strains of music echoing out from kitchen radios. Palm trees and crepe myrtles nodded under hazy sunshine.

"Doesn't look like a mad scientist's lair," Scoop noted from the backseat of Cliff's Packard, eyeing the little tan bungalow with the dark wood trim, neat lawn and hibiscus bushes.

"Yeah..." There was nothing special about the house at all. A driveway at the side led to a separate garage.

"Think anybody's home?" Betty asked.

"I don't know," muttered Cliff. "There's no car in the driveway, but the garage is closed." Cliff made a decision and turned to face his two companions. "Look, one of you has to stay in the car."

They both started to protest, and Cliff raised his voice to cut them off. "If anything goes wrong in there, we need somebody out here as backup."

Sullen silence ensued. Finally Betty spoke up. "Scoop..."

"Okay, fine. I'll stay put."

Cliff tossed her a quick, grateful smile. "Thanks, Dahlia. Okay, Betty, let's go."

They walked up to the door and then hesitated. "So," Betty whispered, "do we just ring the doorbell and ask if they've stolen a rocket pack recently?"

"No..." Cliff looked around and fixed on the driveway. "Let's scout the back first."

Checking to make sure they were unobserved, Cliff and Betty made their way to the side of the house. At one point they glanced back at the Packard, and Scoop gave them an encouraging wave. Cliff returned the gesture, and tripped on a paving stone.

"Pay attention," Betty hissed.

"Sorry."

Around the side of the house, they peered into a kitchen window. The cupboard doors were all open, and many of the shelves were empty.

"Looks like somebody's clearing out," Betty whispered.

Cliff tried the kitchen door and found it unlocked. He opened it gingerly while Betty watched, then tiptoed in.

Together they made their way stealthily through the kitchen, out a swinging door and into a dining room and living room beyond. There were cardboard boxes piled on the floor, and a bookcase near the front door was mostly empty.

"Definitely moving day," said Betty.

"Look at that." Cliff pointed to a box labeled SOLVENTS.

But Betty was already kneeling beside a carton of books. "Oh, I've got something even better here." She reached into the box and produced an ornately engraved folding leather box, slightly larger than Gross's stolen tome.

"Is that...?"

Betty grinned and unfolded the clamshell-style case. "Mister Gross's book, all right. This is the special case it's kept in. I guess they didn't want to damage it."

Cliff moved onto another box, he pried the flaps away and his eyes went wide at what he saw. "Holy moley!" He held up an almost exact copy of his Rocketeer mask. "Pay dirt!"

"So what do we do now, Cliff?"

"You put your hands up and make like statues, that's what," said the female behind them. Cliff and Betty whirled around to face a small woman with short blond hair and a simple blue dress. She stood in front of the swinging door, aiming a modified rivet gun at them. Cliff now saw that it was attached via tubes to a pack she wore on her back, and he had to admire the ingenuity that had gone into its creation.

"Miss McAuliffe, I presume?"

"Yes, but we've already met. Twice, in fact."

"Of course. Both our meetings left my head spinning."

The swinging door opened, and a new woman entered. She was dressed in men's khakis that looked surprisingly stylish on her short figure, she was pretty but wore no makeup and she carried herself with confidence.

"Hello, Cliff. And this must be the lovely Betty."

Cliff's jaw dropped as he stared in disbelief. "Rose?"

Yes, it was the hostess he'd met at the party, but "Rose" had lost the red hair, which he now realized had been a wig, and when he saw her with her real, dark brown hair cut close around her face, he knew her. "Millie Marker! Of course. You're the one who's been flying the rocket suit!"

Executing a curtsey, Millie answered, "Miss Rocketeer, at your service."

Betty's eyes widened. "You know her?"

"Yep. We've done a few air shows together, but you flew for the WASPs before that, didn't you?"

Millie nodded. "I was one of the best."

"But you never saw any actual fighting, did you, Millie?"

Frowning, Millie answered, "About as much as you saw on the sidelines training pilots in Glendale."

Cliff clapped his jaws shut.

Betty asked, "So what happened? Sounds like you were a hero. Or a heroine."

Two other women appeared behind Millie and Doris: one was a thirtyish woman with skin the color of black coffee, and the other was younger, thin and ragged-looking, as if she never ate. Millie motioned to indicate all of them. "The war ended, that's what happened. We were all working for our country. We believed in what we were doing and thought the country believed in us, too. That we'd have jobs after we kicked Hitler and his cronies back down, but we were tossed away like used gum wrappers."

Cliff said, "But that's not fair. The war ended. You were building war machinery. Of course you'd be out of work."

"Why couldn't we be building cars now instead of tanks?" Millie laughed bitterly. She waved the dark-skinned woman forward. "Martha, tell 'em what happened to you."

Martha's voice was deep and hoarse around the edges, as if she'd been shouting for years. "I was a welder, trained and everything. After the war, I applied to a shipyard that was hiring, and they told me they would've hired me in a second if I were a man. Meanwhile my husband got killed overseas in the fighting, and I got me three babies to support. Sure, I get some benefits, but I used to earn a man-size paycheck. Now I'm supposed to work for tips? I ain't no hostess."

Cliff's resolve drained instantly. "That was wrong. They should've hired you."

Millie ignored him and gestured at the skinny young girl. "Tell 'im your story, Jane."

"I was working a factory up in Detroit. When the war ended, they offered me the same job...at half the pay. I refused, and then they told me I couldn't get unemployment, because I'd turned a job down. So I came out here, looking for work. My mom's elderly, and I need to send her money."

Millie hooked a thumb at Doris. "Doris here was smarter than all her male co-workers, but they canned her without so much as a thank you. And me...they decided the WASPs didn't qualify as military because we flew mainly transport missions, so no pension. As if military flying is one hundred percent safe to begin with."

"Look," Cliff said, "I'm sorry you all got a raw deal, and you're right—it wasn't fair. But that doesn't mean you can go on stealing from other folks."

The four members of the Rivet Gang all exchanged quick, confident looks. "Oh, this isn't a career, numbskull. We have no intention of continuing with this," Millie said. "We just needed enough to get set up. One last job, really hit 'em where it hurts, and we'll be able to disappear forever."

Betty said, "So, what now? Use your rivets on us?"

"Not if we don't have to. Cooperate, and we'll just tie you up and leave. If you'd have come ten minutes later, we'd have been gone anyway, as planned." Millie turned to Doris. "Rope?"

"In the garage."

Millie nodded at Martha and Jane, who left through the kitchen.

Cliff knew this was his one chance, figuring he could take just Doris and Millie. But how? There was a large oak dining table between them. He knew Doris would peg him with rivets if he went right or left. Slide over the polished table? Maybe...but going *under* would mean the heavy surface would be over his head, protecting him...

He had to try it. All he needed now was a distraction.

"You were right all along, Betty," he said, trusting her to catch on.

She didn't. Instead, she eyed him in surprise. "Of course I was. About *what?*"

"About the Rivet Gang being women. Sorry I ever doubted you."

"Well, thanks, but..." then she saw something in Cliff's eyes, and she understood. "Oh, right—I was. That'll teach you men to listen. Isn't that right, girls? Don't suppose you have room in the Rivet Gang for one more?"

Millie laughed. Doris smiled.

Cliff moved.

He dove down and hit the table as he heard the loud, rapid *THOOK-THOOK-THOOK* of the rivet gun firing. He scrambled between chairs and table legs, saw Doris's feet in front of him and reached out to yank. She went down, and the gun flew from her grip, landing several feet away. She was already pulling it back toward her...

But Cliff was more worried about Millie. He scrambled from under the table, jumped to his feet and found himself a foot from Millie, who was momentarily stunned. He drew back his arm—

Everything went into slow motion: he heard Betty screaming, he curled his fingers into a fist, his arm muscles tensed...and all he could see before him was a pretty brunette who had flirted with him at a party, who was six inches shorter than him and looking startled and scared.

He couldn't hit her. He froze. And in that instant, Millie regained her advantage and landed a powerhouse right into Cliff's jaw that sent him flying backward across the table to land at Betty's feet.

"Owww!" Cliff and Millie—nursing her bruised knuckles— moaned simultaneously.

As Betty bent down to check on Cliff, Martha and Jane rushed in with the rope. "Tie 'em up," ordered Millie, rubbing her fingers.

"Why didn't you hit her, dummy?" Betty was livid.

"Aww, jeez, Betty, she's a *girl*."

Cliff and Betty were positioned seated on the floor, back to back and tied up with a length of sturdy rope. Once they were secure, the girls ran out with the boxes while Millie paused long enough to kneel down before Cliff. "Thanks for everything." Then she shocked Cliff by planting a soft kiss on his lips.

"Hey, what's going on back there?" That was Betty, trying to crane her neck around to see. Millie smiled, stood and walked around to where Betty could see her. "Take good care of that one, doll—he's a catch." She offered Betty a wink and followed her girls out. They heard the back door slam and a car engine start.

"You should've hit her, Cliff."

"Let's just concentrate on getting out of these ropes, okay?"

They fidgeted and squirmed, but neither could reach the knots. The back door slammed open, and they tensed, expecting the gang's return—but instead they heard Scoop's voice on the phone in the kitchen. After a few moments, she hung up and rushed into the living room.

"Well, don't you two look comfy," she said, starting to untie them.

"Did you really have to stop to make a phone call before you checked on us?" Betty asked. "What if we were dying in here?"

Scoop smirked. "Those girls aren't killers. Besides, I got their license number as they left—that's what I called the police about."

Cliff added, "You can give 'em more than that: the Rivet Gang is led by Millie Marker. She was a WASP in the war, and she's the one posing as the fake Rocketeer."

Scoop paused from working at the knot to ask, "How do you know that was a *fake* Rocketeer?"

Cliff's mouth worked, but nothing came out. Fortunately, Betty covered for him. "Oh, c'mon, Scoop. The Rocketeer's no robber. And besides, I doubt he has the right *equipment* for membership in the Rivets."

The affection that surged through Cliff made his knees weak, as did the smile Betty turned on him when they were freed and standing again.

Then Betty added, "But you still should've hit her," and they were back to their usual place.

Cliff tried not to dwell on his failure to retrieve the rocket pack—he had other things to think about, like the big air show Peevy had booked him for the next day. It was to celebrate the opening of the new Los Angeles Airport in Westchester. It was early December, and the day would be clear and cool. Perfect flying weather, in other words.

For the show, Cliff was going up in his old Stubby. It was a quaint relic now, and the way it handled always provoked anger from Betty ("Isn't it time for a new plane, Cliff, one that actually flies *straight?*"), but Cliff had perfected a few airborne antics that always drew laughter and applause from the crowds.

He got up early, he picked up Betty on the way and they made their way to the hangar where Peevy waited with the Gee Bee Stubby and a new rocket pack. "Try not to lose this one, will ya, kid?"

Betty went to pick up coffee at the Bull Dog while Peevy finished tinkering with the plane. At one point, he looked up from the engine and said, "Oh, get a load'a this tidbit I got via the grapevine: the air show today is gonna get a surprise visit from the Bell X-1."

Cliff froze, gaping. The Bell X-1 was the military's top experimental flying craft. They said it would break the sound barrier, an idea that set Cliff's heart pounding in admiration and envy.

"The X-1 is playing a regular air show?" he asked.

"Well, kid, this ain't just any air show. This is the whoop-de-do opening of L.A.'s new airport. I guess that was big enough to warrant showing off the X-1. Of course you know it needs a bigger plane to launch it, so it's coming with a Boeing B-29 Superfortress."

Cliff's eyes grew dreamy for a moment, as he imagined himself in the X-1's cockpit, dropping out of the belly of the B-29 at thirty-five thousand feet, G-forces tearing at him as the four rocket engines kicked in, becoming the first pilot to break the sound barrier...

"Hello, Cliff? Control to pilot..."

Yanked from his reverie, Cliff saw that Betty stood by the side of the Stubby, her flying jacket, scarf and goggles in place. Peevy was just finishing his maintenance, using a cloth to wipe away a final smudge. Cliff and Betty climbed aboard, waved to Peevy, taxied out and took off.

It was a short flight, and they landed without incident. The new airport didn't look like much yet—some of Cliff's pals had derisively referred to it as the "hareport" because of its chronic problem with rabbits on the runways—but four of the major airlines were opening for business here today, and it was said that it would soon be one of the busiest air terminals in the world.

They taxied the Stubby to a row of other performing planes parked near a hangar. Betty climbed down, took off her flying gear and went into the hangar to primp. Her agent had made arrangements for her to sign autographs later today as part of the opening festivities. Some of the pilots whistled and grinned as she walked by, and a few who knew Cliff laughed when his face flushed.

All of the pilots were buzzing with the news about the X-1. It had flown in the night before, stowed away in the belly of the Boeing B-29 Superfortress that would take it up and then launch it in midair. The B-29 with the X-1 was parked in Hangar 6, the new airport's largest structure, which stood a few hundred yards away on the other side of a runway. From this angle, they could just make out the nose of the massive B-29. "Anybody actually see the X-1 yet?" Cliff asked.

"I did," volunteered a flier Cliff didn't know. "They're not kidding when they say its design was based on a bullet. Doggone thing looks like hot lead with wings, except it's orange."

"I know the pilot, Slick Goodlin," volunteered another. "He says they're gonna pay him a hundred fifty thou to hit Mach One."

"He's full'a baloney," said a mechanic.

"Nah, the X-1 ain't even a real plane," shouted another voice. "It's nothin' but a glorified glider, can't even take off on its own. Big deal."

Cliff tuned out the conversation, peering in the direction of Hangar 6. He wanted to see the X-1 in action as much as any kid out in the crowds today. He could only imagine the craft must be a thing of rare beauty.

"Wonder what's going on?"

Cliff managed to pull his attention away from Hangar 6 to Betty, who was looking the direction of the audience gathered for the air show near the front of the concourse. Shouts and police whistles were coming from that area, and a man broke from the crowd and ran toward them, waving his arm. "Some lady says her baby's been stolen!"

All of the pilots and mechanics around Cliff broke off their conversation, staring. After a shocked beat, most of them started jogging for the crowd. Cliff was about to follow when he felt Betty's hand on his arm, holding him back. "Wait, Cliff...look at that."

Following her gaze, Cliff saw a maintenance truck, unnoticed in the commotion, rolling up to the X-1's hangar. It drove in and disappeared behind the Boeing.

Betty asked, "If the X-1 is this big military experiment, you'd think they'd have their own crew, wouldn't you?"

"Yeah, they would...well, maybe they're just fixing a problem with the hangar."

The crowd noise grew louder—men shouting directions, a woman screaming—but beneath it all they heard another sound, a familiar sound, wafting across the runway from Hangar 6.

"Did you hear that?" Betty sounded hushed, slightly breathless. The sound came again:

THOOK-THOOK-THOOK.

Cliff's pulse slammed into high gear. He jerked forward involuntarily, caught himself and thought furiously.

"It was them in the maintenance truck," Betty said. "The baby thing was just a distraction. Now they're going for the X-1."

"Yeah. Rose said they had one big last job."

"So what now?"

Cliff leapt up into the Gee Bee's cockpit, where he had a certain duffel bag stashed. "Find the airport's security, and get them over to that hangar."

"Right. What are you going to do?"

He showed her the duffel bag. "Let the *real* Rocketeer set things straight."

Betty gave him a smile. "Good luck."

She ran into the hangar, where there was a phone, and Cliff rushed to the side of the building, which was away from most of the pilots. He didn't have time to worry about who might see him or not. He slipped on the rocket pack and helmet and shot up into the air.

He wasn't interested in altitude right now, but only cared about getting to that hangar as quickly as possible. He soared across the runway and narrowly missed colliding with an incoming stunt biplane. He pulled up out of the plane's path at the last second and caught a glimpse of an angry pilot. He waved apologetically and headed for the hangar.

As he approached, the B-29 came into view, its four propellers starting to spin as it prepared to taxi out. He zoomed around the curved cockpit, and although the pilot's headgear made identification difficult, he felt sure it was Millie in there.

The B-29 was already edging out of the hangar, and Cliff suddenly realized he had no idea how to stop the world's biggest aircraft. He circled it, got a quick glimpse of the real crew tied up inside the hangar, but knew he'd have to leave them to someone else. He had to stay focused on the B-29, which was now completely out of the hangar and moving toward the runway.

He flew around to the plane's front, wondering if he might be able to break in through the cockpit. Then he heard the *rat-a-tat* of machine gunfire. He hit the controls and blasted straight up, looked down and saw that Doris was inside the blister that connected to the B-29's mechanized top-gun turret, trying to aim the twin guns mounted there.

Looked like the Rivet Gang was playing for keeps now.

Cliff sped to the rear of the plane, zigzagging to make himself as difficult a target as possible. He had to rule out a frontal attack on the B-29 and tried to think of other possibilities. A hatch? A wing?

No. An engine. If he could damage one, the B-29 wouldn't be able to lift off.

Cliff pulled his Mauser from its holster—a few well-placed shots into a fuselage should do the trick. He'd have to do it quick— the B-29 was already picking up speed.

He was taking aim when Doris opened fire again. He dodged right, left, cut his speed to fall back slightly, until he was right above the far left engine...

BAM! BAM! BAM! He emptied the Mauser into both engines on the left wing. Fuel sprayed from the holes, and Cliff shot up to avoid being doused. A few seconds later, the plane's forward motion slowed and then halted; the B-29 wasn't going anywhere soon.

Cliff caught a glimpse of the gun turret swiveling, and he was about to swoop when he saw Doris, wearing a look of surprise, yanked from out of the gunner's blister. He had no idea what had just happened, but he breathed a little easier, knowing he was no longer a flying bull's-eye.

He heard sirens approaching and allowed himself a second of relief—*the jig's up for the Rivet Gang!*—but then he saw a figure drop from the belly of the B-29, run a few feet across the pavement, and abruptly zoom straight up.

Millie had donned the stolen rocket pack and was trying to make her own escape.

Cliff tightened his grip on his own hand controls, racing after her. Millie veered from a straight ascent to heading west toward the Pacific Ocean, and as Cliff corrected his own trajectory to follow, he was dimly aware of hundreds of upturned faces and pointing hands below. The air-show crowd was certainly getting its money's worth today. The two Rocketeers were putting on a hell of a fight for them.

Within seconds, both fliers were over the roiling blue water. Millie pulled up, startling Cliff, who slowed. She released her controls with one hand, reached into her jacket and withdrew a gun. Cliff dove just as she fired, and he swooped low in a long curve, figuring he made a harder target if he went beneath her. It worked, and he saw her trying to maneuver to follow him.

But he was faster, and a second later, he was inches from her as she lowered the gun again. He reached out and grappled for the weapon as they hovered in midair, hundreds of feet above the sea. They twisted and turned, falling, trying to use only one hand to control their rocket packs. Millie was strong, and her arm was moving inexorably down, the gun barrel lowering, almost on a line with Cliff's helmeted head—

He had to do something, and quick. He didn't like doing it, but it was either this or good bye, Cliff Secord. The woman had lost all reason. She would destroy Cliff, if she could. So he simply released Millie's hand. In the split-second when the action threw her off, he drew back his fist and hit her as hard as he could.

The punch was good, although Cliff cried out as his knuckles broke against Millie's own metal helmet. She went flying back, the gun fell from her hand and, unconscious, she plunged toward the sea.

Cliff instinctively zoomed down after her, but when she hit the water, he had only a split second to pull up before he was also engulfed. He felt his boot toes catch the tip of a wave before his arc carried him back up. When he looked down, he got a quick glimpse of Millie sinking beneath the water.

She vanished beneath the waves a second later.

By the time Cliff returned to the airport, Betty was posing for photos with the rest of the captured Rivet Gang. The airport cops had even given her a gun.

The crowd cheered as Cliff swooped over their heads, but Cliff barely had enough energy to wave. The fight with Millie had exhausted him, and he didn't feel like much of a hero.

He found the quiet spot behind the hangar, set down, tore off the rocket pack and helmet, stashed them in the duffel bag and rushed off to find the nearest phone. He had the operator put him through to the Coast Guard, told them where he thought Millie had gone down and hung up. Then he went to join Betty.

The photographers weren't bored yet, though, and Cliff waited while she finished. He enjoyed watching her easy grace and natural charisma, even if his blood boiled a little whenever the cameramen flirted with her. At one point he heard a particularly piercing wolf whistle and surveyed the crowd, ready to give the stink-eye to whoever had offered up that mating call, when he saw Monk and Ham nearby. The red-haired Monk still had two fingers to his lips, and he winked once at Cliff before turning away. Ham doffed his hat, and Cliff relaxed, knowing that the Big Boss would be getting a good report, even if he had just lost a second jet pack in one week.

When she could surely no longer turn up the wattage on her smile, Betty stepped aside and walked up to Cliff. "So, what happened with Millie?"

"We fought. She hit the ocean. I had no choice."

"Did she get away?"

"I doubt it. The last I saw of her, she was three feet below the surface and sinking fast. I couldn't save her, Betty. I just couldn't."

Betty gave Cliff a reassuring look that eased some of his anxiety. "I know, Cliff. I know."

"How about you? Looks like you did okay."

"It was so exciting! The airport police let me come with them, and we arrived just as the girls were trying to make a run for it." Betty looked back, and for a moment an expression of regret crossed her face. "I hope they go easy on Martha, though. Jane was the one screaming for her baby, but Martha was on the plane and stopped Doris from firing on you. They never meant to hurt anyone."

"Good. If not for them, the Rocketeer would still be in some pretty big trouble."

"You know what their plan was? Jane spilled it. They were going to head west in the B-29 until it ran out of fuel, let it and the X-1 drop into the ocean, and then ransom the location back to the Air Force. They would probably have gotten away with it, too, if we hadn't been here."

Cliff considered for a moment, then said, "Hey, we won, so let's go celebrate! What do you say to a nice steak-and-cocktails lunch? I know this great place—"

Betty cut Cliff off as she waved at someone in the crowd. "Oh, Cliff, I'd love to, but I've already got a meeting with a producer at RKO who wants to discuss my next picture."

Cliff's blood pressure shot up. He wanted to find the producer and give him a talking-to; he wanted to tell Betty to forget that movie stuff, that he was her only fella and that he'd take care of her. But instead he clamped his jaws shut for a moment, and finally managed, "Oh, that sounds like a good break for you."

Betty tilted her head back and gave him a look of astonishment. "What, no argument? Is this the new Cliff Secord?"

"It might be."

"Well, in that case...you may buy me dinner tonight."

She leaned in, gave him a kiss, long and true, and by the time she turned to walk away, Cliff had decided that he would never doubt any woman ever again.

Or at least not today.

THE
END

409

Booksox: 1-800-
930-2241